The Cost of Freedom

The Cost of Freedom

A novel of the Civil War

James R. Arnold

Napoleon Books
2013

Copyright © 2013 by James R. Arnold

Napoleon Books
616 Little Dry Hollow
Lexington, Virginia 24450
U. S. A.
www.napoleonbooks.com

Designed by Roberta Wiener

ISBN 978-0-9670985-7-9

Printed and bound in the United States of America

Table of Contents

Contents

Contents

The Characters

*Richard Ashby: Brother to Turner, Confederate officer

*Turner Ashby: Charismatic Confederate cavalier known as "The Black Knight of the Confederacy," rising to general shortly before his death

Kinlock Barton: Min Carter's friend and sergeant in Loudoun Grays

*Alfred Barbour: Superintendent of the Harpers Ferry Arsenal

Charles Becker: Son of Sigmund Becker

Rachel Becker: Daughter of Sigmund Becker

Sigmund Becker: Former German revolutionary, then federal agent

Andrew Bennington: Plantation owner

*John Brown: Freedom fighter or terrorist, depending upon perspective

Arminius "Min" Carter: Cousin to Armistead and Amanda, a southern patriot

Armistead Carter: Cousin to Min and Amanda, a Union-loyal Virginian

*Benjamin Franklin "Grimes" Davis: Alabama-born, Union loyal cavalry officer

*Frederick Douglass: Former slave, escaped in 1838; thereafter prominent anti-slavery leader

Robert Duchesne: Federal agent

*Richard Dulany: Captain, then colonel, Seventh Virginia Cavalry; in 1853 founded the Upperville Colt & Horse Show, the nation's oldest horse show

Patrick Flannery: Drill master, U.S. Mounted Rifles, then Union Army

James Gooch: Loudoun resident, corporal, Loudoun Rangers

Gordon: Holland Hall's English manager

*James Gwyn: Lieutenant colonel, One Hundred and Eighteenth Pennsylvania, "The Corn Exchange Regiment"

*Herman Haupt: Chief engineer of the Penn Railroad then Union general in charge of military railroads

Amanda Holland: Mistress of Holland Hall, a southern patriot

Boyd Holland: Son of Randolph Holland, brother of Amanda

The Characters

Squire Randolph Holland: Proprietor of Holland Hall, father of Amanda and Boyd

*John Imboden: Skilled Confederate artillerist

*Thomas "Stonewall" Jackson: VMI professor, then Confederate general; Lee's indispensable lieutenant

Travis "Jones": Volunteer guide, then private in Loudoun Grays

*Thomas Kane: Abolitionist, friend to Mormons moving to Utah, then colonel of Thirteenth Pennsylvania Reserves, the "Bucktails;" promoted for gallantry at Gettysburg

Major Judson Kerfoot: Mexican War veteran, commander of the Loudoun Grays

Hendrick Kupper: Sergeant, Loudoun Rangers (Union)

*Robert E. Lee: U.S. colonel in 1859, Confederate general thereafter

*John Letcher: Virginia governor, 1860-1864

Kate Luckett: Amanda's neighbor and friend

*Dixon S. Miles: Colonel D.S. Miles, commander of Harpers Ferry garrison in 1862

Elizabeth Milton: Amanda's neighbor and friend

Brook Morgan: Baltimore merchant, Confederate officer

Abner Means: German revolutionary, grain merchant, Underground Railroad agent, subsequently with Federal intelligence

Benjamin Overmeyer: Union cavalry colonel

Lucy Paine: Amanda's closest friend

Otis Polk: Planter's son, Confederate staff officer

*Charles Prevost: Colonel of the One Hundred and Eighteenth Pennsylvania, "The Corn Exchange Regiment"

Anne Rix: Proprietor of Meme Richard's Dance Hall

Arthur Rixey: Leesburg lawyer, adviser to Randolph Holland, brother to Clarence

Clarence Rixey: Leesburg banker, business partner with Randolph Holland

*Moxley Sorrel: Volunteer Confederate staff officer rising to become Longstreet's indispensable adjutant general

*George Sykes: Union general, rising to corps command

The Characters

*James E. Stuart: U.S. Lieutenant in 1859, thereafter, Confederate cavalry commander under Lee

Liverne Taylor: Free black, Underground Railroad operator, then Federal agent

Jolina Taylor: Free black, Underground Railroad operator, then Union nurse; wife to Liverne

*George Thomas: Virginia-born, Union-loyal general rising to fame as "The Rock of Chickamauga"

Buck Underwood: Captain of Wildcat Roughs, a Confederate partisan band, brother to Bush

Bush Underwood: Private, Loudoun Grays

*Elizabeth Van Lew: Prominent Richmond resident, Federal agent

*Elijah "Lige" White: Commander of the Thirty-fifth Battalion of Virginia Cavalry known as "White's Comanches"

*John Winder: Confederate provost marshal general in charge of Richmond prisons

*Henry A. Wise: Virginia governor from 1856 to 1860. His signing of Brown's death warrant was one of his last official acts. Ardent secessionist, then inept Confederate general. In this war of divided loyalties, his brother-in-law was Union General George B. Meade, the victor at Gettysburg

Hannah Yoder: Abolitionist, conductor on Underground Railroad, then Federal agent

The names marked with a * are recorded in history.

Part I: The Terms of the Race

Chapter 1. Harpers Ferry, October 16-17, 1859

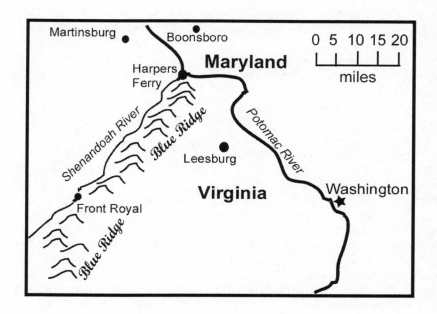

The eastbound train arrived at Harpers Ferry on Sunday morning. While passengers filed toward the car's exit, one person hesitated. He was a smallish man in his early thirties, dressed in a travel stained business suit with a battered slouch hat pulled low onto his forehead. His unsmiling face did not invite close scrutiny. Had anyone dared, he would have seen an unshaven face sprouting a week's growth of whiskers framed by red-rimmed eyes that suggested he had gone without sleep for some time. Such presumption, however, carried risk. Abner Means was an experienced duelist and just now he was fingering a Maynard revolver that lay hidden beneath the folds of his overcoat.

Means's eyes darted over the crowd standing on the Baltimore and Ohio platform. They appeared little different from the civilians he had been seeing at other stations throughout his travels during this autumn of 1859. His assessing gaze ignored the small throng of women and children, passed over an elderly farmer and the negro baggage handler, and lingered on a pair of middle aged men. Among this crowd only they might be federal agents. Means saw a smile crease the face of one of the men. A woman with three children in tow – Means had seen them board in Wheeling – walked toward the smiling man. His arms embraced her while the other man knelt to hug a child. Means released his grip on his revolver.

Rising from his bench he seized his carpetbag and exited the car. He felt foolish to have feared a scene so innocent. He knew it was a sign of fatigue. For the past two months he had crisscrossed Ohio, western Pennsylvania, and upstate New York to attend meetings organized by the Anti-Slavery Society. His own work took place after the speakers had energized the crowds and successfully urged them to contribute their purses. It also took place outside the crowd's view, behind closed and guarded doors because Means did not wish to become known to more than a handful of people. That select handful included men with money who were ready to change America. To them he said that the cost of freedom required hard money to buy guns and munitions to supply an army of soldiers ready to perform the Lord's work by sacrificing their life's blood to end the scourge of slavery.

Today he intended to deliver his stuffed carpetbag as a final payment that would ignite insurrection. He was uncertain whether the fire would catch. He had divulged his doubts to no one, least of all to the cause's prominent backers. He did not tell them that the man they had selected as Captain of the Provisional Army seemed unable to master the myriad details so necessary for success. It was bungling pure and simple that had prompted the Captain's plaintive appeal for more funds. The Captain had spent the money provided by his New England sponsors to purchase crates packed with Maynard revolvers, like the one Means carried, but had failed to buy the correct percussion caps. The mismatch of cap to revolver rendered the weapons useless. Means intended to assess whether the Captain had recovered from this stumble when they met later today. As he stood on the loading platform, Means wondered if the Captain had managed to provide a horse and map to take him to the army's secret camp. Means was too aware of complex plans spoiled by the most obvious omissions.

The locomotive's whistle screamed. The conductor climbed aboard the last passenger car. With a hiss of steam the giant pistons lurched into motion. The train slowly gathered momentum and rolled toward the covered bridge spanning the Potomac River. The platform was clear of everyone except the negro porter. Means approached him and said in a low voice, "A man named Cook said he would leave word with the station porter about where a Mister Gabriel could find a horse. My name's Gabriel."

The porter beamed. "Yes suh. There's a fine Morgan tied up in the stable behind the Gault House Saloon. A friend is there holding him for you."

As Means walked toward the Gault House he casually glanced to his right toward the United States Arsenal. It appeared empty. He crossed the tracks of the Winchester and Potomac Railroad and found the stable where his horse was tethered. At least the Captain had managed this much. A stable boy handed him the reins, gestured toward the saddle blanket with a knowing nod, and left. Mean's probing fingers found the coded directions beneath the blanket. Before beginning the last leg of his journey, he rode west along Shenandoah Street to Hall's Rifle Works. Since it was Sunday, its employees were absent and it too was empty. Retracing his steps, he rode up North Potomac Street to the Musket Factory. Empty. Cook's reports had been accurate so far. His reconnaissance complete, Means turned his horse onto the covered toll bridge leading to Maryland. Riding out the Boonesboro Road he looked back at Harpers Ferry. It had begun to rain which surely meant there would be fog tonight. Perfect. Confidence renewed, he urged his Morgan into a canter and rode to meet the Captain.

Means had last seen him two summers ago in Canada. They had met in secret convention to write a new constitution and to establish a Provisional Government of the United States. The delegates had created a Provisional Army to end slavery and nominated the Captain to lead it. Back home in Germany during the revolution of Forty-Eight, Means had seen paper armies form and dissolve because leaders lacked backbone. Eloquent orators had been ever so bold in the beer halls and wine gardens as they schemed, drank, and debated the details of the revolutionary government they would create. Yet when the time to strike came the erstwhile rebels had hesitated, preferring discussions of high political philosophy to the sound of musketry at the barricades. In Canada, Means had seen more of the same. Then he met the Captain. His first impression confirmed all that he had heard and read: here was a man of action. So Means had labored to collect the necessary money. Yet he had avoided recruiting fighters for the Provisional Army because he knew that while federal agents would find it hard to trace funds, it was simplicity itself to force a prisoner to name his leaders. He suspected that his adopted country would treat treason no more gently than the Germany he had fled.

Means pondered the Captain again; the man's iron faith, his belief that the righteousness of the cause would overcome all obstacles. Surely such a man could recover from his small misstep over the revolvers and provide the soldiers to strike the spark for freedom. Abner Means felt a surging excitement that dispelled fatigue. His Morgan caught his mood and picked up his pace with ground eating strides that rapidly covered the miles until he entered the lane leading to the Kennedy Farm.

Means found that the Captain had grown a thick beard since that Canadian summer. Better to disguise himself he explained. Means saw that the beard did nothing to hide the messianic fire that burned in his eyes. The Captain had already killed at least five people in Kansas. His eyes shone with the resolve to kill more. His countenance informed Means that this insurrection would not falter for lack of backbone.

The Captain proudly produced his arsenal for Means's inspection, explaining that the crates held 198 modern Sharps rifles, 200 Maynard revolvers, and 950 pikes with which to arm the black recruits.

"Why pikes?" asked Means.

"Because, without long training slaves are incapable of using firearms."

3

While working as a grain merchant, Means had traveled widely in Maryland and up Virginia's Shenandoah Valley. He had witnessed slaves fabricating intricate metal work at plantation forges near Shepherdstown and free blacks serving as foremen at iron foundries around Lexington. What he had seen convinced him that the Captain was wrong about slaves' inability to master firearms. But it was a detail. At all events, neither 400 rifles and revolvers nor any number of pikes would overthrow the slave masters. It would take many more weapons, which was why the first objective was the arsenal at Harpers Ferry.

Means completed his inspection. He was well satisfied with the iron fruits of his labors. The soldiers of the Provisional Army would use them to capture the Arsenal.

"This is a splendid collection, Captain. Where are the men to wield these weapons?"

John Brown stared unblinkingly at Means. He raised his arm and gestured toward the men gathered in the room. "We are few in number, but mighty in spirit. We are performing the Lord's work, and will strike the first blow against slavery on the Sabbath, and this will assure His blessing."

Means counted sixteen whites and five blacks. He listened patiently while Brown described his plan. He would lead them to the Ferry where they would divide: some to the Arsenal, some to the rifle works, and the balance to spread out over the countryside to summon the slaves to battle. Brown's son Owen, crippled by a withered arm, would remain behind along with simple, one-eyed Francis Meriam and a frail boy named Barclay Coppoc. They would wait at the farm to hand out pikes to the slaves who would flock to the Ferry when they heard Brown's call for freedom.

Means spoke: "It's a good plan. When I passed through the Ferry there were no federal troops at the Arsenal. However, I overheard someone in the telegraph office say that he expected a train from Washington later today with a detachment of United States Regulars. I doubt it's true but let me scout the Ferry one more time. I'll report to you on the Maryland side of the bridge."

Brown's brow wrinkled thoughtfully. "Very well. The Lord be with you."

Still carrying his filled carpetbag, Abner Means departed. It was late afternoon and the rain had resumed. The anticipated fog began to fill the low ground at the end of the farm lane. Captain John Brown and his eighteen-man army would turn south to march six miles to Harpers Ferry. Without pausing, Means turned north toward Boonesboro and spurred his horse hard.

The arrival of the 1:25 A.M. Baltimore express woke Shephard Hayward from his sleep in the lobby of the Wager House. His first conscious action was to reach into his pocket. His probing fingers encircled the silver coin. Yes! It was still there.

Because of his status as a free black, Hayward considered himself one of the Ferry's privileged men. Some days were better than others, and yesterday had been one of the good ones. A white gentleman named Cook had hired him to tether a horse until a man named Gabriel came to claim it. Cook had paid up front with the silver coin. It was far more money than the job justified, but Hayward had learned long ago to avoid questioning white folks about anything at all.

Hayward saw the conductor enter the lobby. Irish Pat Higgins, one of the night watchmen, spoke to him: "I was to relieve Bill Williams and could na find him. I'm walking along the tracks and someone grabs me. I break free and run. Someone yells 'Halt.' I didn'a know what 'Halt' meant any more than a hog knows about a holiday. Then bang. I feel a sting. And lookee here."

Hayward saw Higgins dabbing at his scalp with a bloody cloth. With a laugh Hayward stood up. "It was whisky that caused you to cut your head Pat. I'll go find Williams."

The baggage handler slowly walked along the track peering through the fog.

From the gloom came the command "Halt!"

Badly frightened, Hayward whirled about and began to run. A weapon discharged. Hayward felt a burning pain. With legs wobbling, he stumbled back to Wager House where he collapsed.

Armistead Carter was upstairs when he heard the muffled retort of a gunshot. It was the evening's second unusual event. Earlier, as he finished a nightcap at the bar, one of the working ladies, a fine looking, dark haired young woman, had casually propositioned him. He had politely declined. She asked if he preferred a young boy. Having traveled a fair amount – he had been to school up North – the question did not shock him. He smiled and explained that he very much preferred the company of women but that he was betrothed. The former was true, the latter pure invention and it had not dissuaded the young woman whatsoever.

Armistead guessed that her third proposition came because Sunday evenings were slow. It did not occur to him that women found him attractive. Although he had declined again, her breadth of imagination had kept him awake, albeit alone, in his hotel room until the gunshot and the gathering commotion downstairs caused him to climb into his clothes to investigate.

He arrived to see a doctor pronounce the hotel's baggage handler beyond medical help. The doctor and a railroad man went outside. Minutes later they were back, the railroad man ashen faced, trembling with fear; Doctor John Starry, alert, composed. Starry reported that a group of armed men had seized the arsenal. They were apparently not bandits because their bearded leader had permitted the Baltimore express to continue unmolested. Starry urged Armistead and the other men to circulate through the streets to warn the townspeople. The doctor announced that he would head to the telegraph office to raise the militia.

Armistead spent the night knocking on doors, telling people to stay inside. Church bells tolled the alarm, accompanied by sporadic gunfire. With daylight came the bodies: Irish Tom Boerley, a strong fisted bully who missed his shot and fell to the raiders' return fire, blood gushing bright from a mortal wound in his groin; Dangerfield Newby, one of Brown's six negroes, shot in the head by a townsman, his body stripped, throat cut, genitals sliced off; Brown's son Watson, shot in the bowels while carrying a flag of truce. George Turner, a visiting businessman, made the mistake of crossing Shenandoah Street within view of the engine house where Brown and his men waited. A killing bullet from a Sharps rifle tore open his chest. Mayor Fontaine Beckham, struck in the head while scouting the raider's stronghold.

By the time Armistead returned to the Wager House a throng of armed townspeople had gathered; some in the hotel, others across the tracks at the Gault House Saloon. They carried hunting rifles, ancient muskets, squirrel guns. Some fingered sharp knives and a few brandished rusty cutlasses. They exchanged news around the bar and Armistead began to understand what was taking place. A master machinist told how he had been stopped from entering the Rifle Works by an armed guard who explained that his army had seized federal property in Harpers Ferry in order to give freedom to every slave in Virginia in the name of God. The machinist's report stimulated angry conversation, punctuated by demands for another round of drinks. Fueled by cherry smashes, juleps, and straight corn liquor, they agreed that when Doc Starry returned from Charles Town with the militia they would sort out this gang of damned Abolitionists right quick. After all, they had already captured one of the thieving cowards and placed him under guard up stairs.

"So, there's two groups, one at the Rifle Works and another at the engine house, as well as a few guards on the Potomac bridge. It seems like there's not more than thirty." Armistead's words trailed off as a man burst into the lobby shouting, "We got one, come see!"

Armistead followed the throng into an alley where he saw a tall man standing over Dangerfield Newby's mutilated body.

"I loaded with a rail spike and shot the son of a bitch clean in the head," the man boasted.

No one attended his words. Men and women kicked at the naked body. Some jammed sticks into his wounds. A man knelt and neatly cut off Newby's ears. He stood, grinned, and pocketed his treasures. The crowd pushed the body into the gutter. A pair of hogs came running and began to feed greedily.

Armistead followed the mob back inside to hear the news that the mayor had been shot. He saw Harry Hunter's alcohol blotched face turn purple with rage. Hunter shouted to the saloon keeper, "They killed my uncle. Come on!"

The pair climbed the stairs and returned with one of the raiders, Will Thompson. As they dragged Thompson outside someone protested that he had been captured while trying to parlay under a flag of truce. Hunter retorted, "Mister Beckham's life is worth ten thousand of these damn abolitionists." The mob followed as Hunter led his prisoner onto the Potomac bridge. Hunter placed his revolver against Thompson's head and fired. Thompson's body fell between the trestles. As it descended several more townspeople took aim and fired again. Armistead retraced his steps to the hotel. Behind him came a renewed fusillade of gunfire as the townspeople practiced their marksmanship on the crumpled target lying on the rocks below.

Armistead had seen individual acts of brutality committed by irate farmers against balky plow horses; by a schoolyard bully toward a crippled boy; by a drunken husband toward his wife. Princeton had taught him how the streets of Paris descended to mob rule during the French Revolution. Neither his own experiences nor all the history books had prepared him to see such things in Harpers Ferry.

The Martinsburg militia arrived in the afternoon. They charged against the rear of the engine house. The raiders had cut loopholes through the bricks and their rifle fire repulsed the attack. Thereafter, armed civilians and militia surrounded the engine house to contain the raiders, but they did not dare charge again. The standoff persisted past nightfall, a precarious equilibrium waiting for some new force to tip the balance.

It came an hour before midnight. A commotion behind the Wager House interrupted Armistead as he picked at the remnants of a late supper. He glanced up to see a well-built, middle aged man stride into the saloon. Behind him marched two uniformed officers and a file of blue-coated United States Marines. Although the older man was dressed in civilian clothes, he was clearly in command: "Lieutenant Stuart, close this saloon down and then attend to the rest of them."

The young lieutenant saluted and the leader spoke again. "Now, can someone please tell me what is going on here?"

A babble of besotted voices poured out a confusing account of the day's events. The man interrupted, "So, you say there are about five hundred of them, and that they are in that little brick building over there. They must be packed in pretty tight."

After the nervous chuckle subsided, Armistead rose and pushed his way through the drinkers until he stood before the older man. "Sir, I believe there were never more than thirty and that they have lost about a third of that number today."

The man fixed Armistead with an intent stare. Armistead returned his gaze. Close up, he saw that the man's dark hair was graying, particularly around the temples.

"And why do you say that?"

Armistead concisely related what he had witnessed. He had just finished speaking when one of the officers returned.

"Colonel Lee, the saloons are closed down. As you ordered, I've stationed a reliable sergeant and a file of men at each."

Lee nodded and then extended his hand toward Armistead. "Thank you for that most lucid account. What is your name, sir?"

"Armistead Carter."

With a hint of a smile Lee said, "You have the makings of a first class soldier, Mister Carter."

The officer named Stuart reappeared. "Colonel, I have deployed the men to contain the raiders inside the armory yard."

"Very good. We will wait for daylight before we move."

The sun rose from behind Loudoun Heights. Its rays penetrated the mist to illuminate a growing throng of spectators on the slope above Harpers Ferry. Women in bonnets and shawls, children in tow, vied with farmhands and businessmen to find a place to observe the unfolding drama. From his vantage point in the cemetery, Armistead looked down upon the small promontory formed by the confluence of the Potomac and Shenandoah rivers. To the north, a high trestle railroad bridge spanned the Potomac, its northern end emerging from a tunnel that had been blasted through the rock cliff of the Maryland Heights. The bridge's southern end rested on the promontory and led to a fork near a small, red brick fire engine house. Here the tracks divided. The Baltimore and Ohio – the commercial lifeline that brought the bounty from the western farmlands to the great cities of the Atlantic seaboard – ran through the lower part of Harpers Ferry and continued west into the Virginia mountains. The other line, the Winchester and Potomac, headed south toward the Shenandoah Valley.

The brick building in which John Brown and his men waited stood alone some forty yards from the eastern end of Harpers Ferry. Armistead saw that Colonel Lee had positioned the marines to surround the engine house. He pondered the raiders' plight. They had struck on Sunday evening. It was now Tuesday morning. They had been isolated for more than thirty-six hours. The isolation must have magnified their fears. Surely by now they understood that the might of an aroused federal authority opposed them and whatever madcap scheme had brought them here could not succeed. Logic dictated that they surrender, yet apparently logic did not apply. They had witnessed their own men shot down while under flag of truce and had themselves callously fired at innocent bystanders. The scene made Armistead think of a theater, the audience now in place in a semi-circle above the stage, the light growing in intensity, the actors waiting for their cues.

A voice disturbed Armistead's musings. "Look, look! Something's happening."

Armistead trained a borrowed opera glass upon a figure in blue uniform, shako, brass epaulets, sash and sword. He walked briskly toward the door of the engine house. Armistead saw that it was Lieutenant Stuart.

"He's a cool un," someone observed, marveling at the officer's erect posture and precise gait.

Stuart stopped at the door. It opened slowly. Someone poked a rifle barrel at his face. Stuart did not flinch. Armistead's breath caught. He thought he was about to witness an execution. Instead, a hand reached out to snatch a piece of paper from Stuart. Armistead guessed that Stuart had delivered a final demand for surrender. Stuart spoke briefly, paused, and shook his head from side to side. Still preserving his erect carriage, he stepped back from the door, removed his shako, and waved it slightly.

What took place next occurred with startling suddenness. Twenty-four marines, arrayed in a two-deep line, emerged from the town and charged toward the brick building. The leading rank hefted sledge hammers, the rear rank carried muskets with fixed bayonets. Nearby townspeople began to cheer. The spectators along the heights reinforced the cheer with their own voices. Two particularly large marines beat the heavy wooden door with their sledges. The door swayed, but it seemed to have an elasticity that deadened the force of the blows. A file of marines carrying a stout ladder charged the door. Wielding the ladder as a battering ram, they delivered a solid strike. Wood on wood, the thud echoed up from the street. The marines stepped back several paces, surged forward again and the door gave way.

A sword-wielding officer led the marines through the breach. Shouts. A flurry of shots. Thin wisps of gun smoke rose from the engine house to meet the morning light. Unable to see clearly, Armistead ran down the cemetery steps, crossed Clay Street, and continued toward the engine house.

He smelled the acrid smoke seeping from the shattered door and saw marines tensely aiming their muskets at the opening. From within came a commanding voice: "Make a lane there. Make a lane."

A marine emerged, his shako slightly askew, a smudge of powder smoke streaking his cheek. Behind him came three men, two black and one white, prodded along in stumbling step by marines who held lowered bayonets at their backs. A pair of marines, supporting an obviously injured white man emerged next, followed by four more marines carrying a small, haggard-looking, elderly man. The marines laid him down on the grass. He had white hair and a full, gray beard. Armistead was close enough to see his eyes. In spite of the man's apparent pain, they burned with an intense light.

"Are you Captain Brown, of Kansas?" a marine officer inquired.

"I am sometimes called so," he replied.

"Are you Osawatomie Brown?"

"I tried to do my duty there."

"What was your present object?"

"To free the slaves from bondage."

Overhearing these words, the crowd, which had grown in number since the shooting stopped, surged inward toward the old man and his marine guards. Someone called out, "Lynch him, lynch the nigger loving bastard." Others picked up the cry. Armistead felt a sharp elbow dig into his side as a small, sallow-faced man tried to push past him. He had a pronounced stutter and a wild look as he picked up the chant, "Lynch him! Lynch him!" Armistead saw a fine foam of spittle issue from his mouth with each repetition.

Lee's voice rose above the crowd noise: "Friends, friends, it is over. Go back to your homes. It is over."

Most people in the crowd checked, but a few – including the sallow-faced man – still pressed forward, chanting all the while. Another officer, it was Stuart, barked out a command. The second rank of marines wheeled about to face the crowd, their muskets held at right shoulder shift. Almost as one, the mob leaders hesitated and then stood still. Lee repeated: "Friends, it is over. Go back to your homes."

A junior officer approached, saluted stiffly, and reported, "Colonel Lee, the prisoners are secured."

"Very good. The saloons will remain closed. Maintain a guard detail at each. I must notify Washington and tell them it is over."

The crowd began to disperse. Armistead accompanied the flow back toward the hotel. He heard a woman's nearby voice, a distinctive German accent conveying emphatic conviction: "It is not over. It has just begun."

The sun burst through a hole in the clouds. In spite of its warming rays, Armistead felt a chill pass through him.

Chapter 2. Loudoun County and Harpers Ferry, October 16 to December 2, 1859

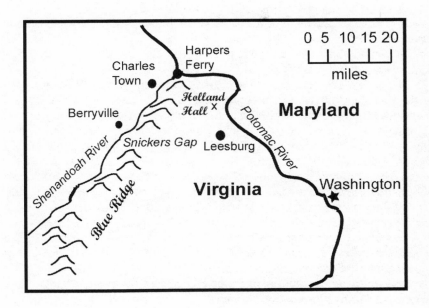

"We've already done a heap of work, Miz Amanda. The morning is nearly half gone."

Amanda Holland sat up, an angry frown half-formed on her face. She saw the servant opening the heavy curtain. The shower had passed and the emerging light seemed to carry Nell's throaty chuckle throughout the high-ceiling sleeping chamber. Amanda's frown receded and then dissolved fully when Nell turned to deliver a silver tray covered with an imported French linen. Puffs of scented steam rose from beneath the linen.

"Your favorite, honey," Nell said. "Fresh from the oven." Nell placed the tray on the bedside table. She removed the tea cozy to pour the brown English tea into a china cup. She delicately wielded a silver pincer to select three flakes of loaf sugar. Replacing the pincer with a spoon — the same spoon that Nell's mother had used to stir the tea for Amanda's mother — Nell added milk to the brew. "Agnes was right near with her milk this morning, but I reckon she gave enough for your tea."

The order was important; first the sugar stirred, the milk added, then stirred again. It was the way tea had been made at Holland Hall since time out of memory. Nell carefully replaced the tea cozy and removed the linen covering the tray. She cut and buttered the hot scone.

Amanda sat motionless, watching the ritual. Her mouth watered. "How would I ever awake without your tea and scones Nell?"

"I reckon you would find a way Miz Amanda. You usually do." Again came Nell's laugh.

Amanda took a first sip. "Ooh, it's too hot."

"You have always been impatient, Miz Amanda."

With an exaggerated pout Amanda replied, "Papa says the same thing."

Nell smiled and walked toward the wardrobe.

"It will be the work clothes today, Nell."

While Amanda studied the list she had drawn up the night before, Nell retrieved the garments: silk underclothes but not the newest; a blue muslin frock made up North instead of the imported French blouses; a long, sturdy skirt sewn by Nell's sister rather than fancier clothes made off the plantation. Work clothes indeed, thought Nell. Nell gave a slight sigh and caught sight of herself in the oak-framed glass that dominated one corner of the room. The reflected image showed a heavy bellied, wide hipped woman. A not unattractive servant's uniform concealed weathered, threadbare clothes stained with barn-yard muck from the pre-dawn milking.

I was once more shapely, Nell thought as she stood waiting for Amanda to finish her tea. But that was before my first, five years ago. Thank God it had been a boy, much better chance he would stay at Holland Hall or at least somewhere nearby. The child inside gave a vigorous kick. She smiled inwardly. Only a boy could give a kick like that. If so, that will make three boys out of four. I've given them what they wanted. I'll be eighteen next year. Will they give me what I want? Will they let me marry this child's father?

The sound of Amanda rising stirred Nell from her reverie. Amanda stood, arms outstretched while Nell dressed her. She continued to study her list, the chores she intended to accomplish today or certainly by tomorrow. She forced herself to focus, to ignore the inner knowledge that the list might as well be blank.

Since the death of her mother, Amanda had applied herself to filling a void. In a surprisingly short two years she had mastered the duties of the mistress of Holland Hall. People said she had done well; at age twenty undertaking the not easy task of replacing a competent woman of business while supporting a father lost to grief and the bottle. In truth, Amanda knew that she had surpassed her mother. The domestic side of Holland Hall now practically ran itself. Which was why the list she held meant so little. She had molded her life to be as unvarying as the tide only to come to the realization that it was not enough.

The slate roof deadened the sounds of falling rain. In spite of the soporific sound, Arminius 'Min' Carter slept fitfully. A bugle's blast brought him to full consciousness. Anticipating a prank, he carefully parted the curtains that opened onto his sleeping balcony. Instead of the expected egg barrage hurled by his militia comrades, another tremulous bugle call greeted him. Gazing down into the yard, he saw Kinlock Barton looking pale and anxious. He walked out on the balcony and called out: "Kinlock! What in the blazes are you doing?"

"We're being called out! There's been an invasion. Someone's captured the arsenal at Harpers Ferry. Major Kerfoot says to assemble in town without delay." Barton wheeled his high-stepping palomino around and rode off at a gallop, leaving Min's incredulous questions half formed on his lips.

Ninety minutes later, seventeen troopers belonging to the Loudoun Grays rode west toward Harpers Ferry. Old Major Kerfoot had told Min everything he knew, which was precious little. They rode fast, through Snicker's Gap and across the Shenandoah River to Berryville where they overtook small columns of marching militia. They too apparently had little idea of what was taking place twenty-five miles to the north. The consensus seemed to be that a serious slave rebellion had erupted.

Entering Charles Town, the Loudoun Grays encountered a body of cavalry. Min spoke with a junior officer and learned that they styled themselves the Mountain Rangers under the command of Captain Turner Ashby. Min whistled appreciatively. Although he had never met the man, the name Turner Ashby was well known. Back in Fifty-Three, Irish laborers working on the Manassas Gap Railroad had rioted. What began as a fight among themselves turned into an assault against their bosses, and then an attack on the townsmen. The people of Markham sought help and summoned Turner Ashby. Thereafter, whenever something needed doing, people had called for Ashby.

Ashby's Mountain Rangers looked like a collection of planters riding to the hunt. They neither wore uniforms nor marched in formation. Indeed, the officer told Min that they had been attending a ring tournament along the banks of Pantherskin Run when the news came from Harpers Ferry.

Min surreptitiously appraised the unit following the Rangers. What he saw made his eyes stare. Warrenton's Blackhorse Troop wore finely tailored uniforms and possessed matching equipment. Deflated, Min gazed back at his Loudoun Grays: rodent-faced Bush Underwood riding his sway-backed sorrel; fat Ned Beattie propped awkwardly in his saddle, already feeling the effects of his covert tippling; earnest Welby Smallwood, his father's huge Revolutionary War saber strapped across his scrawny back. Min shook his head and sighed. He wondered how they would perform if it came to fighting. And, while trying to conceal his inner doubts, he wondered how he would behave.

Still, it was heartening to see their numbers grow as they approached Harpers Ferry. It reminded him of the history books describing the Minutemen at Lexington and Concord Bridge. Min straightened in his saddle and silently pledged to do his duty.

They arrived in Harpers Ferry to learn that they were too late. A regular army officer ordered Major Kerfoot and Captain Ashby to deploy their troopers as pickets on the roads leading to town. They were to report any suspicious movements and await further orders. For the remainder of the day, and for weary nights thereafter, thoughts of Minutemen and Redcoats, of distinguishing himself on the field of battle, gave way to hunger and drowsiness as Min fought to stay awake in order to watch for an invasion that did not come.

On December 2, 1859 a crowd gathered to watch John Brown's journey to the grave. Whereas most, the ghouls excepted, were present for the simple satisfaction of seeing a wrong righted, Armistead was uncertain why he was here. Newspapers throughout the land had made much of the trial of John Brown and Armistead had read them religiously. From New York came Horace Greeley's impassioned defense of Brown's conduct. From Richmond, Edward Pollard responded with a bloody-minded demand for Brown's execution. Like many of his friends and neighbors – particularly the German immigrants whose thriving small farms and shops boomed without use of slave labor – Armistead was opposed in a general way to slavery. But he understood change could not occur overnight, and this view did not put him in the same camp as the northern Abolitionists who demanded an immediate end to slavery. Above all, he found neither sense nor nobility in the murders John Brown's men had committed nor in the ugly backlash of violence the raid had triggered. He concluded that he was here to witness the end of a tragedy in which fate had compelled him to assume a minor role.

The Loudoun Grays trotted into position along one side of an open field across from where Armistead stood. Armistead saw his cousin Min riding next to the elderly major who commanded the unit. The cousins had grown up on adjacent farms. They had been best friends through childhood and remained close even when, to Min's dismay — "Why do you want to go live up among the Yankees, Armistead? There's nuthin they can teach you that you need to know." — Armistead had left to attend Princeton. Armistead wondered what Min was thinking now. In contrast to their well-to-do Holland relatives, neither his family nor Min's had ever been wealthy enough to entertain the possibility of owning slaves. In recent conversations Min had said that since Virginia Governor Wise had called out the militia, his duty required that he help ensure the fulfillment of the court's stern judgment. Min added that he personally believed that John Brown and his ilk deserved their fate.

More militia units arrived to complete a cordon around the execution site. Governor Wise did not want any civilians within earshot of the gallows in case Brown attempted a final speech. To obtain his vantage point, Armistead had borrowed a uniform so he could pass as a militiaman. The militia formed a square around the gallows. They were supposed to face outward and remain vigilant in case of a last minute effort to rescue the condemned man. Min saw that most had turned toward the center of the field. Steadying his horse, Min also shifted in his saddle to look.

It was a crude affair, featuring thirteen steep steps ascending to a platform of unpainted planks. Two posts extended upward from the platform, connected by a horizontal wooden bar. Centered on the plank floor beneath the bar was a trap door. As if anticipating a feast, a pair of turkey buzzards soared over the gallows.

The muffled sounds of drumming floated through the December air. A pair of white draft horses easily pulled an old furniture wagon into the field, their huge hoofs stepping delicately over the torn, half-frozen mud. The wagon carried a walnut coffin trimmed in light colored poplar. Atop the coffin sat the condemned man, his arms bound at the elbows. John Brown wore a tattered, black frock coat over a black vest, a black-brimmed hat, and a baggy pair of black pantaloons. An incongruous pair of red carpet slippers worn over white socks added the only color. When the wind blew, the loose fitting pantaloons shuddered in the breeze. As the wagon neared the gallows Min saw that the old man had a solemn expression.

Yet he was apparently unafraid. Brown stepped down from the wagon, waved one of his pinioned arms in the direction of the newspaper and journal reporters, and climbed the gallows' steps with firm tread. He stopped and stared down at the officials assembled in the front row. Directing his gaze at the prosecutor and mayor, he said, "Gentlemen, goodbye."

Brown awkwardly shook hands with his executioners. The sheriff removed Brown's hat, adjusted the noose around his neck, and placed a white muslin cap over his face. Min heard the sheriff tell him to move over to the trap.

Brown replied, "You will have to guide me there." He shuffled toward the center of the platform. The sheriff offered a handkerchief, explaining that the condemned man could drop it as a signal to cut the rope that would open the trap.

"No, I don't care," Brown replied. "I don't want you to keep me waiting unnecessarily."

The old man's last wish was not granted. It seemed that the militia were unready. For the next ten minutes more troops wheeled into position around the gallows. The sheriff nervously fingered his ax. The crowd seemed to hold its breath as if they were one being; alert, anxious, expectant. Through it all, Brown stood erect and motionless with the noose around his neck.

A cavalry officer mounted on a snow-white horse cantered back and forth. Min saw that it was Turner Ashby. From his time spent patrolling around Harpers Ferry he recognized some others as well. There was John Imboden and the Staunton Artillery, manning a pair of howitzers on either side of the gallows. Nearby stood Professor Tom Jackson with a company of cadets from the Virginia Military Institute. In total, Governor Wise had summoned over one thousand soldiers to ensure that no one interrupted the execution of John Brown.

Finally a militia colonel shouted to Sheriff Campbell, "All ready."

The sheriff hesitated and the colonel repeated his remark. Silence descended on the field. Campbell raised his ax and swung downward with a short, compact motion to cut the rope. The trap opened. Brown fell a short distance, his pinioned arms jerked upward until the rope straightened and came taut. His knees were now on a level with the position occupied by his feet before the rope was cut. For several minutes his hands clenched and twitched. After a last convulsive spasm, John Brown's arms fell limp. Colonel John Preston of the Virginia Military Institute called out, "So perish all such enemies of Virginia! All such enemies of the Union! All such foes of the human race!" Cheers erupted from the crowd.

They did not cut him down just yet, because the old man's pulse continued to beat. For thirty-five minutes the Blue Ridge wind blew over Brown's body, causing it to sway at rope's end until the last ember of his physical life faded. Only then did the Loudoun Grays exit the field.

Min advanced only a few paces before reining in his horse. Someone had blundered. Or perhaps the different militia units had rushed things a bit in order to be at the head of the column on the triumphant return march through Charles Town. In any event, a column of immaculately uniformed infantry blocked the route.

"What unit, y'all?" Min inquired.

An infantryman replied, "The Richmond Grays."

"Don't they drill you down in Richmond how to face about without tripping on your muskets?"

A slightly built private sporting a thick mustache replied coldly, "What do you mean by that mister?"

Min felt a surge of anger. He looked at the man more closely and then forced himself to relax. He realized he had merely wanted to make small talk to distract himself from the spectacle he had just witnessed.

"Nothing at all. My apologies. Say, aren't you the man who was performing the dramatic readings from Shakespeare at the Episcopal Lecture Room the last couple of days?"

The private nodded.

"You were very good. My apologies to the Richmond Grays again."

It was undignified to quarrel with a private. It would be shameful to duck a fight if the man came looking for him. He offered his hand and said, "The name's Carter, Min Carter."

The private returned his clasp saying, "My name's Booth, John Wilkes Booth."

Armistead Carter did not linger at the execution place. When the sheriff had cut the rope he heard someone say, "depart ye wicked into everlasting fire." He was fairly certain that he agreed with the sentiment, but he could not help but admire Brown's calm courage. Now, to complete the cycle, he returned to the Wager House. The saloon buzzed with the latest news. It seemed that John Brown's last words had not been spoken on the gallows but rather he had addressed the nation once more after his death. He had left a message with a jailer. It read: "I John Brown am now quite certain that the crimes of this guilty, land: will never be purged away; but with Blood."

Chapter 3. Holland Hall, June 1860

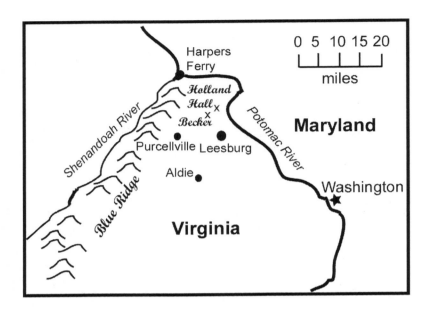

The weeks following the hanging of John Brown found the Loudoun Grays patrolling the roads and farm tracks north to the Potomac and west to the mountain passes. Rumors abounded that abolitionists were coming to finish what Brown and his rebels had begun. In Leesburg, people chased an abolitionist preacher from town; in Charles Town they put northerners in jail. Some prophesied that Brown's death would ignite a massive slave revolt. Around Holland Hall, local gossip seemed to confirm this dire prediction. Reports circulated that slaves were assembling at isolated farms to engage in strange, nocturnal rituals that surely presaged murder and rebellion.

When a barn burned near Aldie and a wheat field caught fire in Purcellville, men nodded knowingly. People became reluctant to travel at night. Fearful plantation owners barricaded their homes. It was said that over in Clarke County, Judge Parker loosened his hunting dogs at night to patrol the grounds of his farm. If anyone was a marked man, people agreed, than surely it was the judge who had presided over Brown's trial. Zealously, the Loudoun Grays questioned all strangers they encountered and, like young men throughout the South, attended to their drill with newfound zeal.

When the spring of 1860 passed uneventfully, the ripening days of early summer brought promise that life's routines would resume. Conversation among neighbors returned to the familiar subjects associated with the progression of the seasons. The wheat was off to a fine start. After a meager winter's diet caused by a shortage of acorn mast, the market hogs had been brought back from the woods and were fattening up nicely. The apples had set fruit; it should be a good year for cider. If some were bold enough to talk about the politics of the coming national election, their voices were drowned out by the majority who preferred to discuss when to make a first cutting of hay, the likelihood of rain, and the rapacious conduct of the big city merchants.

Among the plantation gentry, anticipation accelerated apace with the lengthening days as Holland Hall's annual mid-summer's eve fete approached. It was the social highpoint between planting and harvest, a celebration of the change of seasons and the continuing promise of prosperity, a statement of time and place, renewal and tradition.

The manor house sat on a grassy knoll overlooking fertile hills and fields. Built in the Federal style, Holland Hall featured a Flemish-bonded brick exterior. Inside, broad passages separated twenty-six furnished rooms. The westward facing parlor opened onto a balcony that provided a magnificent view of the distant Blue Ridge. Here, on the long awaited fete day, three cousins discussed the relative merits of two superb horses.

Min spoke with a bantering voice, "Armistead, I don't believe that blue roan of yours can ever head Rattler, not today, not ever."

"Cousin, you'd best make ready to race, because I say Blue and I can gallop to Catoctin Creek and be back here having tea with Cousin Amanda before you and Rattler reach the creek."

"You're not going to let Armistead get away with such a boast, are you Min?" asked Amanda.

Min looked at her with an affectionate smile. Some of his first memories of this quick witted cousin were of how she goaded two boys into contest and prank. That she was doing it again mattered not.

"Rest assured Mandy," Min replied, "Not only will I win, you had better retire any plans to dance with Armistead tonight, for he will be in no shape for any funning once I'm through with him."

"Such talk," laughed Armistead. "Pay him no mind Cousin Amanda, we shall dance tonight, and more than once!"

News of the race spread quickly throughout the household. Early arriving guests swarmed onto the veranda to observe the impending contest. The wagering began before they had departed the parlor. They were men and women who well appreciated good horseflesh and superior riders. Indeed, they tolerated nothing less.

In spite of his uncharacteristic boast, Armistead had not spoken casually when he proposed a race to Catoctin Creek and back. Knowing his cousin's horse, Rattler, had superior speed, he relied on a lengthy course to tire his rival. Then Blue's superior stamina would tell. Knowing also Min's brashness, he was confident his cousin would not deign to change the terms of the contest, particularly when challenged in the presence of Cousin Amanda. He did not know that the impending race would enter local legend, told and retold by those who saw it and those who claimed they had, until a new year brought sights that obliterated memories of all that had gone before.

"Four miles then, gentlemen," proclaimed Squire Randolph Holland, the host and Amanda's father. "You should know the terrain well enough by now, seeing as how y'all been hanging around here for the better part of the spring."

Titters arose from the crowd. Although less attractive than some of the comely women in attendance – she had heedlessly exposed her skin to the sun since childhood and received, her exasperated mother primly explained, her just reward; a collection of freckles to offset her auburn hair — her lack of a porcelain complexion did not seem to deter suitors.

Conscious of the friendly scrutiny from the boisterous gathering, the two riders gathered their mounts. They were well matched; Min, lithe, sandy haired, relaxed – Armistead, one year older, more thickly built, dark haired, intent. Nearing the start line, both horses jigged with excitement. Min's Rattler, renowned for his speed, showed his fine-tuned nervousness as his nostrils flared, his grey flanks quivered, and flecks of foam gathered on mouth and brisket. In contrast, the Blue Roan showed a purposeful, controlled power.

The Squire's commanding voice spoke again: "At the signal gentleman." Pointing his heavy, imported LeMat revolver in the air, he squeezed the trigger.

Anticipating the loud report, Armistead sunk his weight onto his heels to control his mount. Min's Rattler, more familiar with the sound of firearms, needed no such restraint. Consequently, as the discharge echoed off the nearby Blue Ridge foothills, Rattler uncoiled with a great first stride. Before taking a half dozen more, he had a three length advantage. Shouts of encouragement, addressed equally to both riders, and a few good natured criticisms directed at Armistead for having given the early lead to Min through his cautious riding tactics, filled the air. Crossing a gently climbing open meadow that led north to the creek, Min cocked his head back and grinned: "Come cousin, catch me if you can!"

Rattler's dark grey tail waved like a flag briefly lifted by the first breeze of dawn. Armistead pursued this banner, his Blue running effortlessly toward the end of the meadow. The tall field grass parted before the racing horses, its vibrant insect life noise drowned out by two sets of pounding hooves. The riders rapidly approached a woodlot delineating the end of the cleared meadow. Here a split rail, locust fence angled sinuously along the meadow edge, its open gate off to the right. Armistead knew a well-worn path extended from this gate down to the creek. Yet his cousin continued straight on, seemingly headed directly for the trees. Without breaking stride, the grey easily cleared the four-rail fence and disappeared into the enveloping greenery.

Ignoring the inner voice warning that it was too early in the race to hazard an unknown jump, Armistead urged his horse into the air. The jump lacked peril. An old cattle path provided a safe landing, allowing Blue to ground easily, the impact absorbed first on his forelegs and then cushioned by the descending hindquarters. Ducking a low hanging branch, the roan sped around a curve to regain sight of the frontrunner. A fox hunter's yip reverberated back to the pursuing rider, and then was strengthened and repeated when Armistead returned the yell.

After the riders disappeared over the first rise, Squire Randolph Holland turned to his guests: "I propose we move to the grand balcony where I'm confident with the aid of my glass we can see the boys as they return. Also, I see James has some lemonade for the ladies and perhaps a brandy punch for the gentlemen."

Ascending the veranda steps, the guests gladly received a libation from the silver tray held by a straight-backed black man dressed in neat butler attire.

"Thank you James," murmured Squire Holland, helping himself to a brimming wine glass full of punch. As the crowd continued up the spiral staircase, he sipped fastidiously.

"Yes, I recommend this most excellent punch to your attention. The drinks master has outdone himself," he jovially said to his son Boyd and Boyd's friend Charles Becker. Then, unexpectedly, a small frown darkened the Squire's face, quickly replaced by the accustomed, well managed open look that tended to conceal from all except his closest acquaintances his inner thoughts.

"I see Charles that your father has arrived."

Charles' small groan was drowned out by the noise of crunching gravel as a stocky draft horse pulled a black carriage up the elm lined drive. While most neighbors rode the blooded horses for which Loudoun County was famous, or if traveling with family came in elegant carriages, Sigmund Becker traveled in a stained and worn small carriage. Becker was one of the many immigrant Germans who, along with the Quaker community, seemed so ably to complement the older, landed families that inhabited both sides of the Potomac River. Through hard work and wise investments Becker had amassed considerable holdings. Yet the prosperous German apparently felt that showy trappings were unnecessary to his station. Dismounting, with assistance from one of the ubiquitous footmen, he solemnly climbed the stairs onto the veranda.

"Welcome Mister Becker. I see you have not brought your pretty daughter."

"Good day to you Mister Holland."

Controlling his double irritation at Becker's failure to bring his daughter and his disrespectful omission of his host's honorific title, Squire Holland continued: "We were just gathering on the grand balcony to watch Min and Armistead. They left moments ago, a race to the creek and back."

An expression of interest crossed the German's face. Becker bred blooded horses. Moreover, his fine stable attracted buyers from throughout the Shenandoah Valley. "Ah, a race you say?"

"I'm not sure how much of a contest it will be. Min's on his Rattler while Armistead has that big blue roan."

"Ja, I know the roan well," replied Becker as he lapsed into the accent of his native Westphalia, "he foaled from one of my own."

"I know your abilities, Mister Becker, but this time I'm afraid Rattler's his superior."

"I cannot agree, Mister Holland. That roan was bred for stamina. Ja, that race the roan will win."

"Not to insult you, Mister Becker, but Rattler's speed will win this race. Why he already had five lengths on Armistead as they cleared the rise there." Squire Holland's face grew a bit more flushed than the June heat and brandy punch warranted.

"Then I say I have twenty dollars gold that the blue roan is back here first."

"You surprise me Mister Becker, I didn't think you were a gambling man, what with that religion of yours and all. But if I am to wager, I want a greater prize. If Armistead's nag comes in first I'll pay you twenty dollars. But when Min wins, as win he shall, I shall insist you summon your daughter and that she partner my son Boyd for the first dance."

A brief pause ensued, then a tight lipped scowl showed on Becker's face. Finally he extended his work worn hand toward the Squire, "So be it."

The crowd filled the second story balcony. The riders' many friends jockeyed for a viewing position to observe better the panoramic vista. Amidst them, Amanda pushed forward to secure a place in front. There she lifted her father's spy glass – a family heirloom used by Great Grandfather Holland during the Revolutionary War – and focused on the open field near the creek. Two riders came into view, in front the blond rider still, his lead narrowed to a mere fifteen feet. "There they are!" she cried, and the jostling throng pressed toward the rail.

Foremost among them came Squire Holland. "I believe, my dear, that I have the right," the Squire said in a tone that belied his smile. Amanda handed the glass to her father and he described what he saw.

From a distance it seemed that the riders continued effortlessly, and so Squire Holland reported. In fact, with the race more than half run, both horses showed signs of strain. Their glistening, sweat soaked necks and flanks appeared almost black. Min concentrated on the upcoming fieldstone wall, a jump he knew would be the most difficult so far. Rattler could surmount the five-foot high stone fence. The problem was the ditch on the far side. For the first time that day he touched his heels to the grey's flank.

Armistead's blue roan continued to gallop comfortably. So far the race had gone much as Armistead expected. Now was the time to begin to challenge the front running grey. He asked his horse to accelerate. The distance between the rivals decreased until they were nearly abreast. Only then did Armistead realize his mistake. Having concentrated on catching Min, he had failed to notice that behind the fieldstone wall was a wide ditch.

As Rattler jumped in perfect stride, the competitive roan also left the ground in an effort to match. Armistead silently cursed the premature jump, while knowing the fault was his. Casting style aside, Armistead leaned well forward, grabbed Blue's mane, and held on.

"He's left too soon!" the Squire exclaimed to his anxious guests. "By God, he won't clear the ditch."

Apprehension gripped the crowd. They could only too easily visualize the ugly, possibly deadly consequences of a soaring race horse careening into the opposite bank of a ditch; the heretofore effortlessly working machine realized as a great animal supported on four slender legs, a graceful rider reduced to a catapulting rag doll.

The roan almost, but not quite reached the far side of the ditch. His scrambling front legs hit first. Armistead pitched forward. For a moment his head extended beyond Blue's neck. But his strong grip on the mane arrested his forward momentum. By driving his feet into the stirrups, he managed to force Blue's hindquarters down. As a result, the roan's back legs sank to the ditch's floor instead of continuing to rise in cartwheeling catastrophe. The roan staggered onto his front knees, all momentum lost. Then slowly he climbed out of the ditch.

"No, he's still saddled, he's all right," said the Squire, his concern for horse and man apparent to all. "I must hand it to you, Mister Becker, that is one exceptionally strong horse. Any other would have been broken by that ditch."

"Is he again running?" asked the German.

"My God man, what difference does it make? He came to a complete stop. This race is over." The Squire set his spy glass down on the balcony rail with a decisive bang.

"It was a gallant try from Armistead, but now I believe I'll have a victory cup."

With a whoop, one of Min's militia comrades exclaimed, "Back down stairs to greet the conquering hero!"

"Back down to fill your glass I expect, Ephraim Beattie," retorted Amanda's friend Elizabeth Milton.

"To be sure, to do both Lizzie."

The crowd cheerfully descended, their glee heightened by the release of anxiety caused by the narrowly averted accident. Amanda trailed the group heading down the stairs. "Aren't you coming Mister Becker?"

A long pause ensued. The German peered through the spy glass he had seized after his host's departure. Finally he replied: "Ja, I believe I shall."

Becker turned toward Amanda, a bare flicker of satisfaction crossing his usually grim face.

Trailing the crowd filing back onto the veranda, seventeen-year-old Boyd Holland spoke to his friend Charles Becker: "Did you see how that lout Ephraim had his hands all over Lizzie as they were coming down the stairs?"

"You're not a lout unless caught. He had sense enough to wait until the older folk had left. Not like some we know!" replied Charles.

Blushing slightly, Boyd good naturedly pummeled Charles. "We will see who dances with whom tonight."

"It's not dancing we came for. I at any rate intend to do some regular skirmishing in the garden."

"Enough, lest we overheat," Boyd grinned. "Look over there, we should see them in a moment, coming through the opening in the trees."

The guests overheard this last remark as they stood on the expansive veranda fronting Holland Hall. They turned to welcome and applaud the popular winner.

"There he is!" someone shouted as Min's laboring grey came into view. But before this remark registered, several other voices hallooed louder. The entire crowd matched their cries until a cacophony of shouts, whistles, and clapping hands issued from the veranda. For unexpectedly, not just one rider had appeared. Two approached, with Armistead's roan again only three lengths behind.

Min had slowed for a moment to make certain his cousin and horse were unharmed. He then experienced a flush of pleasure as the realization of victory replaced concern for his rival's safety. With another fox hunter's cry, he pushed Rattler back into a gallop.

As before, Armistead repeated the yell, slightly weaker, slightly more distant, but a ringing challenge still. And then the Blue Roan showed his quality and Min realized that his rival was closing with ground eating strides. "Let's go Rattler," he spoke into his grey's ear. "We're almost home." He leaned forward to stroke the rippling muscles protruding above the forelegs. In complete harmony with his horse, this tactile urging told Rattler to run again. The grey responded, his ears laid flat, teeth bared. Not content with merely running faster, the spirited horse stretched out as if to reach the finish all the sooner. Taking hold of the bit in his teeth, Rattler shot forward toward the last fence beyond the tree line, and in so doing deprived the rider of his ability to control the horse's speed and direction with the reins.

Armistead saw Rattler accelerate and so for the second time touched his hand to Blue's flank. Blue's head jerked up as the horse looked back briefly, as if reproaching his rider for this lack of confidence. Displaying a reserve of strength that only Armistead and the breeder, Sigmund Becker, had known, Blue surged forward.

So it was that two riders emerged, separated from the watchers at the mansion by the last four rail locust fence and two hundred yards of freshly mown field. The crowd noise came to the riders, inspiring the blooded horses to fresh efforts. Thirty yards from the fence and Min still struggled to reinsert the bit. Twenty yards from the fence, he stood and leaned forward, a feat made difficult because his heavily breathing horse no longer ran with a smooth gait. Min extended his arm and hit Rattler in the jaw. Startled, Rattler's mouth opened. Min immediately jerked back on the reins thereby pulling the bit into place. Then, too late, the grey jumped, angling almost sideways over the top rail.

This time, Armistead had approached the fence prudently, closed to within two lengths of the grey, kept his roan well in hand, and prepared to jump in stride. But Rattler's unexpected response to Min's blow carried the grey in front of Armistead. Committed to the jump, he saw Rattler's hooves heavily strike the top rail, knocking Rattler into Blue's path. Armistead tugged hard on the reins. His horse side stepped in mid-leap, cleared the top rail, and landed. The unbalanced grey landed much heavier, but Rattler also had a hidden reserve, a strength enhanced by a master equestrian's skill and determination. Min settled his horse and then used the flat of his hand to summon his mount's last energies. During the awkward jump his Rattler had been passed.

The crowd's excitement reached a high pitched crescendo as the racers ran the last one hundred and fifty yards.

"By damn, they're going to collide!"

"Rattler's jumped too soon!"

"Oh he's struck the rail, wait... he's over!"

"Look at Armistead yank that pony around. Wonderful."

Individual words were lost amidst the roaring din. Thus, no one heard an uncharacteristic "God's Wounds! He's done it," spoken by Sigmund Becker.

With a hundred yards to go, Min had closed on his rival so that they ran neck and neck; the blue roan still powerful, grey laboring with uneven gait. Both riders slapped their mounts with each stride, yet neither gained. The grey's rasping breath alerted the cousins. Min felt a rippling shudder between his knees. Armistead's eyes turned toward his cousin in warning. Before their eyes met, Min had made his decision. With a heavy tug he reined in his exhausted horse as Blue shot ahead. Amidst a thunderous acclaim the blue roan crossed the finish. Behind came Min, leading his horse home on foot.

On the veranda the Squire handed Becker a note and then angrily poured himself another glass of punch. Becker accepted the winnings with a vindictive gleam of pleasure. Nearby, Amanda stood motionless, her wide eyes missing nothing.

Chapter 4. Loudoun County, July 1860

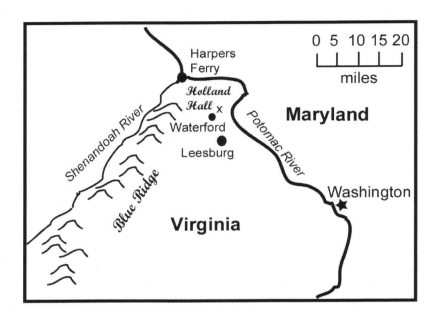

Talk of the race dominated conversation for weeks. In the telling and re-telling, Armistead and Min's good natured bantering and fox-hunting salutes became the chivalrous challenge of courtly knights. The narrowly averted disaster at the stone wall grew into a leap over a steep-banked, rock-filled stream with an enormous rattlesnake on the far side. Armistead barely evaded the snake's deadly strike when Min cast his cloak to cover the reptile, thereby allowing his cousin to cross safely. Only the account of the last jump did not expand with the telling. Here the truth was enough; a surpassing equestrian feat requiring no embellishment.

Likewise, there was no debate over Min's decision to stop. All knew that to continue once a horse had broken his wind – for that was indeed what had happened to the over-stressed grey – cruelly risked a life-impairing breakdown. A disappointing climax perhaps, but no one doubted that Min and his mount had given their all.

The end of a hot, muggy July day found Sigmund Becker waiting inside the stone cool of his grist mill. As one of the certified witnesses to the race, he had been called upon again today to describe what he had seen. The telling was satisfying, a guilty pleasure earned from an outsized, winning wager that commanded respect even from the gentry. The mournful creak of the waterwheel jerked Becker from his reverie. Standing with his stout arms folded, he waited for his daughter to answer his summons.

Rachel Becker entered the mill and instantly saw from her father's expression that this confrontation – the latest in a series that had begun four years ago when she was thirteen – required something more than her usual ingenuous dissembling. Nonetheless, her initial tactic was the same as always. She approached her father, stood on the toes of her five-foot two inch frame, and lightly kissed him on the cheek. "Papa, I think you have been working too hard for such a hot day as this."

"Rachel, I did not call you here to discuss my work or the weather. I expect you know what we must talk about."

Rachel quickly reviewed the past several weeks, searching for evidence of revealed indiscretions. Three nights ago she had climbed out her window, descending through the thick limbs of the Tennessee Coffee tree that loomed over her bedroom, and met Boyd Holland in the barn. But her father had been asleep, of this she was sure. She struck a petulant look, gave a toss of her long, auburn hair, and spoke: "Now father, you know how I have applied myself to my studies. I have read nearly all you have recommended, but I cannot yet read your mind."

"It's you and that Holland boy I mean to talk about."

"He is not a boy, he is almost eighteen," Rachel snapped, her green eyes flashing. "But I don't know why you wish to talk of him, we hardly know each other." She looked closely at his face, searching for a hint to explain his attack.

"You may not know him, but he and his family know a great deal about us. I did well to forbid your attendance at their fete last month."

"What do you mean the Hollands know a great deal about us?"

"Isaac Lassiter, the clerk of records, tells me that Holland's adviser – that Englishman Gordon – has been looking up land deeds and asking questions. You know Rachel, I own a great deal of land here, and hold a large note for property at the ferry crossing."

"And you know Papa, that Charles and I are so proud of you. You have given us everything since Mother died. I'm sure she is proud of you too." Rachel made her breath catch audibly and cast her eyes heavenward. Usually mention of her mother, who had died three years ago when the fever swept northern Virginia, deflected her father's attention to those handful of subjects; business, religion, and horses, which consumed all his waking attention. But not this time.

"Isaac also tells me that Holland's business does not go well. While many hereabouts use freemen to till the land, Holland retains his slaves. He gets less and less each year from his land compared to others. I think he realizes the only way to maintain his position is through marriage. And I think he means his son to marry you."

"But I hardly know him. Besides would it be so terrible a thing?"

"Yes!" spit out her father, in a voice filled with venom. "The Hollands own human flesh, and that is against the will of God. You mustn't see that boy again, Rachel. I forbid it. Their kind and ours shall be forever divided."

Thankful that her father's tirade had come from well trod ground rather than from knowledge of her activities, Rachel embraced him tightly. "Father, you know I try hard to be your dutiful daughter."

Relief crossed Becker's normally taciturn face. "Thank you Rachel, thank you."

As Rachel departed the gristmill, she saw her father's eyes had filled with tears.

"Troop! Count off by fours." Lieutenant Min Carter sat stiffly erect waiting for the next order.

"Right face, trot!" croaked Major Judson Kerfoot. The Loudoun Grays advanced to the designated pivot point – indicated by Min's motionless figure – and turned to face the church at the end of the town square. As the groups of four passed the lieutenant, they vied with one another to break Min's composure. Long familiarity – the entire unit had grown up together, many were relatives and friends, most schoolmates – did not seem to promote respect for rank.

"Sit up straight Min, Old Iron Ass is looking your way."

"Hey Min, that ramrod you got tied to your spine is showing."

"Look at him, ever since that race the whole town been bragging on him. The boy's done gotten stuck up. What we going do with him?"

Ignoring it all, Min maintained his soldierly bearing. As the last section passed he spurred Rattler through an interval in the troop's waiting line, and took position at the unit's right front. Here he could see Major Kerfoot – Old Iron Ass, the gout-ridden but respected Mexican War veteran – had indeed focused his attention on Min, his second in command.

"Draw sabers," commanded the Major.

A small thrill of anticipation swept through Min as the scrape of highly polished steel withdrawn from metal scabbards echoed off the houses surrounding the square. The troop prepared to pass in review at the charge, sabers held high. John Brown's raid up river at Harpers Ferry had underscored the need for martial readiness. The Loudoun Grays had responded with a regular schedule of drill. The Friday pass in review was the highlight of the weekly routine. Lifting his blade, Min saw sunlight reflect off its curved surface. Glancing back, he saw the other riders wait at attention. Old men sitting in their comfortable porch rockers leaned forward to witness better the coming spectacle. Children stopped their games and stood quivering with excitement, brandishing brooms and sticks as they prepared to storm the neighboring hedge where similarly armed playmates readied a stout defense. Doors opened as wives left the kitchen to observe the Grays' charge, accompanied by more than a few interested daughters.

"Troop ready. Charge!"

Ferocious fox hunter's yells filled the square as the riders spurred forward. But the martial sounds were interrupted by hoots and catcalls. For only nineteen riders continued beyond the first few paces. One lay sideways in the dust, cursing his fate and friends alike. He stood and brushed the dirt from his well tailored grey and buff uniform. Level eyed he looked into his horse's offended eyes. "It's not your fault Rattler," Min said.

The horse blew out his nostrils and rested his head companionably on Min's shoulder. Min tightened his horse's girth, loosened undoubtedly by his horse holder and friend, Sergeant-major Kinlock Barton, after Min had dismounted to inspect the troop before the final maneuver. With a tight lipped laugh, Min mounted to return to his commanding officer and request permission to dismiss the troop. While annoyed, his inner voice acknowledged that the promised pride-reducing revenge had come with sublime timing.

Before her death in the great fever of 1857, Armistead's mother had bequeathed many things to her only child including a deep love of book learning and a relentlessly logical approach to problem solving. She had also extracted a promise that he would continue his education. He had attended Princeton with the belief that he would become a lawyer. His father's death aboard a Manassas Gap Railroad train that derailed outside of Strasburg put a sudden end to his formal education. Three years ago, at age nineteen, he had returned to his home place to build a new life.

There were loans to repay and no immediate source of income. So he had leased his parent's house to the first suitable family possessing ready cash. The fact that Madison Jefferson and his family were some of the thousand or so free blacks living in Loudoun County mattered little to Armistead. Likewise, he had ignored the hisses of disapproval from most of his acquaintances living around Leesburg, and the compliments from the heretofore remote Quaker neighbors in Waterford. He had moved into the cabinet making shop abutting his father's cherished chestnut grove and slowly created a successful lumber business.

Through it all he continued to honor his mother's request. It was her influence that stimulated him to collect and read newspaper accounts from all around the country in an effort to make sense of the event at Harpers Ferry. Then he proposed the subject of John Brown when the seminar next met.

His mother had founded the original seminar because she worried that her promising son would become too enamored with the people she disdainfully described as 'the riding set' simply because he shared their passion for horses. She organized a monthly meeting to discuss some important topic and called it a seminar because she had seen the word in a book and liked what it promised. At first it had been a meeting of two, but when her bright relative, Amanda Holland, heard about it she had clamored to participate.

Upon returning from Princeton he and Amanda had resumed the seminar. Those held at Holland Hall were particularly lively because there were always interesting visitors in attendance.

Tonight did not disappoint. Among the guests was Robert Duchesne, a French naturalist who was touring the south to complete his portfolio of North American birds. The Frenchman was already well lubricated by the time Armistead arrived. Nonetheless, his engaging enthusiasm for his subject charmed Armistead. It also apparently charmed the ladies because they had pressed tightly around the naturalist to admire his depictions of the local birds.

"It will be my opus magnum," Duchesne explained enthusiastically. Elizabeth Milton had wedged herself into position directly across from Duchesne. She wore a tight-fitting, low cut dress. Her evident interest in the naturalist's work as she leaned forward to examine closely his drawings seemed to have a startling effect upon Duchesne.

"I never realized that Lizzie had such an interest in nature," Armistead dryly commented to Amanda.

"Oh," replied Amanda, "she is truly a woman of substantial parts."

The seminar convened in the parlor. Since he had proposed the topic, Armistead spoke first. He began with a simple account of John Brown's death. No one who witnessed it could fail to be impressed by Brown's courage. Armistead had been raised to believe that courage was an admirable quality, but he could not respect what Brown and his men had done at Harpers Ferry. On this, he and his cousin Min agreed.

"Yes, he died well, did Osawatomie Brown," Min commented.

"And good riddance," added Amanda.

Armistead passed around several northern newspapers and asked that they be read aloud. A eulogy delivered by a New Hampshire reverend, was typical: "The gallows from which John Brown ascends into heaven will be in our politics what the cross is in our religion. And from his sacrificial blood, the temporal salvation of four million of our people shall yet spring. To be hanged in Virginia is like being crucified in Jerusalem; it is the last tribute that sin pays to virtue."

Min rolled his eyes. The Squire guffawed and took a sip from his glass. Before he could speak Amanda observed, "Here is exactly the problem. We southrons would have treated Brown's raid as one fanatic's mad effort except for the endorsement of so many leading men in the North."

So far Duchesne had been quiet, except to murmur thanks when someone passed him a glass. The alcohol seemed to have removed his polite veneer: "You slave holders have lived so long on your plantations with no one to gainsay or contradict you, and the Negroes only looking up to and worshiping you, that you expect to govern everybody and have it all your own way. I have seen this repeatedly during my travels."

Squire Holland reddened with anger and started to rise from his chair. But the furious indignation of the others overwhelmed the challenge that came from his lips. Aided by Amanda's gentle push, he collapsed back in his chair muttering curses against "damned foreigners."

Armistead regretted the Frenchman's remark because it ended all chance of closely reasoned discussion. Instead, the seminar banded together to oppose Duchesne, making up for lack of eloquence or logic with volume and repetition. Armistead observed that the only surprising feature of the argument was Duchesne's ability to parry the thrusts. If Duchesne was poorly informed about the birds of Virginia, he possessed a great deal of knowledge about the political arguments that were cleaving the nation. It was also notable that his command of English seemed to improve as he neatly trapped members of the seminar by pointing out their inconsistencies.

After the last of the guests had departed, Armistead and Min prepared to leave as well. "That was a disappointing exercise. I am truly sorry Amanda," Armistead said.

"Until his outburst, he had seemed like polite company. He will not be welcome here again, I am sure," Amanda replied.

"There is more to Monsieur Duchesne than I originally thought. There is some steel beneath that French charm and something mighty strange about him," Min observed.

Both Amanda and Armistead looked at Min sharply. They knew their cousin usually accepted people at face value.

"He seemed powerfully well informed and very certain that this secession congress is going to cause a heap of trouble," Armistead said.

"Damn South Carolina hotheads with their ultra views," Amanda said.

"Amen to that cousin," Armistead and Min replied in unison.

Later Amanda returned to the parlor to make sure the servants had completed the clean up. She saw that Duchesne's portfolio of drawings remained open on a table. In the hurry of preparing the evening's entertainment she had not yet looked at it closely. The illustrations were of decent quality, albeit slightly fuzzy and smudged around the borders. She turned several pages. She beheld a drawing of a large raptor, a Mississippi kite. It was not native to Virginia but still looked oddly familiar.

She went to the shelves and took The Natural History of the Birds of the United States. When she was a young girl, a New York merchant had taken a shine to her. After learning about her special interest in animals and especially birds, he had sent her this book as a gift. When snowbound in the winter, or confined to bed sick, she had studied John James Audubon's wonderful color drawings. His rendering of the Mississippi kite was a mirror image of the one in Duchesne's portfolio, its orientation changed one hundred and eighty degrees, exactly the same in shape and detail.

In his room upstairs, Duchesne stood before his night stand and removed the palate piece. It enabled him to maintain effortlessly an accented English. And, as he had reported to his employers, the typical southerner became far more unguarded and garrulous when conversing with a Frenchman than with a man who spoke with the down east Maine accent of his birth state.

Chapter 5. Loudoun County, early August 1860

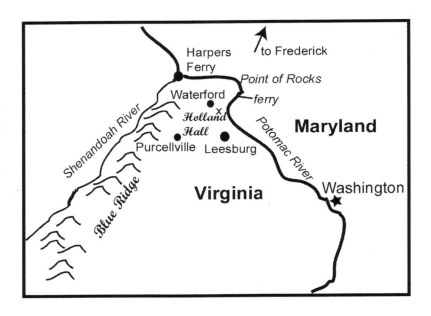

The Loudoun Grays attracted the young, generally idle sons belonging to Loudoun County's landed gentry. Their ranks included neither the
region's Quakers nor the German immigrants, whose sons spent their time
minding the shops and small farms that were a passport to a better life.
Sigmund Becker exemplified the rewards available to immigrants who
made hard work and thriftiness a religion. Yet he had interrupted his routines to stand talking with an old classmate whom he had first met back in
the tumultuous days of Forty-Eight. Twelve years ago, Becker had been an
advanced student of moral philosophy at Heidelberg University when he
encountered a first year student, already marked by a dueling scar, who possessed a gift for conspiracy and commitment to action that awed his fellow
students. Whereas most saw the world through a prism of grey, this young
man saw the same world in the stark relief of black and white, or perhaps
red, for then and thereafter his solution to tyranny was the sword.

Like most of the German revolutionaries who had fled to the United
States after the debacle of 1848, the two men became ardent abolitionists.
Becker reflected how their shared conviction had kept them in contact. Yet,
during the past year it seemed that their regular visits had nearly ceased.

He was not sure that he minded, because involvement with this man had too often led to trouble.

"I passed through Purcellville on my way here. They were drilling again," said Abner Means.

"Again! That's the third time this month. How many?" asked Becker.

"Twenty-one including the Major and his aide. Sigmund, things grow serious."

"What do your friends in Washington say?" In his role as trader and merchant, Means frequently traveled back and forth across the Potomac. An observer might have said his travels were predictably routine. Whereas the Secret Six, John Brown's backers, had been exposed to federal agents when a search of Brown's base uncovered incriminating documents, no evidence and no witness had linked Means to the raid. Accordingly, Means maintained his regular routines while simultaneously carrying funds from Northern sympathizers to the people who maintained the Underground Railroad. Involvement with this covert network of freedom had introduced him to powerful figures in the nation's capital, including some who expected to enter important posts after the upcoming national election. They convinced him that if Lincoln became president, war would ensure. This prospect had changed Means, in his own mind at least, from a courier to military spy.

The current national government's unwillingness to prepare for war angered him; an inconvenient obstacle placed by that indecisive Maryland fool, Buchanan, who seemed oblivious to the machinations of his Secretary of State, the Virginia politician John Floyd. At such times, true patriots stepped forward and, as had been the case in his native Germany, in his zeal to reform the nation, Means acted without legal authorization, or indeed without direction from anyone at all. He had learned many hard lessons at Heidelberg, but one stood out above all others: for a conspiracy to succeed, the number of participants had to be kept as few as possible. The larger the group, the greater the likelihood of betrayal. Means had reduced this observation to a personal maxim: the ideal conspiracy was a conspiracy of one.

Yet sometimes action required helping hands. In that event, Means would select carefully and never divulge more of his plans than his recruits required to achieve his goals. Those goals had shifted since John Brown's raid and now encompassed tracking the activities of the Virginia militia who served along the borders of the Potomac River. When war came, Means expected this border would become a strategic military frontier. The detailed intelligence he and his select agents collected would provide the key to secure this frontier.

Recently, Means had sounded out his old comrade on his attitudes toward war. He came this day to determine if he had another recruit. Means spoke, "My friends in Washington say war is a matter of time. We must prepare by doing two things. First, keep munitions from reaching the militia and second, keep detailed accounts of numbers and arms."

"We are older, wiser now Abner," replied Becker, "We are no longer naive students. This time we can either influence events, or allow ourselves to be swept up by them. What can I do?"

Means solemnly clasped Becker's hand. "I knew I could count on you Sigmund. You may be too old to go riding about the countryside, but you can help in other ways. Next week we expect that bandit Slater to bring his wagon down from Philadelphia through Frederick. It's full of Enfield rifles, still in their English shipping crates. I expect Slater will try to cross at the ferry under cover of night. I intend to stop him, but I'll need the help of a local, someone who knows this area. Someone who is steady."

"I think I know just the man," replied Becker.

"Your son?" asked Means, a note of skepticism entering his voice.

"Bah, not that worthless one. He has taken too much to the young bucks at his school. It's all I can do to keep him too busy to join the militia. No, someone else. A resourceful fellow who I think believes what we believe. Let me talk to him."

"But hurry, Sigmund, hurry. Slater is due soon."

"I'll have your answer in three days."

As Becker watched his friend depart, he wondered if he had pledged too much.

"I thought you would be drilling with the militia, Armistead?"

"No time for that, Mandy."

"You have time for drinking lemonade on my porch!"

"That's different. While the others are engaged in that foolishness, I can be here with you, enjoying your manifest charms."

"You talk pretty Armistead Carter, but you will not distract me. You should be with them. You're a natural leader. Virginia may need you."

"Seriously Amanda, you may be right, trouble may be coming. But I think it makes it worse if everyone goes around playing soldier, getting people all riled up."

"Playing soldier indeed! Those boys are doing their duty and if they are getting people riled up then perhaps you need some riling yourself. They way you talk and stay aloof, why you could become a disgrace to our town and your own family name."

Stung by his cousin's remarks, Armistead flushed angrily. Swimming well in the full flood of life, a rip current had seized him and he knew not what to do. He opened his mouth to respond, but regaining composure, paused. "I'm sorry to have offended you Cousin Amanda. I'd best be on my way. Sigmund Becker has been kind enough to let me use his library and I have a book of his to return."

"Just like you Armistead. Reading books while others prepare to defend their state. I believe I'm ashamed of you." Picking up her skirts, Amanda rose from the porch swing and rushed through the doorway of Holland Hall.

She almost knocked into the butler who was bringing a tray laden with fruit and drink. The butler was startled to see his normally self-controlled mistress in such a state; pale, eyes brimming with tears. He continued to the porch.

"Is something the matter Master Carter?"

"Yes James, I rather think there is."

Sigmund Becker would have preferred to have spent at least one of his allotted three days contemplating how to recruit an assistant for Abner Means. But when Armistead came trotting up to his home on the same day as Mean's visit, Becker realized that the time for action was now.

"Good day, Armistead."

"Hello Sigmund. I'm returning your book and I've come for more."

"Why don't you stay for supper and let us talk. About that book and perhaps some other matters."

"That's kind of you to offer. I think I will," replied Armistead as he dismounted. The two entered Becker's modest but neat home. From somewhere in back a door slammed.

"Rachel, is that you?" shouted the German. Receiving no answer, Becker turned to Armistead.

"Why don't you take a look at my library while I attend to the kitchen for a moment?"

Entering the kitchen he saw his daughter leaning forward over a plank table. Her bosom seemed almost ready to fall out of the partially untied bodice of her dress. Annoyed but preoccupied, Becker snapped: "Where have you been?"

"Picking beans. Isn't it obvious," replied his daughter while motioning toward a laden basket.

"And where is your brother?"

"I think he just set off with Boyd Holland. At least I saw someone ride up to the barn and later Charles departed. But I'm really not sure, I was busy in the garden."

"It's just as well, I don't want Charles...never mind. Armistead Carter is staying for supper. We will have some of the young porker I slaughtered last week along with the red cabbage, potatoes, and those beans. Put a bottle of my Rhinegau and one of the Chambourcins in the icehouse and make yourself presentable. I'll expect you to serve."

As her father left, Rachel's eyebrows arched in surprise. The Rhinegau represented the last from a small hoard that her father had brought over from Germany many years ago. It was only drunk on special occasions. And a second bottle! Why now? wondered Rachel, as she reached up to grab a shiny metal washing basin used to clean the garden produce. Setting the basin on the table she paused to look at her reflection. "Damn!" she exclaimed, seeing her untied bodice strings. Drawing the strings tight and vowing to be more careful, Rachel hurried along with her chores.

While Rachel prepared supper, the two men sat on the porch chatting. Looking west over the rolling fields toward the Blue Ridge Mountains, Armistead said: "See those clouds building up over the mountain, looks like a storm might be coming."

"A storm is coming, Armistead, and its going to sweep this entire country."

"What do you mean?"

"You tell me, you have just read a book about it."

Armistead responded, "I agree, what that woman writes about is very troubling. But people around here are not like those in Uncle Tom's Cabin."

"I'll grant you that the Hollands, Beatties, and other locals treat their slaves well. They don't often split up families, nor do they punish like in the book, but they still own human flesh, and that is wrong."

"As you know Sigmund, I agree it's wrong. But it will end soon. It's clear for all to see, the farms using slave labor are failing compared to those employing freemen."

"If it were just economics, you might be right. But an entire way of life is threatened. People like Squire Holland will never yield without a fight. Their children want to hold onto it just as much. And then politicians in Washington get to arguing about states' rights and that just mixes everyone up. Politicians use states' rights to preserve what they want to keep. But it gets the young hotheads excited, thinking they have to defend their homes."

"Hold on Sigmund," interrupted Armistead, "it's not as bad as that. I agree the stiff necked idiots in Washington will twist any point to suit their own ends. But people around here have plenty of common sense."

"Is it common sense that sets them to drilling throughout the county?"

"They are just playing at soldiers. They like the uniforms, it attracts the girls, they feel like patriots. Why those boys don't even have weapons. Most just have their granddaddys' relics from as far back as the Revolution."

"You've grown up with them Armistead. Do you think your friends would run from a fight?"

"No, of course not. But how much trouble can a bunch of boys carrying old sabers and a few shotguns and pistols cause?"

"Do you think it would be different if they had modern weapons?"

"Well I admit I wouldn't want to see the likes of Nat Grierson or Hawk and Bush Underwood toting something much more deadly than their fists. But why do you ask, Sigmund?"

The German lowered his voice. "I'm going to tell you something that I trust you will keep to yourself." As Becker paused, the breeze stiffened, bringing the smell of rain. A rumble of thunder boomed in the distance.

"You have my word on that Sigmund," answered Armistead.

Fixing the younger man with his eyes, Becker continued. "Richard Slater has a contract to deliver English Enfield rifles for distribution to the militia in both Loudoun and Clarke Counties. He will be bringing them over the ferry sometime next week."

"Are you sure?"

"I have friends in Washington who have followed the shipment ever since a British vessel docked in Baltimore. They say Slater is one of the purchasing agents. Do you think it's a good idea if the militia, including the Loudoun Grays, get their hands on those rifles?"

Armistead started to speak but waited as the wind gusted, raising the hen-scratched dirt in front of the porch into swirling, brown clouds. The flash of lightning and crack of thunder grew more frequent. "No, I guess I don't," Armistead finally said. "Some of those boys could get into real trouble armed like that."

"Just so," nodded the German gravely. "And my friends intend to see that they don't get into trouble. They plan on stopping Slater at the ferry. Abner Means is one of them. He needs someone local to help him."

"Stop Slater!" exclaimed Armistead, "Stop him how?"

"You know Means as a shrewd businessman but he was once much more. He was a most resourceful officer in the Prussian Army before coming to this country." Remarkable how easy the lies flow, reflected Becker, and not entirely disagreeable. It is just like Forty-Eight. He felt more alive than he had in a very long time. Without perceptible pause, he continued.

"Means says Slater travels alone. It shouldn't be hard. Means plans to take those rifles up to Point of Rocks and drop them off the cliffs into the river."

Unbidden, Amanda's stinging criticism echoed in Armistead's head. He found himself responding, "It might work. Means and I could probably do it. But I would want it agreed before hand that there is to be no violence. The whole reason we are doing this is to stop fighting from happening."

"Ja, just so," replied Becker vigorously, the emotion of the moment causing him to lapse back into his native accent. "It will keep your friends from hurting themselves and others."

"But will Means agree to let me arrange how we handle Slater? I think I can devise a way to avoid trouble."

An explosion of thunder drowned out Becker's reply as the clouds opened up. The wind-blown rain deluged the porch, driving the men inside. By the porch steps, the rain turned the dusty Virginia clay into a succession of small, red-brown pools that spread atop the ground before seeping into a damp stain.

The strong wine seemed to have a most satisfactory effect, Becker observed. Trust the Fatherland he thought. Conversation had flowed effortlessly from the time Rachel had presented a groaning sideboard with seven sweets and seven sours, and on through the main serving of roast pork until finishing with the cheese platter, laden with double skimmed Gloucester and his cherished favorite, the imported Camembert. Now, with the meal finished, the sated trio pushed back from table and relaxed. Not unaffected by his own wine, Becker began to grow confident that his plans would succeed.

As the diners rested, the storm passed. Outdoors, the evening sounds of a Virginia summer filled the air. Seated opposite his host, Armistead marveled at the German's loquaciousness. Seldom a man easy to talk to, Becker had been positively verbose, particularly as the meal progressed. And there was a heretofore hidden fire lying beneath Becker's stolid exterior. When the talk had turned to the upcoming election, Becker has spoken with surprising conviction about its importance. And his daughter – whom Armistead had formerly passed off as young, pretty, and insipid – had contributed informed opinions. Armistead turned to face Rachel and found her staring at him.

For most of the meal Rachel had concentrated on providing attentive service. Feeling that her earlier carelessness had risked her father's wrath, Rachel hoped to distract him by the excellence of the meal; pork poached in Madeira, red cabbage baked with apple and onion, morel mushroom gravy. She had even taken the trouble to make spaetzle, the small, cooked pieces of dough that so delighted her father. Furthermore, she had entered into the boring political conversation because she knew that this too would please him. But as the meal ended, Rachel had grown quiet and slightly sleepy. She supposed that the warm dreaminess she felt came from the wine. With her work largely complete, Rachel sat back from the table to watch the flickering shadows cast by the dinner candles and found her gaze fixed on Armistead. I've never really noticed him before she thought. He's surprisingly good looking. I wonder.

Then he turned to meet her eyes. As he smiled, Rachel smiled back. Slightly parting her lips and blinking her long lashes, she slowly turned her gaze downward to her plate.

Becker had seen the exchange of smiles. Perhaps his wine had performed double duty, confirming Armistead in his resolve and introducing him to Rachel. But the future would see to that. At the moment, Becker felt exceedingly tired. "Rachel, please clear the table and then we wish to be left alone to conclude some business."

"Of course father." Standing up, Rachel walked around the table to where Armistead sat. Seeing her father's gaze following her she said: "I think you had better attend to that candle Papa, it is guttering a bit."

As Becker glanced down to adjust the barely smoking candle, Rachel leaned past Armistead to take his plate. In so doing she slightly brushed against his shoulder. Pausing for only an instant, she gathered his plate and utensils and moved on around the table, confident she had been noticed.

Armistead had startled at the contact. He did not fail to perceive her perfumed scent and her slender arms and waist. And while gazing appreciatively, he also saw on the top of Rachel's bosom, briefly exposed when she had bent to take the plate, a prominent discoloration, seemingly a small wound. Flustered, he had looked away, and then Rachel was gone.

Becker spoke. "You have no doubt entertained my proposition during our meal. What do you think?"

Armistead's head felt heavy with wine. A blurred mixture of Rachel's presence, an overly large meal on a humid evening, and Becker's insistent tone overcame him. "I'll have to think about it, Sigmund."

"Can you be back two nights from now? Then you can talk to Means."

"That is a good idea. And now I must thank you for your excellent meal and be on my way." Rising, he shook the older man's hand.

Becker called out. "Rachel, come and say goodbye."

Receiving no answer, Becker muttered something about unpredictable women with heavy good humor.

Armistead slowly he unhitched his horse and walked Blue to the gate. He shook his head to clear the fumes and took several deep breaths. Mounting, he looked back at Becker's house. Two lights shone. From beneath the porch he saw his host extinguishing the dinner candles while holding a night lantern, his silhouette showing behind the cloth curtain. Another figure on the second floor stood sideways behind a window curtain. Her body outlined in sharp relief, illuminated by a single candle positioned somewhere behind her, Armistead saw Rachel Becker slowly undressing.

Chapter 6. Loudoun County, early August 1860

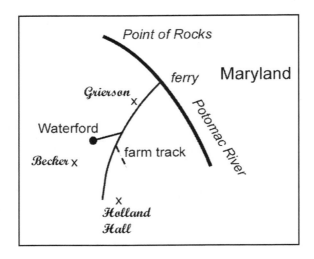

Two evenings later Armistead returned to Becker's house. As he approached he saw a fine black gelding secured to the hitching post. He intently examined the strange horse because it obviously received attention from someone who cared. The worn horse furniture was neither elegant nor expensive. It indicated efficient serviceability over appearance, an attitude he wholly appreciated.

"Welcome Armistead, I am glad you have come," Becker said. "Allow me to name my good friend, Abner Means."

"Hello Sigmund, good evening Mister Means. That's a nice horse and kit you have."

Means fixed Armistead with a penetrating look. "The saddle is a new design. An army officer named McClellan invented it. I expect it will become standard military issue soon. Not fancy, but it suits."

Armistead studied the speaker. Means looked to be about forty years old. His weathered, travel-lined face coupled with thick thighs indicated a person who spent much time in the saddle. A jagged scar extended from his right eyebrow downward along his cheek. The scar, along with his bushy eyebrows and a closed cropped, Vandyke beard, framed a face that brought one's gaze to a pair of arresting, dark eyes, set deep into his skull. It was these eyes, which reminded Armistead of pieces of coal about to burst into flame, that made him realize that here was a hard man. As they exchanged handshakes, Means's firm grasp completed the picture of forceful competence.

"You've come with an answer?" Becker inquired. As they sat on Becker's porch, Armistead had the uncomfortable feeling that Means's unblinking stare was gazing into his soul.

"Yes and no, Sigmund. I think Slater should be stopped. But I also think there might be a legal way to do it. I went to Leesburg yesterday and read up about the laws empowering the formation and equipping of the militia. In a few days Judge Clarke will be through on his circuit and I thought I'd ask him a question or two."

Becker glanced at Means who nodded. "There won't be time for that Armistead. Slater is coming through tonight."

"But you said..."

Means interrupted. "That shipment must be stopped. You well know how some peoples' backbones get stiffened when they stand behind a gun. Give those people modern firearms and they will be looking for an excuse to use them."

"Then I guess you will have to deal me in. What's the plan?"

"I'll explain on the way to the Ferry, we had best be off."

As Armistead and Means stood up, Becker spoke again. "One moment gentlemen, first I propose a toast to the success of our God-given mission."

He produced a small silver flask. Carefully worked in beneath the cap was an inscription Armistead could not make out, although he recognized it as German. The three drank in turn.

After the pair departed, Sigmund Becker remained behind on his porch. He took one more small pull at the flask then held the container at arm's length. Dating from his student days, it was one of the few items he had managed to carry with him during his flight from Germany. In a firm voice he read the inscription aloud and then added, "then as now." Turning he went back inside his home, leaving his solemnly intoned 1848 motto of the German Revolutionaries – "death to the squirearchy" – to be swallowed by the evening air.

Three miles away, Squire Holland's only son Boyd also prepared to depart. His father had asked him to ride to Waterford, where his sister Amanda had been staying for the past two days, and escort her back home. Amanda had gone visiting — "set sail" as she called it — in an effort to overcome the summer lassitude that had recently afflicted her. Her journey to friends and relatives in Waterford was part of the continuing round of visits that, coupled with Sunday church and the occasional grand parties, composed the social calendar for the unmarried, well-born daughters of Loudoun County.

For Boyd, Amanda's visit provided a welcome excuse to visit Rachel Becker. Knowing that Amanda would prefer to travel in the cool of the evening, Boyd reckoned that a moonlit journey home would appeal to her while providing time for another of his increasingly heated encounters in the Becker barn. From the Beckers', Boyd intended to travel across country to Waterford. On the return, he could gallant Amanda's carriage along the direct route from Waterford to their home, a route that shared the Ferry Road that rose up from the Potomac River.

The last eerie calls of the mourning doves ceased as darkness came. Replacing their cries came the full throated bugles of the frogs patrolling the Potomac River banks. The river itself flowed sluggishly with August's torpor, its monotonous murmurs providing a backdrop to the frogs' singing. Overhead, a three-quarters moon danced amidst the clouds, alternately illuminating the countryside and casting it into long shadows.

During the day, old man Noland and his son used their raft to carry travelers dry-shod across the river. At night, for lack of customers, the ferry closed. Because of the summer drought, the river could be crossed without using the ferry. Could be, but seldom was, since there was no reason to do so, until perhaps tonight. So thought Armistead as he waited on the heights overlooking the Virginia shore of the great river. He still wondered if he really should be here to commit what was essentially a crime. He reassured himself that his effort was intended to prevent even larger crimes, but possessed sufficient self awareness to see the essential falseness of this alibi. Had he allowed deeper introspection, he might have concluded that his presence had a great deal to do with Amanda's caustic commentary about his lack of participation in the great events of the day. Instead he focused on the sounds of a horse drawn wagon entering the river.

Armistead reviewed Means's plan. The older man would intercept Slater a mile or so from the ferry on the Maryland side. Claiming a chance encounter, Means would accompany Slater over the ferry and up the heights onto the Virginia side. When the wagon reached level ground, Armistead would gallop up to the travelers to create a distraction. Under cover of this diversion, Means would clamber onto the wagon and overpower Slater. After securing him, they would continue to the nearby cliff at Point of Rocks. The rifles would be tossed into the water, broken on the rocks, and lost in the depths. The part about overpowering Slater bothered Armistead, but he supposed Means had experience in this sort of thing.

Armistead mounted and lightly spurred Blue onward. Committed to action, he felt no hesitation, only a thrill of excitement coursing through his body. Cantering forward, he dimly made out four toiling horses pulling a creaking, heavily loaded wagon. The clouds uncovered the moon, allowing Armistead to see the driver accompanied by a horseman. Suddenly, the driver stood and dropped his reins. He appeared to be shouting, but Armistead's own voice drowned him out.

"Say stranger, have you seen my…"

"What the hell?"

Reining Blue in abreast of the driver, Armistead realized that the seemingly simple plan had collapsed. Means had moved too soon. Armistead saw furious surprise in Slater's eyes. Even clearer, he saw a large pistol firmly pointed at him.

"Hijack my wagon, damn you," Slater snarled. His finger tightened on the trigger.

Armistead tried to jerk his horse around, but left it much too late. A loud explosion split the air. Immediately Blue reared high and neighed a panic stricken call. Armistead fell backwards from the saddle. As he dropped he heard another sound, the muffled report of a firearm. Head first he fell, striking a large boulder by the side of the road, and then, heard nothing more.

As the echo of the twin shots dissipated in the night air, Means tensed and listened. An unnatural silence took hold as even the frogs stopped singing. From across the river a dog barked fitfully, then a light appeared from the ferryman's house and the barking became urgent. At that Means acted quickly. He pushed Slater's body back into the wagon, covering it with a canvas. Pausing to reload his pistol, he jumped down from the wagon to find Armistead lying on his back unconscious, a deep gash in his skull spilling blood onto the ground. Awkward but not fatal, Means concluded. He dragged Armistead to the wagon and hoisted him aboard with difficulty. Cocking an ear towards the river, he noted that the barking had been joined by excited shouts.

Means secured his horse to the wagon and looked back toward the Maryland shore. Two figures stood on the ferry raft, poling steadily toward the Virginia shore. Five minutes to cross, another five to climb the heights Means estimated. He briefly and fruitlessly searched for Armistead's horse. He vaguely recalled hearing hoof beats following the struggle with Slater. He mounted the wagon, seized the reins, and whipped the horses into a fast trot. As the wagon gathered speed, Means wondered how he would explain himself: a cargo of firearms, festooned by one dead and one injured man would strain even his practiced powers to dissemble.

Behind him, the ferrymen arrived at river's edge. As the raft grounded in the Virginia mud, two men stepped ashore, each carrying a lantern. The younger man also carried a rifle. Born and bred in Virginia, the Nolands did not let the incidental fact that they now lived across the river in Maryland interfere in their duty, as they saw it, to their neighbors on the south bank. They had heard shots. They meant to find out why.

They saw fresh ruts in soft mud. Kneeling, the older Noland examined the ruts closely. The dirt was soft and damp. Any marks of passage from earlier in the day would have been sun-dried hard. The old man pointed up the road. The younger man nodded, and together they proceeded. At the top of the climb they found fresh horse dung showing that the unknown party had come at least this far. Swinging their lanterns left and right they examined the ground. The confusion of tracks told them nothing, until Noland's son came across a plate-sized dark spot near a boulder that jutted out almost into the road. A creeping vine covered most of the rock. As the older Noland closely studied the rock he saw fresh blood on the vine leaves. For the first time he spoke: "There's bin trouble alright. Run ahead up yonder to the Grierson's, them's the closest folks hereabouts. Roust 'em up, saddle some horses and git moving up the road. That wagon ain't too far ahead. Have the young'un fetch a horse for me. I'll catch up. Now git."

With no sounds of pursuit, Means reined in his team. The draft horses were built for endurance, not speed. Besides, he knew that hurrying might attract attention. As his horses continued at a steady walk, Means reviewed what had transpired. He felt no regret for shooting Slater. He had learned to kill during his dueling days at Heidelberg and found it came easily enough. Slater had drawn a weapon on Carter and the young fool had just sat there. Shooting Slater was really self-defense, and besides the man deserved it. Before Slater had become an arms dealer he had been a slave trader down south. No, Slater deserved to die as did many more like him. Only then would the country be cleansed.

Now, Means concluded, the only thing to do was to continue along the Ferry Road, past the turnoff to Waterford, and then turn right to Becker's home. The trip should take about an hour. Won't old Becker be surprised, Means chuckled to himself. He leaned back to check on Armistead. Finding him still unconscious, he figured it was just as well. Covering Armistead with the canvas, Means drove on, his soft humming completing the picture of a farmer returning from a nocturnal errand.

Approaching the Ferry Road, Boyd Holland throbbed with frustration. The candle in Rachel's window had not been lit. This meant she could not meet him in the barn as they had planned. Instead Boyd now escorted his sister and one of her friends back toward Holland Hall. Because there had been no signal, Boyd had not entered the Becker barn. If he had done so he would have been surprised to see Armistead's horse tied to a post, his coat still splotchy with the sweat of a hard gallop.

Shortly before Boyd's unnoticed visit, Sigmund Becker had been startled to hear pounding hooves galloping up his drive. Expecting the worst, Becker anxiously stepped outside. It was with some relief that he saw a riderless horse. The horse neighed while nervously pawing the ground. A new anxiety quickly replaced Becker's temporary calm. He approached Blue, speaking soothing words. Reaching to pat the horse's neck, his hand came away sticky. Turning Blue's neck so it was illuminated by the light coming from his house, Becker peered closely. A shallow, bloody furrow creased Blue's neck.

"Mein Gott!" exclaimed Becker, "Shot you have been." Composing himself, Becker took Blue into the barn where he stanched the wound and secured the roan to a post. Stunned and frightened, Becker returned to his house.

The lead draft horse's ears pricked alertly. Then Means heard it too; the sounds of fast approaching horses. While riding with Armistead to Noland's Ferry, he had interrogated the young man about the local paths and byways and learned that near the Waterford turnoff was an overgrown farm track stretching into the woods. Standing, Means turned and pulled back the canvas. He lifted Armistead half over the wagon's side. With a final shove Means pushed him out onto the road. Resuming his seat, he whipped his team into a canter. For the first time, Means noticed the humid warmth of the night air.

Galloping along the Ferry Road came the pursuit; Noland's son, Nat Grierson and Nat's father. At one time the Griersons' large estate had conferred some degree of status upon the family. Years of mismanagement had caused their status to decline, but they retained a belligerent pride in family and place. Equally comfortable at a Holland Hall fete or a Mudtown cockfight — the former served liquor, the latter provided blood sport — they were known as men of action. Before the Noland boy had completed his explanation, the Griersons eagerly joined the hunt. The only delay came when Nat insisted on going back into the house to get his saber.

"What the hell you doing with that thing?" protested his father, who carried a large dragoon pistol strapped to his thigh.

Nat stiffened, glared, and replied that he had been drilling with it for months and reckoned it gave him an advantage in a close-in fight. A sleepy-eyed slave brought their horses and the three set off. In their excitement they forgot entirely about sending a horse back for old man Noland. Rounding a curve on the Ferry Road, they found Armistead's body sprawled in the dust.

Dismounting, Nat exclaimed, "Well I'll be!"

"What, you know him?"

"Yup, it's Carter, Armistead Carter. It looks like he's done dead." This brought the other two riders off their horses.

"Shit, he ain't dead, but it does look like he be shot," said the older Grierson. "What we going to do?" he asked, scratching his head and spitting into the dirt.

As the three paused to consider, the sounds of horses and creaking springs penetrated the air. "It's that wagon!" Noland exclaimed.

"What wagon?" replied the Griersons in unison.

"The one I told you about."

"You ain't said nuthin about no wagon," rejoined Grierson senior.

"Never mind you fools. Quick, into the bushes."

With some difficulty the elder Grierson pulled his son, whose clenched fists and swelling chest indicated the imminent explosion of anger, into the ditch. "Not now," he ordered.

Shrugging off his father's restraint, Nat stepped forward, only to pause in mid-stride when again the sounds of an approaching wagon washed the air. Concealing their horses, the trio waited, the only sound the scrapping of metal upon metal as Nat drew his saber.

Amanda had occupied most of her time in Waterford in contented companionship with her best friend, Lucy Paine. Lucy's unflagging optimism had carried Amanda along through relaxing days spent sewing, laughing, and talking, with evenings devoted to music. Last night, in a gathering of friends, Lucy prevailed upon her to participate in a silly game of fortune-telling. While the other girls took it quite seriously, Amanda viewed such a game skeptically. Nonetheless she joined in.

The girls wrote the names of several sweethearts, either real or desired, upon a piece of gilt paper. They folded each name in the shape of a heart, then dipped the hearts into a gill of red wine. After drinking the wine the party dispersed, each taking the stained hearts home to place under their pillows. As they slumbered, the one they would marry would appear in their dreams, or so claimed Lucy.

All the girls except Elizabeth Milton had prepared two or three hearts; she had written down an even half dozen names, to the others' good natured but partially genuine jealousy. Amanda confined herself to two names, two hearts. One was her cousin Min for whom she felt great affection, but of the same type she gave to Boyd. The other was Benjamin Settle, an older man who was a circuit preacher and for whom she felt a different emotion, perhaps even a small infatuation. She thoroughly doubted Brother Benjamin, as everyone called him, had ever particularly noticed her. But she included him because the others seemed to have no trouble thinking of possible beaus.

Climbing the stairs to her room, Amanda wondered why her heart had never plunged into the frenzied excitement her friends claimed to often experience. At one time, she had begun to believe that Armistead would provoke that response. His thoughtful attentiveness and many practical skills attracted her. But her attraction lacked the consuming passion her friends so vividly described. Perhaps it was Armistead's hesitant inability to act decisively. Or perhaps it was his curious disinclination to rally with the others to defend their home. Since the cousins were native Virginians, from a family with roots dating back more than one hundred and fifteen years, Amanda found his behavior unfathomable.

Yet, she had been greatly troubled by the cooling of her relationship with Armistead, particularly the incident on the porch at Holland Hall. And for the first time, at age twenty-two, she had begun to feel old. The possibility of becoming an unwed maid, like Aunt Naiomi — or Auntie Hag as she and her cousins had called her behind her back — did not horrify her, but it held no appeal.

It was Lucy who insisted, as she reached her bedroom door, that she place the hearts beneath her pillow, and because it was Lucy, Amanda complied. She had dreamed, a dark, brooding dream in which a muscular rider galloped along a narrow, winding road. His cloak flowed in the wind, his dark horse stretching out with great, ground eating strides. He seemed to be passing before a storm, because she could see bright flashes, lightning she supposed, on the not too distant horizon, and hear the peal of thunder. But try as she might, in the dream and when she awoke, she could not identify this rider. A small cap, rather like those worn by soldiers she later decided, pushed down over his eyes to conceal his face. A thick, full beard obscured the rest. Only one other detail could she remember before the dream merged into a thousand confused images. The rider carried his reins in his teeth. One arm reached for something along his saddle; he did not appear to have a second arm.

Amanda's cry of terror had brought Lucy running. As they lay in bed, Amanda described her frightening vision. Lucy comforted her, claiming it was her fault for this superstitious game. Moreover, she avowed that the bad dream had probably been caused by too much red wine. But Amanda had not failed to notice that her dream had also shaken Lucy. Only Lucy's warm presence as they shared the bed for the remainder of the night permitted Amanda any sleep.

The next evening, as if to make amends, Lucy insisted on accompanying Amanda on the trip home. The shock of seeing armed men emerge from the shadows to stand over a body lying in the road caused Lucy to gasp with fright. Amanda also felt a stomach-churning fear. Yet, all the while she was looking, counting, assessing; preparing for she knew not what.

To his chagrin, Boyd had startled as well. But the men recognized Boyd and he, in turn, once recovered from his surprise, recognized them. Their excited, confused story related how they had just come upon this body in the road, and how, by the way, it happened to be cousin Armistead. This news caused Lucy to gasp again. But to Lucy's even greater surprise, Amanda proceeded to interrupt loudly the men.

With a commanding voice Amanda calmly told them to put away their weapons, because someone might get hurt. Then after dismounting to examine Armistead's wound, she had them carefully lift his body into her carriage. Finally she ordered her brother and the others to escort them to the Becker farm. Boyd suggested they head back to Grierson's house, which was a little nearer. Amanda looked at the Griersons. They were as ever; dirty, disheveled, wearing grease stained clothes. "We go to the Beckers," she said.

And because Boyd had never heard Amanda speak in this way before, he obliged. As they trotted along the winding road, Amanda looked up at the bright moon and the now clear sky and thought, no, this is not my dream.

Chapter 7. The Becker Farm, early August 1860

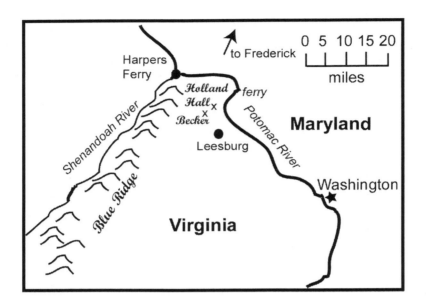

Sigmund Becker again heard approaching horsemen. They've come for me, he thought. Instead, the mysterious riders materialized into the welcome vision of recognizable neighbors. Before Becker could stammer out a relieved greeting, Boyd cried out: "Mister Becker, sorry to trouble you. It's Armistead Carter, he's been hurt. Can he stay here while we summon the doctor?"

Bowel jolting fear returned to Becker. An unrecognizable German curse escaped from his lips.

"Say what, Mister Becker?" Boyd asked.

"Ja, certainly, of course. Bring him in."

Amanda organized the sick room with cool efficiency and dispatched her brother to seek the doctor. The breeze had increased, bringing with it a slight chill. She returned outside to collect a shawl and then heard the whicker of a horse. Because she had often listened for that particular sound, she recognized it. Glancing around to ensure she was alone, Amanda quickly walked to the barn. There, as expected, she found Armistead's Blue. She spoke soothing words to him, but he uncharacteristically turned his head away. She placed her hand on Blue's chest. The racing heart confirmed what she had detected by his appearance. "You have been running hard, or badly scared, or both, haven't you old Blue," she softly whispered.

Reaching up, she gathered his mane to turn his head. The fractious animal jerked his head free. Before Amanda could investigate further, a faint voice called from the house. Hurrying back she did not see Blue turn his head to watch her depart, an angry red welt on the far side of his neck now revealed.

Within the hour Doctor Ferguson arrived. He drove everyone out of the sick room except Becker, his daughter, and Amanda. After a short inspection the Doctor spoke: "A blow or a fall, I can't say which. There is a great deal of swelling, but I don't detect a fracture. He should recover. Unconscious like this is probably the best thing, the brain can rest. And so can y'all. I'll stay the night to watch over him."

"But he will regain his health?" asked Becker.

"I expect so. Young bucks like him can endure a great deal. But I reckon he'll have a powerful headache the next few days."

Before departing, Amanda asked Becker if they could return in the morning. After a brief hesitation, Becker assented.

During the homeward journey to Holland Hall, Boyd spoke up: "Old Becker seemed none too happy when you asked him if we could come again."

"I don't think he has ever held us in high regard, that includes most of us over in Waterford," snapped Lucy.

The 'us', Amanda knew, referred to the non-Germans who inhabited the area. "That could be it, I suppose," replied Amanda. "I wonder. Brother mine, they say that when a horse gets a large scare, it will often run blindly back to the place it last was. Is that true?"

"Yes, sometimes. Particularly if the horse is riderless. Why?"

"Oh just wondering." Instantly alerted by a tone of voice they knew so well, Lucy and Boyd confronted her.

"What do you know that we don't?" asked Lucy.

"Come on Sis, tell," added Boyd.

"No, I'm just puzzling something out," Amanda responded. And because they also knew this tone, they did not ask again.

The successful diversion delighted Means. From a hidden vantage point he had observed the encounter between Amanda's party and the pursuing horsemen. As the entire group continued along the Ferry Road, Means performed a neat calculation and made his decision. He urged the draft horses back onto the Ferry Road to retrace the route he had traveled. A veteran of many tight encounters during his activities along the Underground Railroad, Means had developed a keen understanding of his fellow man's predictability. Since there were no turnoffs from the ferry to this point, and his pursuers had already covered this stretch of road, it was extremely unlikely that they would search back toward the river.

Thus the appearance of a lone man emerging from the shadows bordering the Ferry Road surprised him. The man approached. He unshuttered a dark lantern and stood gazing up at Means. Because he had often crossed the ferry on business, Means recognized him. It was old man Noland.

Noland spoke. "Say don't I know you?"

Mimicking the local accent that he found so disagreeable, Means replied, "I reckon you do," and discharged his pistol into Noland's face. Loading the body into his wagon, Means calmly continued to the ferry where he again crossed the Potomac, disturbing no one except the ever vigilant dog who stood chained in a side yard. Old Miz Noland was partially deaf. But she usually managed to hear what she wanted to hear and had been expecting the dog's barks. Muttering curses, she rose from her rocker, seized the house's remaining firearm, and headed for the door. Instead of exiting from the front, she went out the back way to her garden, determined to kill the marauding raccoon that she felt certain had returned to her ripening corn. She neither heard nor saw the wagon pass along the road.

Means buried Slater and Noland in an abandoned quarry four miles into Maryland and proceeded to a familiar destination, an Underground Railroad way station near Frederick operated by an utterly reliable woman named Hannah Yoder. Here he exchanged his horse team and gave a brief verbal message to convey to Becker.

He drove on until he intersected the National Road leading to Washington. After a moment's hesitation, he turned east toward the capital. He would personally present the men in Washington his wagon load of solid evidence showing the extent of Virginia's treacherous perfidy. Maybe then, he thought, the fools would realize how serious matters had become.

Armistead awoke at dawn. He slowly focused his eyes and became conscious of a pounding headache that superseded the worst he had ever known. As his eyes cleared a figure arose from a nearby rocking chair.

"Good morning young fellow. I imagine your head aches a bit?"

Armistead made out the owlish face of Doctor Ferguson, the Doctor's large friendly eyes framed between thick, bushy eyebrows and a long, flowing beard.

"Yes, where am I?"

"You're at Sigmund Becker's house. How you came here is quite a story. For now, tell me how you feel."

"My head feels like a ringing bell, but other than that I'm fine."

Ferguson performed a quick inspection. His probing fingers elicited a loud groan, to which the Doctor responded: "Good, you sleep some more and I'll check back this afternoon. Becker will know where to find me if you need any help. Now rest."

Armistead wanted to ask many more questions. But the Doctor's reassuring words calmed him, just as they had calmed all the sick and injured along the river for the past eighteen years. Armistead slept again.

He awakened several hours later. This time his vision returned more quickly. Rachel Becker sat in the rocking chair. She smiled at him. Smiling back Armistead said, "Have you been sitting there long? It was not necessary."

"Oh, but I wanted to. We have all been worried."

"I'm alright. But thank you for your concern."

She spoke again, her voice soft, low, and sweet. "The Doctor said to make you rest, feed you if you get hungry, and make sure you have no fever. Now sit still and let me feel your wrist and forehead." She leaned forward to place her hand on Armistead's wrist. At that moment a voice came bellowing from outside.

"Rachel, is he awake?"

Withdrawing, Rachel replied: "Yes Papa, he just woke up."

The sound of heavy, clumping strides coming up the porch steps announced Becker's imminent arrival. Rachel stood and smiled again, "I'm glad you are well." Then her father barged through the door.

"I told you to get me as soon as he awoke," Becker said irritably.

"Oh father," Rachel pouted.

"Go, make us breakfast," Becker commanded. After closing the door, he asked, "Are you alright?"

"Yes, I'll be fine."

"Thank God, now what happened?"

Armistead explained what had occurred up to the moment of his fall. He then asked. "Where is Blue, where is Means?"

"Your Blue came back here. He had been shot, but just a scratch. I have heard nothing from Means." Becker then told what had happened as described by Amanda.

"So they must have come across me where I had fallen," concluded Armistead.

"Yes, I suppose. But what do we do now?" inquired Becker, perspiration collecting on his lip.

"We start," replied Armistead calmly, "by me getting up. Then we eat, I'm ravenous. I'll think of something, but I think better on a full belly."

So saying, Armistead rose, a bit unsteadily at first. Alone, as he cleaned himself in a washbasin, he reflected upon something unusual. Since the death of his parents in the great fever three years back, Sigmund Becker had acted in many ways like a father to him. More importantly, he had been his teacher, opening his great collection of books to Armistead's eager scrutiny. Before, Armistead had asked the questions, and Becker had either provided answers or directed him toward a book that explained the issue. But on this critical morning, Becker had turned to him for guidance. And to his own surprise, Armistead had provided reassurance, that yes, he would think of the answer.

During the meal, a young boy rode up to the porch. Becker rose, pale-faced, and flew to the door.

"Thou art Mister Becker?" the boy asked in the distinctive Quaker locution.

When Becker nodded, the boy continued, "May I have a word with thee?"

After a short conversation, Becker returned to the table. "It is about business. Rachel, get on with your chores, you have already whiled away most the morning."

"But father..." Seeing his stern glance, she halted. How I hate you sometimes, she thought. As she departed, Rachel muttered to herself, "I'm no better than one of the Holland's slaves."

Becker eagerly relayed the news: "Means is fine. He has the wagon and is in Maryland at a Quaker safe house. He says that he is fairly certain no one saw him, so we should say nothing to anyone about what we have been doing. Means will be back here in a few days."

"That explains all and it explains nothing," responded Armistead. "But it will have to do for the present. Now this is what we are going to do." In great detail he explained to Becker how they would respond to a variety of questions or challenges.

Had either one paused to reflect, they might have noticed Armistead's transformation from acolyte to leader. Instead, it was Rachel, who had remained in the kitchen listening intently, who comprehended the change. Standing up to her father and telling him what to do was something of which she thoroughly approved. Just as the men made several resolutions based upon their conversation, so too did Rachel. I think I shall learn more about this boy, she promised herself.

Later that morning, when Amanda and Lucy arrived, they found that Armistead had departed. Becker assured them he was well and had gone home to attend to business. Because Armistead's home was some distance away and Lucy did not feel keen to travel during the increasingly warm, muggy day, the two returned to Holland Hall and Amanda's questions remained unanswered. Her curiosity piqued, she resolved that sooner or later she would piece together what had taken place. Smiling to herself she remembered her father's words spoken to her at age fifteen: "you have the impatience of your sex, but never forget all good things come to women who wait." That might have been true then, she had conceded, but now, with time running out, merely waiting no longer sufficed.

Chapter 8. Holland Hall, early August 1860

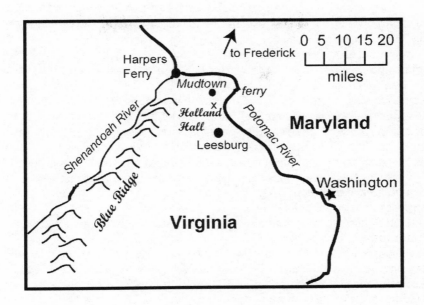

Squire Randolph Holland, his English manager Gordon, and Major Kerfoot of the Loudoun Grays had spent the previous evening waiting at the rendezvous. Time had passed agreeably enough; card playing, smoking, and sharing a neighbor's barrel of newly fermented corn mash. By the time they had concluded that Slater was not going to deliver his cargo, they were in a high flow of spirits. A visit to Mudtown seemed the ideal capstone to a patriotic vigil.

The area's church-going people tried to ignore Mudtown and its easy living population of poor whites and free blacks. They suspected that the village offered dangerous enticements and they were correct. Leaving the major prostrate and snoring like a contented hog, the Squire and his manager entered Meme Richard's Dance Hall. In the back room they found one of things they had come for: a poker game featuring card dealers wearing revealing clothes and who, for a price, would wear less still.

The name of the establishment's proprietor was Anne Rix. No one called her by that name. She herself was uncertain whether it actually was her name and never used it. She had once been pretty, until hard living replaced the glow of youth with a lined, almost coarse face topped by hair that too often had been drenched in cheap chemical color. Yet she retained her figure and more than a few customers still found her attractive.

She told anyone who asked that she had been born and raised in New Orleans. This served several purposes, one of which was to account for her complexion, which hinted at negro blood. In fact, she had spent her mature years in Wheeling, Virginia, having been sent there as a young child in company with her mother and a small amount of money. At the bedside of her dying mother, yet another victim of the great fever of Fifty-Seven, she had learned a little about her home place. In response to her penultimate probing question, her mother had fallen mute. A sad, haunted look had appeared in her eyes and she had said: "For your own safety it is best that you do not know, my love." Only at the end, amid her mother's fevered, lunatic ravings, had she produced a name that Anne suspected was her own. She snipped a strand of hair and thereafter kept it in a locket around her neck, and, she vowed to return to Loudoun County to discover the truth.

As the Wheeling years passed, she encountered railroad and rivermen who frequented the saloon where she worked and who had indeed been to the Crescent City. Their tales fired her imagination. Taking the name Meme Richard — she understood Meme to be French for owner, Richard was the name of the man she believed had sired her second child — she left Wheeling to establish a business like those she had heard about. She had selected Mudtown because she believed it was near to her birthplace.

How well Meme Richard's imitated a New Orleans Dance Hall she did not know. Except for the occasional wandering fiddler who performed for food or drink, the house featured no music. Without music, there was no dancing. But Anne Rix thought that calling her place a dance hall provided class, and class was something she was acutely aware of. In recent memory only one customer, a Baltimore businessman, had complained that Meme Richard's was not a dance hall but rather a fifth rate whorehouse. He had been tied to the bar by two large employees and pistol whipped savagely by Meme Richard herself. Regardless, her customers came for the unbeatable combination of the county's smoothest whisky, the choice of young and handsome girls, and high stakes card play.

Just now it was the latter that was on Randolph Holland's mind. Willingness to take chances at the gaming table, sometimes even reckless chances, fit his notion of how a Virginia landowner should comport himself. Lately his skill had failed to match his enthusiasm, and so it proved again. He found himself in the familiar position of writing another note of hand to cover his substantial losses and sharing a bed with a mulatto girl with whom he had often found solace. Morning came too soon, bringing a difficult headache and a confrontation with Meme Richard.

She spoke in a low voice without inflection, biting off her words in a measured cadence. From experience, Holland knew she was in a towering rage.

"Your man Gordon beat one of my girls again. That's twice in the last month."

Blast and damn, Holland thought. What eats at that man? Over the past year, he had felt his control over his manager eroding. Two obstacles prevented him from sending Gordon packing: first; the Englishman understood the complicated finances associated with maintaining Holland Hall and had a natural gift for fobbing off irksome creditors; second, he owed Gordon a considerable sum stemming from his ugly run of luck at cards. Because he possessed little hard money — no plantation owner did for God's sake! — he had written several notes to Gordon. Lately, the man had refused to accept them, which made matters damnably awkward. He had been forced to sign over deeds to several choice parcels of land. God forbid that the children should ever learn about this, but when his luck turned he would reacquire the deeds.

The squire realized that Meme Richard was done speaking. She stood impatiently waiting for an answer. Damn Gordon, he reflected again. How could he not understand that here in Virginia a family's name was everything? Even Mudtown rumors could beget scandal among the landed gentry.

He reached for his purse and dimly recalled losing it to Gordon sometime during the evening. Trying to ignore his pounding temples, Holland spoke casually, "Just so Madame. I regret it extremely. If you will name a sum in addition to what we agreed upon last night, I will write you a note." And then he had no choice but to accept the large figure she named.

By late morning he had returned home to learn that there was still no message from Slater. Instead, he found his two fellow investors, the men who had actually paid for the shipment of Enfields, waiting for answers. With them was a representative of Governor Henry Wise, the man who had originally proposed the scheme. The Squire invited them into the walnut paneled office he called his war room. It was dedicated to the Squire's two heroes, George Washington and the Duke of Wellington, and contained paintings of their battles along with a collection of weapons. Taking his place at the head of the table beneath his cherished painting depicting the charge of the Scots Grays at Waterloo, he wearily attended to the conversation.

"The man's reliable," stated Gordon for the third time.

"Then where is he, blast it?" responded Clarence Rixey, a Leesburg banker.

Clearing his throat, Major Kerfoot sent a stream of tobacco juice sluicing neatly into the brass spittoon. "My boys need those rifles if they are to train effectively."

"Precisely," agreed Holland. "Ah, thank you James." The butler placed his tray on the sideboard and departed.

"Gentleman, I think a drink may help us to see our way clear." So saying, the Squire poured brimming glasses of port. "Now Gordon, let us review events."

Gordon repeated how the transaction had come about. He was in an excellent position to do so, having organized the business arrangements. Conveniently, these arrangements had involved shipping the rifles aboard an English sailing vessel on which Gordon's nephew served as supercargo. This position had allowed him a small amount of storage space for personal use. Moreover, although the investors had paid full price for the cargo, in fact the shipping fee had been avoided by using Gordon's relative and Gordon had pocketed it himself.

At the end of Gordon's review, Holland spoke again. "Something may be amiss. I suggest we send a message to our friends in Frederick and see if Slater arrived there yet. We should have an answer by tomorrow. I suggest we adjourn until then."

"Agreed, Holland," said Rixey. "But damn it, we want those rifles. You were due only two cases. But I paid a pretty penny for eight more and the..." His voice trailed off when the heretofore silent governor's man gave a small cough.

Rixey glanced at him and then continued. "Er, right. Ah, the others are, er, just as eager as you all to receive their weapons. We need to find Slater."

As the group broke up, Holland called his servant back to the room. "James have one of the reliable boys take a message to Frederick for me. He is to wait for a reply."

The slave waited for the Squire to scrawl a short note, barely able to suppress his elation. So the information he had sent had been acted on. Good, very good. Taking the sealed envelope James headed for the stable. He summoned his son Wellington, a boy of fourteen.

"Take this message to the Lehmans in Frederick. You have been there before." Then, lowering his voice he said: "It worked boy, it worked! Praise be. Now we must finish the job. On your way drop this off at the Yoder place, give it to the missus."

He handed his son a second note, written in his own hand. It informed the reader, the same person who had received his first warning about the militia's efforts to purchase firearms, what steps were being taken to locate the missing shipment. "Now hurry boy," James concluded.

James relaxed, his face losing its eager intensity, regaining the look of a dutiful servant.

Chapter 9. Alexandria, late August, 1860

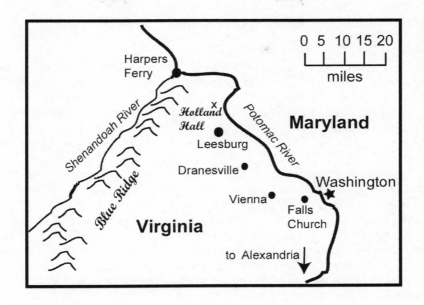

Two weeks later Amanda awoke at an unaccustomed early hour. As the entire household knew, the early morning was far from her favorite time. But on this morning she dressed hurriedly — Armistead had told her she must not be late — and skipped down the stairs to the breakfast parlor. Lilain, the cook, smiled as she entered and motioned toward a place setting. For as long as Amanda could remember Lilain had been a fixture at Holland Hall. She was mute, a fact that Amanda's father had not realized when he had purchased her as a young girl. Later, when sober, he had insisted that he knew of her condition all along and that it would make her the ideal house servant. She had risen from dairy maid to head of the kitchen by dint of cheerful hard work and superb talent for baking.

The appetizing aroma from one of Lilain's creations wafted through the room, propelled by a slight breeze blowing through the open window. Amanda saw a cloth covered basket from which an apple cinnamon scent rose. She sat down by the window and caught the bouquet of the trumpet vine that crawled up the porch trellis. The two smells merged to create a marvelous perfume. Lilain poured her a cup of dark, rich coffee — for an early morning like this tea would not do — and pulled the cloth corner away from the basket to reveal the contents. With a smile as bright as the sun streaming into the room, she waited for Amanda's signal. Amanda smiled back and Lilain reached with her tongs to place a roll onto her breakfast plate. While she ate, Amanda heard the melodic murmuring of the bluebirds and the wren's pure, simple refrain. It was if everything was combining to make this a perfect day, a day in which she hoped to restore her relationship with her cousin and to investigate further the strange combination of Armistead's injury and the disappearance of Old Man Noland.

She heard the sounds of a horse trotting up the drive and shortly thereafter Armistead's voice: "Cousin mine, are you ready?"

She picked up her day pack, which she had prudently prepared the night before, seized hold of the bulging picnic basket that Lilain handed her, and stepped out onto the kitchen porch. With a slight flounce of her skirts, she replied, "Of course!" Armistead's surprised look easily repaid her efforts at punctuality.

"In all our years, Amanda, I have never known you to be ready on time."

"Fie cousin," she answered with the exaggerated, simpering drawl employed by many of the local girls — a coquettish tactic that had prompted derisive, shared laughs when the two cousins gossiped about their neighbors — "I am older now, and becoming a most proper woman." Changing her accent to that of Mister Yesbera, the school master under whose tutelage most of the neighborhood children had suffered, she intoned, "Punctuality is one of the seven attainments of a proper woman, as you should know."

Armistead replied in the same tone: "And persistence one the seven attainments of a proper gentleman." They both laughed.

They walked past Armistead's horse, who was being led to the paddock by one of the boys, and Amanda glanced over to see a scar running along Blue's neck. Amanda paused and Blue gave a friendly whicker of recognition, straining his large muzzle toward her. She reached into a pocket to find a treat that the horse had known would be there. While Blue greedily devoured his apple, Amanda stroked his neck and asked, "What happened to Blue?"

There was a short pause before Armistead replied, "He received an injury, but it's alright now."

"That night when you got thrown?"

Another hesitation. "Yes."

In all decency she could probe no further. She released Blue and walked toward Armistead. Slipping her arm around his she said, "Let us take advantage of our early start on this fine day. I don't guess that the train will wait, even for two like us."

He handed her up into the light dogcart, walked around to the opposite side, and climbed aboard.

His color had returned. He spoke to driver, "Briskly now Ben, if you please."

The locomotive arrived in Alexandria shortly before noon. It was not often that the inhabitants of Loudoun County visited a large commercial center. Although Armistead had invited Amanda to accompany him on what he described as a pleasure trip, they both knew that it would also provide a rare opportunity to conduct business. Not only did they have errands associated with his timber business and her plantation, but they had spoken with their neighbors and received a long list of orders to place, overdue shipments to investigate, merchants to meet, contracts to deliver.

They set about their chores with cheerful efficiency. Although Amanda's father permitted her to participate in selected aspects of the plantation's management, he still limited her to areas that could loosely be called women's business. Here in Alexandria she was unfettered. As the day progressed, she revealed to Armistead a shining business capacity he had never seen exhibited. At first he tried to assist. Her sharp look had clearly told him not to intrude. He then stood back to enjoy the spectacle of various businessmen adjusting to the need to negotiate not with him, but with a woman. She let him know that she was grateful for his tolerance, and he, by long habit ceased his frank admiration and entered into good natured competition. In this too she shone.

After Armistead skillfully teased out the truth from a supercilious merchant about why Harry Crawford had yet to receive his promised shipment of iron bars — between the time the blacksmith had placed his order and it had arrived in Alexandria, the merchant had found another buyer willing to pay a considerably higher price — Amanda entered the conversation. In a completely convincing exhibition of a guileless farm girl recalling an amusing incident, she related how Crawford, "handsome perhaps, but really too brawny, though the other girls admired his huge muscles, too quick tempered for her taste," had confronted an overdue shipment. She told how Crawford, red-faced and swearing revenge, had dropped his tools, jumped onto his horse, and set off on an overnight ride to sort out the supplier whom he suspected of cheating him.

Her tale was pure invention, but her vivid depiction of Crawford's implacable Irish temper and amazing strength served its purpose. The merchant discovered that he had another shipment that he just might divert in order to supply Crawford's forge. He would send it out next week.

"You had best be the one to let him know, Amanda," said Armistead thoughtfully. "He won't be happy to wait a week and I don't want to be the one to bear him bad news."

"I reckon I might, no I will, send it out on tomorrow's train," interjected the anxious merchant.

"That's probably a good idea," Armistead intoned solemnly.

The cousins managed to restrain themselves until they had departed and walked around the corner. The image of Crawford the ill-tempered titan was false. In fact, his back stooped from years of horse-shoeing, Crawford was far from a tough Irish pugilist but rather a genial fellow who enjoyed passing time with anyone who happened into his shop.

Armistead dissolved into laughter. "And that part about his overnight gallop, that was rich Mandy!" he said. "Why he can hardly stay aboard that fat walking horse of his when he rides to Mudtown and back."

Between errands they found time to enjoy Lilain's picnic basket by the shore of the Potomac. They found time for Amanda to purchase some imported French patterns that she assured Armistead were the latest in fashion, for Armistead to buy some chocolate cherry cordials that he had found irresistible since childhood, and time for both to buy several books at a good second hand shop. They were sitting on the veranda of a hotel, finishing a small decanter of wine, when Armistead announced that he wanted to make one more stop. His serious tone of voice reminded Amanda of the way he had spoken earlier that morning when answering her query about Blue.

"This had been such a splendid day, I think I will sit here until it is time for the train," she responded.

"Yes, but there is something I want to see and I think you should see it as well," he replied.

They walked two blocks before Armistead paused. Amanda saw the sign, Slave Auction, even as she felt Armistead engage her arm and gently pull her onward. They passed beneath the sign into a small crowd of loud, boisterous businessmen and planters.

"Say Colonel, where's this lot going?" inquired Armistead as he motioned to a group of slaves.

The auctioneer glanced his way, gave a gap toothed grin, and replied, "These be prime field hands and sturdy breeding stock. I reckon they'll make somebody down Carolina way right happy." He spat a thin brown stream of tobacco juice. "Lookee here." He selected a well built young man and ordered him to move forward. As the slave shuffled into position, the chain dragging from his manacled feet scraped piercingly along the elevated, wooden platform. The colonel looked at Armistead and asked, "You be interested?"

Before Armistead could reply, a beefy, well-dressed, young man carrying a highly polished, ivory walking stick, elbowed him aside.

"Let me see what ya got there, Colonel."

"Show him your muscles boy," the auctioneer said.

The slave stood motionless with a vacant stare fixed on a distant horizon as the buyer ran his stick along the well-defined muscles of the slave's shoulder and upper arm. The auctioneer interceded. "Pard' me mister." He was a smallish man. The slave towered over him. The auctioneer had to strain to reach up and slap the slave across the jaw. "I said show him your muscles." Armistead felt Amanda stiffen at the sound of the blow. He also saw the slave briefly fix the auctioneer with a burning stare, and then lower his eyes, change his stance, and flex his biceps and legs.

"Nice," said the buyer. This time he ran a hand slowly along the slave's shoulders and upper arms. Prodding his legs wider apart, he almost caressed the slave's prominent thigh muscles. Slightly flushed, the buyer straight-

60

ened up and said, "Nice, very nice. Let's see his teeth." Gently he prodded the slave's mouth with his stick. The slave remained still. The buyer smiled, but Armistead noticed that he smiled with his mouth alone. The auctioneer said, "Achilles doesn't seem to be on form today," and hit him again.

"Oh, I think he's in fine form, it's just he hasn't quite learned his manners," replied the buyer. Armistead saw the buyer's index finger move and heard a sharp click. A pointed blade appeared at the tip of his walking stick. The buyer gently pushed it against the slave's lower lip.

The slave's mouth opened as the buyer pushed the blade forward against the slave's tongue. Armistead saw the buyer's own lip tremble and a thin line of spittle emerge. The auctioneer stiffened and took a half step forward. Armistead could see he was undecided whether to intervene. The auctioneer then relaxed as the buyer withdrew his stick. Another snap and the blade disappeared. After lightly running one hand over the slave's forearm, the buyer turned away and said, "My name's Polk, Colonel, Otis Polk. I might be interested in this one."

The auctioneer nodded and spat. Meanwhile, his assistant escorted a group of slaves onto the platform. Buyers gathered to poke and prod, running practiced hands along muscles, looking at the women's breasts and hips while commenting lewdly.

"Armistead! Take me away from this place," hissed Amanda. As they departed the slave pen, the auctioneer's sing-song voice washed over them: "Here's a cotton nigger for you! Genuine, believe you me. Look at his shoulders! There's a pair of legs for you! If you have the right soil and the right sort of overseer, buy him. He's a good un, a right bargain. He's just as good for ten bales as I am for a julep at eleven o'clock."

The return train trip home passed in silence. Armistead bleakly reflected on what had taken place and how it had gone wrong. He supposed he could blame Sigmund Becker. Becker had responded to Armistead's claim that the local slave owners generally treated their slaves well by asserting one fact and one challenge. Becker said that one of Virginia's largest businesses was the breeding of slaves for sale to the lower south. Armistead had learned that this was true. Becker's challenge had been for Armistead to visit a slave auction. So he had planned a trip to Alexandria and invited Amanda. He had thought that a visit to the slave market would prompt a closely reasoned discussion, the type of engagement the two so enjoyed. Instead there was this: an unexpected, shared magic followed by a disgusting spectacle; and an uncomfortable, hollow feeling that he knew Amanda shared.

Falls Church and Vienna passed. By the time they approached Dranesville, Armistead resolved to ask Amanda if she would like have supper at the inn, as they had planned. An astonished expression passed Amanda's face. She swallowed once, then again, and answered simply, "No."

The train chugged into Leesburg where they saw Ben with a two-horse team and the light, traveling carriage. Wordlessly, Amanda accepted his proffered arm as she climbed into the carriage.

The ride home also passed in silence. When the carriage ground to a halt at the front entrance, Amanda spoke, "I trust you will not be calling for me again, Armistead Carter?"

"If that is what you wish, Amanda."

"How could it be otherwise?" she replied. Turning lightly on her heel, even now displaying that grace that caused a catch in Armistead's throat, Amanda ran up the stairs and through the door of Holland Hall.

Chapter 10. Fountain Rock, the Shenandoah Valley, September 1860

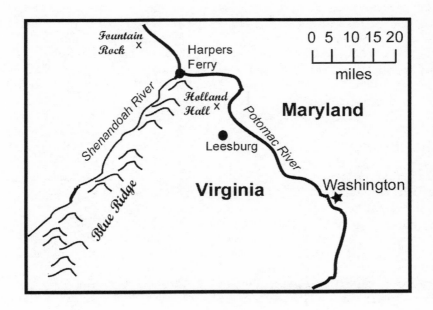

Amanda gazed out her bedroom window to see the neatly fenced fields with their hand-dug livestock ponds extending like a necklace of pearls to the distant tree line. Beyond lay the Blue Ridge mountains, their slopes gradually revealed by the rising sun. Since her trip to Alexandria she had not slept well. One consequence was that the saw a different world; a dawn and a predawn vista, a familiar scene transformed into something new; distant peaks washed by a light that made them float on a hazy, red-yellow aura, separated by dark slashes where mountain brooks carved hidden paths leading she knew not where. She was not prone to somber or black moods, but when they came she thought of the mountains as her lodestar, inviting her for a visit or perhaps for something more permanent.

During happier summers she and her friends, accompanied by Armistead, Min, and their comrades, would ride to the mountains to picnic. Before Christmas, the boys would hitch up the big sleigh and they would set off on a joyous run to find one of the shapely hemlocks that grew in a sheltered place on the heights. Alas, not today, she sighed.

She supposed that she had always preferred the company of men. It was not that she was like so many of her friends who since the age of twelve had embarked on husband hunting with single-minded seriousness. Neither was her pleasure of male company like the tempestuous emotion of those who claimed to fall into and out of love several times a month. Rather, she admired the way men appeared confident and decisive, willing to accept uncertainty, to seek risk, to mold life's events to suit themselves. As she had lain awake last night and the nights before, she had come to realize that most of the boys of her youth were now absent, some with new families to tend, many thoroughly occupied with the militia. Since John Brown's raid, Min and his unit had been patrolling, intercepting and questioning all strangers, preparing to resist what to Amanda seemed the implausible possibility that the northern people would want to cross the Potomac to impose their will on Virginia.

In the absence of male friendship, she had tried to engage in plantation business. Whereas in the past her practical business questions had caused her father's eyes to spark with fond admiration, lately he had responded with irritation and sometimes anger. Worse, he had resumed his heavy drinking. And then there was Armistead. The trip to Alexandria had revealed something that both cousins suspected; a widening schism, an apparently irreconcilable difference of opinion and attitude.

In an effort to banish these brooding thoughts, she remained in bed for another hour to read one of the books she had purchased in Alexandria. Written in 1852 it was an examination of national issues from a southern point of view. It was tedious going. When she found her mind wandering, she forced herself to read aloud: "Let the North enjoy their hireling labor with all its..."

What was that commotion outside? Had she heard a rider turn into their lane? She continued to read, "pauperism, rowdyism, mobism. We do not want it. We are satisfied with our slave labor. We like old things — old wine, old books, old friends, old and fixed relations between employer and employed."

Someone, she did not recognize the hoof beat, entered the lane. She went to her window to see a negro boy rein in his horse and wait expectantly. One of the house servants — it was James's daughter, young Gwen — emerged from the front door and walked down the steps toward the rider. He smiled winningly, spoke, and Amanda saw Gwen laugh. He reached into his saddlebag, withdrew some kind of parchment, and handed it to Gwen with a flourish. Gwen spoke to the rider and he grinned. She turned on her heels and sashayed up the stairs with an exaggerated outward thrust of her hips. Then Gwen turned to face the intently watching rider, placed her hand on her head, struck a pose, and spoke again. Both the rider and Gwen dissolved in shared mirth. Amanda found herself smiling as well as she reflected upon the all too short joys of youth. She dressed and went down to investigate.

"Good morning missy," James said. "This just came for you."

"Good morning James. Thank you."

He handed her a rolled parchment. Sitting down to breakfast, she unbound its leather tie, and unrolled it to read: "Fairest Miss: You are hereby invited and most reverently expected to attend a grand gala at Colonel Fenton's Fountain Rock. There will be a Lance and Ring Contest featuring the most gallant Knights of the Shenandoah and selected knights from parts beyond. The Champion will crown the Queen of Love and Beauty. Please come and help reign over our humble gathering." The invitation was penned meticulously in an old script and signed in large, bold letters "Ivanhoe." Beneath it was the signature "Turner Ashby."

Amanda smiled again. She recalled Turner Ashby from a visit to his home in Fauquier County. Her father had some important business to transact, or so he said, and had taken her along so she could see some of the country. Only later had she realized that he had wanted to show her to a new set of eligible men. Whether she had made a favorable impression she knew not, but she easily recalled Ashby's powerful charm. At that time Ashby had been a grain dealer, planter, and local politician with a growing reputation as a man to watch. Her father's business with him, Amanda remembered, seemed to involve a considerable amount of drinking, shooting, and hunting. On the carriage ride home the next day, Amanda had asked her father how business had gone and been brought up short with a terse rebuke not to shout when she talked.

Her father's voice interrupted her reminiscing, "What have we here?"

"Take a look," she answered.

The Squire read the invitation and chuckled as he rubbed his hands together. "Well, well, you will want to go, of course."

"Oh father," said Amanda. Striking a pose she continued with a little girl's voice, "I do so dislike you making decisions for me. And I would have nothing to wear."

They both laughed. It was a battle they had fought repeatedly since Amanda had been dressed in skirts and had said, with a child's implacable firmness, that she preferred breeches. Only the strong-willed presence of her mother had triumphed over Amanda's nearly equal sense of self. Ever since, particularly after her mother's death, he had lavished gifts of clothes upon her. And she, in turn, had generally resisted his efforts to introduce her to his 'special' gentlemen friends — friends who seemed always to have two attributes in common, age and wealth — with the claim that she lacked the proper clothes.

This time he had detected her teasing tone of voice. "You know," he said, "I do have some business with Ashby."

"If it's anything like before, perhaps you had best avoid it."

The Squire gave Amanda a sharp look, but her sweet smile dispelled all anger. He grinned in return.

"I do have some business and had reckoned on sending Gordon out that way anytime soon."

"Well then father," Amanda interjected, "I could do double duty by acting as your agent and wearing that new Parisian gown to represent Holland Hall at the gala."

Squire Holland understood that he was involved in a negotiation and she had just stated her best terms. Well, he thought, she did seem to have a fair head for business and any man she met at Fountain Rock would be a suitable match.

Nell glided around the table to pour some more tea for Amanda.

"Agreed," the Squire said. "You will need one of the girls, of course. James, who should we send?"

The slave replied, "I do think, sir, that Gwen would suit well. It's time she began to see something of life."

"Fine, very well. We'll need an escort as well. It ain't safe these days traveling to Leesburg, let alone over the mountains. Do you really want to go Amanda?"

Surprised that her father had agreed to her proposal, she sipped her tea and considered. She had awakened with the mountains beckoning but lacking a reason to visit or anyone with whom to travel. Now she had both. It was fate, she decided, and her pulse quickened with the expectation of journey and adventure. "Yes, thank you father. I believe I do."

So it was that six days later Amanda departed Holland Hall in the company of an excited young Gwen. Amanda rode with the men. Behind, Gwen rode in the plantation carriage. Progress was slow, the carriage labored beneath an implausible amount of baggage, but no one was in a great hurry. Clattering alongside rode the escort the Squire had arranged; a cheerful, laughing group of young men belonging to the Loudoun Grays, their minds already anticipating the contest and their certain victory at the Lance and Ring Contest. A fox hunter's horn sounded. "Ho! For the tournament!" one of the Grays called, and the procession set off toward the gap leading to the Shenandoah Valley.

A gaily colored awning sheltered the spectator's gallery from the sun. Servants dressed as pages brought refreshments, strolling minstrels provided music. There were jugglers, acrobats, a sword swallower; everything a wealthy Virginia planter could conceive that was appropriate to medieval pageant except for Fountain Rock's proprietor himself, Colonel Lafayette Fenton, who strutted among his guests wearing his father's Revolutionary War uniform.

A trumpet fanfare brought Fenton's manservant, a slave named Ajax, onto the field. He was dressed in what Fenton thought a Grand Chamberlain should wear; bright fabrics, ruffles, and pleats on arms, torso, and hem. Ajax hoisted a colossal gonfalon up a tall chestnut mast. The wind caught the banner and blew it taut to reveal Fenton's coat of arms. "Let the tournament begin!" Fenton cried.

For the first round, the knights rode a straight course toward four posts. Each post had a protruding arm from which hung a wicker ring six inches in diameter. Beside each post stood a slave boy dressed in a multi-colored outfit of a court jester. At the start and end of the course were identical wooden tables laden with small pewter tankards. Ajax, who appeared to be enjoying himself hugely, explained that the riders had to complete two passes during which they would attempt to spear the rings with their lances. After each pass the knight would be expected to salute the gallery by draining a goblet of mead. The top half of the riders, those who collected the most rings, would advance to the tournament's next round. The skill lay in managing one's horse while accurately aiming a lance, and this required a fine match between the horse's gait and the rider's balance. Whereas many of the participants could aim a pistol with rough accuracy while cantering across a field, few had experience wielding a ten foot long ash lance. And fewer still possessed a head for the large drafts of mead – at Fountain Rock, a heady beverage comprising beer and corn mash spirits.

Introduced as Sir Lancelot, the first knight entered the list amid polite applause. Since he was bare-headed, the spectators could see that he was only a youth. He wore vaguely medieval garb and had a lady's glove pinned to the breast of his tunic. Sir Lancelot rode a fine-boned palomino who demonstrated an athleticism that more than compensated for her size. Charging down the lists at an easy canter, the knight secured three rings on his first pass, picked up a goblet, and with courtly gesture saluted the pavilion. Something of the effect of Sir Lancelot's salute was lost when he gasped and choked while taking his drink. Laughter lightly rippled through the gallery. On his return pass the knight captured two more rings, drank his second cup, bowed, and retired with a slightly unsteady step.

Amanda learned that he was Ashby's nephew and saw that his skill had been exceptional when, thereafter, most of the knights scored more misses than hits. Meanwhile, the spectators chatted about the small things that made plantation life: a promising first cutting of hay; the amazing fecundity of the swine since the passage of last winter's comet; Laudable McLeod selling off his slaves to pay his debts. Amanda overheard an older man, a northerner as revealed unmistakably by both the speed with which words issued from his mouth and by the accent itself, intent upon more serious conversation. She faintly heard the words "Lincoln, Douglas, Bell" and "that scoundrel Jefferson Davis" and knew he was trying to discuss politics. A few people nearby gently scolded him for bringing up such weighty matters during a Knight's Tournament. The young woman next to Amanda hissed, "filthy, damned Black Republican." Then the babble of voices drowned out the northerner's voice.

Someone inquired, "My, who is that handsome man?"

It was Min, mounted on his Rattler.

"Sir Roderick is next," intoned the Grand Chamberlain.

Min rode with relaxed reins, his horse responding to unseen, gentle pressure exerted by his thighs. At first pass Min managed to spear only one ring. Amanda overheard a young, pretty, black-haired woman say to her rather stoutly built, coarse-featured companion, "He rides well, don't he."

Her stout companion pushed back a long lock of hair that had escaped from the blond bundle of her meticulously plaited tresses and replied, "I wish he'd ride me."

"Mary Jo!" the dark haired girl exclaimed as they both giggled.

For Amanda, the idle chatter, the competition itself, seemed to be occurring at a distant remove. She was present, but the distracted feeling that had persisted since the trip to Alexandria remained. Still, she knew that a contestant needed at least three rings to advance, so her cousin would have to double his total on his final pass. She sat up straight to see Min seize his first tankard, face the pavilion, and raise it in salute.

Amanda stood, waved her handkerchief, and called out, "Hooray for Sir Roderick!"

She saw Min smile. Then he wheeled Rattler about into a canter and precisely speared his second ring.

"Oh, he is wonderful!" the blond girl with the plaited tresses cooed.

She threw her glove onto the field. It could not have come at a worse time for Min and Rattler.

"You idiot, Mary Jo," the dark-haired girl hissed. "You wait until they are done before throwing your favors."

The distraction of the flying glove caused Rattler to jig and Min missed his second mark. Silently Amanda willed success to horse and rider. The horse's jig had carried him slightly out of line. Min's lance caught the third ring off center, held it for a moment, and then it dropped. The crowd groaned. However, with Rattler back on gait, Min cleanly captured the last ring bringing his total to three. He wheeled about and speared the glove off the ground. Riding to the front of the pavilion, he reined in.

With his lance he proffered the glove toward the blond girl and spoke, "You dropped this, I believe ma'am."

The fat girl stammered, "Ah, ah, it is my, ah,"

She was searching for the correct word and Amanda could not help herself. In a soft undertone she uttered, "Garter."

"It is my garter, Sir Knight. I meant it for you."

Min's face remained impassive but Amanda saw his eyes reflect his mirth. He replied, "Then I shall belt it to my bosom, fair maiden. I am sure it will bring me luck."

The crowd applauded enthusiastically, the noise permitting Amanda to dissolve in helpless laughter without notice. As Min drank off his second draft, a spectator shouted, "Bravo, Sir Roderick."

Then the blast of a fox hunter's horn compelled silence.

"The Black Prince, Knight of the Shenandoah," intoned the Grand Chamberlain. It was Turner Ashby, wearing a full suit of knight's armor, astride a magnificent white stallion. Even in his armor it was apparent that he was a short, compactly built man. As soon as he put his stallion in motion it was equally apparent that he was a superb horseman.

Ashby put his mount into a trot. The spectators gasped. Every contestant so far had cantered through the course because this gait provided a much smoother platform for aiming the lance accurately. The up and down motion of the trot trebled the difficulty. Ashby caught the first ring, then the second, missed the third and speared the fourth. A wave of applause swept over the field as he saluted the gallery. He opened his visor to reveal a swarthy face with jet black hair and a flowing beard. He drained his tankard. He trotted his mount on the return pass as well, and this time captured all four rings. Again applause enveloped the field and Amanda found herself standing and clapping as enthusiastically as anyone.

Chapter 11. Fountain Rock, September 1860

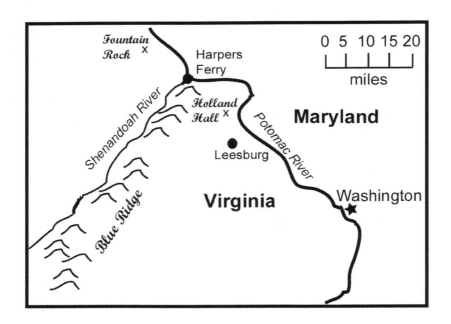

Ajax's stentorian voice lifted above the cheers to explain the new rules for the top flight riders: "This time, my lords and ladies, this time the knights will compete to capture rings three inches wide, half the size of the rings in the first round. Let the contest continue."

Eight knights remained. Amanda recognized Turner Ashby, his nephew, and Min, but the balance she did not know. In contrast, most of the gallery, who lived on nearby plantations, were well acquainted with the riders and now the wagering began in earnest.

"I'll lay two to one that Sir Roderick captures three rings."

"Ten dollars gold that Piedmont advances to the next round."

The distinctive accent of the northerner cut through the babble of voices. In a challenging voice he said, "I have one hundred dollars gold, sir, that says the Black Prince wins the entire match."

The northerner was addressing a smallish, stoutly built, red faced man who sat near him.

"What do you say to that, Bennington?" laughed another man.

The commotion had attracted attention. Amanda heard Bennington respond, "I don't guess that I'll wager against Turner Ashby."

Amanda recognized Bennington's voice as the one who had been arguing politics and then heckling the northerner with increasing passion.

The northerner spoke again. "Then I'll take the field against the Black Prince for a thousand."

A gasp issued from the crowd. The sum named was well beyond a gentleman's wager.

Bennington flushed an even deeper red, the veins on his neck outlined sharply against the fleshy folds of his skin. He stared at the northerner, sent an expert stream of brown tobacco juice onto the ground next to the northerner's boot, and said disdainfully, "I don't reckon I want to wager with a yankee."

The crowd laughed appreciatively.

Amanda asked. "Who is that man?"

"That's Mister Andrew Bennington. He owns Belle Grove, six hundred acres and close to one hundred niggers. He's a crack shot who has been called out more than once. Nobody around here steps afoul of him. They know better. I reckon that varmint might be cooling his toes before the night's over."

The blast of the hunting horn again silenced the crowd. "The Black Prince to enter the lists."

This time Ashby set his horse at a canter. As he swept down the course his horse's mane and tail streamed like a banner, joining the plume on the rider's helmet to create a flowing whole, horse and man. Ashby speared all four rings as the crowd cheered. He raised his tankard in high salute, turned it upside down to show that he had emptied the contents, and returned at a trot. He captured only one ring, but it did not matter. He had won over every spectator.

Min was next. To enter the lists after such a performance was difficult. But Amanda knew that her cousin backed down from no man, and admired those few who could best him. Min speared two rings on his first pass and drank his cup. Had Amanda been closer, she would have seen that his eyes had a slightly unfocused look. But Rattler now comprehended what his rider expected and ran with smooth strides along the return course. By virtue of fierce concentration Min captured two more rings. As he reached down to clutch his second tankard his hand came up empty. He smiled, and then laughed. Gathering himself, he firmly took hold of his tankard and raised it in salute to the pavilion. He then gestured toward Ashby and spoke with commanding presence, "Sir Roderick salutes the Black Prince, a peerless knight." And then he tossed back his drink.

As the last contestant completed the course, the crowd of servants and horse holders parted to reveal a rider, his head encased in a metal helmet and visor, trotting toward the lists. He reined in and spoke loudly, "Monsieur Black Prince! A thousand pardons, but I was sadly delayed at the fords of the Shenandoah by a dragon most fierce. Permit me to join your contest."

Ashby replied, "And who might you be called, Sir Knight?"

"My name is Don Quixote."

"Allow me to seek the consensus of my fellow knights," responded Ashby.

The knights appeared welcoming, although Amanda noticed that Min remained silent, a wide grin on his face. One man whom Amanda did not know, shifted uncomfortably, opened his mouth to speak, and then snapped it shut. Ashby said to him, "Speak up, Sir Galahad, speak up. We are all equal here."

"That's my point, Turner," the man slurred. "We have, ah, ah, been strengthened by mead, which surely puts Don Quixote at a disadvantage."

Ashby explained to the stranger what had taken place so far. Don Quixote spurred his blue roan to the table, and drank off two tankards in quick succession. Looking at the man who styled himself Sir Galahad, he spoke, "And now sir, I believe we are more equal."

"Let him compete, let him compete," the crowd shrieked.

Beneath the shouts and calls, Amanda heard the plump blond girl ask her sister, "Who is he anyway?"

Amanda leaned forward. "Pard me, I believe his name is Armistead Carter."

Armistead carried a banner with the inscription, 'Tyrant Slayer'. He plunged the staff into the ground, accepted a lance from one of the servants, and set off down the course. After spearing two rings, he lifted the requisite tankard in salute to the pavilion. He fixed Amanda with a winning smile, poured the mead down his throat, looked again in the same direction, and gave an exaggerated bow as he set the tankard back down on the table. He gently urged Blue into a canter and captured three rings on his return. Although Amanda saw that he was unnaturally flushed, and he had taken a considerably longer time to finish his fourth draft, the crowd cared not. For them, Don Quixote had introduced an unexpected element of competition, the final outcome uncertain.

A brief consultation between Turner Ashby and Ajax yielded the names of the four knights who would vie to crown the Queen of Love and Beauty: the Black Prince, Sir Roderick, Piedmont — one of Ashby's neighbors — and Don Quixote.

Ajax spoke, "For the penultimate quest, the knights will attempt to capture the rings after they are released into the air. Piedmont, Knight of Belle Manor, to the lists."

That this quest would be difficult was clear to everyone after Piedmont's first pass. When he approached the first post, the negro boy tossed the ring into the air. Piedmont tried to track it with his lance but missed entirely. His lance struck the outside of the second ring and sent it tumbling to the earth. He captured the third cleanly while missing the fourth. Lifting his tankard to the pavilion, he tried to maintain a fierce scowl.

A thin female voice called out, "Disregard the fumes, Sir Piedmont. Faith and a steady hand."

The young man's scowl dissolved. He grasped the tankard with both hands, held it over his head, and poured its contents steadily into his open mouth. He speared a second ring on his return. He drank off his last tankard and dismounted awkwardly.

Min had watched intently. It seemed to him that Piedmont's effort to track the moving ring kept him slightly off balance. From behind, Armistead's whispered voice came to him, "I think we aim steadily at the place the ring will be at the top of the toss. About the mead, I will tell you nothing."

Min smiled. Years ago, during a visit to Min's family place, they had wheedled some hard cider from one of the hired hands. They had been playing a game they called cavalier, in which first one cousin and then the other named a challenge — a climb, a leap, a race — until a winner clearly emerged. Min had explained to Armistead that the cider was like the mead they had read about in stories of King Arthur and the Roundtable. He had matched Armistead cup for cup until Armistead had become violently ill. Not until years later did Armistead learn that Min had pre-arranged it all. Whereas Armistead's mead had been true hard cider, the hired hand had given Min sweet cider.

"Sir Roderick! Are you ready, sir?"

Min startled. Ruefully he wondered how long he had been sitting there. Breathing deeply to clear the haze, he nodded and set off. Rattler's familiar gait seemed to bring him to another place. With careful concentration he pointed his lance at an upward angle and approached the first post. He caught the ring's outside edge and failed to capture it. But as he headed toward the second post he better appreciated Armistead's advice. The true aiming point came at the moment of equilibrium when the ring reached the top of its ascent and before it began to fall. He captured the second, third, and fourth rings.

Cheering and applause washed over him as he raised the required tankard. "Disregard the fumes, Sir Knight. Faith, a steady hand, and old Rattler will see you through."

It came to Min's mind that the voice belonged to Amanda. He looked toward the pavilion but could not clearly make out his cousin. In fact, he realized, he could hardly make out the four posts. Whereas before they had appeared in neat linear order, now they seemed strangely out of line. He felt the latest tankard explode in his belly. He had little chance of spearing the rings and but for Rattler's sure step might have speared one of the jesters instead. Arriving at the table near the start, he drank off his tankard and then impulsively seized another. He spoke loudly, "I salute our fair maidens, and my fellow knights. But most of all I salute this noble mead," and finished it without a blink.

If it was a bit slurred, no one seemed to mind. More than one woman called out the name "Sir Roderick" in approbation.

"Don Quixote is next," Ajax announced.

Armistead set Blue down the course. Min had shown the winning technique. He caught the first, second, and fourth rings at the zenith of their ascents. The obligatory mead was more of a struggle. He had consumed his beverages in a shorter time span than the others. This latest drink was far from settled as he returned on his final pass. Nonetheless, he again speared three of the four rings. By an extreme act of will he quaffed the final tankard and dismounted with what he hoped was knightly dignity.

The hunting horn's blast announced Ashby's entry into the lists. The spectators stood to watch.

He gently urged his horse into a canter, raised his lance, and methodically speared the first three rings. The fourth briefly hung on the tip of his lance until falling to the ground. The crowd groaned as one.

The mead seemed to have no effect on him. He saluted the pavilion with the same compact grace that he had exhibited more than an hour earlier. Ashby began his return pass. The crowd counted as he came to each post.

"Four!"

"Five!"

"Six!"

"By God they're even."

Whether Ashby deliberately missed the winning ring no one could say with certainty. His lance seemed to pierce the ring's empty center, but somehow it slipped off the lance tip. Reining in his horse, Ashby reached for a tankard. He saluted both the pavilion and Armistead. With a bright grin creasing his face, he said, "Don Quixote, we seem unable to settle the issue with a contest against the rings. Therefore, may I suggest a knightly joust?"

The challenge pulsed like a current through the crowd.

"A joust. Oh I have always wanted to witness a joust," sighed the plump blond girl.

Behind her a man asked his neighbor, "A joust, what in hell's a joust?"

Amanda strained to hear Armistead's response, but the crowd noise was too great. However, it was apparent that he had accepted.

The horn blew a dramatic fanfare. The Grand Chamberlain silenced the crowd and then spoke: "Don Quixote and the Black Prince have agreed to a joust. They will carry blunt lances and seek to unseat one another."

To make the contest even, Ashby had discarded his full armor. Both riders wore helmets and padded jerkins. Ashby turned toward the gallery. "May I carry any favors on behalf of a fair maiden?"

Several women responded by tossing a delicate glove onto the ground in front of the pavilion. The plump girl, who had long ago divested herself of all her readily tossed garments as first one and then another handsome knight paraded before her, turned to her dark haired companion. "Let me have your glove, sis."

"I will not."

"Oh you trollop you." She had no clear idea what a trollop was, but was fairly certain it was more bad than good. She sensed the moment disappearing and changed her tone. "Oh Kate, you have a way with words. Say something for us both. Please."

Kate stood. Her voice was surprisingly large for a small woman. "Black Prince, on behalf of my sister and myself: "ayez courage et bon chance."

Ashby had been reaching down to accept the gloves that the jesters had collected. He straightened up and looked in the sisters' direction. He said simply, "merci" and bowed.

"What's that mean?" the plump girl inquired.

Before her sister could respond, a loud, male voice spoke: "I don't know 'bout this 'ah a coo raage', but I reckon you could use a little of this Ashby." It was Bennington. He flung a half-filled goat skin bladder toward Turner Ashby.

Ashby gestured toward one of the boys to retrieve the bladder. He took it, unscrewed the cork, lifted it into the air and sent a steady stream of liquid into his open mouth. Emptying the bladder, he handed it to the slave and bowed deeply in Bennington's direction. He then gazed expectantly at Armistead, mounted on his horse forty yards distant.

For Armistead, the crowd's babble had merged with all surrounding sounds into a persistent, disagreeable din. He had welcomed the chance to collect himself, to remind himself to accomplish what he had come for. Now his opponent seemed to be looking at him as if he was supposed to say or do something.

Amanda saw Armistead's perplexity but said nothing.

Min's voice filled the void. "Be quick about it, won't you Armistead? Ashby shouldn't be the only one to enjoy a refreshment. We all knights are getting powerful thirsty."

To aim a light ash spear through the center of a wicker ring was one thing, to wield a long, heavy elm pole, something else again. To get the feel of it, Ashby proposed that during their first pass they each aim at one another's shield. He also suggested that they adhere to the rules of chivalry and refrain from aiming at horse or head. So now, Armistead reflected, he was about to joust with one of the best riders in Virginia. It was not quite what he had planned.

He had learned of Amanda's intention to attend Turner Ashby's fete two days after she had received her invitation. He had been returning a book to Becker when the German mentioned it. It seemed there was very little occurring in the neighborhood about which Becker did not know. Armistead seized upon the news because he believed it offered a chance to make amends. He could at least show that he was as much a Virginia cavalier as any other in Loudoun.

He had three days to practice, plot, and to obtain, at a ridiculous price, a metal helmet. His plan had almost miscarried when the mule carrying his baggage cast a shoe while fording the Shenandoah. A fortuitous encounter with a farrier who was making his rounds had allowed him to proceed with small delay. He had been unready for the gut-busting mead, but ever since he had fallen ill to cousin Min's hard cider trick, he had conscientiously practiced until acquiring a stronger head for drink. Over the span of his life, Armistead had found that practice and planning provided the ability to surmount most challenges. And to his surprise, he had discovered that when challenged, he wanted to win

The Master of the Hunt sounded a fanfare. Armistead and Ashby, Don Quixote and the Black Prince, lowered their visors and charged.

To the spectators, the rapidly converging knights appeared certain to collide. Woman gasped with fear and averted their eyes. The lances struck the shields nearly simultaneously. The double impact of wood on metal sounded. Then the horses sped by, the riders still mounted. The crowd roared its deep approval.

The horn sounded again. Both riders wheeled their horses about. In two strides their superb horses accelerated to a fast canter. Again the lances contacted solid metal at the same time. Ashby gave a quick twist of his upper body and took most of the force of Armistead's blow on his shield. Armistead had been so intent on delivering his thrust that he had failed to protect adequately his right shoulder. Ashby's lance struck him flush above the breastbone, knocking him backward. For a brief moment it seemed as though he would hold his seat. Then, slowly at first but with increasing momentum, Don Quixote toppled from his saddle and landed hard on the ground.

He next saw Ashby's concerned face peering at him from close quarters. A terrific ringing reverberated in his ears. He turned his head with leaden difficulty only to realize that he still wore his helmet and was looking through its upraised visor. He suddenly felt both sick and foolish.

"Are you all right," asked Ashby.

"If you'll help me up we'll both find out," Armistead replied. "But first, help me with this damn helmet."

The fresh air caressed his sweat-streaked face. Armistead felt marginally better. He grabbed Ashby's proffered hand and hauled himself to his feet. The relieved crowd began to cheer. Ashby carried Armistead's hand into the air. The two knights stood facing the pavilion as the cheers continued. Blinking away some blood from a cut caused when the mis-sized helmet had snapped down against the bridge of his nose, Armistead said out of the side of his mouth. "I believe now we bow. You might help me with this."

Ashby gave Armistead an affectionate gaze and the two knights lowered themselves into a courtly bow.

They walked slowly toward their fellow knights. The men swarmed around the two heroes, shaking their hands, slapping them on the back. Someone offered Armistead a tankard. He managed to say, "Not just now, thank you", before his knees buckled and he began to fall. Suddenly there was a strong arm wrapped around his upper torso, supporting him from beneath his armpits.

A voice spoke. "Make a lane there cousins. Make a lane."

Min guided him through the throng. "A few steps more," he urged softly.

Then, behind an outbuildings, Min gently lowered Armistead to the ground. Min took a few steps to the side and looked away. He began to sing softly an old Scottish tune they both knew well. "Say Johnny Cope, are you walking yet?" Armistead managed a smile of recognition before he was overcome. His violent retching sounds filled in the empty places of Min's homage to Scottish martial revenge.

Chapter 12. Fountain Rock, September 1860

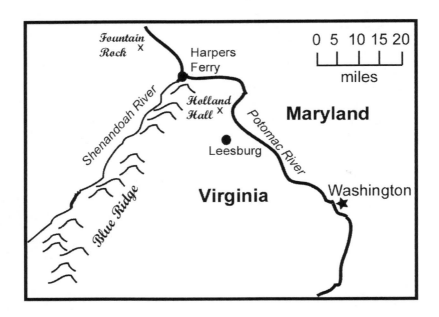

With nightfall came the ladies' opportunity to shine. Most had watched the Lance and Ring Contest with polite attention and some with genuine interest. All passionately attended to the details of preparing for the Grand Feast.

They gathered in a great room on the manor's second floor. In the winter this room served as a ballroom. In the summer its two cavernous stone fireplaces stood as silent sentinels, guarding opposite ends of the oblong room. Instead of roaring oak logs, their iron anvils supported blooming red and pink geraniums. The heavy, brocaded curtains had been drawn back, the ornate French doors leading to the veranda opened to admit a warm breeze. The veranda faced west. As the sun sank toward the distant Allegheny mountains, its rays entered the room to be reflected first by the highly polished maplewood floor and then again by the numerous mirrors strategically located around the room to assist the women while they dressed.

A fluttering, excited group collected in front of the mirrors to assess the fall of the hemline, the placement of a fur pelisse over a shoulder, and more covertly, the costumes worn by the others. Numerous servant girls stood behind them, their outstretched arms laden with tunics, capes, and sashes. Because the handful of women who knew her also knew that Amanda was well read, they consulted her regarding appropriate medieval costume. Her sometimes sardonic answers, "No Sandy, I believe medieval ladies sought to mystify a bit more" — this to an acquaintance who was displaying an excessive amount of bosom — only attracted more queries. In spite of her closely held suspicion that much of this preparation was empty show, she could not help herself from being caught up in the cheerful good flow of humor, a humor that became increasingly ribald when the women discussed the young men who had competed in the contest.

At last, breaking away from her inquisitive new friends, she said, "Come on Gwen," and moved to a corner mirror. Dispassionately she assessed the figure before her. She had chosen to dress as a shepherdess. The simple, dark green tunic hung gracefully from her shoulders. The brocade on sleeve and bodice matched the color of her coral earrings, a gift from a Baltimore clipper captain with whom her father traded. Her hair was gathered in a closely woven grapevine circlet. Whatever effect the whole created, Amanda received one overwhelming impression: she was growing old. Reflected in the mirror behind her, she saw Gwen discretely turning first one way and then the other to examine her own costume. The bright, white muslin dress well set off her shining ebony skin. With something of a shock, Amanda realized that indeed Gwen was no longer a little girl but had blossomed into an attractive woman. Turning slowly so as not to catch her preening, Amanda said briskly, "This will have to do." Softening slightly, she smiled at Gwen and said, "You look very pretty."

A hunting horn sounded a sweet fanfare, the notes of its final flourish summoning knights and ladies to the feast. The guests assembled beneath a huge tent that had been erected on the side lawn of the manor house. In the center of the tent, a hand-hewn chestnut mast supported the ridgepole. A second, smaller mast protruded toward the sky. Secured to it was a brightly colored gonfalon with the manor's coat of arms. The 40-foot-long banner streamed gaily in the breeze. Two oak pillars formed an entrance portal. From one flew the Virginia state flag with its familiar motto, "SIC SEMPER TYRANNIS": Thus Ever to Tyrants. At the column's base stood stacked muskets forming a small pyramid, their sword bayonets catching sun's last rays. An imposing knight in a full coat of mail armor guarded the opposite column. Next to him was a tripod formed by a ferocious appearing collection of medieval weaponry. Here too, a banner flew, but it expressed a different sentiment: "Let love and beauty rule."

Inside, a plank table extended nearly the tent's length. At the table's center was a large confection baked in the form of a swan. Atop the swan's head was a gold crown, the conqueror's crown to be awarded to the Queen of Love and Beauty. The guests found their places, each person flanked with someone of the opposite sex, and the feast began.

Slaves delivered course after course to the groaning side tables. Behind each male diner stood a 'man at arms' – Fountain Rock had borrowed the most reliable house slaves from nearby plantations – dressed in the livery of their plantation, while behind the women stood 'ladies in waiting', slave girls dressed in simple, medieval costume. The servants brought soup tureens, platters of iced oysters, steaming cuts of roast pork in a continuous shuttle from side table to dining table, exchanging fresh servings for half empty plate and bowl and steadily refreshing the accompanying wines and champagnes.

It was now permissible to discuss important matters, so talk naturally focused on the forthcoming national election. An elderly planter observed, "I have seen much of life and I cannot believe we will ever have such a man as Abraham Lincoln President of the United States."

Arthur Rixey, the Leesburg lawyer, nodded agreement. "Southern men and Southern women will not sit down with folded hands if the masses elect a Black Republican President."

Amanda had heard such opinions time and again and they held little interest. Instead, she listened intently while a Baltimore merchant recounted the latest news. It appeared the Democratic Party had irretrievably fractured, with northerners nominating Stephen Douglas while the southerners had selected Vice-President John Breckinridge.

"There's a good man," said the merchant's neighbor, "experienced and one of us."

"But he can't get enough votes in the north," retorted the merchant. "Douglas can, and he's solid on slavery."

Another voice interjected: "Bah! Douglas is as bad as Lincoln. He would do just as much to undermine the South and slavery."

During a pause in the ensuing babble Amanda spoke: "What about this new organization? It seems to support a good middle ground."

A brief silence fell over the nearby diners. Politics was men's business and few of the local menfolk expected their women either to know about candidates and parties or to care. The merchant was different. His business had taken him north. In New York and particularly Boston he had seen and heard women take part in lively discussions of national issues. To his chagrin he had experienced first hand a cogent, point by point refutation of his political philosophy delivered by a small, keen-eyed Quaker woman. Until that time he had never disputed anything with a woman beyond the details of household economy, his drinking habits, or his amorous inclinations. In Boston he had discovered debate with an intelligent woman to be surprisingly enjoyable. Taking a sip of wine, he fixed Amanda with a not unfriendly gaze and replied, "The name's Morgan, ma'am, Brook Morgan. I don't believe we've met."

Morgan continued, "You allude, I believe, to the Constitutional Union Party and its candidate John Bell. Bell is a good man also. He and his party offer a moderate course between the firebrands on either side."

"The name's Holland, sir, Amanda Holland." With her gift for mimicry, she captured perfectly Morgan's inflection. "I understand Bell acknowledges states' rights within the framework of respect for the Constitution, the Union, and our laws."

Amanda observed that while she spoke, Morgan looked her straight in the eyes. It was not like it was with most men, who seemed to use their eyes as if they were undressing her. His forthright gaze, his apparent attention to what she said reminded her of Armistead. Morgan began to reply when the gentleman to Amanda's right — a man whose roving foot had repeatedly sought contact with Amanda's foot — interrupted.

"I don't know nothing about this Bell, but I do know we've got to stop that nigger loving, Black Republican son of a bitch Lincoln. Pard me ma'am," he added, turning to Amanda with a leer.

From across the table, Bennington, the ill-mannered man who Amanda had overheard abusing Ashby's northern guest, spoke with an alcohol slurred voice.

"If Lincoln wins, God rot his soul, we southrons will leave the Union. What do you say to that, Mister Yankee?" He fixed Ashby's guest with a blood shot glare.

Amanda saw Morgan roll his eyes and give her a wink.

"I say," the northerner firmly replied, "what Mister Lincoln himself says. The threat to leave the Union if the Republicans triumph, is like a footpad holding a pistol to his victim's head."

Bennington exploded from his chair. "You call me a common thief? I'll call you out you son of..."

Ashby's strong voice intervened. "I'm a Bell man myself. But gentlemen, I sense that we bore the ladies. A glass of wine with you both, and I implore you, no more political discussion."

Lowering himself onto his chair, Bennington motioned for his servant to refill his glass. He sat fidgeting irritably, an angry flush suffusing his face. His servant brushed against his shoulder, spilling a few drops of wine on Bennington's bulging waistcoat.

Bennington snapped at the servant. "I'll have the hide off you tomorrow, see if I won't."

With fear in his eyes, the servant anxiously patted at the spill with a linen napkin.

"At the rate you're going, Andrew," laughed a woman across the table, "you'll be in no kind of shape to whip anyone."

The feast wound toward a close. While his neighbors carried the conversation, Morgan took discreet opportunity to study the woman across from him.

She was a trifle old, he concluded, but he had always been attracted by older women ever since his father's second wife, a buxom, lively woman of twenty-eight had displayed a thirst that Morgan's fifty-eight-year-old father had seemingly been unable to quench. She had appeared at his bedside when he was fifteen, to show him things he had never again experienced outside the confines of a select bordello in Paris. Morgan concluded that Amanda Holland, although perhaps a bit thin, was attractive enough, particularly when she engaged him with her open, long-lashed look.

He heard a stir from Ashby's party near the head of the table. He continued to look at Amanda and saw her gazing toward Ashby. Her eyes widened and a slight flush showed on her face. Quickly she turned her head back and downward to her plate. Almost without pause she then raised her head and resumed a conversation with the gentleman seated to her left. Morgan was confident of his ability to read people. His livelihood and sometimes his life itself depended upon it. He was certain that this interesting woman was in a high flow of emotion. Yet she had barely displayed it, recovering her composure with a skill Morgan could not help but admire. He casually glanced toward the head of the table to ascertain the source of her discomfort.

The man who had jousted with Turner Ashby had arrived at the table. He saw Ashby spring to his feet, shake his hand, and motion to the empty place setting at his right hand. It was the only setting along the entire table where two men sat side by side. Morgan took a sip of wine and saw that Amanda was continuing an animated conversation with her neighbor. Softly he inquired of the woman next to him, "I see our gallant has re-appeared. Would you know his name?"

Armistead was far from fully recovered. A dull throb persisted around his temples and he felt strangely sleepy. Emptying his stomach had helped. What had helped even more was a foul-smelling beverage brought to him by a grinning black boy.

"Sir Knight?" the boy had said, "my master reckon youse need this."

"Min, you drink it," Armistead had replied.

"God! It smells awful. What in the world is it?"

"Master gets it from Europe. It's called Fernet Branca. It do smelt bad. But Master says it fixes a man right up who done been poisoned by drink. I've seen my father serve it to Master Ashby himself."

Armistead looked at him sharply. He realized the boy was in earnest. "Right, you're the Grand Chamberlain's boy. What's your name?"

"Sam," the boy answered.

"Sam, you tell your master that I have not been poisoned by drink. What I have been is knocked off my horse while wearing a ridiculous, God damned suit of metal and furthermore..."

Armistead's voice had begun to swell. Min interrupted.

"Fine then," he laughed. "Since you are feeling so well, just drink this off so we can go to supper."

Armistead sputtered out a few more half-hearted curses, took the glass, and drank it down.

To his surprise, he felt the Fernet Branca's soothing warmth spread through his belly. Five minutes later, when he and Min entered the feast tent, he felt a faint hint of an appetite.

His arrival caused an embarrassing stir. Ashby had been concerned and solicitous, delighted to learn that the roborative beverage had done the trick. As Armistead sat he glanced down the table and found Amanda. Briefly their eyes locked. He had never been particularly able to dissemble in front of his cousin and so it was here. Armistead then sat down to food, more drink, and to dismissing gracefully the adoring attention of the lovely, empty-headed woman next to him.

The servants cleared the table in preparation for dessert. The clatter of dishes and silverware provided Amanda with a chance to remove herself from the conversation and to ponder the conflicting emotions racing through her. She had been delighted to be admitted, however briefly, into the men's conversation of business and politics. She had felt Morgan's eyes gazing at her and discovered, to her surprise, that she did not mind. She had been relieved to see Armistead appear, apparently unharmed. The look he had given her had been far less welcome. It was as if he were on the verge of resolving something about which she knew nothing. She sighed to herself. She had traveled west to free herself of brooding thoughts. Instead, she seemed to have substituted one set of troubles for another.

The discordant sounds of angry debate intruded into her thoughts. It was the northerner again, being baited by Bennington and his cronies into increasingly strong statements about politics, slavery, and union. From the top of the table came the sound of a fist firmly striking the table followed by the hushing clucks of women striving to silence their male companions. Gradually everyone quieted. Ashby rose to speak.

"It is the obligation and honor of the victor of the Lance and Ring Contest to select the Queen of Love and Beauty. By fortune most kind, nay by a mere whiff of chance, your host had the luck to defeat a most worthy knight. I name, of course, Don Quixote."

Ashby smiled at Armistead while the guests applauded.

Ashby continued: "It would be ungallant of me to claim victory. After all, I have had more practice than most with the mead."

The crowd laughed. Several of Ashby's friends chanted, "Hear him! Hear him!"

"Therefore it is only right and proper, that Don Quixote here name his Queen. Stand Sir Knight and tell us who she is."

Armistead slowly rose to his feet. An expectant silence fell across the table. The guests gazed at him intently.

"Amidst such beauty it is nearly beyond this knight's ability to name just one." His eyes found Amanda.

Because she had anticipated it, Amanda was ready with her response before Armistead went any farther. With her eyes, and a subtle but firm inclination of her head that went unnoticed by all but one guest, she communicated what she had to say.

Armistead's voice caught and then stumbled into a throat clearing cough.

"Give him some more mead, Turner. He grows faint!" the old sea captain hooted.

"Fair maidens, gentlemen, and fellow knights. I give you Amanda Holland, Queen of Love and Beauty."

His eyes shifted to salute her. She was gone.

Most of the guests did not recognize the name of the anointed one. They searched the table eagerly for first sight of the blushing, radiant beauty. "Who is she? Who is she?" several voices loudly asked.

The woman seated across from Min had previously concluded that he found her champagne-infused wit attractive. Emboldened, she thrust again: "Sir Knight, I am shocked to observe your family capable of such atrocious manners. Can you account for it?"

Min looked at the empty chair, at the figure of his cousin who appeared sad and confused, and flatly replied, "I rather think it in the nature of a feud," and then stared bleakly down at his plate.

Perplexed, the crowd stared at Armistead. An uncomfortable silence intruded.

Ashby recovered first. He addressed Armistead. "Sir, if this is your idea of a joke, I think it sadly out of place."

Morgan was one of the few guests who was hugely enjoying the drama. He had seen Amanda's jaw tightening with anger and then resolution. He admired her proud carriage as she retreated from the table. What will that witless boy do now? he idly wondered.

Armistead stood like an actor on center stage, his carefully rehearsed, climactic denouement suddenly revealed as farce. "Monsieur Black Prince, I meant no disrespect to you and to this table. I am afraid my fall has addled my senses. The joke, however sadly misplaced, I know, is directed at me."

Outside the tent, Amanda leaned against a tree. She allowed the reviving air of the mountain breeze to blow gently across her moist cheek. Then, with firm step she walked to the manor house to pack for departure.

With effort and charm Turner Ashby rekindled his mid-summer's eve fete. He grandly announced that all the ladies present deservedly shared the title Queen of Love and Beauty, ordered the musicians in, and made sure he danced with every woman. He could not help but notice the queen's unclaimed crown collapse in a pool of confection as the swan centerpiece melted in the late summer heat.

Out of earshot of the tent, another man's plans were preceding smoothly. Bennington and his cronies had encountered Ashby's northern guest and were again hectoring him.

"It's a damned piece of impudence for a Yankee and a Black Republican to come down here and accept the hospitality of a Virginia gentleman." Bennington spoke with a slurred tongue. He took another pull from a flask and continued, "What I have just said had reference to you and was meant to be insulting."

The northerner slapped Bennington's face with his glove. Bennington growled a curse and took a swing at him. Before a brawl erupted other guests intervened. One of Bennington's cronies spoke: "It is usual among us to resolve these matters with pistols."

"I expect it is," replied the northerner. "I'll meet your man anytime he wishes."

"Now!" said Bennington, all traces of a slur gone.

Word of the pending duel reached Ashby while he danced with the plump, vapid woman named Mary Jo who clung to him far too closely. As soon as the music stopped, he excused himself and went outside. He saw a file of men carrying torches wending their way through the formal garden. Approaching them through a side gate, he intercepted the duelists as their seconds paced out their positions on the level surface of a lawn croquet court.

Ashby entered the band of flickering light to overhear a man say to his northern guest, "Mister Means, Bennington is an experienced duelist. He has shot down more than one man. No one around here challenges him."

"I understand," replied Abner Means.

Ashby confronted his neighbor, "Mister Bennington, what is the time fixed for your meeting with Mister Means?"

"I am to fight that son-of-a bitch directly," Bennington answered.

Ashby did not particularly like Means either. He doubted if the German merchant possessed any capacity with firearms. He knew Means as a skilled businessman who found northern markets for produce at prices higher than Ashby himself could secure. Still, had it not been for Means's unexpected appearance the day of the contest, Ashby would never have invited him. None of that mattered now. To Ashby, something fundamental was at stake.

"I beg your pardon, Mister Bennington. Mister Means has nothing to do with this affair. He is at this house tonight as my guest. When I invited him to come, the invitation was Turner Ashby's word of honor that he should be treated as a gentleman. In turn, his presence is my voucher for his character to my neighbors and other guests. I am sorry to have to explain these points of good breeding to you, Mister Bennington, but you have shown your ignorance of them by insulting my guest."

The torch light reflected off Bennington's now perspiring face. He slowly clenched and unclenched his fists. Unblinking, Ashby stood in front of him and continued.

"The insult is mine, not his, to resent. As my guest he is here under my protection. If you are not prepared to make a satisfactory apology both to my guest and to me at once, you must fight Turner Ashby. The time and place previously agreed upon will answer just fine. What do you say, sir?"

Bennington had approached the duel with mounting excitement. He had confidence in his own skills. He doubted that Means possessed any. He had stopped drinking mid-way through dinner. He had thought the discrete substitution of water for his flask's brandy an inspired stroke. When he had baited Means, the northerner's willingness had surprised him. Nonetheless, the sense of fight was on him, pulsing through him like a fever, providing a joy that he found he could only duplicate upon occasion in the bedroom. Ashby's intervention changed everything. He was not prepared to fight such a celebrated marksman.

"I'm sorry Turner. I'm not myself. I admit I've been drinking heavily. It's your damn mead you know." Bennington spoke in a wheedling, slurred voice full of false gaiety.

Ashby snapped his fingers and his man servant appeared. He handed Ashby a writing tablet and pen. Ashby wrote a few short sentences, signed his name, and passed the sheet on to Bennington.

"If you sign this apology, Bennington, and if Mister Means will accept it and your hand, then I think we can dismiss all of this."

Bennington signed his name. A baleful glare accompanied his perfunctory handshake with Means. He departed with the words, "Come on boys, I reckon the ladies are looking for us."

When he was out of Ashby's earshot, Bennington spoke again. "This ain't over, Mister Turner fucking Ashby. I'll sign your death warrant one day, you'll see."

Chapter 13. Leesburg, Holland Hall, Richmond; November 1860 to April 1861

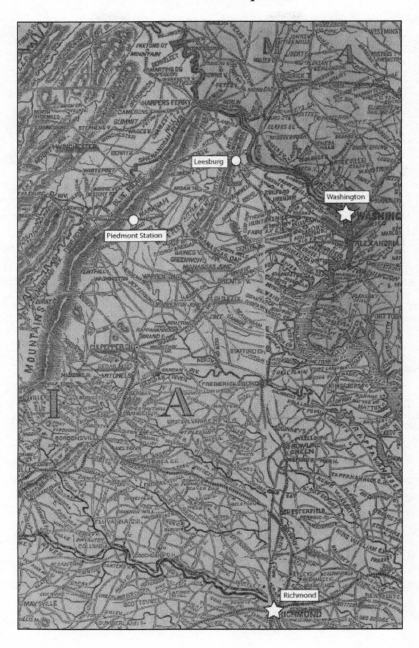

The Abolitionist had been speaking for less than five minutes and already the crowd was restive. Unfazed, he continued: "You in Virginia are the lowest of all."

Scattered hissing came from the crowd. At the back of the room, Armistead shifted uneasily and pulled his hat low over his face. God don't let anyone recognize me, he thought.

"You have more slaves than any other state. A half-million in bondage, yet you want more. Why? Because you breed them as you do your farm animals. You breed them for sale."

"What's wrong with that?" cried an angry voice.

An egg, thrown by someone in the crowd, exploded on the lectern.

The speaker ignored it and persevered. Impressed by his composure, Armistead shouldered his way forward. He heard the Abolitionist speak more plainly:

"You breed them for sale to the other slaveholding states. You hold onto them until after the harvest and then sell them south. Breaking up families. Condemning young and old, mere boys and girls to a life of labor and the lash."

"Read these, my friends. These advertisements from respected newspapers in Vicksburg, New Orleans, and Mobile, and tell me it is right:

"Ranaway, my negro man Sam. A reward will be paid for his apprehension Dead or Alive.

"Ranaway, a negro woman named Martha, some scars on her back occasioned by the whip.

"Ranaway, a negro woman and two children. A few days before she went off I burnt her with a hot iron on the left side of her face. I tried to make the letter M."

"Then I'd try her again on the other cheek and get it right," hooted a florid faced, well dressed young man.

Laughter filled the room, almost drowning out the speaker's words. Armistead found himself straining to hear the Abolitionist's conclusion.

"The Almighty has no attribute that can take sides with the slaveholder."

Another egg splashed against the wall behind the speaker. Then another, and then came the thud of a rock striking the lectern. A barrage of eggs, fruit, and rocks pelted the Abolitionist as the surging throng closed in. Amidst the noise, one distinctive voice, higher pitched and obviously feminine, came to Armistead's ear. It pleaded, "Friends, hear him, hear him." He turned to see a woman holding out her arms to try to restrain the crowd. He could not see her face. Then, a large, loutish looking farm hand pushed her aside and she disappeared from view.

The Abolitionist was still striving to speak but the crowd shouted him down: "Ranaway. Ranaway. We'll run this yankee son of a bitch back to the arms of his nigger woman, won't we fellas?"

Startled, Armistead recognized the voice of Bush Underwood. Bush led the advance toward the Abolitionist. As always, his weasel-faced cousin hung slightly back, waiting for a clear opportunity to hurl a rock.

Armistead turned again to see the Abolitionist calmly dab his face with a handkerchief to wipe away the bright blood that flowed from a gash on his cheek.

The crowd bayed: "Let's tar and feather him."

"Flog the miserable bastard!"

"Hang the Yankee dog!"

Armistead saw the crowd drive the Abolitionist out the door into the street. He felt someone squeeze his elbow. It was Means.

"It's time to leave," Means said. "He'll be alright."

Armistead allowed Means to guide him into the street. He did not hear two of Means's colleagues speak:

"Hannah told him that it was useless to address this crowd," said one.

The other replied, "It was a waste of breath. When has one hard-headed Yoder listened to another?"

The presidential election of 1860 came at last. Although Loudoun, like the balance of Virginia, voted for the moderate candidacy of John Bell's Constitutional Union Party, it only served to divide further the South's voice.

"The radicals control events now," Armistead glumly commented to Sigmund Becker.

"Yes!" replied Becker, "And they will cleanse the nation of the curse of slavery."

"That's not what I meant," Armistead said. "The moderate voice of most Virginians will be overwhelmed by the din made by those South Carolina hotheads. They will not hear conciliation in Lincoln's words, they will hear challenge."

In January the deep South joined South Carolina in her call for secession. In Virginia, leaders traveled to Richmond to debate the future. Because of a request from his commanding officer, it fell to Min to convey two local delegates to Piedmont Station where they would take the cars for the state capital.

"The entire nation has always looked to us for leadership," observed the delegate from Loudoun County.

"Which way will we go?" asked Min.

The second delegate, Alfred Barbour, the Superintendent of the Harpers Ferry Armory and Arsenal, spoke. "As you know, young man, I am a Unionist delegate. I think, in spite of fools like Arthur there," he gave his traveling companion a sidelong look of deep disapproval, "we can hold Virginia steady."

Min wondered if this could be. Within his own family he had seen feisty belligerence opposed by implacable determination. He sensed Virginia's choices narrowing to an all too likely end.

On April 16, 1860, with the Virginia Convention on Secession still deadlocked, news came that the South Carolina hotheads had indeed prevailed. After a thirty-four-hour bombardment, Fort Sumter had surrendered. Hard on its heels came Lincoln's call for the militia to muster to defend the Union.

When Amanda heard the news she went looking for her father and found him, as she had expected, in his war room. He was opening the walnut case that hung beneath the painting of George Washington. The case contained the saber and horse pistols his father had carried during the Revolution. He drew the saber from its sheath and began instructing James on how to sharpen and polish it when he saw Amanda approach. "You've heard the news," he said, his eyes shining bright. "Why, that damned Black Republican had the gall to claim that Virginia owes 2,340 men to fight against the Southern Confederacy. Except for a few traitors in the western mountains, no Virginians will ever enlist in the national ranks."

His manager, Gordon, interjected, "You may be wrong about the number of traitors who will worm their way to the surface. Remember, Holland, it had to be a traitor or traitors who stopped our shipment of rifles."

"Well, we will get them back and more when the boys capture the Ferry," the Squire replied.

Turning to his servant, the Squire continued, "Now James, as you very well know, these weapons date to Cincinnatus Holland's service with Lighthorse Harry Lee's cavalry. Your grandfather sharpened this blade. He went on campaign with my father, and served him in camp and field. Just as duty to Virginia has passed on to me, so it has descended to you."

Unnoticed, Gordon rolled his eyes. Christ, he thought, how these fools love their darkies. These ridiculous sentiments undid the discipline he sought to instill. Well, things would change when he was fully in charge.

The Squire concluded, "If I am to wield this blade, it will require some attention."

Amanda spoke, "Father. If anyone is to use it I'm sure it will be Boyd. And yes, he will want it sharp. Come out to the forge and show us how it is done."

She paused to allow her father and James to leave the library. In a quiet voice she said, "Mister Gordon, I am surprised at you. You seem to have forgotten your manners. As you are employed by my father, you are to address him as Squire or Mister Holland."

Their eyes locked. Amanda's gaze did not waver until Gordon looked away. "Yes missus," he mumbled.

"Good, I am glad we understand one another," said Amanda.

She neither saw Gordon's malevolent look nor heard him mutter, "There are some things you don't know, missy, but your time will come. Gordon will teach you, oh yes, oh yes he will."

Some one hundred and twenty-five miles to the south, Min studied the mirror in his room at the Exchange Hotel. The image he saw — a tailored gray uniform with ornate sleeve embroidery, two gold braid bars on his collar indicating his lieutenant's rank, gray trousers with a cavalryman's yellow stripe, plumed hat — reflected a certain martial authority. Inwardly, he wondered if he should even be in Richmond. Min well knew that for more than two months Virginia's best known politicians had been in the city deliberating the state's future, in or out of the Union. It was hardly the place for a young militia officer, Min said to himself for the hundredth time.

He was here because Governor Wise had sent a courier to request that the governor's old friend, Major Kerfoot, attend a special council. Kerfoot was strictly enjoined to keep the meeting secret. Moreover, before departing, the courier had demanded that Kerfoot destroy the message. Kerfoot had told Min that when he protested, "surely among gentlemen there is no need," the courier had stiffly insisted and had not departed until watching Kerfoot burn the message.

After explaining all of this to Min, the Major added that the whole affair seemed odd, almost frightening. Wise was no longer the governor. But Kerfoot had little use for the newly elected Governor Letcher. "Hesitant, indecisive, a trimmer. Need a firm hand at the helm just now," croaked the bedridden major. At any event, Kerfoot could not travel to Richmond. Furthermore, he had come to realize that his gout and advanced age invalidated him for field service. He had done his part in Mexico. It was time for Virginia's young sons to step forward. It was Min's duty to represent the Loudoun Grays at the meeting.

With considerable trepidation, Min had accepted. On the train ride to Richmond he reviewed his own military experience. To date it seemed to involve pointless nocturnal patrols to suppress mythical slave rebellions and intercept nonexistent yankee raiders; that, along with periodic assemblies to watch men hang. Before he had seen John Brown meet his fate in the muddy field near Charles Town, Min had never seen humans die outside of their beds. Since that time he had returned to Charles Town to see four more of John Brown's men hang on the gallows. Whereas Min had no doubt that Brown and his followers richly deserved their fate, he was far less at ease over the circumstances of a more recent death he had witnessed.

He had been with a detachment of five men in pursuit of a supposed yankee agent. They had ended up charging a campfire. In the confusion one shot had rung out. Bush Underwood claimed that the man was about to draw on him and he had fired in self-defense. The others had backed him up. When Min had searched the black man's body he had found no weapon. Min would have welcomed the chance to talk this over with Armistead, to unburden himself of the guilt he felt. But Armistead had been strangely absent in recent months and Min had been extremely busy with mustering in new recruits to the Loudoun Grays. And now this. His commander had selected him to represent the unit in Richmond and he felt unworthy.

It was 7 p.m., time for the meeting to convene. He knocked twice on the door, paused, and knocked four more times in rapid succession.

The door swung open. Min found himself staring into the face of Turner Ashby. A broad smile emerged from beneath Ashby's swarthy features. "Welcome lieutenant. The governor asked for brave, reliable boys. I see he picked well."

Ashby made the introductions. Min knew Ashby's younger brother Richard, as well as Oliver Funsten who lived not far from Min's home and commanded the militia in Clarke County. Across the table he saw Alfred Barbour from the arsenal at Harpers Ferry. Judging from his reddened features, Barbour was already well along in his evening drinking. Among the others, he also recognized Frank Imboden of the Staunton Artillery. The remainder were strangers.

"Governor," said Turner Ashby, "May I present Lieutenant Arminius Carter of the Loudoun Grays."

Virginia's former governor was a slim man, neither tall, nor short. As he exchanged a perfunctory handshake, Min was struck by his unusual complexion. As Min later described it to a friend, his skin was the color of rigor mortis. Wise spoke in a shrill voice, "Where's Major Kerfoot?"

"Sick, and unable to be present. I am his second in command."

"Tell me sir," inquired Wise, "do you consider yourself a patriotic Virginian?"

"A great grandfather at Guilford Courthouse, a great uncle wounded at Yorktown. Kin who served with the regulars at Chippewa and Lundy's Lane. My father killed with Charlie May's dragoons at Palo Alto. If called, I expect to do my duty." Min resented the question. He paused for a long moment before adding, "Sir."

"Where do you hold on states' rights?"

The question took Min by surprise. Moreover, he was still angry and made little effort to conceal it. "As a soldier, I do not believe it appropriate to meddle in politics. As a free citizen, I do not choose to discuss my views before an inquisition. Sir!"

"Well said young man."

Min turned to see Alfred Barbour nodding approvingly. Barbour took a long pull from a flask and then added, "Here's someone you are not going to intimidate, Wise."

"He's the sort we will be wanting," quickly interjected Turner Ashby. "I'll vouch for him."

"Gentlemen," Wise said, "I will be brief."

"That will be a first," observed Barbour as he took another pull at his flask.

The governor gave him a baleful look and continued.

"Our deputation to Governor Letcher has failed. Yet the crisis is coming sure as the wind. Exactly how and when no one can say. But as it was during the great days before our First War for Independence, when the crisis arrives, the nation, and more particularly our cousins throughout the south, turn their eyes on Virginia. We, the leaders of this great state, must not waver. As the south will depend upon us, so I will depend upon you. I will not deceive you. Bold action may be required. Are you willing and ready to act on your own responsibility? Tonight, I want your pledge that you will heed my call."

"Hear him! Hear him!"

Min found Wise's manner of speech annoying. It was as if he was acting in a Shakespearian tragedy; thrusting forward on one foot, gesturing with a hand above his head while pointing skyward with one finger; in sum, portentous and unconvincing. Yet as Min looked around the table, he saw that Wise's speaking style had won them over.

The governor's aide placed a document in front of the officer who sat closest to the head of the table. Without reading it, he signed his name and passed it along. In turn, each officer added his signature.

As Min observed this, he could not ignore the disquieting knowledge that it was a mistake to sign something he would barely have time to read. Yet he had also been trained to believe that a gentleman was judged by the company he kept. Admittedly, he did not like this officious gasbag Wise, and really knew only one other man in this room. But what he knew about Turner Ashby he liked and respected. Would Ashby be willing to place his name on this document?

Ashby, sitting next to Min, signed his name with an elaborate flourish, and passed it to Min. Their eyes locked. From beneath his heavy black brows, Ashby's eyes burned with a fevered intensity. Min felt as though he was at the junction of a strange road, forced to make a momentous choice without knowing where either route traveled. He sensed the eyes of the entire, impatient table focused on him. It seemed as if his ears were on fire, the back of his neck hot. It was almost an unreal suspension of time during which he could see someone else named Arminius Carter writing out his signature. Then he was himself again, breathing deeply and passing the document along.

Every man present signed. The governor spoke. "Gentleman, on behalf of Virginia, I thank you. I will be sending orders shortly." He rose from his chair. The others stood up after him. His aide opened a side door through which the governor departed. The officers filed out through the hall door.

Min's questioning eyes engaged Turner Ashby. Ashby smiled, winked, and said, "Later."

Chapter 14. Richmond, April 1861

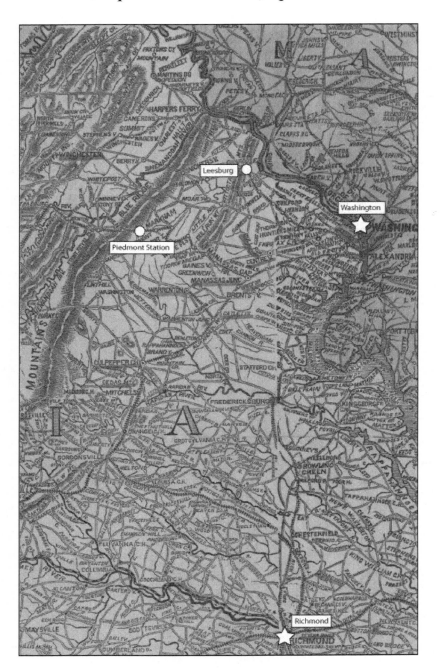

At one time the Swan Tavern had been the preferred lodgings for Virginia's elite. Situated diagonally across Capitol Square from the Exchange Hotel, the Swan's simple two-story frame structure with a long, front veranda was a typical eighteenth-century inn. More modern establishments like the Exchange Hotel, built in the classical style with three-story, fluted stone columns, or its twin, the recently completed Ballard Hotel, with which it was linked by an iron bridge of Gothic design, eclipsed the old-fashioned Swan in design and convenience, but not in heritage. Delegates to the Virginia Convention of 1788 had stayed at the Swan while debating ratification of the Federal Constitution. At the foot of the tavern's six wooden steps, Patrick Henry had greeted his great political antagonist, Edmund Pendleton, when the latter arrived in his elegant phaeton. Thomas Jefferson, two months removed from his presidency, appeared unannounced at the Swan in 1809. Richard Ashby and Min Carter perused page after page of the Swan's guest book and saw the names of these leaders, and many more, a chronology of Virginia history.

"Great men, great events, and now us," Min quietly observed. "It's sobering."

"Come now, Min, anything but that. I'll go fetch us another round of cherry flip."

More officers converged on Min's table and a loud, animated discussion began. Nearby, a small, middle aged man dressed in a travel-stained business suit with a slouch hat pulled low over his face inconspicuously edged his chair closer.

"For God's sake, Wise did not have to go through all of that ridiculous tomfoolery," drawled Richard Ashby.

Frank Imboden interjected, "It's the way he is. He's a cagey politician. Two years ago he helped me obtain a pair of brass cannon for my artillery company. He told me I could retain the guns provided that whenever he called for them I would obey the call, regardless of whether he was in office and regardless of whether the call be private or official. You see, he likes to have his followers committed before he chooses which way to go."

"Say what you like, I think he is a pretentious ass," concluded Richard Ashby.

Amidst the table's general laughter Turner Ashby spoke. "I agree with that comment, of course, but I don't quite agree with Imboden's assessment. A few weeks back, I was talking with Andrew Hunter, John Brown's prosecutor. He showed me a letter from the governor. I remember part of it because the words chilled me thoroughly. Wise wrote, 'If the people were ready I am ready today to go out of this house of bondage with the North, whose freedom is tyranny.' No, I believe Wise has already decided which direction he wants to go and when the time comes, he wants us to get him there."

"And where exactly is there?" Min asked.

"Well, for them," responded Turner Ashby as he gestured at the officers representing the tidewater, "the navy yard at Norfolk. For us, did not you recognize Alfred Barbour?"

"Was he that sodden, red-faced man?" inquired Oliver Funsten.

"Yes," replied Ashby, "Ain't he a hard drinking piece of work. Well, he is the superintendent of the United States Armory at Harpers Ferry. So for us, it will be Harpers Ferry, of course. And here, I expect, are our orders."

The governor's aide strode into the tavern. With studied nonchalance, he looked around the room, before slipping a parcel to Turner Ashby.

Ashby perused the papers and whistled softy. "They mean business. Wise is returning to the Convention to try to force Letcher's hand. Regardless, they've arranged transportation with the presidents of the Central Railroad and the Orange and Alexandria and Manassas Gap Railroads. Barbour is to return to Harpers Ferry and prepare. Imboden to move with his artillery immediately. Harman to Staunton to rally volunteers. Funsten to do the same at Berryville. Carter to rouse his unit in Loudoun while I go to Fauquier to bring the Black-Horse Cavalry. By the way, Wise has just received a telegram that Federal troops are on the move to Harpers Ferry. That's it gentlemen."

Abner Means remained slumped in his chair until after the officers departed. Last summer he had allowed himself to be baited in the presence of some of these same men. He had made the blunder of becoming too well known, and nearly compounded it with an even larger mistake. Bennington's challenge had rekindled a long-suppressed passion unlike all others. At the time he had regretted Ashby's intervention. Later, he realized that it was for the best. However satisfying to have spilled Bennington's bowels, it would have brought him widespread notoriety, something an intelligence agent could not afford.

Since that time, he had concluded that the magnitude of the traitor's plot required an expansion of his own resources. He had used the money he had never delivered to that idiot Brown to build an intelligence network. He had also come into contact with men in Washington who understood what was at stake. Indeed, one of their detectives, a man named Duchesne, had tracked the Wise plot to the Exchange Hotel. At that point Means himself had begun his surveillance.

Although he was a deeply calculating man, at the end of the day Means believed that an agent's success was inextricably linked to things beyond his control. He reflected that tonight proved how his luck was still in, but he knew that his wellspring of fortune could only be tapped so many times before running dry. My star is still rising, he thought, but less fast and with less certainty. He finished his drink and waited five more minutes before departing.

Outside, he paused briefly beneath a lamp post and nodded imperceptibly toward a negro boy who stood across the street. The boy followed him into an alley. Means wrote a short, coded message. He instructed the boy to take it to the telegraph office and then hastened toward the railroad station. As he walked, he wondered if the telegram's ultimate recipient, Abraham Lincoln, had the backbone to act.

Chapter 15. To Piedmont Station, April 1861

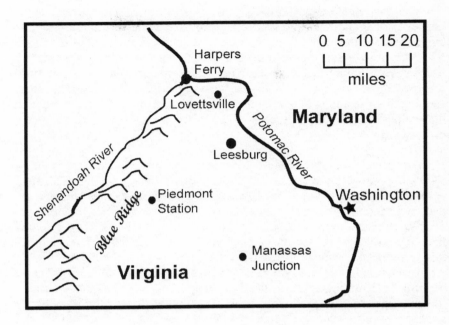

The change in the train's motion jarred Min into partial consciousness. Until now the mission had progressed smoothly. At the Richmond Armory Captain Dimmock, although a northerner by birth, willingly fulfilled their requisitions and even included several crates of muskets for the Martinsburg Light Infantry. Someone assembled draft teams to haul the weapons to the station. There, an express waited on the siding, ready with a head of steam up.

Frank Imboden prodded Min fully awake. "Come on," Imboden said, "Something ain't right."

The train had stopped. "Where are we?" Min asked.

"Somewhere near Manassas Junction," Imboden replied.

They stumbled alongside the cars toward the front of the train. Four steps up an iron ladder and they entered the locomotive. Inside was the engineer.

"What's wrong?" Imboden asked.

"Fire's dead. Don't have no steam." The engineer spoke with a flat, northern accent.

Min looked into the hopper and saw that it was full of logs. He opened the boiler door and saw dying coals.

Imboden, who had been watching him while simultaneously keeping an eye on the engineer, pulled out a heavy navy revolver. "Why don't you just put some of this good dry wood atop that grate and see what happens," he drawled. "We'll even help."

The engineer thought quickly. The man in the slouch hat had given him five dollars gold with twenty more promised and asked him to see if he couldn't make the train a few hours late. He had intimated that he needed the extra time to sort out an unfortunate confusion regarding a woman in Martinsville. Slouch hat hadn't said anything about these revolver brandishing young officers. Sighing at a fortune lost, the engineer reluctantly stoked the stove and kept adding wood until the locomotive roared along at better than forty miles per hour.

Armistead had been staying close to his family farm, in hopes that by remaining rooted to the soil he could reacquire his balance. He had declined several invitations to supper at Becker's and confined himself to periodic trips to Leesburg to purchase the most recent newspapers. He had read the words put out by the Confederate government in Montgomery and weighed them against those of Lincoln's new government. Then, he had looked deep into himself and decided where his conscience lay.

When a neighbor brought Min's horse and a note asking Armistead to care for him until his return from Richmond, Armistead had obliged. Today Min was due back so Armistead rode to Piedmont Station, Rattler trailing impatiently. Min's short telegram explained that he had been delayed and asked if Armistead would please leave Rattler at the station. While arranging for Rattler's care, he encountered Ephraim Beattie, one of the militia officers, leaving the telegraph office.

"Morning Ephie," Armistead said.

Beattie wore a distinctive uniform, a gray shell jacket over an unusual pair of white trousers with a tawny, beige seat. He held a crumpled telegram balled up in one fist. He looked pale, the absence of color contrasting with his customary red and swollen features. Beattie hissed, "Your time is coming nigger lover," and brushed past him.

Startled, Armistead watched Beattie untie his horse and mount. Later, he supposed it was the cruel way Beattie raked his spurs along his horse's flanks to force it from a standstill into an abrupt canter that caused him to return to the telegraph office.

"Say Judson," he said to the operator, a kindly old man whom he had long known. "What's eating at Ephie?"

"Lookee here Armistead. It appears things are going to get right lively." He handed the rough copy to Armistead.

Initially, Judson's dense, hurried scrawl was hard to decipher. Slowly the letters emerged: "Muster the Grays at Lovettsville by 4 p.m. By order of the governor we will take the cars to Portsmouth Navy Yard." The signature line spelled out his cousin's name.

Portsmouth was well east of Richmond, down on the coast. It made no sense and because it didn't, when the locomotive arrived in mid-afternoon, Armistead was waiting at the station. Together they rode toward Lovettsville. It did not take Min long to relate what had occurred.

"So, as you can appreciate, I am pledged to obey the governor. In a nutshell, Armistead, I've committed myself and the Loudoun Grays to helping seize the federal arsenal."

Min could see that his cousin was deeply shocked. After a long hesitation Armistead replied, "But that makes you no better than John Brown."

"I know, cousin, I know," answered Min glumly. "I mentioned as much to Turner Ashby. He told me that we had done what we could for national reconciliation by first supporting Bell in the election and then selecting a fair mix of representatives to the special meeting in Richmond. Did you know that Alfred Barbour, the superintendent of the armory, served as a pro-Union delegate at the state convention in Richmond? But Lincoln's call for the Virginia militia to help put down the rebellion proved too much. Too much for him and many others. Barbour's with us now. At any rate, Ashby concluded that if war ensues, we will have the consolation of knowing that we have done all in our power to avert it."

Min's tone of voice sounded dubious. He continued, "I can well imagine your response but here it is. The Loudoun Grays have been called and I must lead them."

There was a slight pause. Casually, too casually Min asked, "Will you be joining us?"

Armistead heard the clearly expressed hope embedded in his cousin's question. Ever since the bombardment of Fort Sumter, he had been hearing this question, spoken or implied.

"Min, you know I will not. I bow to no one in my love for Virginia. But when it comes to the question of preserving slavery, that is a cause I cannot support."

"Armistead, we have lived together boy and man. I have seen the negro from my youth upward in all circumstances and I know that his tendency, if left to himself, is constantly back toward barbarism. The negro is far better off in bondage."

Min's manner was hesitant; he had seldom engaged his cousin in deep debate, their relationship was on an altogether different plane.

Armistead replied, "The men meeting in Richmond are deeply divided between union and secession, but as a group they are wrong about slavery, although I grant you that they are right about most everything else. I have hope that the notion that Virginia should stay in the Union will prevail and we Virginians will show the rest of the South the correct path."

There was another, longer pause.

"Armistead, I told you that our orders came from the governor."

"Yes, well Letcher blows with the wind. At day's end, his views matter less than Wise's."

"I should have explained. When I said that we met with the governor, I meant Wise. Our orders come from him."

A silence ensued. Finally Armistead spoke. "Min, I cannot wish your raid a success, but you have been candid with me and I will not betray your trust. Take care of yourself, and..." His voice caught. He reached across his saddle to clasp Min's hand. In a soft voice he finished his thought, "And, and, take care of the others."

They separated. Armistead clucked at his horse, "Come on Blue, we're going home."

Min remained motionless. He breathed deeply. Armistead's use of the word raid, an obvious reference to John Brown, rankled. Yet his concern for the well being of the Loudoun Grays — his kin and friends — remained. Min urged Rattler into a trot and then a canter and like some 2,500 other Virginia boys and men headed toward Harpers Ferry.

Chapter 16. Loudoun County, April 1861

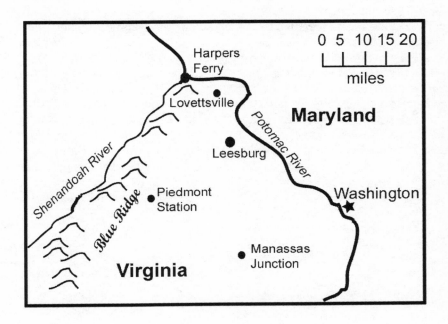

Throughout the following morning Armistead worked at repairing a fence that some rambunctious calves had toppled in their bid for freedom. Occasionally, during his journey from barn to field, he heard the clatter of hooves and would look up to see a soldier hurrying toward the muster in Lovettsville. Once he heard a voice give a fox hunter's view hallo. It was his cousin, Boyd Holland, resplendent in full uniform, waving a greeting which Armistead returned. The galloping horse carried Boyd through the woodlot and then he was gone.

By afternoon the land lay unusually quiet. The only sound Armistead heard was the action of his hoe as he attacked the already prolific weeds engulfing his pea patch. He heard the hoof beats before he saw the rider. Someone was coming fast across the fields from the direction of Becker's farm. He savagely continued to chop at the weeds, willing the rider to go elsewhere. The hoof beats relentlessly approached. The voice was not the one he had expected.

"Are you going to help a lady off her horse, Mister Carter?"

Sitting astride a man's saddle, Rachel Becker wore a fawn colored riding tunic, gathered at the waist with a wide belt so as to pull the material taut over her shoulders and chest. She wore neither a bonnet nor hat, nor apparently a blouse beneath the tunic. She had a fuller bosom than he remembered.

He realized that he was staring and moved quickly to offer a hand. "My apologies, ma'am; when I heard someone approach I rather thought it would be your father."

She gave an appreciative laugh, tossed him the reins, and sprang lightly from her saddle. She landed easily, only to stumble against him. With his free hand, he gripped her waist to help her regain her balance.

She straightened and gave him a radiant smile. Her eyes hinted at some secret amusement. "My, how clumsy of me. Thank you, sir knight." She pressed her fingers lightly against his wrist and disengaged.

The scent of her perfume he now remembered as well. So, she had heard of his escapades at Turner Ashby's fete. Reclaiming the reins, she turned away to stroke her horse's neck. Armistead admired her close-fitting, white riding breeches with a superbly stitched, fawn colored seat. It reminded him of the cavalry trousers he had seen Ephraim Beattie wearing yesterday.

Rachel turned and smiled again. "I take it you are not disappointed that it's me instead of father?"

Surprised once more, Armistead found himself saying, "No Miz Becker, I'm not."

"Pa's in town. It seems that's where the boys are gathering, getting ready to play at war again. Anyway, he felt he had to go and watch but wanted me to come fetch you for supper. You know we've both noticed you've turned us down lately and this time he wanted me to say he won't take no for an answer."

She looked downward and added, "Besides, neither will I."

"It's planting time. I've been real busy. You know I don't have any help, so the chores really pile up."

She replied softly, "Yes, I often think of you here alone."

Unsure what to say or do, Armistead returned her gaze.

She spoke again, "Well, while you contemplate" — it was a big word, but she wanted to impress, and she mispronounced it — "our invitation, I do believe Belle here," she motioned to her fine boned palomino, "picked up a stone in her right front."

Armistead led her horse into the barn where he cross-tied her. He lifted up her hoof and examined it carefully. He probed with his hoof pick. Releasing the horses leg he said, "There's nothing I can find."

Rachel stood in the barn's half light, the shadows playing across her face. Again Armistead observed her look of wry amusement. She approached and stood next to him. "Are you sure?" she asked. Instead of looking at the horse, she turned her head up toward him. Her perfumed scent washed over him. He started to lean towards her when he heard the sounds of a rider coming fast up the lane.

From outside the barn came the call, "Mister Armistead! Mister Armistead!"

This time it was Armistead who gave a wry smile. He walked to the barn door to see that the rider was young Wellington, James's son. The boy looked frightened.

"My pa sent me to find you."

With a tightlipped smile, Armistead replied, "Well, you have done that."

"Major Kerfoot has been visiting our place quite often. He, the Squire, and that man Gordon drink, play cards, and talk. Until today, Pa could not figure out what they wuz fixin' to do. Our boys, I mean the Loudoun Grays, plan on attacking Harpers Ferry sometime today. Pa said you would know what to do."

Time seemed to stand still. Later he would come to realize that he had been caught up by events greater than himself. For the present, he was self-aware enough to realize the situation's irony. Meticulous planning had led to an unwanted falling out with Amanda, to public humiliation at Turner Ashby's. Yet, when Wellington delivered his message, Armistead understood that his efforts to avoid planning by secluding himself on his farm had likewise failed.

"Thank you Wellington, that is news indeed. You tell your pa that I do know what to do."

Having learned about the mission of the Loudoun Grays from an independent source, Armistead judged that he was free to act without compromising his bond with Min.

Rachel was not happy to be abruptly dismissed. Her eyes hardened with anger as Armistead firmly explained that just as the Loudoun Grays had their duty to attend to, so he had his. She sat stiffly in the saddle while he concluded, "And Miz Becker, please tell your pa to stay home. I'll send word when I can."

She gave him a disdainful look and departed.

While Armistead saddled Blue, a developing resolve hardened: he would follow the dictates of his conscience, consequences be damned. He wondered if Amanda, who so often had tweaked him about his passivity amidst what she saw as a clear dictate for action, would approve. Then, concentrating at the task in hand, he set off on a hard ride to Harpers Ferry.

Another man also learned about the mustering of the militia that day. Across the mountains, Andrew Bennington summoned his cronies to explain his plan. "There's likely to be shooting when they get close to the Ferry. When there is shooting, folks sometimes get hurt. Let's see if we can't arrange a little pain for Turner Ashby."

Chapter 17. Harpers Ferry, April 18, 1861

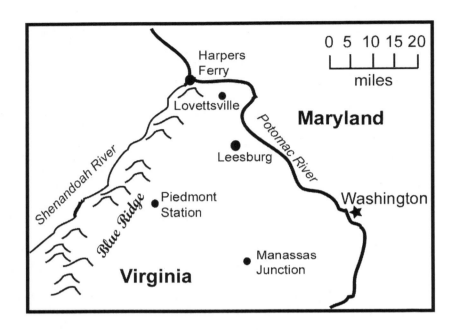

Like clouds gathering before a storm, throughout the lower end of Virginia's great valley groups of men met at crossroads to merge into dust-streaked columns of march heading north. Because they were inexperienced, the march proceeded fitfully as officers argued over who was in command and debated exactly how to proceed. The slow approach march provided ample time for men who yesterday had been walking behind plow or laboring at forge and grindstone to grow anxious. Rumors circulated the length of the column: the Massachusetts regiment was in Harpers Ferry, one thousand strong; United States regulars were dug in across Bolivar Heights waiting to take on all comers; the Marines were en route with orders to take no prisoners among those who would rebel against the national government.

The Loudoun Grays had united with Turner Ashby's men and together they had maintained high spirits until a hard-spurring courier reported that several hundred reinforcements from across the western mountains refused to march. They said they lacked muskets. As this unwelcome news spread, Min felt the column's spirits deflate. Ashby addressed the courier in a voice that carried far:

"Tell your comrades that a man who will not go unless he has a musket is worse than a coward, he is a renegade. If you can do no better, get a spear or a lance. Take a lesson from John Brown. Manufacture your blades from old iron, even though it be the tires of your cart wheels. Get a bit of carriage spring, and grind and burnish it into the shape of a bowie knife. But if possible get a double-barreled shot gun. If the enemy's guns reach further than yours, reduce the distance; meet them foot to foot, eye to eye, body to body, and when you strike, strike home. Your true-blooded Yankee will never stand still in the presence of cold steel!"

The Mountain Rangers, the Loudoun Grays, and everyone else within earshot cheered, and Min found himself shouting as loud as anyone.

Some three miles short of Harpers Ferry, Ashby halted the column and ordered the men to dismount. While his brother rode back to try to force the men to remain quiet — a task that proved impossible given their high spirits and the fact that more than a few troopers had been liberally dosing themselves from their flasks — Ashby issued orders. Min's mission was simple: take a handful of reliable men and cut the telegraph wire linking Harpers Ferry to Maryland and Washington.

Ashby concluded, "We're late as is. We were supposed to arrive well before dusk. I can give you only sixty minutes and a local boy who knows the way. How many men and weapons do you want?"

Min rapidly considered. Since he wanted to evade contact, more men would simply make more noise. But if something happened to one rider — a horse casting a shoe, a stone in the hoof — he needed a reserve.

"In addition to the guide, one, my troop's sergeant-major," Min replied. Besides being a dedicated prankster, Sergeant-major Kinlock Barton possessed one other dominant attribute. Although Min had known him since childhood, he had not realized it until three years ago when Kinlock had plunged into raging flood waters, while everyone else held their ground, to rescue a stranded Mudtown widow and child who clung to the limbs of a fallen tree. At that time and twice since Kinlock had shown that in an emergency he possessed an utter indifference for his own safety. Min knew he could depend upon him.

About the guide he was far from certain. He was a scrawny boy of perhaps fifteen who apparently worked at the railroad station. He wore an oversized hat that nearly came down to the bridge of his nose, a tattered jacket, and breeches wore clean through in several places.

"What's your name, son?"

"Travis."

"Travis what?" Min asked.

"Just Travis," the boy replied as he sent an expertly directed stream of tobacco juice sluicing into the nearby dirt.

They followed Travis in single file, separated by ten yard intervals so a single volley would not strike them all. Because the moon had not yet risen, it was dark. Once they approached the looming cliffs outside of Harpers Ferry it became blacker still. The only sounds came from their horses' hooves and from the frogs singing in the nearby canal.

Min spoke softly. "Travis, would you know of any place near where anyone has been working on the railroad?"

The boy cocked his head and considered. "They bin repairing the bridge leading off of Upper Hall Island right over there. I know because I saw them when I was hooking cats there last week." He spoke in a distinctive, up-hollow mountain accent.

"You two wait here," Min ordered. Kinlock raised an eyebrow but remained silent. The boy showed no expression at all.

Min walked carefully along the canal. As his eyes adjusted he moved with more confidence and found what he had been looking for. The laborers had piled their building material near the bridge. Min picked up three railroad spikes and reversed direction.

"Here boys," he said and handed each a short, heavy spike. "We can't afford to make noise and we're not at war yet."

They proceeded until the outlines of the armory lumber yard on Upper Hall Island appeared. Soon they would turn left onto Boundary Street to approach the town from above. Min saw Travis check his horse from a trot to a walk. Min moved beneath the cliffs and stopped.

In the roadway, facing Travis, was a man on a horse. He appeared to be holding a weapon.

"Evening mister," Travis said.

"Halt! Who goes there?" came the reply.

Travis continued to advance toward the man. "Who goes where, what do you mean?" Fifteen yards separated the riders.

"Halt or I'll fire!" the guard exclaimed.

"Mister, I'd stop her if I could, but she's barn sour and we're almost home, and she ain't stopping now. You know me, I work at the station."

"That you Travis?"

"Yep. There I got her under control." He stopped alongside the guard. "You want some baccy?"

"That's mighty kind of...what..."

Min saw the guard tumble from his saddle and plunge face first toward the ground. He and Kinlock joined Travis. They looked at the still figure of a soldier lying on the ground and then back at Travis.

"He ain't dead," Travis said. Min saw him return the rail spike to the folds of his shirt.

Kinlock dismounted. He rolled the body over, nodded to Min, and dragged the man into the bushes.

"Well done boy," Min said.

Travis looked at him silently. The boy spat, crammed some more tobacco into his jaw, and spat again.

"I'll have a chaw if you don't mind."

Travis broke off a solid wedge and silently handed it to Min.

They continued through side streets along the top of the village. Twice they halted when they heard people moving, but in both cases it turned out to be civilians. They hobbled the horses between the railroad tracks and the Potomac River and moved cautiously downstream, pausing outside a large building.

"That's the Rolling Mill," Travis said softly. "Then the Musket Factory, Wager House, and the bridge. That's where the line is strung. If there's anymore guards, them's likely to be at the factory."

"You reckon we can skirt 'em by taking to the river?" Min queried.

The boy hesitated and then slowly nodded.

"You know how to swim?" Min asked.

Travis shook his head no.

"Right then, we'll take our chances moving along the river bank."

They were huddled close together. Travis looked at Min without expression. Min looked back, nonchalantly turned his head slightly to spit, and again fixed the boy with his eyes. Travis broke eye contact first. He shrugged and led the way down the railway embankment to water's edge.

They passed a series of empty shops, their progress unmarked except by the frogs who fell silent in the nearby river. Apparently there were no guards here. The lit windows of the Wager House came into view. As they neared the hotel the boisterous sounds of men arguing carried out onto the water. Suddenly Travis moved his hand slightly, signaling them to stop. He entered the shallows, splashing and stumbling noisily.

"Halt! Who goes there?" came a sharp voice.

Travis stopped. He stooped forward and answered with a slurred voice. "It's me, Travis. Leave me alone, I'm fixin to be sick."

The guard chuckled. "Drinking again, boy. You're too young you know."

Travis retched loudly, and cried out, "Help me!" and fell into the water. The guard shouldered his musket and hurried to assist him. Because he was entirely focused on the boy he did not see Min stalk behind him and lower his spike onto the back of his neck. While Kinlock dragged the guard into the reeds, Min helped Travis up. When their eyes met this time, Min turned his head to spit, engaged Travis's eyes again, and winked.

Something like a smile creased the boy's heretofore expressionless face.

They continued past the railroad platform and reached the base of the Baltimore and Ohio bridge undetected.

"The wire's strung there," Travis said, gesturing up toward the bridge.

"It's my turn, I reckon," Kinlock said. He carried a large bowie knife strapped to his thigh. Kinlock climbed up into the trestlework. He called down, "I found it. Wish I could tap a message on it. I know what I'd like to say to Mister Abe the gorilla."

"Stop messing about Kinlock," Min hissed, "and get the damn line cut." He heard the sounds of blade sawing on metal. Suddenly a snake-like strand fell, its looping descent startling both Min and Travis. They looked at each other sheepishly but said nothing.

Kinlock climbed back down.

"Right, let's get back to Ashby as direct as possible," Min said.

Min felt a surge of elation. The Loudoun Grays had struck the first blow.

The need to evade the numerous militia columns had forced Armistead to abandon the road and travel across country. It was ten at night by the time he entered the Ferry. Riding down Shenandoah Street he dismounted at the Wager House. The saloon was full of excited men speaking loudly. He forced a passage to the bar. "Barkeep, are there any troops in town?"

"Who wants to know?" the man replied.

Armistead lowered his voice and motioned with a discreet nod of his head. The barkeep leaned toward him.

"We're just outside town and I'm here for a final scout."

"Right. There ain't many, maybe sixty or seventy."

"Whereabouts?" asked Armistead.

"Don't know for sure, but I reckon most are holed up with their commander over in the arsenal."

Armistead found a solitary, scared sentinel guarding the arsenal gate.

"Is the commander inside?"

"Yes sir, but you can't bother him."

"I'm carrying very important intelligence."

The guard's eyes widened. "Are they coming mister, are they really coming?"

"Yes, they'll be here soon. I must go report."

Armistead hurried past. Before he entered the arsenal he heard the sounds of running feet as the sentinel abandoned his post.

Lieutenant Roger Jones glanced up from his desk to see a civilian enter his office.

"And who are you sir?" Jones asked.

"My name doesn't matter. I'm here to report that the militia are only a mile outside of town and that they mean to capture this place."

"Already?" Jones replied. "In what force?"

"Several thousand with more coming fast. How many do you have?"

Jones looked drawn and haggard. Still he managed a wane smile, "Forty-two. I wired Washington requesting reinforcements and am waiting for a response."

Together they heard the sounds of footsteps. A compactly built, sturdy-looking sergeant entered. He drew himself erect and delivered a salute. Although a full, roguish mustache obscured the sergeant's face, Armistead could see that he was an old man, at least in his forties.

Jones returned the salute. "Word from Washington, Flannery?"

The sergeant replied with an Irish burr. "No sir. And the telegraph has gone out."

"Just so," replied Jones. The lieutenant stood up. "You know our last orders, sergeant. Let's get to work. We will muster at the bridge." Jones began to salute the sergeant and then paused to look at Armistead. "You know mister, we could use a few loyal men just now."

The question seemed to hang in the air for an eternity before he responded in a quiet voice, "What can I do to help?"

"Go with Flannery here, he'll show you. All right sergeant. At the bridge in thirty minutes. Dismissed."

Armistead followed the sergeant outside.

"Do you have a horse lad?" Sergeant Flannery inquired.

"Yes sir, over at the Wager House."

"Fine, that's on our way."

"Where are we going?" Armistead asked.

"To the Rifle Works," Flannery replied.

"What are we going to do there?"

"Blow it up."

Chapter 18. Harpers Ferry, April 18, 1861

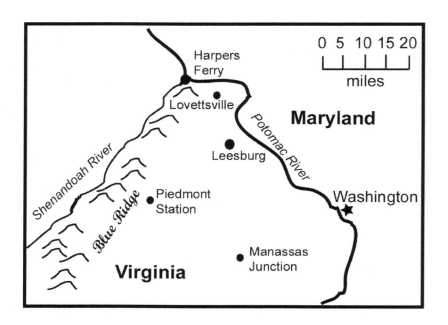

A solitary sentinel dressed in civilian clothes stood guard outside the Rifle Works.

Sergeant Flannery spoke to him: "Good job Donovan. I knew I could count on an Ulster lad. The rebels are coming fast. Your work's done here. You'd best be off."

They crossed the canal and walked through the deserted grounds. Flannery unlocked the factory door and motioned Armistead to enter.

"Wait here," Flannery said before disappearing in the shadows.

At first Armistead could see nothing inside the darkened factory. While he waited for his eyes to adjust, Flannery's words returned to him. He had called the Virginia militia rebels, the proud label with which Great Grandfather Carter had ridden to Carolina to defeat the British at Guilford Courthouse. Which side would he be with now? Armistead wondered.

Slowly the shadows began to take shape. Overhead were the dim outlines of machinery. In the building's center he saw stacks of crates. Restlessly he began to edge forward.

A voice spoke sharply, "Hold hard, lad!"

Although badly startled, Armistead obeyed the commanding tone.

He turned to see Flannery, illuminated by the light of the two storm lanterns he carried, slowly approaching. Flannery stopped. "Now then, if you will just carefully back out the way you came, we can get on with it. You see that black dust next to your foot. You really don't want to step on that with your hob nailed boots, because, you see, that's gunpowder."

Armistead looked down to see a narrow trail of finely ground gunpowder extending from the side of the door to the base of the stack of crates. Here it intersected several much wider bands that criss-crossed over and through the crates and led to a central core. Eight large powder barrels with their lids removed composed that core.

Armistead stood motionless and drew two deep breaths. He slowly raised one foot and removed his boot. While repeating the process with his other foot he spoke conversationally: "You might have warned me."

"Oh but I did," answered Flannery. "I told you to wait, over there." The sergeant's eyes looked toward the door, the small smile playing across his face at odds with the disapproving emphasis on his last two words.

In his stocking feet there was no danger of creating a spark. Armistead backtracked to stand next to the sergeant.

"Right then, perhaps now we can get to work?" Flannery asked.

Armistead nodded and then queried, "The crates contain muskets?"

"Oh the lieutenant had us pile the rifles and pistols in here as well, but very good."

Armistead nodded again.

"So," the sergeant continued, "I'll hold the lantern if you will climb up that ladder and open those high up windows. I'm not as spry as I once was."

For the first time Armistead noticed that Flannery walked with a slight limp. Side by side they stepped over the gunpowder trail and approached a long ladder that ascended into cobweb-shrouded darkness.

Armistead began to climb. He quickly realized that Flannery's lantern would not reach above the roof trusses. He called down, "Are they sash windows?"

"Louvered, both sides," Flannery replied.

Because he had often stacked hay in a cavernous bank barn late into the night, he half expected the sudden eruption when he disturbed a family of rats. He ignored their scrabbling as they ran atop a massive beam.

"What was that?" asked Flannery with an anxious voice.

"Just some rats," Armistead replied.

Three rungs from the top he saw the dusty windows silhouetted against the night sky; outside, that the moon had risen above the heights surrounding Harpers Ferry. Reaching through the mesh of cobwebs, he opened the first set of louvered panes. As he descended he felt a rush of warm air rising toward the opening. Ventilation, he thought, to make the fire burn better.

They carefully moved the ladder to position it beneath the next set of windows. Armistead climbed one step and paused. Cheerfully he said, "It will be bats or maybe snakes this time."

"Jesus, Mary, and Joseph," Flannery sighed and crossed himself.

As he continued to climb Armistead considered how, amidst real danger, this soldier feared harmless, natural nuisances. Perhaps it was fear of the unfamiliar. Maybe overcoming fears was a matter of practice. He found the thought comforting.

When they were done Flannery spoke, "I'll ignite the powder train and then we best hurry away. You kept your wits in there. I'll remember that. Where are you heading next?"

"I don't know. I did what I came to do."

"Well lad, there's a place for you in the Mounted Rifles if you want it."

"Thank you sergeant. And I'll remember that."

They shook hands and then Flannery lowered his lantern to the ground. He blew gently and a flame stretched outward, sizzled, and caught. Inexorably it advanced along the powder train toward the stack of crated weapons.

One after another, a series of detonations reverberated off of the ridges surrounding Harpers Ferry. Rattler nervously pawed at the ground. "Easy fella, easy," Min said.

Richard Ashby inquired, "Cannon fire?"

"I don't know," Min replied. "Look there!"

A reddish glow had appeared in the sky over Harpers Ferry.

"I bet those Massachusetts men set the town on fire," someone angrily called out. "Let's go."

The men surged forward, anxious riders communicating their excitement to their horses. Turner Ashby reappeared.

"Steady men, steady!" he roared. He stood alone in a patch of moonlight and addressed the officers. Unseen, on a slope overlooking the road, Andrew Bennington drained his flask and leveled his rifled musket.

Ashby spoke: "We are going to go hard into town. I think..."

From the shadows above, a rifle discharged. Min heard the impact of a bullet striking the roadway near Ashby's horse and braced himself for the volley he was sure was to come. After the echo receded, he heard scrabbling sounds. Along with several others he started to turn his horse toward the sounds.

Ashby spoke again. "Steady all!" Gesturing toward the town, he addressed his officers: "Our business is there. I believe that the Massachusetts regiment is a myth, but I do know there are close to fifty regulars belonging to the Mounted Rifles in town. If they offer resistance, we ride them down!"

On the hillside, Bennington paused to catch his breath. With shaking hand he reached for his flask, realized that it was empty, and threw it down with disgust. His nephew spoke, "let me have a shot at him. I reckon I'll have a steadier aim."

Temper flaring, Bennington raised up to slap him. "Damn your insolence!" He paused and collected himself. "It was the bad light. The conditions weren't right. I'll arrange things more certain next time. Come on." As they breasted the crest they heard Ashby's voice from below.

He was speaking loudly so as to be heard by all his troopers. "Men! The eyes of Virginia are upon us. Do your duty. Obey your officers. Follow me!"

The troopers raised a cheer. Ashby spurred his horse into a canter and the horsemen charged along the Charles Town pike.

It seemed to Min more like a race than an orderly military maneuver. The pace kept quickening as the Loudoun Grays vied with the Mountain Rangers to enter Harpers Ferry first. As they approached the town, the red glow brightened and the first smell of smoke came. The cavalry rode down Washington Street. Min realized that if a fight began here, marksmen manning the buildings could destroy the closely packed horsemen in the street below. But instead of hostile soldiers, Min saw cheering civilians leaning out of doors and windows, waving hats, handkerchiefs, or just hands alone. He saw the main arsenal and carpenter shop engulfed in flames. Suddenly, motion from a small mob attracted his attention.

An angry group of men, armed with revolvers and squirrel guns, stood surrounding a huge man. They had bound his hands and slung a rope around his neck and were steadily driving him with kicks and blows toward a large tree.

Ashby reined in next to the mob. He was alone. Min remained ten paces behind him.

"What's the meaning of this?" Ashby demanded.

"We're going to hang the son of a bitch! What's it to you?" retorted a florid faced man.

"I'm Captain Turner Ashby and I represent the governor. We are here to capture the armory in the name of Virginia."

The mob ignored him. Min glanced over his shoulder. Most of the men had dispersed to combat the spreading flames. To his relief he saw Kinlock and three of his men still mounted. He called them to his side.

"Boys," he said softly. "Draw your weapons but don't use them unless they fire first. We can bluff 'em. Follow me."

He led them four abreast to support Ashby.

"Sir," Min said, in what he hoped was a strong voice. "Shall we charge?"

For the remainder of his life, Min remembered Ashby's brief look of surprise, his dancing eyes revealing barely contained mirth, and above all, a shining joy that, as Min was to learn, Ashby always exhibited when confronting danger.

Ashby addressed the mob's apparent leader. "No, I don't think we are going to have any trouble. Do you sir?" He stared hard at the florid faced man.

The man lowered his eyes and mumbled, "No sir."

"Hand over your prisoner," requested Ashby.

Min felt the tension diminish. Someone removed the rope from the large man's head and prodded him forward.

Looking at the prisoner, Ashby asked, "Now sir. Who are you?"

"Jeremiah Donovan. I enlisted with Lieutenant Jones."

"Ah, the federal officer commanding the detachment of Mounted Rifles?" asked Ashby.

Before Donovan could reply, the florid faced man spoke. "You did no such thing Jemy Donovan, you lying Irishman." Speaking to Ashby, the man continued, "He's lives here in town and has been spreading yankee lies for weeks now. When Lieutenant Jones asked for volunteers, Donovan here," he jerked his thumb in the Irishman's direction, "took a musket and mounted guard at the armory gate. So me and the boys took the musket back and were fixin' to hang the traitor."

The crowd buzzed with renewed anger. They surged forward a few steps. Someone called out, "Let us hang him, sir." Other's picked up the cry.

Again Ashby spoke in an authoritative voice: "My friends. We are here on the governor's orders to seize the armory, not to capture friend Donovan here. You sir," Ashby looked down at the Irishman, "are free to move north and seek employment under the government of your choice. Lieutenant Carter, you and your men escort him to the bridge. Friends! The rest of us have a fire to suppress. Let's get to work."

Min addressed his sergeant-major: "Kinlock, you see to the boys helping put out the fires. And sergeant, best behavior, hear! We are off to a fine start, let's not sully the reputation of the Loudoun Grays. I'll conduct Mister Donovan to the bridge. "

"Come on Donovan, let's go." He realized that he was tired. The intense excitement caused by the stalk to cut the telegraph line and the wild charge into town had been replaced by an overwhelming urge simply to find a quiet place and rest.

A voice spoke up next to him: "I reckon I'd best show you the way." It was the boy, Travis.

Min gave him a slight nod and they began walking down Shenandoah Street toward the bridge. The town was alive. People lined the street, talking, laughing, pointing. Behind them stood small knots of quiet citizens, some grim-faced, others revealing no expression at all. The spirit of unexpected holiday, of celebration, among those who welcomed the militia's arrival, contrasted with the contemplative, sometimes sullen mood of many others. The light from torches and lanterns intensified. People noticed his uniform, noticed his prisoner, and cheered loudly. Min saw that Travis seemed to puff his chest out with pride at every cheer. He enjoyed the skinny boy's transformation from reserved child to strutting hero.

They passed the brick engine house already known as John Brown's fort. With Travis showing the way, they turned onto the Ferry lot and approached the Gault House Saloon. Min forced himself to remain alert because here was another possible trouble spot that he had heedlessly entered. But most of the men had left the saloon to watch the fire, leaving the bar maids and professional ladies standing alone to wonder what could happen next to interrupt their nocturnal commerce. Min nodded politely to the women and ignored their cheerful solicitations.

Turning to the left a final time, they approached the covered bridge's toll house, now deserted, and stopped abruptly.

Lining the bridge's entrance, ten paces to his fore, stood a double rank of soldiers. Slightly in advance was a single figure holding a short saber. Min's appearance had apparently interrupted a conversation, because another man, his back turned toward where Min stood, was addressing the sword wielding figure as if in argument, gesticulating forcibly, and pointing back over his shoulder. Even before this man turned to face him, Min recognized him. Still, the half second's recognition did not erase his shock. He hoped his voice did not betray him when he spoke, "Good evening cousin."

Armistead's eyes widened and Min had the satisfaction of seeing him gulp once, and then again, before responding, "Good evening Min."

Armistead had been arguing with Lieutenant Jones that their efforts to burn the arsenal were being thwarted. No sooner had the regulars departed than the townspeople entered the burning buildings to extinguish the blaze and save the weapons-making machinery. Min's appearance, which had to mean that the Virginia militia had entered Harpers Ferry, ended the debate.

Jones nodded toward his sergeant. In a loud, steady voice Flannery issued the order, "Front rank, about face, column of fours, march."

Armistead realized that time was running out, yet he remained at loss for words. He stared at his cousin and saw the unspoken question on Min's lips.

A second command. "Rear rank, about face, column of fours, march."

The tramp of soldiers' boots echoed from the covered toll bridge as the regulars marched toward the safety of the far bank. Armistead felt the presence of a remaining soldier and knew it was Sergeant Flannery. He supposed he had made his decision when he had set out with Abner Means to intercept Slater and his wagon load of rifles. There was no point in prolonging it. Again he heard himself say, "Take care of yourself Min, and the others as well."

This time it was Min's voice that caught when he replied, "And you, cousin."

When he reached the Maryland shore, Armistead turned to face Harpers Ferry. He saw Min, now backlit against the dwindling fires at the Rifle Works. He appeared to be gazing straight at him. Reflexively, Armistead raised his hand to wave goodbye and then caught himself. What an incongruous gesture he thought. He walked into the shadows beneath Maryland

Heights and began the trek north toward Frederick. He wondered if he would find Means there, and figured it was inevitable that he would.

Across the river, Min had been barely able to see the departing soldiers. But because the profile was so well known, he had recognized his cousin as he briefly stood alone, silhouetted against the rocks. He had seen his cousin raise his arm and shake his fist. Anger overcame his fatigue. He no longer cared he told himself. Armistead had promised not to violate his confidence. In spite of his pledge, he had come to Harpers Ferry ahead of the Virginia militia and aligned himself with the federal soldiers, with Virginia's enemies. Lies, betrayal, and then defiance.

A slight pressure of his thigh urged Rattler around. Silently they walked south into Harpers Ferry. His order, snapped out between clenched teeth, told Travis to follow.

Travis did not understand Min's anger nor why he visibly slouched in his saddle. But he did not care. On this night, when some seemed to be losing their way, he had found his. Happy for one of the few times in his life, the boy hurried to catch up.

Part II: The Empty Sleeve

Chapter 1. Holland Hall and Leesburg, May 1861

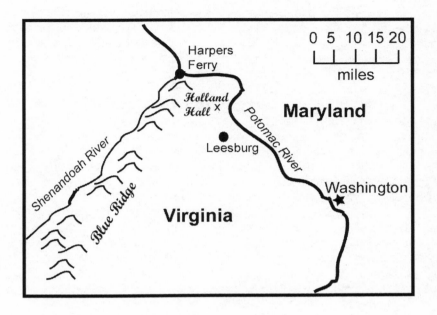

Amanda Holland carefully examined the manifest. Over a period of decades, a younger, more vigorous Squire Holland had built far reaching commercial ties that were the envy of his neighbors. Three months ago those neighbors had selected Holland Hall to act as purchasing agent for many of the Loudoun County militia. Occasionally, Amanda's father perused some of the enormous quantity of documents generated by this activity. More often he summoned Amanda and breezily explained that everything seemed in order, that he and Gordon had other important business requiring their attention, and could she just give these papers a look. On such days Amanda had learned not to expect to see him again. The manifest before her was the plantation's third large contract. It itemized everything from shako plumes to horseshoe nails, the long list of material necessary to ready the Loudoun Grays for war. This time all was in order.

Two months ago she had confronted Gordon over a set of improbable numbers related to the purchase of canvas and cloth. The unprecedented sums had raised Amanda's suspicions but she had been unable to identify readily what was wrong. It required close study to detect Gordon's fraud. A discreet trip to Leesburg to meet with her father's lawyer had confirmed her conclusions.

"Mister Rixey! We will dismiss Gordon immediately!"

The normally glib Arthur Rixey started to answer, tripped over his own words, gathered his breath, gulped and finally replied, "Miz Holland, that might not be wise. I'm afraid that the plantation's affairs are at a delicate stage just now. Perhaps you had better sit down."

Because of his patronizing tone she remained standing. Later, she understood that for Rixey it had probably been as pleasant as having his teeth drawn. By the time the interview concluded Amanda believed that she possessed only parts of the story about how Gordon had nearly come to control Holland Hall's finances. At first shame replaced her anger. Then came the resolution to defeat the Englishman.

It was like a game of chess, she decided. Her mother had taught her the game, explaining with a laugh how her repeated victories over a young Mister Holland had prompted her father to propose marriage: "It's the only way I see to avoid regular public humiliation," he had said. In turn, Amanda and her friends challenged the local boys. For many it was a safe way to be close to a boy, to occupy his attention, to flirt without consequence. Amanda enjoyed the games for their pure exercise in skill.

This time, Amanda understood that she played for something more serious. Her father's unwise moves had given Gordon the advantage, he was up a piece, probably a powerful one. Her position was too poor for a direct attack. So she planned to move carefully until she understood thoroughly the strength of Gordon's position. She might even have to sacrifice another piece to gain time.

"Daughter, are you ready?"

Amanda hurriedly set down the sheaf of papers. The work had so thoroughly absorbed her attention that she had forgotten that she had another duty today.

"Just a little longer, papa. You do want me to look beautiful, don't you?"

"Yes, yes. Of course. But for God's sake, Amanda, do hurry. We absolutely cannot be late." His tone of voice told her that she had charmed him once again.

Amanda fled upstairs to change. She ducked into the great room to see the girls cutting cloth for fatigue jackets. "Keep 'em at it, Granny. I promised our boys we would be done by this Saturday."

"Don't you worry none, Miz Amanda. We'll be ready." Amanda looked at the old woman with great affection. When her father had purchased her, she held the reputation as the best seamstress in Loudoun County. Rheumatism had finally slowed her hands, but not before she had chosen the most promising young girls to learn her skills. Amanda ran into the room, kissed her on the cheek, and said, "Thank you Granny. I know we can count on you."

As she dressed, she listened to the conversation. Some of the slaves were making a tent for Boyd to take on campaign. Amanda heard one of the children ask, "What are yankees, sister?"

120

"Yankees! Why that's them rampaging folks that will come a-cussin' and a-swearin' to our homes like they was gwine to take the plantation!"

The child was clearly scared. His sister soothingly added, "Don't be fretting. Master Boyd and the others will take care of them. Particularly if you stop a shaking and get back to helping us finish this here cloth house."

Little did they realize, Amanda thought, that it was not just the yankees that were threatening to take Holland Hall. She swept down the stairs and out the door. James handed her into the carriage, Old Moses cracked his whip, and the team was off. In full voice, with brandy breath, Squire Holland ordered the driver to push hard to avoid being late. The smell reminded Amanda that a third foe had entered the lists to attack her home place.

"How much longer?" Min wondered, but still the speeches droned on. One politician after another denounced the "Black Republican" president, belittled the "vulgar, fanatical, cheating yankee trash" who would certainly run at first chance, and extolled the virtues of the uniformed men who stood before them. The crowd who had assembled in Leesburg's courthouse square seemed to have an endless appetite for such words.

The clatter of a late-arriving carriage distracted the speaker. Min smiled. It was the Squire and Amanda. Won't she be surprised, he thought.

The orator looked down at his sheets and resumed. He ignored the soldier who called, "Say mister, you read that bit already." Min recognized the voice of Kinlock Barton. They might or might not be "Loudoun County's best blood," Min reflected, but they were without doubt young, high-spirited, and lacking respect for authority. Since his election to replace Major Kerfoot, they showed little inclination to obey his orders if they felt like doing something else. Still, he had to admit that after Virginia had joined the Southern Confederacy, the boys attended more earnestly to their drill. Compared to their appearance last year at Harpers Ferry, they also looked more like soldiers. All knew that they had Amanda to thank for this change.

Min reflected that it was typical of his cousin. While the other women sewed and knitted, she worked tirelessly to procure everything the unit needed. If it was un-ladylike, it was also effective. Compared to the other county militia, the Loudoun Grays shone resplendent.

The last speaker mounted the dais. Unlike his brother the banker, Arthur Rixey was a smooth, impressive orator. He quickly captured the crowd's attention. Forty-five minutes later came his conclusions: "Like all of you, I loved the Union. But northern insults, northern aggression, northern assaults against our basic rights demand a response." The crowd roared its approval.

"Like many of you, I have the blood of a soldier of the Revolution in my veins." Light from the late afternoon sun reflected off the highly polished saber that Rixey held high over his head. "The sword! The arbiter of national dispute. The sooner it is unsheathed in maintaining Southern rights, the better!"

Thunderous cheers, a steady drumbeat of applause; Rixey gazed outward, nodding his head with approval. "One year ago our leaders warned that southern men and southern women will not sit down with folded hands if the masses elected a Black Republican President. So it has come to pass. Even while the boys assembled here prepared to fight, our women toiled to do their part."

A color guard passed through the ranks and halted in front of the dais. The color sergeant, the tallest man among a squad of large men, carried a gilt-edged flag pole to which was attached a flag, still furled in its leather case.

Rixey continued, "With loving hands, every mother whose son stands before us, every sister whose brother stands before us, sewed a stitch on this flag. Yet they asked that a woman who has done even more present this flag to our soldiers. I call upon Miss Amanda Holland."

For Amanda the surprise was so intense that time itself seemed to slow. She sensed she was an actress in a play; a play whose beginning she had helped write but whose ending resided in some unknown future.

She gathered herself and walked with firm stride. She mounted the speaker's platform and stood facing the crowd. The color sergeant dipped the flag. Amanda reached forward to untie the leather thongs. The silk banner hung for a moment and then caught the breeze. Amanda saw its hand-painted inscription:

The Women of Loudoun

To

The Loudoun Grays

GO AND FIGHT!

She straightened herself and raised her right hand to salute the banner. She saw the crowd; men, women, children, old and young, all dressed in Sunday finery; soldiers proudly erect holding their weapons in a return salute; faces everywhere shining with emotion. The odor of close packed human bodies mingled with the smell of horse, leather, cigar smoke. But it was the sound she later recalled; the smooth hiss of steel on steel that echoed from the buildings when the Grays drew sabers to return her salute. Then the band began to play but its music could not be heard above the martial cheers of hundreds of Loudoun County men and boys.

Chapter 2. Manassas Junction, July 1861

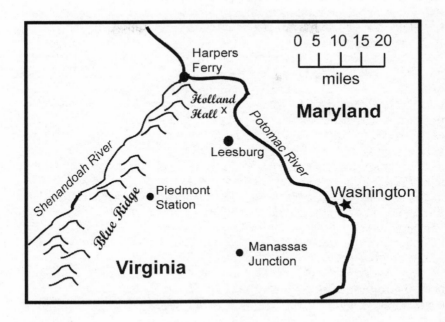

Min walked past a small knot of soldiers gathered around a sutler's wagon. A white-haired man wearing a faded blue uniform was holding forth. Min paused to listen.

"Boys, I tell you, a battlefield is not a drill field. Green troops, men and officers alike, are liable to do about anything when the bullets start flying. The man who boasts the loudest the night before," he paused to stare at a large, strapping sergeant, "might be the first to piss himself and set off for the rear."

The sergeant laughed with mock disbelief. "Ah, what do you know, old man?"

"See this here uniform? It don't look like much now, maybe, and maybe its wearer don't look like much neither. But there was a time in Forty-Six when a heap of folks knew the name of Artillery Sergeant Ebenezer Holcombe. We fought our guns hard that day at Palo Alto. When them Mexican lancers came galloping fast, some men run. You might have run had you been there." He again fixed the sergeant with a stare. "But we'uns of Ringgold's Flying Artillery didn't run. My gunners loaded fast, and I pointed our piece straight. We sent them lancers flying I tell you."

"The next day we caught up with the Mexicans at Resaca de la Palma. Our Flying Artillery led the way until we couldn't move no closer through that thick chaparral. We traded fire with a Mexican battery. It was hot, I tell you. It seemed like no one could survive that fire. You might have run there too, young fella." For the third time he glared at the sergeant.

"Old man, wurst you scairt?" inquired a boy wearing a homespun uniform that was much too large for his small frame.

"Course I was. We all was. You just listen to your officers, son, and do your duty, and y'all be fine. 'Cept maybe him." The old man nodded at the big sergeant and spat. "But I tell you, boys, battle ain't like a drill field."

Min drifted away, the old man's words echoing in his head. The Loudoun Grays were drilled about as best as they could be. And now this veteran of the Mexican War was telling him that it might not be enough. At least it was normal to be scared, Min reflected.

He approached another campsite where well-dressed officers sat on chairs along a laden banquet board covered with a white tablecloth. Each officer had an attentive black servant who moved quickly to shift plates, recharge glasses, and light cigars. Judging from the cheerful burble of conversation, it seemed that these men were enjoying themselves hugely. Min peered at the unit name stenciled on a camp chest; the Second Palmetto, a South Carolina regiment.

Min had never been a regular church goer. Yet on this evening of doubt, and what he candidly acknowledged to himself as fear, he felt drawn to a nearby torchlight clearing where a preacher spoke. He was not alone. A crowd of soldiers packed five deep to form a half circle around the preacher. Many were Virginia infantry, soldiers wearing handsome gray frock coats trimmed in black. Nearby, Min noted some Alabama soldiers who wore dark blue coats with a high collar. They respectfully held their plumed black shakos under their arms. Slightly apart was a small knot of swarthy-looking, colorfully clad soldiers who styled themselves zouaves. They spoke among themselves in a foreign tongue that Min recognized as French. Across the circle, he saw several men from his own unit including the Rixey twins, who, to his certain knowledge, had not spent a day in church since they turned twelve and realized that they had grown taller than their pa. The preacher mounted the ammunition box that served as his pulpit, cleared his throat and began.

"My sermon tonight is on the subject, too late for repentance. A man who puts off religion is like a heedless traveler. The traveler arises late in the morning. He reaches the station just in time to hear the whistle. Toot! Toot! and the cars have left him. He runs after them."

A long pause ensued.

"But they are too fast for him!" The preacher pointed his long bony arm at the soldiers.

"My friends. My friends, he is TOO late!!"

124

As the preacher continued Min found his mind wandering. He noticed that some listened to the sermon with rapt attention while others stirred uneasily, shifting their weight from one foot to the other.

When the long sermon ended, Min turned and jostled an officer who had stood implacably throughout the sermon smoking a thin cheroot. Simultaneously the two spoke, "Pard me, Sir."

They exchanged smiles. The stranger looked to be about his own age. He was a handsome, dark haired man with neatly clipped mustache and Van Dyke beard. Min saw that although he wore elaborate gold braid and highly polished brass buttons, he was without rank. The stranger held out his hand, "Sorrel, Moxley Sorrel sir." Min introduced himself. He found Sorrel's firm clasp and neat, manly air attractive. They walked away from the rapidly thinning crowd.

"Tell me, sir," asked Sorrel, "What did you think of the sermon?"

"Well, it was like many that I have heard, although I do remark upon the appropriateness of the topic. It might be a sad thing indeed for a man who could be killed tomorrow to learn that there is no chance for repentance now."

Sorrel gave a deep throated chuckle. He pulled out a finely tooled flask and offered it to Min. "That was the thought I had, but I am, you see, a Jew, and so am less familiar with these practices."

Somewhat astonished — Min was not sure if he had ever met a Jew, and what he had heard contrasted with this elegant looking, yet friendly officer — he replied, "I do not know about that preacher's doctrines. I attend the Episcopal Church myself, or rather I used to. I have become somewhat lax in recent years, but Episcopal doctrine holds out higher hope for repentance. That is fine brandy. I thank you, sir."

Sorrel took a pull himself before returning the flask to a pocket. "I thought I would take a stroll tonight. I have read about soldiers on the eve of battle. Shakespeare writes, "He that outlives this day, and comes safe home, will stand a tip-toe when this day is named."

Min murmured, "Henry the Fifth on the eve of Agincourt."

Sorrel nodded and continued, "I wanted to see how our men prepare themselves. A great many seem to seek out the preacher's words, but as many again seem to be like those soldiers there."

He gestured toward an intent group gathered around a blanket spread over some barn planks. The rattle of rolling dice sounded above the buzz of conversation. Somewhat ashamed, Min saw that at least half the men belonged to the Loudoun Grays.

As they paused to watch, Sorrel explained that he hailed from Savannah where he was a member of the Georgia Hussars. Becoming impatient with the inaction along the Georgia coast, he had mustered out and then hurried to Richmond to join Beauregard's army. Just now he was without rank or position. Because Beauregard's adjutant-general was a friend of his father's, he hoped to secure some appointment. If not, he was prepared to fight as a private.

While they talked the gaming continued with voices rising in anger and curses becoming more frequent. Sorrel softly spoke, "That fellow there is having most unholy luck. It quite defies the laws of mathematics. He's about to strip his unfortunate opponent bare. I wonder if that man realizes he is being cheated."

Suddenly Sorrel took a half step to the side, pulling Min with him. "Yes, I rather imagine he does."

Min had refrained from mentioning his association with the gamblers to his new friend. In part this was because he had often heard Bush Underwood and his cronies vilify Jews as dirty thieves and worse, and in part because he sensed that Sorrel might not approve of the rodent-faced Underwood's sheer disregard for anything resembling gentlemanly attributes. But beyond noting that Underwood's pile of coin grew steadily, he had paid little attention to the game. He had been taking another sip — his third, fourth? — when Sorrel seized his arm. The motion caused him to spill some of the exquisite liquid.

Sorrel pulled out a handkerchief to pat at the spill. Motioning to the players, who had suddenly fallen silent, he explained, "Excuse me, but I feared we were about to be in the line of fire."

Min saw that the gambler opposite Underwood had trained his revolver at Underwood's belly. In the flickering firelight he saw the blood drain from Underwood's face. With a sigh Min strode into the circle of light and approached the gamblers.

"Gentlemen, this won't do. We will need every soldier when the yankees come calling. Now, Private Underwood, you can return that pile of coin to the center, match it with one of your own and you and your friend will draw a card, high card wins all, or you can simply return him his money."

From the corner of his eye Min saw Underwood's opponent lower his gun and relax. Underwood seemed in shock at the sudden turn of events.

"Come on now Bush, I haven't all night. Which will it be?" Min prompted.

"I don't guess I'll game anymore tonight," he replied as he grudgingly pushed the pile of coin across the cloth.

Fixing the gambler with what he hoped was a steely stare, Min spoke, "Now sir, I suggest you return to your company camp."

After the gambler and his cronies departed Min spoke again, "Private, I'd best not see anymore card playing or dice in the Loudoun Grays."

Underwood continued to slouch on the ground without speaking. Min knelt in front of him, his face pressed so close that the visor on his kepi brushed Underwood's pock-marked forehead. The stench from Underwood's body mingled with his foul breath to cause Min nearly to gasp. He snapped of the words, "Did you hear me soldier?"

126

"Yes."

"Yes what?"

"Yes...sir."

Min stood up and unconsciously brushed his uniform as if to rid it of Underwood's filth.

He rejoined Sorrel who said, "That was well done. But you had better watch that man, he intends no good for you."

"Yes, I know," Min answered.

Before separating, they drained the last of Sorrel's flask.

"Where will you be stationed tomorrow?" the Georgian inquired.

"Some of my boys know the lay of the land around Manassas Junction. We've been assigned to Captain Lay as escort to General Beauregard."

Recalling Bush Underwood's sorry spectacle, Min wondered if the pride with which he spoke these words was misplaced. Regardless, Sorrel did not seem to notice.

"Ah, you will be in the middle of it no doubt."

"And you?"

"I hope to be a volunteer aide to General Longstreet. He is over by Blackburn's Ford. The talk around headquarters is that the yankees will try to force a crossing against our right."

"Then you too will be in the thick of it. Good luck." Min extended his hand.

Sorrel shook his hand and replied, "Good fortune to you as well."

Min returned to the Gray's camp and found the horses securely picketed and the men bedded down. He quietly approached Rattler who whickered his greeting. He stroked him under his neck in the sweet spot he so enjoyed. As always, he rested his big head on Min's shoulder, the breath blowing softly from his nose. "Well boy," he murmured, "tomorrow or maybe the day after we will discover what battle is all about. I know you will do your duty, but I reckon I'd best say a little prayer for myself. Lord, please give this humble servant the courage to do what is right, come what may. Please give him courage and do not let him besmirch his name before his comrades. Amen."

Rattler whickered once more as if in agreement. Using his saddle as a pillow, Min lay down. By the light of a nearby fire, he wrote a short entry in his diary, signed the date, July 19, 1861, and closed it.

Chapter 3. Loudoun County, Manassas Junction, and Carlisle Barracks, Pennsylvania, Summer 1861

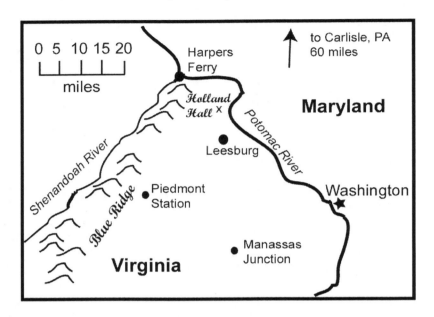

At Holland Hall the first days of summer seemed to last forever. The community had adjusted to the departure of so many menfolk. No one expected them to be absent for long. The older men, her father included, tirelessly proclaimed that there would be a big battle in Virginia, and probably another somewhere out West, the South would comfortably win both, and peace would shine on the Confederate States of America. When Amanda had observed that the first war for independence lasted over six years, her father scoffed affectionately and explained that war was men's business, and wiser men than he had assured him that this war would be short and decisive.

Outside of her devotion to chess, Amanda had never held any interest in war. But nothing was better calculated to provoke her than men's amusement at her ignorance. She began in her father's library. Here most of the books were tales of imagination; battle and war portrayed in a heroic style. Amanda found them unconvincing. She recalled how Armistead had praised the Sigmund Becker's library and decided to visit at first opportunity.

She found him resting on his porch on a late June evening. She had always conceived him to be a taciturn man, this evening he appeared positively morose.

"And how is your family, Mister Becker?" she inquired.

"Gone," he replied.

"Gone, Mister Becker?"

"Charles has run off to volunteer for the Thirty-third Virginia" Becker said with a sigh.

Good for Charlie, she thought. "At least he won't be gone for long."

"Oh?"

She waited, but he did not elaborate. "Mister Becker, I have come hoping that you might show me your library. I am told that it is without peer hereabouts."

Becker straightened in his chair. She saw the first glimmer of interest in his eyes, yet he merely grunted in response.

"Armistead told me that your history selection is particularly strong."

With a heavy sigh he rose and beckoned her inside to a neat, book filled room. The histories were admirably arranged by subject. Those devoted to military history, a surprising number Amanda noted, seemed to march in ranks from early Greek history to the present.

"I see, Mister Becker, that European history is full of conflict. I dimly remember learning about the Peloponnesian War in school and that it seemed to go on for a terribly long time."

"Fifty-six years," Becker murmured.

"Here I see books on the Hundred Years War, the Thirty Years War, the Seven Years War. What strikes me is how long they all lasted. Why should this war be different?"

Amanda perceived that she had engaged Becker's interest.

"There are two pairs of armies facing one another. One pair is around Harpers Ferry, the other in northern Virginia close to Washington. Neither side is truly ready for war, but politicians and the public on both side demand action so soon something will take place. For the moment no one knows when or where the blows will fall."

"Regardless, surely the first battles will decide the outcome?"

"Nein, Bah! Fools think this because they do not know how to think. Do they consider how big this country is? Do they understand how modern weapons wielded by determined soldiers change the historical calculus of battle? Does anyone know the military effect of modern transportation? Just the other day we learn how many men and how quickly they move from Richmond to Manassas Junction. And..."

Becker paused, reddened, and coughed. Amanda had been unable to follow completely his flow of words. The subject was too unfamiliar. Instead, she had gazed into the man; his obvious knowledge and passion for the subject surprised her. She was certain that his awkward pause came because he was about to say, or already had said, something he regretted.

He recovered his composure quickly and then somewhat brusquely asked, "So, is there something here you would like to borrow?"

Amanda realized that the gulf between them had returned. After she had selected three books he escorted her to the porch, went back inside, and closed the door. But the window was open and his muted, Germanic curses escaped.

Old Moses had parked the carriage near the kitchen garden. As Amanda rounded the corner she saw Rachel Becker talking with her servant. She gave Amanda an appraising stare that was rather longer than politeness demanded.

"Don't you miss the menfolk, Miss Holland?"

"Why yes, of course."

"It was such a pleasure to see them in their fine uniforms. Our gallant soldiers, in particular your brother Boyd and cousin Arminius. And what has become of your cousin Armistead? We were becoming such close friends." Amanda felt a stab of pain and saw a gleam of triumph appear in Rachel's eyes when she perceived her bolt strike home.

"We have heard nothing about him. Have you?" Amanda coolly inquired.

Rachel responded with a look that Amanda found hard to read; was it anxiety, perhaps fear? But she recovered quickly.

"Of course not. What an absurd notion."

The journey home mostly passed in silence. Amanda had a great deal to ponder and Old Moses well recognized his mistress's moods. When they did talk, he mentioned how Rachel had been inquiring about Armistead just before Amanda had appeared.

"I guess Miss Becker didn't trust this old darkie to tell the truth," Old Moses chuckled.

"No. I rather think that she had other reasons."

Back in her father's library, it required a solid hour of delving through a German language primer for Amanda to determine part of what Sigmund Becker had said. As near as she could tell, he was cursing himself for being an incautious fool. Since he had again confirmed that he was anything but a fool, Amanda wondered what he had meant.

"Wake up. Min, wake up!" Min stifled a groan and opened his eyes. It was still dark. Kinlock whispered excitedly, "Something big is up. They want you at headquarters."

Min stood and shook his head vigorously to try to dispel the fumes from Sorrel's brandy. As he followed a staff officer to Beauregard's headquarters, it came to him that his effort was not entirely successful. The officer led Min to a tree-lined lane. Ahead stood a two-story farm house. Even though it was two in the morning, light poured from each of the five upper story windows. The front door opened and an officer quickly descended the stairs, brushed past Min, mounted his horse, and cantered down the lane. A pair of sentries eyed Min suspiciously but allowed him to ascend the stairs after the staff officer responded to their challenge with the correct counter-sign.

Min passed another guard standing by the parlor door and paused while the staff officer introduced him. Before him stood a small man with a sallow complexion, a heavy black moustache and closely cut hair. He wore an elegant, buttoned-up coat and a small red cap trimmed in gold. His left hand was jammed into his trouser's pocket, a cigar in his mouth. Min saluted and General Pierre Gustave Toutant Beauregard removed the cigar and extended his right hand.

As they clasped hands, the general fixed Min with a hard-edged gaze. "Lieutenant, we must resist the degrading yoke which those ruthless invaders have come to impose."

Taken aback, Min cast about for a proper reply. A rapid series of images; John Brown twitching from the gallows, Amanda and the flag, Armistead on the bridge at Harpers Ferry, passed through his mind. Min found himself replying, "And we will do it, sir."

Beauregard briskly continued, "We are outnumbered, lieutenant. And don't believe for a moment this talk that one of us can beat ten of them. I know their officers. Hard men. Good soldiers. But just now they are divided, one army before us here, the other still in the valley near Harpers Ferry. I have ordered General Johnston to move his army from Harpers Ferry to join us. Together, we can whip the yankees, but it all depends upon Johnston's men getting here before the attack comes. Deliver these orders to Johnston, or the senior general at Piedmont Station. Don't spare the horseflesh. I depend upon you lieutenant. The army depends upon you."

Armistead lay on his cot staring at the ceiling. The evening gun fired. The post bugler played his haunting salute to the departing sun and Armistead wondered when and where he had lost his way. He had come to understand that his passage north from Harpers Ferry on the night the United States Army abandoned the arsenal separated the time before from the time after. He was self-aware enough to realize that wallowing in self-pity was unlikely either to alter the course of events or his own present unhappiness. Yet, he did not fully comprehend that as much as anything, he was simply lonely.

Having arranged with a Quaker family to care for his farm, he had come north to apply for work at the Cavalry Depot at Carlisle Barracks. The pay for skilled civilian employees was good and the work provided a welcome diversion, especially on a mid-April day when troopers of the Second U.S. Cavalry returned to Pennsylvania. These weathered veterans had been stationed in Texas. While their money lasted, they lit out for Carlisle's saloons with a Texas sized thirst. Thereafter, they entertained anyone who would buy a round with stories about fighting the Comanches, tales of ferocious blue 'northers', seven-foot rattlesnakes thicker than a man's forearm, and gay Mexican senoritas, lissome and obliging. Armistead was among their most attentive audience. He had begun to conceive a plan to travel to the western frontier to escape from a world gone mad when he met the commander of the Second Cavalry, Major George Thomas.

They were physically unlike: Armistead lean, long muscled; Thomas stout, barrel-chested, a hideous arrow wound scarring his jaw. Age and profession also separated them: Armistead a twenty-three-year-old civilian employee at the barracks; Thomas a forty-five-year-old West Point educated soldier. However, they were both Virginians, so they gravitated to one another like cousins. For Armistead, it was like being embraced by family after wandering alone for too long. They talked horses and hunting, about Thomas's adventures in Texas and Armistead's view of the John Brown raid. Armistead learned with amazement that Thomas's family had owned slaves and that when George was fifteen he and his family had fled from the slave insurrection led by Nat Turner.

Their conversation often reverted to the war. Armistead had asked, "Will the war end quickly?"

Thomas chuckled and took a sip of whiskey before replying. "The fools in Washington think so, but consider. In my regiment alone we had Sidney Johnston, Bob Lee — who you mentioned you have met — Earl Van Dorn, showy womanizer that one, Edmund Smith, and some reckless lieutenants like Fitz Lee and John Hood. Every one of them have proven courage and several of them have surpassing military skills. They all went south. The north has many just like them. No one knows how it will all end, but I tell you it will neither be short nor easy."

Inevitably they addressed the question of loyalty. Neither did anything to conceal their accents and both had suffered from the growing northern suspicion of all things southern. Thomas related that already he was being called a Virginia renegade by some of the officers he had once commanded. When Armistead complained about the frequent challenges to his honor, Thomas dismissed him with a curt "Bah." Then, seeing that he had offended Armistead, he elaborated:

"The government is requiring all officers to take an oath of allegiance. Many of my brother officers view this as an insult because every one of us gave this oath when first entering service. I say at times like these we can not stand on pride. I do not give a snap of my finger about it. If they want me to take the oath before each meal I am ready to comply."

Thomas's words gave Armistead much to consider. He wondered if he was confusing honor with stiff-necked pride. The friendship had been too brief. When the Second Cavalry's lieutenant-colonel, Robert Lee, resigned his commission, Thomas received a promotion to replace him. Eight days later, Thomas told Armistead that Sidney Johnston, the regiment's colonel, had also resigned to join the Confederacy and that he had been promoted again. "Nineteen years in the army and service in two wars earned me three promotions. Now two more in a little over a week. Given that our superiors have suddenly become such perspicacious judges of merit, maybe it will be a short war!" Thomas said with a deep-throated chuckle.

Shortly thereafter Thomas led his troopers south to patrol the line of the Potomac River near Harpers Ferry. Thomas's sensitivity was such that he did not ask Armistead to accompany him. He understood that Armistead did not yet know which way to turn and he gave his new friend time to decide for himself.

Armistead's head slumped on his pillow as his recollection of Thomas faded. He resumed his study of the cracks and knotholes on the ceiling. They formed irregular patterns like constellations in the night sky. On too many nights Armistead had stared hard at them and he knew that here at least there was no hidden lodestar waiting to be revealed. With some effort he rose from his cot. There was an abolitionist meeting in town tonight, sponsored by a patriotic society. It would be well attended by Quakers and Armistead wanted to know how they squared their conscience regarding opposition to slavery with opposition to a war against slavery. He was also curious to hear Frederick Douglass speak.

Chapter 4. Carlisle, Summer 1861

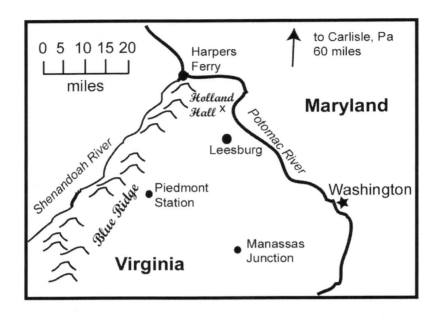

He was unlike any black man Armistead had ever heard. From the start, Douglass possessed a commanding presence. In part, Armistead reflected, this came from his physical self, in particular the thick eyebrows that framed a pair of eyes that glowed like coals. But most of Douglass's aura flowed from the passion of his words. He held his audience spellbound with his life story. Born in nearby Maryland, he had been taken from his mother while still an infant. As a boy he worked as a house servant. Then, one day his Baltimore master discovered that Douglass was learning to read and write.

"He could have had me whipped or worse, because it was against the law for a slave to learn these things." Douglass paused dramatically. The audience seemed to hold its breath as one. The room filled with a stifling heat from their close-packed bodies but no one noticed because the story held them in thrall.

"No, my kindly master did not whip me, my acquaintance with the lash came later when I had graduated," Douglass spoke the word slowly, irony dripping from his voice, "to become a field hand. No, instead my kindly master inflicted a more severe punishment. He told me that 'learning will make you unfit for slavery' and put a stop to it."

The audience groaned. Several people cried out. Armistead saw that many women were weeping.

Douglass waited until they grew quiet. He related how he kept trying to escape until he was successful at last. "I made my way in the world," Douglass explained, "because I did learn to read and to write and people paid to learn what I had to say."

Eventually he earned enough money to purchase his freedom. And later still he met a white man who was as eager to attain freedom for the negro as he was himself. Douglass described John Brown as a saint governed by a higher law than the Constitution. He concluded:

"Until John Brown struck his blow, the prospect for freedom was dim, shadowy, and uncertain. The irrepressible conflict was one of words, votes, and compromises. When John Brown stretched forth his arm the sky was cleared, the time for compromises gone. The armed hosts of freedom now stand face to face with the defenders of slavery over the chasm of a broken Union, and the clash of arms is at hand."

At the reception following the speech, Armistead observed the effects of Douglass's words. Some people were withdrawn and thoughtful. Others felt inspired to go out and enlist tomorrow, or so they said. A small group gathered to listen to a man describe in gripping detail the scene of John Brown's execution. Shaking his head, Armistead turned to withdraw and bumped into a woman.

Before he could speak she sternly asked, "You disagree sir?"

"Pardon me, ma'am. Yes I do, I was there you see."

A mischievous smile briefly crossed her face. "Yes, Mister Potts is a bit on the fanciful side, as I well know since I was there also." Hannah Yoder's accent was unmistakable. It came, Armistead later learned, from the combination of her Pennsylvania Dutch father and Maryland mother. It was the voice he had heard twice before: once uttering a chilling prophecy at Harpers Ferry, a prophecy that had come true when rebel guns opened fire against Fort Sumter; and again when he had attended the Abolitionist meeting in Leesburg. From the first, the voice had stayed with Armistead. He never imagined that he would someday meet the speaker.

She accepted his invitation to step outside into the evening cool while he went to fetch two lemonades. The light from the gas lamp did not show her to best advantage. Regardless, Armistead saw that she would never be mistaken for a pretty woman. She was average in height, rather more plump than not, with an unremarkable face accented by a turned up, button nose. She had a ruddy complexion with unfashionable lines etched by exposure to the sun. Her brown hair was gathered in a disorderly bun, held in place by a simple linen cap. Her loose-fitting dress caught on the swell of her chest and then fell straight down toward the ground. When Armistead came to know her better she would describe herself, without a hint of bitterness, as shaped like the dumplings her family ate every Tuesday and Saturday. At first encounter it was her general cheerfulness and self-deprecating humor that attracted Armistead. It was her lively intelligence that caused him to continue to seek her company.

Over the ensuing weeks, Armistead met with Hannah as often as he could. He was not paying court to her, as they both understood, but there was something more than casual friendship, and it seemed mutual. She was unlike any young woman he had ever encountered. She made no use of her sex, yet she was neither cold nor masculine. She talked to men as an equal and the resultant spirited conversations reminded Armistead of times spent with Amanda. The difference was that Amanda's mind closed when the contradictions became too acute, whereas Hannah accepted well reasoned argument even if it differed from her own views. They learned that they had a surprising number of things in common. Many stemmed from the fact that Hannah had spent time visiting her mother's family in Frederick, Maryland. They knew some of the same places and some of the same people. And then Armistead learned that they both knew Abner Means.

Only later did Armistead appreciate the skill with which she introduced Means's name into the conversation. After they had established that they both knew him, she probed farther and Armistead found himself, for the first time in her presence, consciously dissembling. It was odd how she returned to this topic over the subsequent days. Partial recollections, innocent sounding questions, but always Armistead evaded, becoming more smooth with practice. Then one day in the middle of July, Hannah told him that she knew Means a bit better than she had been letting on.

Armistead caught her unusual tone. "To my certain knowledge, Hannah Yoder, you have never apologized to me for anything. You don't have to begin now." Armistead's laugh died on his lips when he saw the Hannah's exceptionally serious look. Later he wondered if there had been a wistful aspect to her expression, but by that time he had come to doubt his ability to read anyone at all.

"He will be here tomorrow, Armistead. And he very much would like to speak with you." She reached out and lightly touched his arm. "It would mean a lot to me as well."

Means arrived at the rendezvous looking much as Armistead remembered him. He rode a superb horse, fitted with a McClellan saddle. In contrast, Means himself wore a drab, dust-stained suit appropriate for a traveling merchant. Physically, he appeared unchanged until Armistead looked closer. Then he saw a face with more lines, a thinner body, harder muscles.

"So, you have met Hannah Yoder. What do you make of her?" Means asked.

Means abrupt question reminded Armistead that he seemed oblivious to the social courtesies. "She's smart, candid, direct. She seems uninterested in or incapable of using the ploys practiced by the girls back home when they want something from you."

Means chuckled dryly. "Oh I think she is most capable if she thought it would further her aims. But she attended to the report and so knew how best to approach you."

After a moment of shocked silence Armistead weakly asked, "The report?"

"Come man," Means replied. "Are you being willfully stupid or just ridiculously naive? We are professionals. Hannah Yoder was the best conductor in three states. She quickly rose from running her own station to coordinating the entire region. She and I have worked closely together in the past. Now, in a pleasant change of circumstances, we no longer have to conceal what we do from the government. Rather the reverse, in fact, because now we work for the government. Hannah says that you remain sound. That's good because I want you to join us."

It was as if he had been playing a game of blind man's bluff, Armistead reflected, only it was always his turn to wear the blindfold. With effort he mastered his emotions and stared directly at Means. When Means spoke again it occurred to Armistead that his mind was apparently an open book to this man.

"Hannah is not the only one who has been clear sighted about the future. I told you the Potomac would become a strategic line of surpassing importance, and so it has. In war, weapons, soldiers, and numbers all matter, but far more important is accurate intelligence. It can make all the difference and it is what we are lacking. That doddering fool Patterson receives orders to advance on Harpers Ferry. Does he obey? No!" Means practically spat out this last word. "Instead, he says the town is held with too great a force and who can say if he is right or wrong."

"Means, I will not spy on my own people," Armistead said quietly.

Means continued as if he had not heard. "The president of the Baltimore and Ohio suspects that the rebels are planning a raid. True or not, our government stations entire regiments to guard the line. Likewise, the governor of Maryland hears a rumor that the rebels are preparing a strike against Baltimore. Is it true? No one knows but he withholds men to protect the city instead of sending them to join our armies. We are stretched thin, Carter, far too thin."

"I will not spy on my own people," Armistead repeated.

"We are not asking you to. The government has authorized a new unit, the Loudoun Rangers, formed from Union loyal men on both sides of the Potomac. You are acquainted with many of them. Their task is to patrol the river and provide accurate intelligence about what is taking place on both banks. I have in my pocket an officer's commission."

Armistead felt his head sway with the possibilities. Then anger returned. He refused to be manipulated, to be stampeded by these people. "This is happening too fast, Means. It's so, so unexpected." Even as his words trailed off Armistead felt dissatisfied with his explanation.

The older man looked at him with contempt. "Nonsense." Means turned away, paused, and spoke again. "Consider something else, Carter. The Loudoun Rangers will be formed, with or without you. Some of them want nothing more than to settle accounts with their neighbors. Men like Herk Settle, James Gooch, and Ballard Hibbs. You know their type. If they are not kept in tight rein, the Loudoun Rangers will turn that border into a lawless region where pillage and rapine hold sway. Think about it."

The discussion was apparently over. Means mounted his horse.

"Where are you heading now?" Armistead inquired.

Means responded with a disdainful look, as if the answer should be obvious: "South," he replied and rode off into the shadows.

Chapter 5. Piedmont Station, July 20-21, 1861

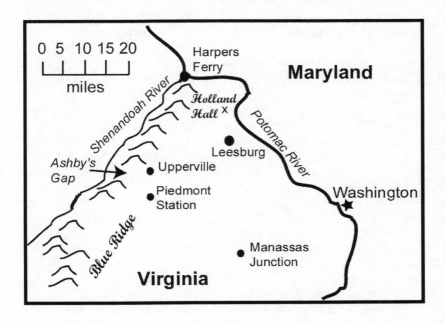

By the time the moon set, Min had ridden twelve miles and still had another eighteen to travel. In the dark there had been awkward moments when he encountered thick traffic — artillery batteries, supply wagons, even a cavalry regiment — over spilling the road in a slow moving flood converging on Manassas Junction. At those times Min took to the adjacent fields, he and his horse as one, running across uneven ground, jumping half-seen fence and hedge. When the traffic noise subsided, he returned to the road and then, because of Beauregard's words, he demanded an even faster pace.

The trouble came during a long stretch of empty road. The warning was the same as when Min and Armistead had raced at Holland Hall; a rippling shudder from between his knees that told him his over-strained horse was near to breakdown. At Holland Hall, Min had stopped immediately. Although fully aware of the consequences, this time he urged the grey onward and Rattler responded nobly. Another mile, and another mile still, his gait ever more choppy until he had no more to give. He dismounted and removed the saddle. Rattler turned, his expression showing disapproval at his seeming betrayal. "I know, fella, you would run if you could." He reluctantly tied him to a tree, took off his riding boots and tucked them under his arm, and began running. Rattler's pained whinnies provided a mournful escort until he passed out of earshot.

The stars in the east grew pale. By the time sunrise came, Min had learned that patriotism and self-interest were often at odds and, at least among the poorer farmers, the latter seemed to triumph. He had approached the first farm to ask to borrow a horse. A large, ugly yellow dog barked furiously, showing every sign of wanting to attack. Finally a voice from inside called the animal off and Min climbed the stairs of a partially collapsed porch to meet a hard faced slattern who scowled suspiciously. She held a lantern in one hand while her other hand remained concealed behind the door. A parcel of staring, grubby children darted around her skirts. Their erratic movements disturbed some scrawny chickens who tried to escape out the door. The woman angrily kicked the chickens back inside and cuffed one of the children. Min explained his need for a horse but the woman denied that she possessed any. Min wished her good day, adding that since she presumably had no use for it, she might want to sell the horse tack that hung just inside the door.

His visit to the second farm was equally unsatisfactory, albeit briefer. An old man's emphatic gestures with a shotgun did not invite closer investigation. As he continued, he began encountering footsore, hungry stragglers and he supposed that they had made life miserable for the local inhabitants. At the third farm he finally managed to borrow a cadaverous, knock kneed nag, but only at the cost of his timepiece, left behind when the suspicious owner demanded payment in advance.

He arrived at Piedmont Station in early morning. Among the throng of soldiers, no one seemed to be in charge. Eager to participate in the battle, senior officers had turned their commands over to their subordinates and boarded the cars for Manassas Junction.

Eventually Min's search led to a plantation house on a hill overlooking the station. Except for a pair of guards standing at rigid attention at the door, the front of the house was empty. Min ducked into the parlor and saw several military chests next to a large office desk. A clutter of formal looking papers and envelopes covered the desk. The slight breeze through the open window had scattered several pages onto the floor. Min moved toward the house's rear where he encountered a bustling stream of house servants carrying laden trays. From the garden came the sounds of laughter and then music as a band began to play.

Min found a young, fat, superbly uniformed officer holding forth before a set of admiring civilians. Min elbowed them aside and stood before the officer.

Plainly annoyed by the interruption, the captain turned to Min and said, "Well?"

"Dispatches from General Beauregard, sir."

The captain opened the cover and casually glanced at the message. "You took your time I see. Just take it back to my office and put it on the desk with the others."

"The others?" Min asked.

"Fortunately lieutenant, the other two couriers displayed greater zeal and have already delivered the general's orders."

"The other two couriers?" Min asked incredulously.

The captain turned to his audience. "I see that the army does not select its couriers for their native intelligence." Having soaked in their approving laughter, the captain turned back to Min. "Allow me to explain. It's the way things are done in the regular army. If there is an important dispatch, you send it in duplicate or triplicate." As if lecturing a school boy, the captain held up first two and then three fingers and repeated his last words. Again his performance amused his audience. "You militia will learn," the officer paused with mock drama, and then added, "eventually. Good day lieutenant."

Before he exploded, Min turned and stalked away. He saw that another train was loading at the station below. He hurried to board it but not before he learned that the corpulent officer's name was Otis Polk.

The rumor spread quickly: McDowell's army was leaving Washington and marching south. The news came to Holland Hall on July 18. The next day, when a traveling merchant reported that Johnston's army was marching east through Ashby's Gap, Amanda decided to act. She consulted with her father and then directed the servants to load a wagon with linens and food. Oddly, James's son Wellington failed to appear to drive the wagon. James himself was plainly distressed but Amanda, because she was very much caught up with the task at hand, did not investigate further. After staying overnight with a family friend in Upperville, Amanda followed in the wake of Johnston's army to Piedmont Station.

She arrived in time to see a single locomotive straining heavily, a collection of freight and cattle cars in tow, soldiers waving from doors and windows, soldiers perched precariously atop the roofs, a large flag streaming rearward from the last car as if delivering a farewell salute. It appeared that half the county had gathered around the station; women lining the track waving handkerchiefs; children capering with excitement, older men respectfully doffing their hats. Amanda recognized few people, although once she thought she caught a glimpse of Sigmund Becker. But before she could approach him he had melted into the crowd. It was easy to do because in addition to the civilians there were hundreds of soldiers belonging to Johnston's army who were waiting to take the cars to Manassas Junction. Amanda had never seen so many soldiers: men from distant parts of Virginia, a regiment of North Carolinians, elegant appearing soldiers from Mississippi, rough hewn mountaineers from Tennessee; but no one who had any news of the Loudoun Grays. She realized that the local boys made a small contingent within this vast horde.

There apparently had been some kind of battle two days ago with a larger battle still to come. Her servant, Lemuel, built a shelter around the wagon, Amanda shared a dinner with some cheerful Maryland soldiers who knew some of the same people she knew, and then she tried to sleep. It was a fitful sleep, interrupted several times during the night when the locomotive returned to carry more soldiers east. Either she or Lemuel would then rise to inquire about the Loudoun Grays, but still no news.

Dawn on July 21 brought the promise of a hot, sultry day. An early morning breeze provided slight refreshment, then it subsided; stunted, apparently, by the distant, dull, basso profundo sounds of discharging cannon.

Chapter 6. Manassas Junction, July 21, 1861

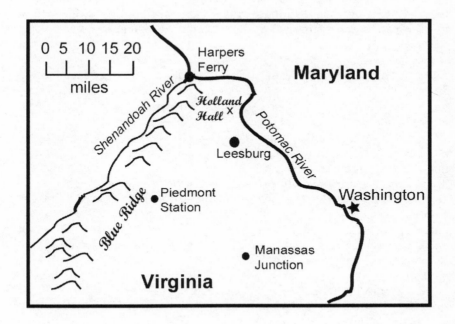

The train carrying Edmund Kirby Smith's brigade stopped at a siding to pick up water and boiler wood. Min had boarded an old cattle car where the smell of close-packed bodies mingled with the reek of manure. The boys had cut holes for fresh air but their efforts yielded little relief. A handful of ladies appeared to offer food and drink. From the east came the sounds of distant thunder, yet the sky was clear. A wide-eyed drummer boy who Min figured could not be more than ten or eleven years old, asked, "Say mister, what's that noise?"

Min replied, "I think it's the sounds of battle."

The boy's eyes flashed with pleasure. "We're going to whup 'em something terrible ain't we."

Min ignored the uncomfortable feeling in his stomach and answered, "Of course."

By the time the train reached Manassas Junction the noise had transformed to a persistent ripping sound like a giant sheet being torn, and then torn again, punctuated by the solid boom of artillery fire. The soldiers scrambled from the cars and assembled in regimental formation. Colonel Smith ordered them to drop their knapsacks and led them north at the double on the Manassas-Sudley road.

Min selected a horse from Captain's Lay's remounts, and set off in the same direction. The dust kicked up by Smith's column was so dense that he could hardly see. After passing Smith's toiling men, Min forced a passage through an ever-thickening crowd of stragglers. A handful of bloodied and bandaged men were among those who clogged the road, but Min noticed that most were apparently unhurt. Some gathered around low spots where shallow pools of water had collected in the numerous hoof prints. They shoved and jostled for a chance to sip greedily from the muddy water. Some sat near the road looking dazed and exhausted. But most joined the head-down shuffle rearward as if they were a herd of frightened cattle determined to move somewhere, anywhere, as long as it was not here. Smoke now merged with the dust to form a sense-stifling cloud.

A group of Confederates crowded around captured and wounded prisoners. Min saw one Union soldier who had been shot in the stomach rolling in agony on the ground, pleading with the guards to kill him and end his misery. A short, rakishly dressed Louisiana zouave elbowed his way through the crowd. He stood over the wounded man and asked, "Put you out of your misery? Certainly, sir!" The zouave swiftly lowered his musket butt and crushed the wounded man's skull. The crowd gasped in horror and backed away. The zouave looked at the remaining wounded and asked in a matter of fact voice, "Any other gentlemen here'd like to be accommodated?"

Shaken by the zouave's casual savagery, Min continued toward the front. The noise grew louder until at last Min reached the battle itself. He passed Imboden's battery which seemed to be trying to reorganize in a sheltered place behind the lines. Min saw that the battery was missing about half its horses as well as a number of men. He was close enough to see Frank himself, his uniform stained with sweat, gun powder, and, on his left side, from sleeve to shoulder, blood.

Closer to the front, closer still. Ahead stood a line of Confederate artillery; the gunners stripped to their shirt sleeves, working fast to swab out barrels, reload and re-point the guns, to fire again and again. The cannons' detonations merged with the individual explosions from hundreds of muskets to create a sustained, overwhelming din. Cheering erupted nearby and Min saw General Beauregard ride up to the nearest battery. "Hold this position and the day is ours!" he cried out to the gunners. Suddenly a shell exploded directly beneath the general's horse, disemboweling the animal and toppling the man. Beauregard kicked free of his stirrups, stood, and gestured to an aide to fetch another horse. As he waited he calmly lit a fresh cigar. Min's voice added to the cheers for the dapper Creole's courage. I suppose I will get used to this, Min reflected, but he wondered if it could be true.

To Min's right was a wooded ravine that sheltered a shaken and dispirited mass of men belonging to Bee's, Bartow's, and Evans's brigades. Here too a steady trickle of men leaked backward from the ravine. Some were wounded, but many, many more were not.

Closer at hand was a more recognizable battle line. Min rode to join a group of mounted officers who stood just behind the line. The Union artillery fire was even heavier here. The Confederate infantry stood along a slight crest, mechanically loading and firing their muskets. Shell bursts thinned their ranks, but they steadily closed on the center where stood their colors.

"What unit, cousin?" Min inquired.

"Eighth Georgia, sir!"

"Why do you stand silhouetted here and take such losses instead of just falling back a few paces and join the others in the ravine?

The officer stared hard at Min and replied, "We did not come all this way to Virginia to run before yankees, sir."

The Georgian took off his kepi and raised his arm to wave it and inspire his men. There was a sudden whooshing sound. Min felt a tremendous wind pass. The officer's arm was gone, ripped from his shoulder by a solid iron bolt. For a brief moment the man looked puzzled and then the blood began to spurt from the torn joint. He screamed and screamed again. Two nearby soldiers dropped their muskets, stood up, and began to run. A corporal, serving as file closer, intercepted one of them. "Stand your ground Black, damn you, stand your ground." While another pair of soldiers carried the dismembered officer to the rear Min recovered from his shock. He realized that he was shaking. He felt moisture around his groin. My God, I've been hit too, he thought. He looked down and saw a dark, wet stain spreading between his legs. He realized he had pissed himself. No one else appeared to notice.

Min peered through the smoke to see the Union artillery that had removed the officer's arm. There were eleven guns positioned in a saucer-like fold in the ground. They were less than three hundred yards away. Min clearly saw the enemy gunners work their pieces. Each cannon seemed aimed directly at him. His every instinct told him to run, to run to safety, to hide, to live. He forced himself to wait until the guns fired again, waited, and discovered that he remained unhurt.

He looked to his left and saw a belt of scrubby trees that partially concealed a line of soldiers. Min recognized the flag of Virginia floating above the battle line. At least I can die among my own, Min resolved, and turned his horse. His mount carefully stepped around a number of prostrate forms, their mangled flesh already beginning to mortify beneath the hot July sun.

He passed soldiers belonging to Jackson's brigade, men from the Shenandoah Valley. He saw Jackson himself leaning against a small pine tree. The general wore an old regular army cap pulled low over his eyes and a shabby coat. He appeared almost inert and reminded Min of a quiet farmer at rest or a country schoolmaster. Min rode on. He was looking for the Thirty-third Virginia because its colonel, Arthur Cummings, was an old family friend and he believed that he would not disgrace himself a second time when in the presence of familiar faces.

As he moved the firing became less intense. Odd, he reflected and then it came to him. The Union guns did not see Cummings's unit and were instead concentrating their fire against other targets. Shamefaced at his feelings of relief, Min approached Cummings.

The colonel shook Min's hand and shouted, "Hot work, Min. Here to join us?"

"I reckon so, if you'll have me."

Cummings grinned and replied, "That battery over there is making our life intolerable. I suspect Old Jack is going to have us charge it anytime soon. I recommend you leave your horse behind."

Suddenly there was a stirring among the field officers in the adjacent regiments. A courier came pounding up to Cummings, the colonel nodded, and shouted out, "Rise up men. Fix Bayonets!"

Min dismounted. So badly was his arm trembling that he had trouble unsheathing his saber. He prayed that no one noticed. And then the regiment was in motion. A slight swell of ground offered some shelter for the first hundred yards. As the regiment climbed the swale the Union battery roared again and Min braced himself for the impact. But the Thirty-third's line remained intact. Min realized that the battery was still ignoring Cummings's regiment. He looked around and saw that most of the men were wearing blue uniforms recently captured at Harpers Ferry. Min guessed that the yankee gunners mistook the Virginians for friends. Ahead lay a high, split rail fence about seventy yards from the Union battery. The men reached the fence. Cummings shouted out the command to halt. The captains echoed the order until the entire line came to stop. "Steady men, give them one good volley and then hard at them."

The soldiers aimed their weapons carefully and at the word pulled down on their triggers. The smoke had not even cleared when came the command to charge. With a cheer they clambered over and through the fence and ran toward the battery. Min saw that their musketry had done great damage. Whereas before the battery had looked like a well synchronized machine, it now seemed to be a churning, confused mass. Many men and horses were down. Several of the still standing horses were rearing up, their hooves flailing wildly.

The man next to Min collapsed suddenly. He fell silently, without even a groan. Then another fell with a shattered leg. As the line passed over the wounded solder Min saw that he had begun to crawl rearward. To his right he saw a mounted officer slump in his saddle even as his horse gave a loud cry of nearly human suffering. The infantry continued to run forward, soldiers ducking their heads like men struggling against a strong wind. Min dodged around a soldier propping himself on one arm, the other arm dangling loosely, attached to the shoulder by a torn, red mass of flesh and muscle. The soldier screamed out, "Forward boys! Forward! Tell them the Thirty-third Virginia is coming!"

Then they were among them, a confused, stabbing stumbling fight. Min later recalled that some time during the charge he was released from fear. He became a wild, savage beast, determined to kill or be killed. A federal gunner swung the pole with which he swabbed out the guns toward Min. Min clearly saw the man's face contorted with rage. His pole descended through a long arc but before it landed, Min stepped forward to plunge his saber into the man's belly. He strained to pull it free. At first it would not budge. It was apparently caught behind a rib. So intent was he that Min did not see another gunner, a smallish man wielding a short saber, advancing toward his side to slash at his unprotected neck. As he extricated his saber a deafening explosion rang in his ear. He felt burning powder against the side of his face and staggered clear to see his foe collapse.

A Confederate soldier stepped through the smoke cast by his discharged musket. Min looked at him. He was a beardless youth, not more than sixteen or seventeen years old. Min managed to croak, "Thank you, cousin."

The boy grinned and continued past him.

The fight seemed over. There was no one left to defend the guns. Then Min heard Cummings shout, "Fall back men. Fall back and reform. Here they come!"

Again Min felt the cold clamp of fear seize hold. He stumbled backward with the others, pausing only to glance periodically over his shoulder. He saw a line of powerful looking men wearing blue uniforms with red pantaloons. The light gleamed from the long sword-bayonets attached to their muskets. The shame of being shot with his back to the enemy competed with his urge to move fast to escape these red-legged demons.

Cummings shouted again, "Reform men. Reform." Min collected himself and managed to take a place in the Thirty-third's ragged line. He heard an officer bellow, "Present arms."

A nearby captain hoarsely pleaded: "Aim low, boys, aim low. It takes two to carry one if you wound one of those red-legged bastards."

Min picked up a musket only to discover that it was unloaded. He saw that the opposing line had halted and was presenting a solid line of muskets aimed at the Thirty-third. The rival lines fired nearly simultaneously. A heavy blow struck Min's shoulder. Pain then burning. As he fell he saw the men around him running to the rear. He tried to shout out, "stop, rally men," but the last thing he heard before losing consciousness was a shrill scream that he realized was his own.

Chapter 7. Piedmont Station and Holland Hall, July 1861

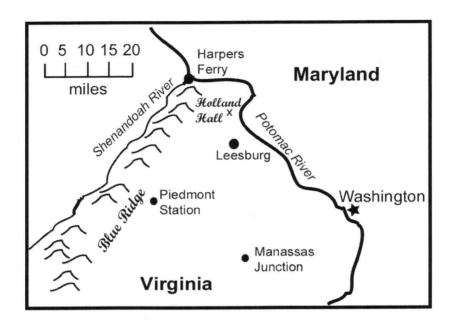

0 5 10 15 20
miles

Shenandoah River

Harpers Ferry

Maryland

Holland Hall X

Potomac River

Leesburg

Piedmont Station

Blue Ridge

Washington

Manassas Junction

Virginia

Amanda stood amidst the large crowd who waited anxiously at Piedmont Station. The sullen boom of cannon had subsided hours ago, but still no news came from the battlefield. Finally, just before sunset, a locomotive's shrill whistle announced the arrival of a train from Manassas Junction. Before Amanda could push her way to the platform she knew that it was victory. Men whooped and cheered, slapped one another on the back, lit cigars, gulped from hip flasks, and then cheered some more.

"Old Bory and General Joe whipped 'em all the way back to Centreville!"

"The valley soldiers behaved like Napoleon's Imperial Guard!"

"Ten thousand yankees killed and another ten thousand captured!"

An officer stood on the platform calling out names. The women gathered around him; wives and mothers, sisters and sweethearts. Amanda saw that the officer was handing out notes written on paper torn from soldiers' pocket-books. Most of the notes carried welcome news that the writer was safe. But as Amanda strained to hear any names she recognized, a nearby shriek of anguish caused her to turn. She saw a lean, weathered woman of indeterminate age dressed in what must have been her Sunday finest; an ill-fitting, faded dress that marked her as a hardscrabble farm woman. Her left hand clutched a piece of paper, her right stroked the hair of a smaller, even thinner woman whose head rested on her bosom. Great, gasping sobs came from the smaller woman. "It will be alright," the older woman kept repeating, "It will be alright. He's in the house of the Lord now."

Shaken, Amanda breathed deeply. This won't do, she told herself inwardly. I suppose I will get used to it. I simply must.

Then she saw that the train carried more than officers dispensing news of the battle because soldiers started unloading the wounded. Amanda hurried back to her wagon to gather supplies and lend help. A medical orderly quickly cut the sheets into bandage-sized strips. At first tear she had to stifle her protest about ruining the imported French linen. Her blankets served as ground cloths for makeshift beds. Amanda saw that the most seriously injured were placed on these beds; the others simply lay down in the dirt. While orderlies established a makeshift hospital, civilians brought food, and most particularly water for the thirst-crazed injured. She stood undecided until a harassed surgeon bumped into her. He wore a blood soaked leather apron and smelt of liquor. "Excuse me, ma'am," he said with a slight slur. "But you are rather in the way."

"I want to help. What can I do?"

The surgeon stifled a rude retort, composed himself and answered, "That lot over there. Most of them are going fast. They're scared and lonely. Maybe you could comfort them a bit. Now, excuse me again, ma'am. I've been at it for some time and with this load just come, I reckon I'll be at it all night." He took a pull from his flask and stalked back to the hospital.

Amanda walked behind the station where a large awning sheltered a score of so of wounded. She paused to stand by a preacher who was kneeling next to an almost faceless soldier; faceless because some terrible injury had removed most of what made him look human.

"How long do I have, sir?" the soldier asked.

The preacher replied, "The surgeon tells me not over twenty minutes."

The soldier exhibited no fear. He put his good hand to his shattered face and closed his eyes with his fingers. He stretched out as best he could, pulled his broken arm across his breast and crossed his good arm on top of it.

"Now fix me," he said.

The preacher pinned the toes of his stockings together, in the way Amanda had seen the dead laid out. Even as she watched, she saw his breathing stop, the hint of a benign smile forming where his lips once had been.

After two days helping to care for the wounded, Amanda returned to Holland Hall. She passed through a country convulsed with joy. Gone were apprehensive looks and anxious talk. Even the black boy who handed her down from her carriage exclaimed, "Ain't it wonderful, Miz Amanda, we whupped 'em something terrible!" Amanda found it difficult to share in celebration. There was still no news about the Loudoun Grays. All too readily she could picture one of them in the scenes she had witnessed at Piedmont Station.

She set to overcoming her fears by dint of hard work. Having observed the field hospital in action, she now knew what was needed and what was unavailable. She wrote letters to procure bandages, splints, potable soup, surgical instruments, and most of all morphine, whose blessed power to reduce pain she has witnessed firsthand. And she sought quantities of everything in amounts that once would have seemed stupendous.

In addition, there was the routine plantation business. She worked on most of these chores later in the day and on into the evening because they were familiar problems which she could cope with them even when her energy was spent and mind dulled. But there was one domestic duty she had to address that was far from routine. She learned about it the day she returned. Young Wellington, the son of their senior house servant, had run away.

While Amanda sat waiting for James to report, she reflected upon this startling intelligence. No negro had ever run from Holland Hall. The plantation held a reputation for treating its slaves well. Indeed, her father took pride in his ability to make most any black become a dependable worker. The Squire had learned from his father a simple approach to discipline. He treated his slaves fairly and seldom resorted to physical punishment. When someone failed to meet his standards, he merely arranged to borrow a slave from a neighboring farm where the conditions were far less kind and allowed him to describe to the recalcitrant slave the consequences of being sent elsewhere. Moreover, families were kept intact whenever possible and there was no objection to a breeding woman having a husband. And now, at a time when they all had to pull hard together, Wellington had betrayed their trust.

Amanda's felt her temper rising. She turned to stare out the window and heard James enter the room. She composed herself and without inflection spoke: "I have heard the news. How can you account for such a betrayal, such ingratitude?" She turned to face James. He looked absolutely wretched. She softened her tone and slowly pulled the story from him.

On the surface it was straightforward enough. Wellington had routinely been entrusted to carry messages to neighbors and even to distant businesses. Early on the morning when Amanda had set out for Piedmont Station, he had delivered two messages to neighbors up the Potomac toward the Ferry. Then he had disappeared. Curiously he had released his horse in a distant neighbor's field and that neighbor had brought it back to Holland Hall.

"Tell me James, do you think there will be more runaways?"

James gave her a sad look. "Miz Amanda, I plain don't know."

Amanda suspected that his story was incomplete but that his last statement was sincere. She dismissed him and returned to her registers.

The Richmond papers came, and with them an account of the Battle of Manassas. Squire Holland seized them, harrumphing and chuckling with deep approval. "See here, see here!" he spoke with great excitement. "At battle's end the Virginia cavalry swept the field and sent the yankees flying back to their hideous capital. Perhaps the Loudoun Grays distinguished themselves."

He read on, paused, and then his expression changed. In a quieter voice he said, "Here are the casualty returns, listed by regiment. The print is small. Amanda you read them. Look for the Grays of course, the Loudoun Artillery, and our kin and friends from Clarke County in the Thirty-third Virginia."

The fine-printed list marched in orderly column by regimental number, by company, A to K, within each regiment, and then alphabetically by name. She came to the Thirty-third Virginia and read: Company A, James Adams, killed; Edward Allen, wounded; John Bailey, killed; and continued to alphabet's end where she reported that George Wilcher, Aaron Wilson, Andrew Wilt, Isaac Wynn, and Archibald Young had all been wounded. The regiment's list seemed endless. She later counted one officer and forty-four enlisted men killed, one hundred and one enlisted men wounded.

On first inspection she saw no mention of the Loudoun Grays. Her relief was brief. Following a list of the First and Thirtieth Virginia Cavalry came the notation "Independent Cavalry Companies." Disbelief and then horror overcame her. With tears streaming down her face she screamed, "Min is killed!"

That evening, Squire Holland summoned the entire family. He said, "We have all suffered a terrible loss, but we know that Arminius is now in the hands of the Lord. Our noble commanders, Generals Johnston and Beauregard, issued a proclamation after the battle. You will all read it. For now, I recite a part that speaks directly to us."

He straightened his spectacles and placed the paper close to his nose: "Comrades, our brothers who have fallen have earned undying renown upon earth, and their blood, shed in our holy cause, is a precious and acceptable sacrifice to the Father of Truth and of Right. We will transmit this land free to our children, or we will fall into the fresh graves of our brothers in arms. We drop one tear on their laurels and move forward to avenge them."

Chapter 8. Winchester and Holland Hall, Autumn 1861

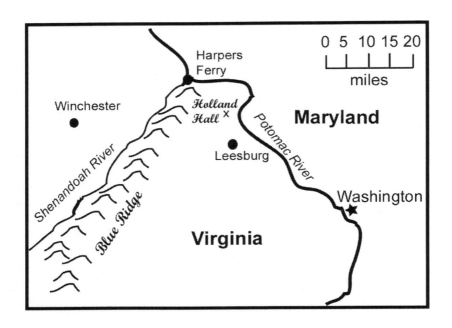

People remembered the autumn of 1861 for battle and storm, although as time passed some came to understand that the storms had been the more lethal, particularly for units commanded by the hero of First Manassas, General Thomas Jackson. To prevent friction between soldiers and civilians, Jackson ordered his men to bivouac in open fields, oblivious to the fact that their shoddily manufactured tents failed to protect them from cold and rain. For those already weakened by fever, mumps, and diphtheria, the autumn storms brought death.

Among the discontented, Sergeant Kinlock Barton saw little reason to remain in camp and suffer when the delights of nearby Winchester beckoned. Old Jack had declared the town off limits and stationed the militia in a cordon around Winchester to enforce his decree. For Kinlock and scores of other resourceful soldiers, this only heightened the challenge. On a late November evening after drill was complete, Kinlock said, "Travis, let's go do us a little listening."

Travis 'Jones' was among the volunteers who came to join the unit following the heady victory at First Manassas. No one knew his true name.

"Come on Travis, if you be going to enlist in the Loudoun Grays we got to enter your name," Kinlock had explained.

"What's that name there?" Travis had responded while pointing to a name in the company ledger.

"Jones," answered the company clerk, Luther 'Fatty' Dudley.

"That will do," Travis replied.

Thereafter, to Kinlock's delight, Travis proved a peerless stalker, able without detection to eavesdrop at a militia post in order to learn the password. Armed with the correct word, Kinlock used chalk to decorate his jacket with officer's shoulder straps, Travis lifted a sword from an infantry officer's tent, and 'Lieutenant' Kinlock Barton and his orderly sauntered up to the militia post, gave the correct countersign, and entered Winchester.

They found the proper ladies who lived along Main Street eager to compete to feed their soldier-heroes. And they found the girls living above the back alley saloons even more obliging. "Ain't this the life, Travis?" Kinlock sighed as he returned to the common room. He saw Travis looking uncomfortable while sharing a small table with an attractive mulatto girl.

"He won't do nothing with me mister," the girl whined.

"What's the matter boy? Don't fancy nigger blood? I'll get you someone else."

The girl walked away in a huff.

"Don't talk about her like that. She's as good as the others," Travis hissed.

Kinlock quickly straightened up. Although he had drunk a great deal, he had seen young Travis enough to know the signs. Some things just seemed to set the boy off and when he lost his temper he fought like a cornered wildcat.

"Look, I didn't mean anything by it. What do you say but we take a last drink and then I reckon we'd best get back to camp."

They sat in the crowded, dimly lit saloon. Time passed in silence. Travis seldom had much to say under any circumstances. Eventually when he spoke, he repeated a question that he had often asked before: "Do you think we'll ever see Lieutenant Min again?"

The question interrupted Kinlock's thoughtful consideration about whether he could afford to have another go upstairs. He answered as he always did: "I hope so Travis."

During the long walk back to camp, when Kinlock became noisily sick, it was Travis's turn to provide comfort. With surprising tenderness the boy cleaned Kinlock's face with a handkerchief and reached under his armpit to steady him. "Come along, old puke, I'll see you home."

Amanda sat at her desk in the library sorting through the most recent post. Most were responses to her requests to purchase medical supplies for the Loudoun Grays. They contained the now familiar apologies for the respondent's inability to oblige. Apparently, supplies were in great demand and had become very expensive, if they could be had at all. She opened a letter from her Aunt Letty in Richmond. She smiled as she read. It seemed like the yankee threats against Richmond had scared her not one bit. She read aloud one choice passage: "out of 1,000 wounded yankees in one hospital in Richmond, one third are wounded in the back! There is valor for you."

Brook Morgan replied, "I don't know about that. Some of them must be fighting well because I saw a heap of dead and dying Confederates."

Amanda started to scold him and then bit her tongue. Brook had appeared on their doorstep ten days ago, pale and haggard, blood seeping through his riding breeches. He had apologized profusely for his unexpected appearance and then slid unconscious from his horse. It turned out that Morgan had joined a Confederate battery recruited from southern-loyal Marylanders and been wounded in a skirmish east of Richmond. Rather than remain at a Richmond hospital — "Amanda," he said, for they were on a first name basis now, "it was courting death to stay there. Crowded hospitals or cold nights in a warehouse, filthy water drawn straight from the James River,"— as soon as he was able he began riding north toward Baltimore. The strain had reopened his wound. When the servants undressed Morgan to lay him in bed, they found his riding boot nearly filled with blood. Since that day, he had made a slow recovery. Because he was still thin and weak, Amanda tried hard not to upset him.

Instead, she continued sorting the post. "This is odd," she muttered. "Brook, you say the main hospital in Richmond is called Chimborazo?"

He nodded in reply. The recollection of misery seemed to sap him of further speech.

She cut open the envelope and her breath caught as she saw the words "Dear Folks at Home." The letters were spelled out shakily, but they were unmistakably written by her cousin. With trembling hand she read Min's report that he had suffered a slight wound at Manassas. Min proceeded to describe what he had done and seen: "I do not know how it is with others but as long as I face the enemy I can stand and fight them or move forward without feeling much if any fear, but as soon as I turn my back to them, and march in retreat, I have a strong inclination to run, especially when bullets and grape and bombs come crashing around us. While charging I didn't think much about getting shot, but while falling back I couldn't avoid looking back every step or two to see if the whole yankee line is taking aim at my back in particular. But if they did they fortunately missed their mark and I hope will never have the same target to shoot at again, the same side I mean."

Amanda exhaled deeply. She realized that she had been holding her breath. She continued reading: "The doctors assured me there would be no lasting damage from my wound. What they did not tell me about was the fevers. But I am well on the mend and now find that I have got to the end of my paper, my candle, and my eyes. I therefore, dearest family, take my leave and go to rest."

Amanda folded the letter and inserted it among the pages of her diary. She looked up to see that Brook had fallen asleep. She started to ring the bell to summon young Wellington to put another log on the fire, remembered, and rose to do it herself.

Chapter 9. Shenandoah Valley, November 1861

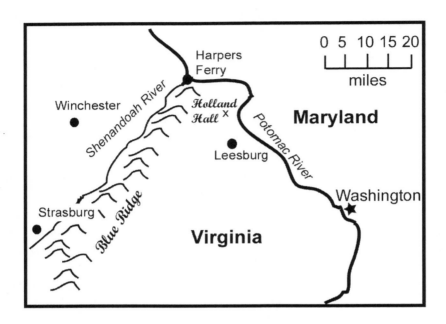

Min stiffly descended the stairs leading to the adjutant's office, his frustration increasing with each step. The long, weak rays from a watery November sun reminded him that another season was passing, yet the obstacles to his return to the Grays still seemed endless. At first he had thought himself one of the fortunate. At the field hospital near Manassas Junction, the doctor had assured him that nothing important was damaged, removed several metal fragments from his shoulder and arm, and moved on to more urgent needs.

Min had lain on a bed of straw but in spite of his exhaustion, sleep would not come. After the surgeons completed their grisly chores, the shrieks and groans finally subsided. The soldiers' stoicism, their lack of complaint, contrasted with the horrible groans of the wounded and dying horses. They were in pain beyond their dumb understanding and their calls were awful.

Toward dawn Min noticed a pair of orderlies approach. They paused by each wounded soldier. One held a lantern, the other wrote in a ledger. When they came near Min asked, "What are you about?"

The man with the ledger answered, "We are moving the men who we can. You are one of the chosen ones."

The orderly looked drawn and fatigued but nonetheless he managed a faint smile. "You will be on the cars to Richmond come morning."

He had endured three months in the hospital, pinned to his bed by a wasting fever that left him thin and weak. Each week had seemed like an eternity, but Min knew that he was still one of the fortunate. For every ten who entered the hospital, four departed the world for good. On his lucid days he read the Richmond newspapers to follow the course of the war. He learned that the Loudoun Grays were now part of the Seventh Virginia Cavalry Regiment serving with Stonewall Jackson in the Shenandoah Valley. Min was able to glean few particulars about his unit because instead the Richmond press focused on General Robert E. Lee's botched campaign in western Virginia.

On the infrequent days he could muster the energy, Min wrote letters home. They went unanswered, a puzzling and deeply disappointing result until he learned that his letters had never been sent. The hospital orderly who controlled the flow of mail demanded extra payment for his efforts. Confused by fever, Min had failed to understand the orderly's business proposition. By the time Min comprehended the extortion scheme, he had recovered enough to leave the hospital. He personally posted a set of letters and took the cars north to Gordonsville and Manassas Junction and west through the mountains.

He observed that there was a dramatic change in the countryside since he had last traveled along this route. Before, everyone had heedlessly rushed to war as if they were preparing for a festive picnic. Now, he found a countryside mobilized with a large military presence spreading along the railroads. There was a giant packing plant at Thoroughfare Gap, making the halt for boiler water a losing battle against noisome odors of dung and blood that permeated the handkerchief pressed firmly against his noise. Each town had a camp of instruction where new recruits busily drilled, each rail station an army corral where cattle patiently waited for the knacker's knife. There were provost guards to check passes, military clerks to stamp permits, and harried officers to direct the flow of men and supplies to the ravenous armies. Min wondered how many men could be at the front with so many on duty throughout the rear. Yet it was odd, he observed while walking from the depot to a headquarters in Strasburg, numerous young men in civilian clothes were apparently conducting business as usual.

His effort to rejoin his unit foundered at the sale barn in Strasburg. Like all Confederate troopers he was expected to provide his own horse. He had asked a relative to search for Rattler, but his uncle had learned nothing; the trail long cold, queries answered by stone-faced silence. Min knew he could never replace Rattler, but the overpriced, miserable screws on offer underscored his loss. While negotiating a purchase he encountered a colonel in charge of the provost guard. The colonel eagerly seized upon Min's unexpected presence to fob off a disagreeable, minor assignment. Min, in turn, had no choice but to obey and so entered the adjutant's office to receive his orders.

"The old man chew hard on you Min?"

Min immediately recognized the voice of Fatty Dudley. Fatty's participation with the Grays had been a source of both amusement and shame;

amusement because the oafish, but good humored young man could barely ride and his seventeen-hand, draft horse cross, staggered beneath his weight; shame because rival soldiers directed barbed jests at his unsoldierly physique. Min discovered that Fatty and the Grays had parted on good terms, both convinced that it was for the good of the service.

"Good God!" Min replied, "The South must be in desperate straits if it still has to enlist the half wits and the disabled."

"Hush Min," Fatty responded sternly, his effort to hide his smile beneath a fleshy upper lip a failure. "The state of Virginia, in her distress, has called upon all true patriots, and summoned each to his proper place. Me to give orders, you to obey."

Min laughed. "So exactly what is it I'm to do?"

It seemed that Virginia had slipped one hundred years back to a time when the Shenandoah Valley was the state's frontier and in the mountains to the west an active enemy controlled the land. Min knew that western Virginia sheltered many Union-loyal people. Fatty's account of how some fifty mountain counties had voted to secede from Virginia came as news. Consequently, while Jackson's Valley Army confronted an organized Union army just north of the Potomac, bands of mountain men were plaguing the army's flank all along the Alleghenies. Fatty explained that one group of bushwhackers, most related to a mountain family headed by Tink McGuire, had been ambushing supply trains sent into the mountains to requisition food and horses.

General Jackson wanted the McGuires suppressed, but until yesterday the band had skillfully evaded contact with the soldiers hunting them. Finally a detachment from the Second Virginia had surprised the raiders and captured one badly wounded soldier. Before he died, that soldier revealed the location of McGuire's mountain hideout. The only troops available to look for McGuire belonged to an irregular unit. Since the provost colonel did not entirely trust the irregulars, he wanted Min to accompany the scout.

Min felt his temper rising. "Accompany? What does that mean?"

Fatty looked down at his sheaves of paper. "Well technically you are outranked by the leader of the irregulars. But I'm sure you can work things out." Uncharacteristically, Fatty's words came out fast.

Min responded sharply, "Come on Fatty, what's really going on here?"

At first Fatty looked down and mumbled. But the long habit of friendship quickly overcame his inchoate sense of duty. Fatty's account ended with a warning, "Be careful, Min. Folks around here tell me that Buck Underwood is a tough customer."

Min examined Captain Buck Underwood and his Wildcat Roughs. So this is Bush's brother, he said inwardly. Underwood's men looked more like outlaws than soldiers, which was probably what they were before the war, he reflected. Min sighed and walked toward the only ranger who wore a semblance of a regular uniform. Three yellow bars on his collar signified his captain's rank.

"Lieutenant Carter, on detached duty from the Seventh Virginia Cavalry, Company C, Loudoun Grays."

Underwood sat on a camp stool. His full beard concealed most of his face, a slouch hat pulled low onto his forehead hid the rest. His dark grey uniform jacket was obviously a private purchase, a quality garment with an officer's gold lace filigree on the sleeves. The light blue trousers had once been worn by a Union soldier. The grease spots on the jacket and pants were recent. He was a huge man. When he responded to Min's salute with his own sketchy salute, Min noted his unusually large hands and thick forearms. His voice was surprising; a whispery drawl discordant with the scale of his body.

"Boys," Underwood said, "I don't reckon Mister Carter likes the cut of our gib." Two or three rangers laughed, several others hawked and spit tobacco-dark streams onto the trail. "Well, Mister Manor Born, we was just fixing to get started but me and the boys don't know if you can make it with us Wildcat Roughs so you're going to have to prove yourself. There's two ways up this mountain. They meet about a half mile below McGuire's camp. You go that way and we all will circle around and meet you."

Underwood paused to spit. "If you make it." Again the rangers laughed. One reached for a jug tied to his belt. Moving faster than Min thought possible, Underwood's sergeant — a fleshy, barrel-chested man — took two steps and drove his fist into the ranger's belly. The ranger emitted a stifled howl and doubled over in pain.

Underwood looked at the ranger and said in his whispery voice, "Later Upton. You know the rules. We'll have our fun when we're done with the McGuires."

Min climbed the mountain slope, following a twisting path only six feet wide that ascended through a green-black, dripping hemlock forest. A swirling mist ghosted over the path, limiting his sight line to twenty, and then ten feet. Min paused, took a half step, and then stepped back. Looking down, he saw that the hard dirt and gravel surface of the path did not take the impression from his riding boot. If someone had walked this path recently he would have left no mark.

The path leveled off and a hint of breeze dispersed the mist to reveal a small clearing. From Min's right a trail emerged from the hemlocks to join the main path. He had reached the intersection where Underwood had told him to wait. To hell with that, thought Min. Underwood clearly considered him a dandified manor man, not realizing that Min had grown up riding and hunting in mountains like these. He would scout ahead, determine if the prisoner's story was false, and report back the colonel. He could not be rid of 'Captain' Buck and his Wildcat Roughs too soon.

Min waited until the breeze died and the fog filled the clearing again. Rather than walk into the clearing, he skirted the forest edge until he intersected the path on the far side. He paused, still no sound, and proceeded. A steep but short climb, a flat place, a rhododendron grove on the left; a burbling sound grew louder as he advanced. Now, his every sense alert, Min stopped. A brief moment before he felt the touch on his shoulder he smelled the body odor and then the fetid breath. At least it gave him warning so he did not startle when the whispery voice hissed into his ear, "I thought I told you to wait back at the clearing."

Shaken — God, the big man moved quietly! — but determined not to show it, Min stood still. In a low voice he said, "the prisoner said below the rhododendron grove," and gestured to the ravine to his right.

"You been any farther ahead?" Underwood asked.

Min shook his head.

"Look." Underwood pointed along the path.

Min saw the same mix of gravel and small stones that held no footprint and so revealed nothing. Nothing except a faint mix of light against dark. Nothing until a hard stare showed the colors resolve into a regular left-right-left pattern where a walking man carrying a heavy load had kicked over small stones with his toes, the stones' moist underside dark in contrast to their light tops.

"I reckon we found 'em," Underwood said.

Chapter 10. Shenandoah Valley, November 1861

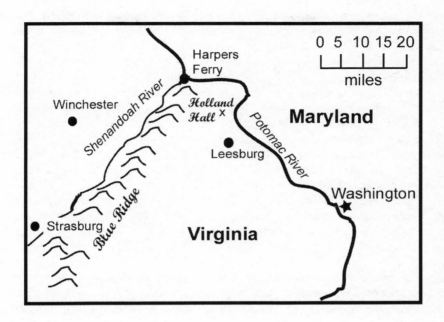

Min followed Underwood down to the clearing. The man had hunter skills, Min reluctantly acknowledged to himself. Unwilling to find too much merit, Min reflected: with practice, any kind of ill-bred, uncouth, ridge runner can track a deer. Let's see what kind of military man he is.

They rejoined the Wildcat Roughs at the clearing's entrance. Underwood looked at a broad built ranger with a fat, fleshy face whose small eyes seemed to disappear into the folds of skin. "How many, Pigeye?"

Gesturing back to the path that Underwood's men had followed, he said, "Three come along that way 'bout thirty minutes ago."

Underwood replied, "Pity we missed them. Would've evened the odds a bit."

"So you knew!" Min said angrily.

"Course I knew. That's why I sent you the long way. I reckoned it would give us time to sort out a little business with Mister McGuire in our own way."

Several of the rangers laughed. Min felt his face redden. Before he could speak Underwood knelt, pulled out his knife, and sketched on the ground. The other rangers squatted around their captain and stared intently at his crude map.

"Boys, the three we tracked are tuckered out. They'll be soaking their feet in the pool here." Underwood marked a place with his knife. "I reckon Mister Lieutenant and Julian and Luke can take care of 'em. That leaves about eighteen or so more. Two for each of us."

Using a few words and his knife, Underwood quickly explained his plan. Underwood and another ranger to enter the camp via the trail, fire, and run back up the slope to lead McGuire's pursuing men into a deadfall where the balance of the rangers deployed in the rhododendrons. Pigeye and three men to move stealthily below the camp to seal off its exit on the far side of the gorge. With a nod Pigeye's group disappeared into the forest. Underwood turned to Min and gestured with his knife, "You get to the pool by moving along the high ground here. I'll give you five minutes to work into position before me and Melvin open the dance. Don't dawdle. Even experienced shooters like my uns can shoot long when firing uphill and we don't want no wild bullets harming the youngsters." Underwood gave a quick grin to Min's two comrades and then said, "This is your first blooding. You'll do fine. Now git."

The two rangers stood up. One's face was deeply scourged by acne, both were grimy, unwashed. With sinking heart Min realized that neither was more than thirteen or fourteen years old.

As they moved carefully into position overlooking the gorge, Min's anger returned. Underwood had given him the easiest task: capture three unarmed, weary men. The captain thought it would be so easy that he assigned children to help. Meanwhile, Underwood himself performed the riskiest part of the mission: luring McGuire's men down the trail to the ambush site.

From the ravine, wood smoke rose from three campfires, the smoke tendrils merging with the mountain mist to form a low, gray ceiling. Scanning the camp, Min saw men tending to chores. Just downhill of his position was a fast running brook, the sound of water over rock concealing any noise that Min's party might make. Min drew his revolver. The older boy already had his in hand, the younger one now reached for his weapon. Then the younger boy wet his finger and turned it to catch any moving breeze. At First Manassas Min had seen the faces of men in battle; the determined patriot, the unnerved coward, the ruthless killer. These boys appeared neither frightened nor over anxious. Rather they looked like eager, questing hunters, testing the wind to adjust their aim, arms relaxed in order to shoot accurately. They have no idea, Min thought. Something had disturbed the men below; shouts, figures moving. Min motioned to the boys and the trio ran down the slope.

The men who had been soaking their feet were slow to react. Their heads were turned toward the trail where Underwood had made his diversion. The quickest witted, a corporal, was pulling on his boots when a volley of gunshots sounded at the head of the ravine. His two companions stood up quickly, one slipping on the wet rock. When he was less than eight feet away Min yelled out, "Surrender now!" He leveled his revolver at the corporal. He sensed the two boys also pointing their weapons at the other pair. Three faces turned toward him, each showing surprise and then fear. Min motioned with his left hand, "Hold your arms up and walk slowly toward that stump."

Min saw the corporal quickly assess the situation and recognize that there was nothing he could do. "I reckon we're sold men. Let's do what he says."

Min felt some of the tension drain away. He noted that after a brief flurry of shooting only an occasional single shot sounded from the head of the ravine. They marched their prisoners to the center of camp. Silence, the smell of wood smoke, frying bacon: "You two guard the prisoners, I'll see what your captain has done."

The first body lay sprawled across the trail, blood oozing from several wounds in the chest. Four steps farther a second body, face down, dressed in civilian clothes, his thigh shattered from a minie ball, a gaping hole in the back of the skull, the collar showing powder burn.

Three Wildcat Roughs appeared. Two supported a wounded comrade who hopped on one leg, his damaged leg dangling at an awkward angle, a crude bandage tinged red tied around his shin. It was not a bad wound, but the injured man moaned loudly. "Stop whining Lenk," said one of the rangers who was supporting the wounded man, "Learn to get your fat ass down next time."

"Where's Underwood?" Min asked.

"Saw him last moving along the swale yonder", answered a ranger.

The other ranger laughed and spat, "He was chasing a McGuire, jist bout had him treed."

Min encountered five more bodies. Two wore uniforms. They lay along the trail, both killed by rifle fire. A ranger knelt by one of them, expertly searching his inside vest pockets. A blood trail and crushed underbrush led to two more bodies; both wearing civilian clothes, both showing leg wounds, both face down, one with a hole in the back of his skull, the other with a skull shattered by a point blank shotgun blast. A rustling in the nearby underbrush caused Min to raise his revolver and move quietly toward the sound. A ranger was straddling the body of a man dressed in civilian clothes. He spat in his face and clubbed him in the cheek with the butt of his revolver. "Where is it you son of a bitch?"

Min shouted, "Leave that man alone."

The ranger turned and glared. Flecks of spittle clung to his mustache.

Another rustle of leaves and a whispery voice, "You have a problem lieutenant?"

"What's going on here Underwood?"

"I believe that's Captain Underwood to you mister."

Min saw that both of Underwood's knees were soiled. A light spray of blood speckled his shirt.

"Sir!" Min spat out the word, "We completed our mission and secured three prisoners. Should I be rounding up the rest?"

"Prisoners?" the word came out slowly, dripping with scorn. A small group of grinning rangers had gathered behind Underwood. Underwood turned toward them, "Sergeant, we got any prisoners?"

"No sir, no prisoners except that one." He gestured toward the wounded man in civilian clothes.

Underwood spoke again, "A hard fight Lieutenant. The bastards winged one of my men." Pointing to the prisoner, Underwood snapped, "Bring him along."

They returned to McGuire's camp. The boys were sitting on crude camp stools brandishing their revolvers at their captives who sat awkwardly in the dirt by a camp fire. Min saw that the boys had tied their hands behind their backs and then linked them together with a picket rope.

Underwood addressed the older boy, "Any trouble Julian?"

The boy rearranged the chaw in his mouth and answered, "No papa. It went just like you planned."

The rest of the rangers shuffled into camp. The men carrying the wounded prisoner dumped him heavily next to his comrades, causing him to groan.

"Take proper care of that man," Min snapped.

"Reckon I slipped," the ranger drawled.

Amidst the chuckling Min heard one ranger say, "Proper care for a McGuire, cut him up for bait."

Underwood spoke: "A good job today boys. We cleaned out a nest of yankee bushwhackers. Now I think we can have some fun. Pigeye, you know what needs doing. The lieutenant and I are going inside to write our reports."

Min followed Underwood into the largest tent. Inside was a partition that divided it into a sleeping chamber and an office. Underwood motioned toward the writing desk. "Write up your report lieutenant. Make it brief and you can get down the mountain before it gets dark."

Underwood opened a camp chest and lifted out a jug. He unstoppered it and took a draft. "Ah," he signed. "The one thing the McGuires could always do was make some mighty fine shine."

The shattering blast of a colt revolver echoed off the ravine walls. Shouts and then three more shots. Min rose quickly but Underwood was already outside the tent.

The rangers stood in a semi-circle. At the open end stood the two boys, each grinning happily, smoke eddying from their Colts. Three dead prisoners formed a bloody, collapsed tripod. The man on the litter lay face down, the hole in the back of his skull seeping brain and blood.

Pigeye spoke to Underwood, "Prisoners tried to escape, sir."

Underwood ignored him and walked up to the boys. He eagerly asked, "So you're blooded boys, are you now?" He knelt down by the bodies, ran a hand against the sodden back of a head, and stood.

"Come here boys."

The boys holstered their Colts, straightened themselves, and stood before the Captain. He painted a bloody cross on their foreheads. "You're men now, real soldiers, and real Underwoods."

"Thank you father," the boys said in unison.

Underwood looked at the lifeless bodies. He began walking back toward the headquarters tent. Before he entered he turned and spoke to his sergeant, "Throw 'em out of stinking distance," and then disappeared inside.

Chapter 11. Holland Hall and the Shenandoah Valley, November 1861

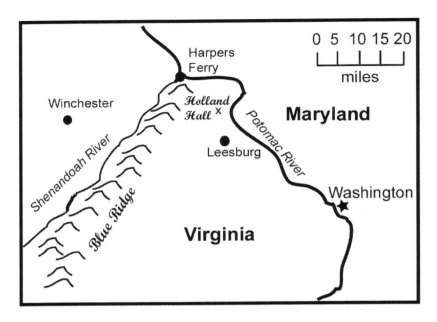

The storm wind shook the glass of the library's bay window. Seated at her desk, Amanda glanced outside to see the swaying limbs of the Tennessee coffee tree. It will probably lose the rest of its leaves tonight, she reflected. She returned to the accounts. They did not present a pleasant picture. Like most plantations, Holland Hall conducted business using a complicated set of trade arrangements. No one relied upon hard money. Instead, there were exchanges of goods and services, most performed on the strength of a handshake with neighbors and reliable merchants. Usually, after the harvest, Virginia plantations sold off their surplus slaves for resale south. This provided the money planters needed to see them through the winter. Home bred slaves replaced those who departed, and in normal times it was a highly profitable business.

But the war had changed much, including the business cycle that kept Holland Hall solvent. No longer did wagons carry the plantation's produce north over the Potomac for shipment by rail to Baltimore and Washington. Instead, the wagons traveled south to one of the army's collection depots. The trip was longer and more expensive, the profit less, and payment was in Confederate dollars, the new national currency. Patriots everywhere accepted the new money, although the county's Quakers and Germans demanded coin. Amanda recalled how her mother had always told her to heed their actions because they were wise business people.

Far more troublesome had been today's revelation. Unbeknownst to Amanda, soon after the great victory at Manassas, her father had visited his banker, Clarence Rixey. He had borrowed a great deal of money, pledging land as collateral, and purchased as many slaves as he could afford. Initially he had hired them out to neighbors to work the harvest. Today, with contracts finished, they had begun appearing at Holland Hall.

Amanda had stood on the porch watching their arrival, her mood changing from disbelief to dismay. Before she could speak her father explained, "A prodigiously smart investment, my daughter. The war frightened people and I bought them at steep discount. What I knew and the fainthearted did not was that Manassas assured our victory. When peace returns we will begin an era of prosperity and slaves will increase greatly in value. And, as you see, I mostly purchased young females of breeding age."

Amanda interrupted his triumphant flow with one question: "Father, was this your idea or Gordon's?"

"Why, er, mine of course," he replied.

Confirmation of Amanda's guess came from her father's guilty expression. The more she learned the worse it became. The bank's promissory note was for the surprisingly short term of six months.

"Yes Amanda, Gordon, bless his wise head, suggested that detail. We pay an interest rate well below what is normal in exchange for agreeing to an earlier repayment date. Peace will come before that date, we avoid paying much interest, the price of slaves climbs tremendously, and we are sitting on a fabulous fortune. Indeed, my children's fortunes and, God willing," the Squire fixed Amanda with a particular expression meant to convey hope but which she read as reproach, "my grandchildren as well will be secure forever. Now Amanda, give your clever father a kiss and another jot of brandy and wipe all concerns away."

Amanda pressed her fingers against her temple. Her review of the accounts had done nothing to reduce the ache in her head that had been growing all day. She closed the ledger. She knew that even though it was late, sleep would evade her.

An aide ushered Min into Colonel Turner Ashby's office. Ashby looked up from his desk and smiled. He stood, extended his hand in greeting, and spoke, "Lieutenant, I am so happy to see you again."

Ashby listened with deep concern while Min recited his experiences at both Manassas and Richmond. Then, with some reluctance, Min related the story of his involvement with Underwood and the Wildcat Roughs.

"That was bad business," Ashby observed.

"I reported to the colonel that Underwood had allowed the slaughter of unarmed men," Min said.

"And what did the colonel have to say about that?" Ashby asked.

"Lieutenant, you can put it in your report and I will pass it along through the proper channels."

Ashby snorted. "Min, as I have had to learn, that is the way the so-called professional army does business."

Ashby proceeded to unburden himself with a torrent of criticism and complaint, most of which he directed at the army commander, General Jackson. He described how he had recruited into his regiment hundreds of willing men, all of good breeding, every one of them an expert rider and a good shot. Ashby's expression made it clear that he believed that these qualities were amply sufficient to make a good cavalry trooper. In a matter of fact voice without a hint of boastfulness, he added, "They will follow me anywhere."

But that was insufficient for Jackson. He criticized Ashby's lack of attention to drill. He complained about the regiment's unreliable roster of men fit for duty.

"You know how it is with these boys, Min. They turn out if there is a fair prospect for a fight. Otherwise, they become bored and skip away to visit home."

The color rose around the edges of Ashby's full beard. "I have saved Jackson's army from being utterly destroyed yet I get no support from Jackson. Instead, he makes my task far harder. He heaps indignities upon me and my men and leaves me in embarrassing, even dangerous situations because he won't inform me about his plans. Frankly, I wonder how much longer I can be of service here."

Min began to interject a comment but Ashby cut him off. "Forgive me, I have taken advantage of you to unburden myself. Now that you have returned to us, you will find you have your own command problems." A hint of amusement played around the corners of Ashby's eyes.

Ashby pawed through a pile of reports. "Infernal paperwork," he muttered. As he continued to sort through the papers he said, "It seems that the Loudoun Grays are not the only soldiers disobeying Jackson's orders to steal into Winchester. According to a Winchester doctor, he has recently diagnosed quite a number of girls in an interesting way. So the war has done something for the increase of the army."

Ashby seized a paper with a triumphant snort. "Now, reverting to your company. Would you know a Sergeant Kinlock Barton?"

Min sighed and nodded.

"It seems that he is under arrest. Welcome back, Min."

"Well here is how it was," Kinlock explained. He spoke in an earnest tone that immediately made Min suspicious. "Some officers in the Fifth Virginia received presents from home."

"Whiskey," Travis interjected.

"There were two kegs..."

"Three," Travis interrupted.

Kinlock looked at the youth with mock annoyance and continued: "So they invited the other officers to their tent to share. Well, it didn't seem gentlemanly of them to forget about us so we pulled up a few tent pins, rolled out a keg, filled our two buckets, and rolled it back in."

"So you were arrested for stealing?" Min asked in as severe a tone as he could muster.

Kinlock sheepishly averted his eyes and Travis continued: "No it was because of the colors."

"The colors?" Min inquired.

"The next morning the officer of the day found the Fifth's colors lashed to the tallest tree in camp," Travis explained.

"How did he figure out it was your doing?" Min asked.

"Well, you know that Colonel Ashby has made me a color sergeant," Kinlock replied.

"He was asleep at the base of the tree," Travis related. "I couldn't rouse him."

"I told him I was guarding the colors," Kinlock added. "Min, you have got to do something. I hear we are fixin' to march against the yankees and you can't leave me here."

"I'll see what I can do, Sergeant," Min responded. "Come along Travis." Min waited until he was out of earshot before he began laughing uncontrollably.

Travis gazed at him affectionately. It's good he's back, the boy thought. Things will be better now.

Chapter 12. The Yoder Farm, Christmas 1861

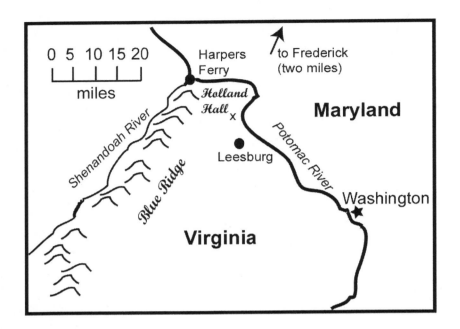

Armistead's boots creaked on the hard snow, sounding like the brakes on the steam locomotive that had just deposited him in Frederick. He consulted the directions written in Hannah's neat hand and began to walk briskly. Months had passed since he had last seen her. At that time he felt anger at the way she and Means had manipulated him. He had avoided all unnecessary visits to town and immersed himself in his job at Carlisle Barracks. When his anger receded and he came to terms with what had taken place, he called upon Hannah's residence. She no longer lived there a black servant explained.

"Did she leave a forwarding address?" Armistead asked.

"No," replied the servant.

So Hannah's invitation came as a complete surprise. She and her family would welcome his presence for the Christmas season if he had no other plans.

The Yoder farm was four miles outside of Frederick. By the time Armistead arrived, the sun had begun to set. A soothing stillness settled on the countryside. Smoke rose from the chimneys of a farmhouse nestled in a hollow. It was an old, L-shaped building built with heavy timbers and field stone. The long arm of the L enclosed stables and a barn. Armistead walked up the fir-lined lane to a gate. As he began to open it he heard the clanking of a chain. A large dog came, barking furiously. Armistead hastily closed the gate and waited. He heard the dog lunge and come up short as its chain jerked it back.

A voice, speaking in German, called out sharply and the dog fell silent. In heavily accented English the voice asked who it was. Armistead answered and was told to wait. He heard another volley of commands followed by footsteps. The gate opened and Armistead saw a black face peering out from a hooded overcoat. He recognized that it belonged to the same man he had met at Hannah's residence in Carlisle. This time his expression was entirely different. Instead of a blank indifference, he smiled and extended his hand.

"Liverne Taylor."

His large hand easily engulfed Armistead's hand. Taylor held the grasp and said, "Welcome."

As he approached the house, Armistead saw that the dog had retreated into a cubby that was built into the thick, stone foundation. Its long chain fastened to a wheel running on an iron rod that was set above the second floor windows. It allowed the dog to guard the entire front and sides of the building.

Armistead nodded toward the animal. "Mean?"

"Let's just say I would not advise wandering around outside without one of us," Taylor replied.

The downstairs had a large common room, dining room, and kitchen. Upstairs were a spinning room, a smoke room full of preserved meats hanging from the beamed ceiling, and a series of bedrooms. A passel of young, black children scampered along the upstairs hallway. "My children," Taylor explained as one called out joyfully and ran toward him. Taylor opened his arms and lifted the child into an embrace. He showed Armistead to his room and explained that Hannah had taken the sleigh to fetch a Christmas tree. He was welcome to wait in his room or down in the common room.

"This must be an old place," Armistead commented.

"Hannah says it was built early last century," Taylor replied.

"I've never seen a smoke room on the second floor," Armistead said.

"Unusual, ain't it," Taylor said. "They built what they knew. In Germany they lived above their animals, so the smoke room helped disguise the odor. We kept it this way for much the same reason."

"I don't follow," Armistead said.

"It hid the scent," Taylor replied as he closed the door.

The book he had been reading on the train, The Cavalryman's Manual, hardly seemed appropriate so he went downstairs empty handed. The common room was dimly lit and cold, although a fire burned in a large stone hearth. A straight-backed wooden chair and small desk stood near each of the three windows so as to catch the light. The inner wall held rank after rank of shelves divided by a partition into two unequal sections. The shorter side was devoted to books on animal husbandry and agronomy. The collection was small but modern, covering both theoretical and practical subjects. Clearly someone in the household took a scientific approach to farming. Armistead reflected that people back home could benefit from this knowledge. Far too many either farmed by trial and error or simply continued to do what their fathers and grandfathers had done.

"Ah, you have found my husband's special passion," said a soft, feminine voice.

Armistead turned to see a large black woman. She looked him directly in the eye without expression. Armistead sensed that she was assessing him.

"Hello. I did not hear you come into the room. My name is Carter, Armistead Carter." Not quite knowing what else to do, he held out his hand.

The gesture seemed to please her. She shook his hand. "I know. Hannah has spoken of you. My name is Jolina Taylor. Time is precious, particularly during the holiday season. Liverne is minding the children until Hannah returns. If you will pardon me, I must study." She gestured toward a reading desk laden with several thick books.

"Please, do not let me interrupt you, Miz Taylor."

Armistead returned to the shelves. The material on the other side of the partition was more broadly focused. The subjects included economics, the law, and politics. There was a complete run of William Lloyd Garrison's The Liberator and the abolitionist paper National Era. Another file contained articles about the Fugitive Slave Law. As Armistead perused the shelves, he saw that the unifying theme was slavery in America. He selected The Cotton Kingdom by Frederick Law Olmsted. He opened it to see that it had just been published yet already, judging from the marks on the pages, several people had read it. As he settled into the reading chair nearest the fire he reflected upon the contrast between the holiday season at home and this place with its huge guard dog, spartan common room, and Jolina Taylor.

Hannah returned before the evening meal. She seemed unchanged and her bright welcome reassured him about his decision to accept her invitation. Better still was the appetizing aroma rising from the kitchen. The ensuing hearty German dinner reminded Armistead of the meal he had shared at the Becker home. Once Liverne Taylor realized that Armistead shared his interest in scientific farming, conversation flowed easily. Hannah seemed pleased that the two men got on well and only occasionally interjected a comment. The bent-backed man who Hannah introduced as her uncle seemed content to limit himself to exclamations in German about some particular delicacy on his plate. The happy burble from the Taylor children filled in any potentially awkward gaps in the conversation.

During one such gap, Taylor's eldest son asked, "Are you a soldier, sir?"

Armistead felt an embarrassed silence. "No, I am not."

Until this point, except for some quiet discipline of her children, Jolina had said very little at table. She looked at Armistead and said, "My man would fight if they let him. Jason, my eldest too."

Although Jason was tall for his age, Armistead reckoned that he was probably only about fourteen years old. "God willing it will be over long before he comes of age," Armistead replied.

"Amen," responded the other adults. And then Jolina spoke again, "Mister Means says it won't."

There was a monastic quality about the farm's routines, with the day divided into segments of physical labor and time for study and reflection. Armistead decided that this well suited the somber fact that although it was Christmas, the nation remained at war with itself. He learned that Jolina was reading medicine. She already possessed a fair practical knowledge, learned from experience with the children, the animals, and, she said, "some other things." She was expanding her knowledge by book learning, particularly military medicine. When Armistead asked why, she responded, "Because Mister Means says we will be needed."

The riders were the exception to the farm's orderly patterns, or perhaps, Armistead mused, they too adhered to a pattern that he had yet to comprehend. They appeared at the farm almost every day and sometimes at night without any apparent regard to schedule. Some were white and some black. Armistead noted that only two came more than once. Usually their powerful horses showed little sign of exertion, occasionally they were well lathered, having been ridden hard. There was one consistent aspect about their visits: the watch dog never barked when they came.

Armistead helped with the chores, and because here he was on utterly familiar ground, he was able to add real skills. By working alongside Liverne Taylor, he learned that the man possessed a wide variety of talents. Woodworking, however, was not one of them. So, after Armistead replaced a crudely splinted wagon axle with a perfectly formed new one and built a sturdy timber derrick to lift heavy rocks from the creek bottom onto the wagon bed so Taylor could repair the farmhouse's foundation, he was rewarded with genuine gratitude. Moreover, Liverne asked if Armistead was partial to any particular spirits. "All of 'em," Armistead replied, and so the two men found another bond when they shared corn liquor or apple brandy together, always well out of sight of the missus.

Before this breakthrough occurred, he had already won over the children. He had always gotten on well with children. He taught them games, played chase and hide, and wrestled with all comers up to and including Jason. It was the combination of Liverne's strong drink and his own frolicking with the children that led Armistead to his one serious misstep.

It came two days before Christmas. After a particularly hard day of work he and Liverne had enjoyed a longer than usual tipple in the barn. In a high flow of spirits, Armistead divulged his 'secret' project. He had built some simple sledges for racing down the snow covered hill above the orchard. Two were child-sized and one was large enough to carry two adults. With some difficulty he and Liverne coaxed Hannah and Jolina outside to join the fun.

The children's cries of delight as they slid down the hill set the tone. Armistead had placed pairs of stakes into the snow to mark gates and led everyone in the construction of a ramp-like jump at the end of the course. Soon children and adults alike were taking turns; each team, Jason and his eight-year-old brother, the twins, Liverne and Jolina, Armistead and Hannah, vying to finish first in a series of trials that would lead to the grand champion of the hill.

It was cold but not bitter. A dry, light snow began to fall. The Taylors were aboard the sleds. Their whoops of delight sounded from somewhere below in the gathering gloom. Armistead and Hannah waited their turn at the top of the hill and they were alone. He had touched her before; holding her lightly in his arms while they flew down the course in the sled, reaching out a hand to steady her when she slipped while trudging back up the slope. But when he reached for her this time it was different and she knew it immediately. His mouth was already close to her face, although she allowed him to kiss her. She did not kiss him back. Instead, she pushed him gently away and with equal tenderness said, "Thank you. I take that as a compliment, but please, no."

They gathered in the common room to celebrate Christmas eve. One of the two concessions to the holiday was a particularly hearty fire that managed, for once, to drive the room's habitual chill off into the corners. In addition, a cloth covered the four small glass panes of the adjacent parlor door. One of the twins tried to creep inconspicuously toward the door in hopes of peering through the keyhole. Hannah reached out and pulled her into her lap. "No, Rebecca, the Christkind may still be in the house and you might be blinded by his brilliance if you were to sneak a look."

The clock struck twelve times. The tinkling of the Christkind's bell sounded. Liverne opened the parlor door to reveal a tall, thick fir. Flames from the beeswax candles fastened to the tips of the branches created halos that reflected in the hanging red and green glass spheres. Stars made of flattened straws swayed lightly on their strings. The children surged into the room, looked at the gifts underneath the tree, and halted. Liverne walked to a wooden stand on which perched a large, leather-covered bible. He began to read, "And it came to pass..."

He completed the familiar passage and closed the Bible. Hannah picked up an old zither and plucked at its strings. She tuned it and then nodded. The children's soprano piping, Jolina's alto, Liverne's deep baritone, Hannah and her uncle, Armistead, German and English intertwined: 'Stille Nacht. Heilige Nacht. All is calm. All is bright...'

Following the Christmas day feast, Hannah and Armistead sat before the fire digesting the heavy German meal. Armistead asked about Abner Means. He learned that Means was actively helping the Union forces stationed along the Potomac River and that he was still pursuing his plans to organize a mounted force of Union-loyal Virginians. "I imagine Hannah that you have a way to get in contact with him?" Armistead drily inquired.

She smiled and nodded.

"I should like to send a few letters home if it is possible. You can read them before they are sealed."

Hannah stiffened and scowled. She quickly composed herself. "Armistead, you are a dear friend. I, we, Liverne and Jolina, trust you. Abner as well. Doing what we do we have learned to trust very few people and we have learned never to make a mistake."

A long, but not uncomfortable silence followed. Then Hannah spoke again:

"When I was young I was taught that precisely at midnight on Christmas Eve all animals could speak in the human tongue to honor the birth of the Christ child. My first memory of this farm is one of tremendous excitement. Because my grandparents kept so many animals — cattle, pigs, horses, chickens — I remember trying as hard as I could to stay awake to hear them speak."

"And what did they say, Hannah?"

Hannah looked at him with surprise. "You know, I have told more than one person this story, but you are the first to ask me that question." She paused before continuing. "They did not speak to me that year or the next. In fact, it was the Christmas of forty-six, I was thirteen. I will not tell you that they spoke aloud but the message was perfectly clear. That night I learned who I was and what I must do."

Armistead waited silently but he did not expect to hear any more. He thanked Hannah for her hospitality and retired upstairs to write his letters. He rose before dawn, reread one of the letters, left both on his night table with the knowledge that Hannah would somehow manage to send them home, and walked to the rail station. Until he reached the outskirts of Frederick he encountered no one except for a solitary rider heading toward the Yoder Farm, a place he had come to realize had once been a station on the Underground Railroad.

175

Chapter 13. Loudoun County and Edward's Ferry, Winter 1862

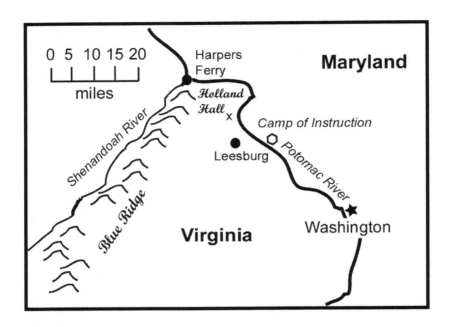

In Loudoun County the Christmas season brought a temporary return to normality. Once again young men were plentiful because, with or without permission, soldiers had come home to enjoy the holidays. Among them was Min Carter. When he visited Holland Hall, Amanda rushed to embrace him and, to the surprise of both, held him hard while dissolving into great choking sobs.

During their shared time together it became readily apparent to Amanda that he had changed. It was not just the unnatural, stiff way he carried his arm as he partnered the girls in dance. Rather, he did not thrust himself forward to participate in the games and charades the girls arranged for the soldiers' entertainment. She saw that he was also less likely to laugh and sometimes when he did his eyes remained distant.

He asked whether anyone had heard from Armistead. Amanda sadly replied, "No, not as far as I know." Only once during the frantic round of balls and routs, while squiring her to a regimental ball at the Picket Hotel in Leesburg, did Min speak to her about the war: "It is an awful thing to be obligated to take another's life, Amanda. I know that it is our duty neverthe- less and the more that are killed in each engagement the sooner the war will close." Soon thereafter, the soldiers were gone, again leaving those who remained behind anxious and worried.

To rally spirits after the boys departed, Lucy Paine invited Amanda and their friends to her home for what she called a quilting bee. Recently, cloth had grown expensive so the women had patriotically pledged to resort to homespun. Furthermore, while their skilled negroes made clothes for the army, they would make their own garments. It turned out to be a noble pledge that most of the girls could not fulfill. Amanda had long disdained the arts of knitting, spinning, and weaving. However, Lucy had always been clever with her hands so she promised to teach the others. They would begin with the simplest of tasks by learning how to knit socks.

They sat is a circle and set to work. "I am glad I live in war times. It makes me feel like a heroine," commented Elizabeth Milton.

"Like this Mandy," Lucy patiently said as she again demonstrated the technique.

"Ow!" howled Elizabeth, stabbing herself with her knitting needle for the third time.

"Lizzie, stop carrying on so," Lucy retorted. "Now you are truly heroic because you are sacrificing blood."

While they worked they discussed matters small and large.

"When my brother came home to recover from his wound he told me I should not get married until the war is over. A girl can end up a widow in a short time," commented Kate Luckett.

"It would not be such a bad thing to be a pretty, young widow," observed Letty Smallwood.

"Such stuff, Letty. You have no idea," Amanda snapped.

An uncomfortable silence descended. I should not have spoken so sharply, Amanda reflected inwardly. Could it be jealousy? she mused. Letty is lovely, only seventeen, and has a world of choices before her while I am almost a spinster, an embarrassment to family and friends.

"Letty, you already are young and pretty, but I really think you do not want to be a widow. As for myself, I intend to become a crone," Amanda said in a rallying voice.

The girls laughed. Their knitting needles resumed their progress and Lizzie spoke:

"Captain Houston and I have an understanding. I think Ma suspects it, and she don't approve, of course. She gave me another long article on marriage to read."

"You always have been the fortunate one!" exclaimed another girl. "Except for you and Letty, I expect that the rest of us may end up crones like Mandy said. Men are getting pretty thin on the ground. I was thinking the other day that on our side of the river there are only three white men around and two are perfectly ancient. Why if the darkies took the notion to run, or worse, there's nothing we could do."

"I overheard Uncle Phil talking to some of the young servant men. He was telling them the direction they must take when they want to run off to join the yankees," Lucy said.

"Oh, such disgusting ingratitude. What did you do?"

"Ingratitude indeed. We had always treated him like a friend rather than a servant. I told Mister Jenkins, our overseer of course. Uncle Phil was shocked, absolutely shocked. He had not been whipped in my memory. But Jenkins laid into him right smart. Oh how he howled." Lucy's infectious laugh spread throughout the room. Only Amanda remained silent.

The Camp of Instruction lay on the Maryland side of the Potomac River near Edward's Ferry. A steady stream of traffic; farm wagons, peddler carts, whites and blacks on horse and foot, had worn deep ruts into the track leading to the camp. The falling temperature froze the ruts, making it difficult for Armistead's horse to pick a path through the traffic. He gently asked Blue to hurry because the north wind gave promise of more snow and he wanted to arrive before the storm's onset.

At the camp's entrance, small knots of soldiers bartered with some negro men. The sentinels were too busy leering at a handsome woman to pay any mind so Armistead passed without challenge. Before him were several neatly aligned rows of tents occupied by New York, Ohio, and Minnesota infantry regiments. He paused to watch the evening drill. The infantry were superbly equipped. They wore voluminous, blue-grey greatcoats and carried large backpacks held in place by pipe clay-polished straps. Linen haversacks and metal canteens jostled against their left hips as they marched in unison to the tap of the drum. An officer shouted an order and the entire mass wheeled as one.

Having completed a complicated series of evolutions at the quick pace, they stood motionless, their shiny rifles held at the high port. The evening gun sounded. The soldiers stacked their weapons in front of their conical Sibley tents and lined up beneath a crudely built arbor of pine boughs to receive their supper. A series of large bonfires around which were arranged long, trestle tables cast an almost holiday cheer to the scene. The food smell coming from the huge iron cauldrons fires reminded Armistead that he had barely eaten since departing Carlisle.

He swallowed painfully and resumed his ride. A soldier darted past. Armistead called out, "Say mister, can you tell me where the Loudoun Rangers are camped?"

The soldier replied with a scornful jerk of his thumb and pointed across the parade ground to a distant hillside. Armistead climbed the hill just as the snow began to fall. The strengthening wind brought the foul smell. The latrines were shallow ditches hacked into frozen soil. He saw a surprising number of men perched awkwardly on wooden planks that spanned the ditches. They seemed oblivious to the rapidly intensifying storm.

The camp itself featured torn, weather-stained tents. Even as he watched, a gust of wind lifted a tent flap and collapsed the entire structure. A groan came from within but nearby soldiers ignored it. Instead, they resolutely huddled in front of their flickering, green-wood fires, their backs to the wind, their attention focused on some barely sizzling sides of whitish-grey, gelatinous meat.

Armistead's horse whinnied loudly and one of the figures turned to give him a suspicious look. The Ranger shook his head, looked hard, and stood up. He was a large, barrel-chested man. He called out, "I'll be damned. It's Armistead Carter." A grin creased his grimy, unshaven face and Armistead recognized Hendrick Kupper.

"Hello Henk. What the hell is going on here?"

The Rangers' story came out in bits and pieces. When the men realized that Armistead was a sympathetic audience, a torrent of complaint and accusation emerged. It seemed that the yankees who had come first had sited their camps in the sheltered hollows close to sources of firewood and good water. The officious New Yorker who commanded the camp had shunted the Rangers to this bleak, exposed hillside. The Rangers had protested that there were better sites available. The New Yorker sneeringly replied that those sites were reserved for more reliable soldiers.

"Boys," Armistead said, "They made me a captain, which as you know is a mighty powerful man."

The Rangers laughed appreciatively.

"I don't reckon I can do much tonight but tomorrow I'll go talk with this New Yorker. What's his name?"

"Colonel Benjamin Overmeyer," Henk replied, "Only we call him Colonel Always Liar."

After feeding and rubbing down his horse, Armistead rejoined the Rangers around the fire. Several men offered him a share of their food. Armistead gamely ignored the nauseating smell of the partially cooked, old pork. He discovered that somehow the more he chewed the bigger the bite became, and ended up nearly choking as he tried to swallow the meat whole. Henk impassively offered him some hardtack. Armistead's teeth made little impression upon the iron-hard cracker.

Henk spoke: "Armistead, I was eating a piece of hardtack this morning and I bit into something soft; what do you think it was?"

"A worm?" Armistead replied.

"No. It was a God damn ten penny nail!"

Chapter 14. The Camp of Instruction and the Becker Farm, Winter 1862

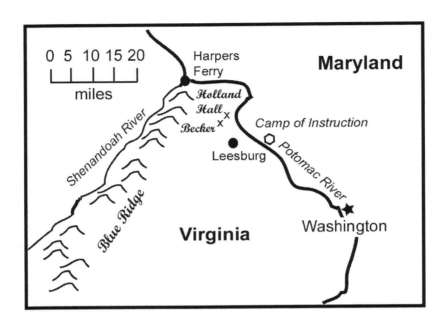

Armistead spent most of the next morning waiting with growing impatience to speak to Colonel Overmeyer. His tribulations began when an immaculately uniformed aide required him to write a formal request to explain why he needed to meet with the colonel.

"He's enormously busy today," the aide brusquely explained. "But if you must you can wait your turn."

It seemed that the colonel liked to spend his mornings attending to matters of discipline. The front room of his headquarters tent enclosed a large table and chairs, several bookcases, and a glowing stove. Overmeyer parted the heavy curtains leading to his sleeping room and closed them carefully. "Won't do to let in a chill," he muttered to no one in particular. He lowered his corpulent frame into a chair at the head of the table. His aides sat nearby. Armistead and the others stood closely packed in the corners and listened while officers presented their cases.

It took time because Overmeyer punctiliously followed army regulations. Occasionally he set his aides to consulting one of the books on the nearby shelves. A period of lengthy deliberation about appropriate punishment followed.

Overmeyer appeared to be a martinet. He sentenced a soldier who had cursed within his earshot to be bucked and gagged for five days. "On the Lord's day we will release him and hope he has learned his lesson," Overmeyer observed. God forbid that he and Henk should ever meet, Armistead reflected.

A soldier who was caught gambling received the sentence of hanging from his thumbs. Armistead heard a nearby voice whisper with a disgusted tone, "It will be the stock and pillory next." Overmeyer sentenced another man who had failed to salute properly the task of cleaning out latrines. An aide leaned over and whispered in the colonel's ear. "Yes, perfect." Overmeyer said. He looked at Armistead and smirked: "He will begin with the Loudoun Ranger's camp since I understand their latrines are the most used."

Amid laughter and stares Armistead bit off a rejoinder. He gathered himself and stood rigidly still without expression. A slight disappointment registered on Overmeyer's face before he proceeded to the next case.

They were a hard-drinking group. Aides regularly refreshed the colonel's glass while other officers drank from their flasks without constraint. Yet alcohol was the cause of most of the camp's discipline problems. Whiskey was cheap and readily available, sold by peddlers or used as trade by local blacks. The results were predictable, and as the morning wore on the more serious cases appeared before the court.

Colonel Overmeyer, his face now flushed a livid red, dealt harshly with most of them until an earnest Massachusetts lieutenant presented a case involving one of his men. Apparently this soldier had got drunk and fired his gun at a black cook. Overmeyer summoned the soldier to explain himself. "Sir, I thought the gun was unloaded. So I snapped it in John's face because he was being disrespectful."

"Did he learn his lesson?" Overmeyer asked.

The soldier looked startled and the lieutenant quickly interjected, "Sir, he killed him."

"So be it," Overmeyer said. "There's too many of these black rascals around camp. Maybe this will be a lesson to them. Fine this worthy man a week's pay. Next."

An aide spoke, "Sir, you recall last week we arrested three niggers who were selling whiskey to the men. To settle on an appropriate punishment you suggested that we consult with their masters. I did so and they recommended that the miscreants be whipped by the men who bought the whiskey."

Overmeyer laughed heartily. "Yes, that is rich. Let the punishment fit the crime, my grandma always used to say. And now gentlemen, I believe it is time for dinner."

The colonel ponderously rose from his chair and passed Armistead without making eye contact. His aide looked him in the face and smirked.

For Rachel Becker, the first winter of the war brought boredom. She was accustomed to having attentive men around. She liked acting out different roles while engaging in subtle games of chase. She enjoyed the challenge of controlling the pace of the hunt and particularly relished the startling effects when she whimsically changed the rules. Most of all she had learned that when she set her mind to it, few men could resist her. The knowledge pleased her. But the war had interrupted her lessons and a recent spate of hard weather had confined everyone to their homes.

With the rival armies patrolling the river, the messengers also came less often. But there were always paths unguarded for the experienced or especially determined, and Abner Means's agents, men and women alike, were both. The messenger's appearance at dusk on a mid-January evening brought welcome diversion. It was beginning to snow again but even before the messenger had unwound the thick scarf that covered his head and neck she dismissed him from consideration. It was that negro man from up Frederick way and she had already learned that he was one of the few who seemed resistant to her charms.

Her father welcomed Liverne Taylor warmly. While he thawed by the fire, Rachel set to work separating the thin sheets of coded messages that had been carefully sewn into the cover of a well-used bible. They dealt with the war and held scant interest for her. However, this time there were also two letters in regular envelopes tucked inside the cover. The addresses, written in a strong masculine hand, were to a bank in Leesburg and to Amanda Holland.

Rachel glanced toward the fireplace. Her father was busy pouring brandy from a decanter and Taylor's eyes were fixed on the filling glass. Rachel slipped one of the letters into her pocket and continued her work. Later, while the men sat at table discussing the boring war, she carefully steamed open the letter — her father's lessons had not, after all, been ignored entirely — and read what Armistead had to say.

She remembered him with annoyance as another of her less successful projects. She disliked Amanda and loathed her even more after reading the letter. It seemed that Armistead was somewhat smitten by his cousin. Rachel's temper rose as she recalled the mousy, flat-chested, Amanda. What could he possibly see in her? she asked angrily. Whatever it was, apparently he wanted to start afresh with his 'Mandy' and had written this letter to start a new accommodation.

Her father's training had encompassed a variety of what he called 'the secret arts.' Among them was the ability to mimic handwriting and at this she excelled. It might be amusing, Rachel conceived, to write a letter to 'dearest Mandy'. So, after Taylor departed she surprised her father by asking where he had secreted a bundle of Abolitionist writings on the purpose and meaning of the war. "Your conversation with Mister Taylor made me realize there still is so much I must learn," she said. Becker gazed fondly at her during the subsequent nights while she read the various documents.

It particularly pleased him that she was so taken up in her study that she meticulously copied certain poignant phrases.

"I am a fortunate father," Becker happily reflected.

The Loudoun Rangers had been recruited from Union loyal men living on both sides of the Potomac River. Some would have been able to see their homes from the camp were it not for the fact that the blowing snow made looking difficult and their cramped posture perched over a latrine ditch restricted their field of view. On any given day nearly half of the Rangers were too ill to report for duty. Armistead had assembled the balance for drill. He knew many of them personally or he knew their families. Familiarity did not seem to breed respect. Armistead ruefully recalled Min's complaints about the difficulty of ordering boyhood friends to do anything unless they felt like it. They certainly did not seem to feel like drilling just now, exhibiting neither spirit nor aptitude.

During his time at Carlisle Barracks Armistead had observed George Thomas's regular cavalry drill repeatedly. At the time he had thought it a largely empty exercise to occupy time. Now he began to appreciate what he had seen. In contrast, the Rangers were incapable of parade ground maneuver. He ordered, he cajoled, he tried to explain why it might someday save lives if they could wheel in unison to face an enemy attack from the right, left, or rear, and his men largely ignored him. Furthermore, he suspected that his newly acquired knowledge gleaned from the pages of the Cavalry Manual might evaporate in the stress of actually meeting the enemy.

He remembered Thomas's statement that the noncommissioned officers, the experienced corporals and sergeants, were the backbone of every army in history. Armistead knew only one such man and after four futile days of drill, he wrote a letter to Means requesting help. To his delight, a beaming Sergeant Patrick Flannery appeared outside his tent eight days later.

After watching yet another exercise collapse into shambles, Armistead said to Flannery, "It's hopeless ain't it."

"Ah, I've seen worse. We'll whip them in shape inside of a month or my name's not Paddy Flannery."

Armistead looked at Flannery skeptically. Surely the man was trying to have some fun with him. But rather than mirth, Armistead saw solid determination in Flannery's eyes.

Weeks later, when he received a summons to attend what Colonel Overmeyer called 'a council of war', Armistead possessed some confidence that the Loudoun Rangers at least understood the rudiments of cavalry drill. He listened as Overmeyer smoothly explained that his plan relied upon surprise and speed. They would cross the Potomac at Edward's Ferry and fan out to accomplish various missions. Overmeyer's New Yorkers would march to Mount Gilead to capture Captain Richard Simpson and his detachment who were busy recruiting for the Eighth Virginia; the First Maryland Potomac Home Brigade to march from Harpers Ferry and raid Upperville and Middleburg in search of horses; the Purnell Legion to intercept a wagon train smuggling supplies from Baltimore to Leesburg. Overmeyer's detailed knowledge about the rebel dispositions impressed Armistead. "Maybe he's a different man when he's actually in charge of the fighting," he mused. Still, it struck Armistead as odd that the men who knew the terrain best, the Loudoun Rangers, were to remain in Waterford. They constituted his 'reserve', the colonel brusquely explained, but his tone of voice left little doubt that he did not trust the Rangers.

The issue of trust came again to the forefront of Armistead's mind as the column filed along the winding track leading to the Potomac ford. The Rangers had been together for less than two months and many had yet to fight. A sprinkling of them came from belligerent Scotch-Irish stock, but the majority were Germans and Quakers who lived around Waterford and Hamilton. The willingness of the Quakers to fight had come as a surprise to Armistead. He did not know that during his time in Carlisle, various Confederate units had visited the farms of Union loyalists to confiscate draft animals, wagons, and forage. One Friend told him, "When they come to the threshold of our homes to take what is ours, sometimes the flesh grows stronger than the spirit."

Yet the notion that he was about to fight his first battle alongside Quakers made Armistead uneasy. He gestured to Henk to let the others pass and then softly inquired, "Henk, will this lot fight?"

"You mean the Friends?"

Armistead nodded.

"God damn right they will. Back when we were helping that fool Baker get over the river at Ball's Bluff, Isaiah Virts was next to me in the skirmish line. The rebels were coming hard. He pointed his Enfield, said, 'Friend, it is unfortunate, but thee stands exactly where I am going to shoot.' He hit him flush." Henk laughed his full-bellied laugh. "No, don't worry about the Hamilton crowd. Our problem is up there." He gestured toward Overmeyer with disgust.

The head of the column passed the last turn before the steep descent to the Potomac. Armistead shook his head sadly, recovered, and spoke in a rallying tone of voice, "Sergeant, I reckon we better join the invasion of Virginia."

"Won't they be surprised," Henk softly replied.

Chapter 15. Loudoun County, April 1862

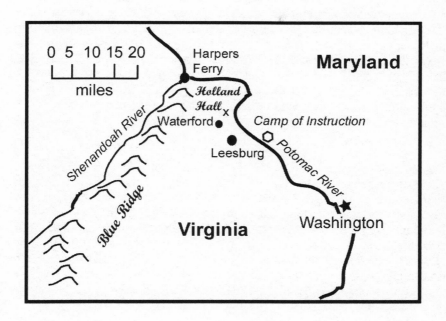

The weather-stained envelope came to Holland Hall in the late afternoon. It had clearly passed through several hands since it had been written. With a strange flurry of emotions, Amanda recognized Armistead's writing on the envelope. She passed through the kitchen and asked Nell to make her a cup of tea. She waited distractedly in the library, the envelope unopened on her desk, until she finished the tea. Finally, she cut the seal and began to read:

"Dearest Mandy, I hope this finds you and yours well and in good health."

This salutation was about the last expression of human warmth anywhere in the short letter. The balance was a condemnation of the secessionist who had "determined on a policy of rule or ruin by waging a cruel and unjustifible war on the best government that ever existed." Amanda paused in angry reflection. Armistead's father had always been quick to pass judgment on the behavior of others. It was a pity that Armistead had grown into this trait. She felt like she hardly recognized the person he had become. She glanced back at the phrase "cruel and unjustifible war" and allowed herself a bitter laugh. During their school days, she and Armistead had always been the last two standing during their hotly contested spelling bees. Yet now he's allowed himself to get so worked up that he's even forgotten how to spell, she bitterly noted.

Armistead reported that he had joined a Union cavalry unit. He had chosen it because it was pledged to visit ruin and death upon all who opposed them. The letter closed with a frightening boast: "Defend yourself if you can, we are coming, carrying the sword and buckler of the lord."

Amanda tossed the letter down in disgust. So he's acquired religion to justify himself, she reflected. The sound of a horse and rider moving fast down the lane brought Amanda to the window. It was Gordon. Odd, he's usually half drunk by this time and sends one of the servants if anything needs tending to. The half-formed resolution to ask Gordon what he was about died when she returned to her desk and read Armistead's letter for a second, and then a third time.

With drawn pistol, the Union rider warily approached the rendezvous. A quarter moon shone through the trees, creating a spider web-like maze of shadows. It was difficult to see, particularly just ahead, where twin ranks of cedars shrouded the lane. The rider continued to the third curve where he paused to let his eyes adjust. So far the colonel's directions had been accurate. Yes, there it was; a clearing on the left with the outline of stone chimney. He slowly tapped the butt of his revolver on his canteen three times, paused, three times more, and then twice in rapid succession.

From the shadows a British-accented voice spoke: "The guide has the directions."

Corporal James Gooch relaxed and replied: "The provider has the gold." He rode forward to complete the transaction.

"They will camp for two nights beginning tomorrow in the Baptist church in Waterford," Gooch said.

"Very good," replied the guide.

He handed Gooch a sheet of paper. Gooch unshuttered his dark lantern to read detailed directions to three places. "The agreement was for five," he said sharply.

"Three for information, five for gold," replied the British voice.

Gooch sighed. He had hoped to pocket a bit of extra profit. He handed over a small pouch.

The guide counted carefully, grinned, and handed over a second paper with two more sets of directions. "Tell your colonel that next time I may be able to offer something more tempting."

Gooch started to inquire but something about the man's face made it clear that further questioning would be futile. On his return journey to camp, Gooch speculated about his share of the haul. Months ago, seizing rebel horses and selling them to the Federal remount bureau had been easy. But recently the rebels had made raiding difficult. Worse, the proceeds, divided among many, had been disappointing. Barely enough to cover two visits to Meme Richard's, Gooch ruefully reflected.

However, Colonel Overmeyer's newest plan promised something far more rewarding. The rebels would light on the Loudoun Rangers like gnats to exposed flesh, leaving the rest of the county safe to work over. And then there was the Englishman's hint about "something more tempting." Maybe he would be able to visit Frederick, or better still Washington itself where it was said the girls were clean, plentiful, and much more interesting than the local talent. Wait till they get a look of James Gooch, the rider chortled to himself.

In spite of his talk about "surprise and speed," after a march of only two hours Overmeyer ordered the column into camp near the bluff overlooking the ford. Everyone was keyed up and the order caused considerable grumbling. Armistead learned from one of the New York officers that Overmeyer had decided he needed to verify the accuracy of his information before embarking upon his "bold but hazardous undertaking."

Thereafter, Armistead watched as a handful of scouts splashed across the ford and disappeared into the evening mist. Brave men, he thought, but we could do that job better.

The colonel's conduct the next morning did not increase Armistead's regard for Overmeyer's abilities. The column deliberately descended the track leading to the ford and then halted at water's edge while Overmeyer and his staff consulted a map. Finally the colonel nodded. A bugler sounded the call to advance. "Good God!" Armistead exclaimed, "Why doesn't he just send a herald across to notify everyone that we are here?"

As the first troopers carefully picking their way across the rock strewn ford, the sound of hoof beats from somewhere to the rear alerted Armistead to the presence of a fast moving rider. It is probably another courier, Armistead thought. Overmeyer can't seem to march anywhere without sending out a regular stream of messengers. The hoof beats grew louder. Armistead glanced back to see a compact rider wearing civilian clothes urging his horse into a fast canter. Four large riders followed close behind but it was the man in front who absorbed Armistead's undivided attention.

He peered at the nearby soldiers as he rapidly passed through the rear of the column. When he saw Armistead, he checked his horse and spoke as if it were the most natural thing in the world to meet him here: "Ah, Carter, a word with you," said Abner Means. Means's escort arrived. They were big, tough-looking men wearing the distinctive orange facings indicating that they were veterans of the Second U.S. Dragoons. They deferentially stationed themselves just behind Means's sweat-streaked horse. "Alone," Means added.

"I come from Washington. There's something we need done. I'll explain along the way."

Armistead impassively stared at him and replied, "My place is with my men."

"A commendable sentiment, I'm sure. However, you are needed in a more important place. Moreover, there's not likely to be any fighting. Overmeyer's orders are to scout, secure horses, and return. Over and back, fast, not stand and fight."

"You seem to understand our colonel's orders better than he does," Armistead said. "So you also probably know that the man is a fool. His stupidity is only surpassed by his arrogance. I'm going with my men, if not to protect them from the Confederates, then to protect them from him."

"I understand what you are saying and I repeat, all my," Means paused as if searching for the correct word, "resources tell me that there are few enemy on the other side. But that is not the point. I too thought I could best serve by leading men into the fight. I thought I was going to be colonel commanding the Loudoun Rangers. But the men in Washington said that the army had hundreds of colonels and that I had," again Means hesitated before continuing, "some things that were more valuable. In the same way the army has thousands of captains but there is only one man who can do what needs doing just now. It's important captain. It's up Valley. You know the land and the people." Means voice trailed off.

Armistead sighed, clucked softly and began riding to rejoin Henk.

"Captain Carter!" Means voice had taken on a completely different, authoritative tone. "I have here," he pulled out a paper, "orders requiring you to accompany me to Harpers Ferry. At that point, you can decide voluntarily whether to participate further."

Armistead ignored him. "Corporal," Means said.

The four regulars spurred their horses to surround Armistead. Henk moved forward to challenge them. Armistead saw the regulars draw their Colt revolvers.

Armistead reined in. "Easy Henk, it's alright. This gentleman has official business with me. Take care of the boys. I'll see y'all later."

Henk watched Armistead depart, surrounded by the burly horsemen. He scratched his head. It plainly was not alright but he did not know what he could do about it.

Henk leaned against the gatepost. "What a god damn ridiculous place to try to defend," he muttered for the fourth time. Six roads led into the town. Lieutenant Luther Slater had stationed a picket of four men on each road. This left just twenty Loudoun Rangers camped in the church, and most of them were new recruits. Henk had questioned these dispositions. Slater replied that he too did not much care for the position but that Colonel Overmeyer's express orders were to camp in Waterford tonight.

Since he was the acting sergeant of the guard, Henk again walked the circuit to ensure that the pickets remained awake. A slight chill was in the air. The moon had sunk. It must be about three in the morning, Henk thought.

Henk froze, blinked, and stared hard. Across the road from the church was the home of the Virts family. Arrayed along a bank on either side of the house was a line of shadow where none had been before. "Halt! Who comes there?" Henk bellowed. His challenge brought no response but it did bring Slater and the reserve scrambling out the church door and into the front yard. Belatedly Henk realized this was exactly what the rebels wanted. His warning shout was crushed by the noise of the rebel's first volley.

Henk ran to join Slater. Several men had been hit and were crying out in pain. They could barely be heard above the howling curses flowing from Henry Hough. "Help me up Henk, we'll get those bastards yet!" Hough demanded. The Rangers seemed to share his fighting spirit and were rallying to the calm orders given by popular Lieutenant Slater. Henk took his place in the line next to James Cox. "They pinked me in the arm, Henk. Help me load."

The Rangers fired an uneven volley towards the Virts' house. Slater's voice rose above the battle noise: "Back! Back into the church!"

Henk dragged the still-cursing Hough inside. Someone closed the door behind him and then cried out as he too was hit.

"Douse the lights!" the lieutenant commanded. Before someone extinguished the lantern, Henk saw that Slater were bleeding heavily from wounds in his shoulder, arm, breast, and hand. Bullets began thudding against the thick door, as if someone was knocking with an iron-tipped hand. The Rangers huddled on the floor, taking shelter as best they could behind the prayer benches. The shots from the rebel carbines easily pierced the church's lathe and plaster walls. Firing blind, they kept the Rangers pinned to the floor and occasionally struck home. A heavy thud and Edward Jacobs writhed on the floor with a thigh wound; ten minutes later, another thud followed by an agonized groan as a ball passed through Henry Dixon's bowels.

After about thirty minutes, Slater collapsed from blood loss. Before he lost consciousness he passed the command to the Ranger's drill master, Sergeant Flannery. Flannery appeared oblivious to all danger. He set the company cook, Black Angus, to caring for the wounded and positioned the Rangers in pairs, weapons pointed toward the windows in all four directions. A bold rebel briefly appeared at a window in an attempt to fire an aimed shot into the church. Henk sighted his carbine and waited. When the figure appeared again, Henk fired and heard a satisfying howl of pain as the figure disappeared.

Suddenly the rebel shooting stopped. From outside the church came shouts: "Cease fire, flag of truce." Someone tapped lightly on the church door. "Who is it?" Flannery demanded.

"It's Missus Virts," came the reply. Flannery looked at Edward Jacobs, a new recruit who lived near Waterford. Jacobs nodded, "I think so."

"What do you want?" Flannery shouted.

"Major White demands that you surrender."

"Tell the bastard to go to hell!" Flannery replied.

The fighting continued for another hour. The calls of the wounded; for water, for their mother, for their God, subsided into a mewling drone of pain. Henk shared the last of his canteen with Hough. "Dumb shits," Hough muttered, "mama and God ain't going to help us now. Got any more water, Henk?"

"Fraid not," Henk answered.

"Just as well, I guess," Hough said. "Don't reckon we got the fixins for a proper julep anyhows."

It was growing light outside when a second flag of truce appeared. Again came the demand for surrender and again Flannery repeated his defiant answer. "Hold on boys just a little longer," Flannery told the Rangers. "I'm sure the sounds of firing will bring help."

Dawn came. Henk looked around he church. He saw that at least half the Rangers had been hit. Charles Dixon, dead near the altar; Slater lying on a pew soaked in his own blood. One by one the surviving Rangers reported that they were almost out of ammunition. "Then make sure each round counts," Flannery replied.

When the third summons for surrender came, Flannery crawled over to Slater. The lieutenant was conscious again. A wound to his temple bathed his face in blood. He said something that Henk could not hear and Flannery nodded.

Flannery put John Hickman's pocket handkerchief on his sword tip, crawled to the door, and bellowed, "Cease fire! Armistice. Cease Fire!"

The rebel fire died down. Flannery bellowed again: "Tell White that our conditions are parole and immediate release and officers retain their side arms."

Time stood still. Then, from outside called a voice: "Send your leader out to arrange the preliminaries."

"It's a trap," someone hissed.

"I'll go find out," Flannery said and walked outside.

Henk waited for the sound of a death shot. Instead silence, followed by conversation.

Flannery returned. "Let's do it in style, boys. March out, line up on the porch, and surrender your arms. We will be paroled and free to go."

The twelve unwounded Rangers formed a line on the porch. In the front yard the troopers of Lige White's battalion gazed curiously at them. Some made eye contact with neighbors, schoolmates, friends, relatives, but no words passed. Lige White entered the church and knelt by Slater. "I am sorry to see you so dangerously wounded, Lieutenant," he said.

Outside, a Confederate trooper moved toward the porch. "I'm going to kill that traitorous son of a bitch," he said.

Henk recognized William Smoots. Several rebels grabbed Smoots' arms to restrain him.

From the porch, Charles Smoots spoke, "Unbuckle your weapons Bill, you cowardly cur, and I'll wipe the grass with your face in two minutes."

White reappeared at the door. "Gentlemen, this fight is over. Thirty-fifth Battalion. Attention. Bugler, sound 'To Horse'."

The clatter of hooves receded. From across the field came a quail's courting song. Missus Virts appeared on her porch to offer coffee. Henk shook himself. It seemed so normal. He shook himself again. I'm alive, god damn it, I'm alive.

Chapter 16. Loudoun County, April 1862

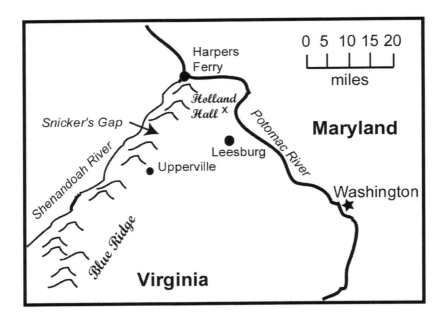

For many years Amanda had dealt with unwelcome moods by embarking upon a round of visiting. The long winter, the presence of soldiers — Confederate, Union, and increasing numbers of deserters without allegiance to either side — curtailed travel. She sought release in work and in reading and found that even these familiar habits failed her. The arrival of Lige White's Virginia cavalry and the return of her brother fortuitously coincided to offer an opportunity for her favorite diversion. The cavalry brought order back to Loudoun County. The roads were again safe, at least during daylight, although few chose to travel far without an armed escort. Boyd's unexpected reappearance stemmed from reasons that were unclear. He said that he had a furlough, but his expression told Amanda otherwise. She knew that he would be more forthcoming outside of the home and away from their father. It was simplicity itself to enlist Boyd by telling him that they were going out on a 'scout'.

At first, as they rode the familiar circuit to friends and family, it seemed little had changed. The dogwood buds were swollen and nearly ready to display their riot of lantern-like blooms, the frogs chorused from their breeding ponds, the pastures showed green promise having absorbed the abundant winter moisture. But the broken fences — their laboriously hewed rails wantonly used for soldiers' campfires — the occasional blackened chimney standing vigil over ash and brick piles where once a manor had stood, and most especially the wary looks of the few people they encountered, all suggested that change had come and that it was for the worse.

Amanda knew that during the winter and early spring the yankees had made several sweeps through the county. They never stayed in one place for long and this made it hard for the Confederates to find them. "If they'd stay and fight we'd lick 'em sure," Boyd glowered in between swigs from his hip flask.

Several neighbors reported that when the yankees did come they knew exactly where to go to find the places where the menfolk were absent. They descended like "a vandal horde," one neighbor said. People guessed that the negroes cooperated with the raiders. Suspecting disloyalty, some had sold their slaves. Others had hired some of the county's hardest overseers. Yet, it made little difference. The yankees continued to find the most vulnerable places. Perplexed, many had begun to blame the Quakers and the Germans. Consequently, when Confederate commissary agents came, people directed them to the farms around Hamilton and Waterford. As they watched the agents' laden wagons depart, they considered the suffering endured by their neighbors as proportionate punishment for their own losses.

Amanda listened to the stories of suspicion and vengeance and felt her spirits plunge. But she refused to be diverted from her plan, which called for the first day of the scout to end in Upperville. Furthermore, to Boyd's distress, she insisted on visiting their Aunt Althea. Aunt Althea was famously argumentative. Family gossip held that she had driven her first husband to an early grave with words alone. If no one else would oblige, she would argue with herself. At one time she had lived in town, but her habit of spending long hours peering out the window had made her unpopular with her neighbors. To their relief, she finally moved to her second husband's small farm on a hill west of Upperville. It enjoyed a superb view of the Blue Ridge, but more to Amanda's purpose it also overlooked the Snickersville Pike leading west through the mountains.

Amanda was uncertain how she would be received. They had never been particularly close. To her surprise, her aunt seemed pleased to see her. After an exchange of greetings, she whistled shrilly. From around the corner came her husband, looking thin, worn, and anxious. "We have visitors," Aunt Althea snapped. "Go and fetch that ham from the spring house. Cider, asparagus, and some fresh-baked biscuits will do nicely."

"Missus Goodwin, I do declare. That might be the last of the meat until the next slaughter. I do wish you would speak with me before making promises.

"There's plenty more for you to do without worrying about that. Now get busy."

Goodwin's shoulders slumped and he trudged off toward the spring house. Boyd went to join him — probably to tipple together, Amanda guessed — while Aunt Althea held forth on the porch: "I received your letter and have kept at it ever since." She proceeded to give a remarkably lucid account of Union activities. Using Harpers Ferry as a base, the yankees moved through the gaps to descend into the Loudoun Valley. They often cooperated with units coming from the Maryland side of the river. From the stragglers who invariably visited the Goodwin farm, Aunt Althea had extracted the names of officers and their units and much else as well. "Now write this down carefully dear," she instructed.

While her inner voice reflected that Aunt Althea had never called her 'dear' before, Amanda dutifully began recording her aunt's information. A page and one-half later her aunt said, "So the last are the Twenty-Eight Pennsylvania, Colonel Geary at Point of Rocks, the Sixth New York Independent Battery at Brunswick, and those villains in the Loudoun Rangers."

"Why do you know, Amanda, that they had the audacity to take possession of Lovettsville and Waterford and begin to recruit from the traitors living in our midst?" Amanda recognized the signs and closed her ledger.

Flushed with indignation, her aunt continued. She described the excesses committed by the raiders. They had stolen horses of course, and taken sides of bacon from the smokehouse, but those were far from their worst of it. At daybreak several riders had appeared in Upperville to tell the inhabitants to prepare breakfast. An hour later, a yankee colonel named Overmeyer arrived at her sister's home. He and his staff expected to find the meal waiting. "They don't know my Gertie very well now do they Amanda?" she said in a voice dripping with venom. Surprised that there was nothing on the table, the colonel asked for a cup to get a drink of milk. Gertie ignored this request as well. An aide opened a sideboard, removed some fine glassware, and poured the milk.

Aunt Althea's face was now suffused with rage. "Imagine that," she shrieked, "why the very idea of a yankee drinking out of a cut glass!"

Amanda waited, with growing impatience, through the subsequent tirade. In spite of everything, she found that her aunt possessed surprising insights. However, her stomach groaned with hunger — it was growing late and somehow her aunt's husband had never brought the promised food and drink — so, when Aunt Althea finally paused for breath, she rose from her chair and spoke, "Dearest Aunt, we really must be on the wing or we will be unseemly late to our lodgings in Upperville. Your intelligence gathering has been peerless. Before I go I would like to ask one more question."

Aunt Althea sputtered, harrumphed, started to glower, and changed her mind. Amanda had thrown her off her stride and she didn't like it, but she did not readily see a way clear of her niece's impeccable manners. She decided to ignore Amanda's interruption and resume her flow. She drew breath to continue but Amanda interjected her question first.

194

"You know the way the raiders seem able to pinpoint our most defense-less homes. People say either the servants, the Germans, or the Quakers are betraying us. What think you?"

Her aunt paused to consider. Her angry flush receded, replaced by a clear-eyed look of cunning. "Why Amanda, you silly goose. It's probably none of them. They have too much to lose. Look instead at who gains by these raids. You will find, I am sure, that it comes down to money."

Chapter 17. Loudoun County, April 1862

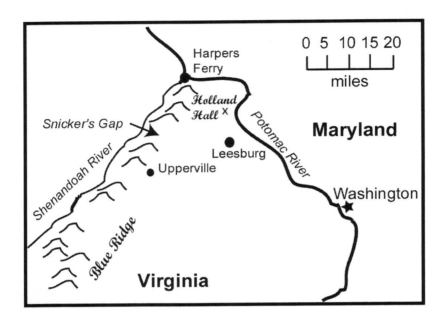

Amanda continued to ponder her aunt's words during the second day of the scout. The notion that the betrayal might come from a seemingly patriotic Confederate, even perhaps from someone she knew, was difficult to entertain. Yes, some of the people living in the German or Quaker enclaves in Loudoun County had been actively cooperating with the yankees, but that was unsurprising; they had always been overt in their opposition to slavery. Yet there was Armistead's strident conversion. If she could be so wrong about him, then perhaps her judgment was less sharp than she had believed. But, the majority of the county had seemed absolutely committed to the cause. Many had sacrificed a great deal already. Has it come to this? Amanda wondered. An enemy within, willing to bring pillage and destruction upon their own neighbors, all in the name of mammon. It seemed too incredible. Still, the niggling worry kept recurring. She retained it in the back of her mind for further reflection, a process her mother had taught her, and returned to the present.

The temperature rose pleasantly throughout the morning. By mid-afternoon it was almost hot. "Boyd, I have an idea," Amanda said.

"You usually do, Mandy," Boyd replied.

"Let's stop at the swimming hole below the bridge. It will be like old times."

After a short, invigorating swim, they sat dangling their toes in the clear pool. Tiny fish brushed against their feet. A heron patiently stalked the reeds. Overhead, a shrill rattle announced the kingfisher's passage. Amanda reluctantly composed herself and spoke about the subject she had been avoiding.

"So how is life in the army?" she asked.

"It's a lot of sitting in camp, marching here, marching there for no reason. We need someone willing to take us into the fight so we can get this thing over with."

"Why I thought Turner Ashby..."

Boyd cut her off. "Him. He's nuthin but a God damn showy ass. Ever since the Grays came under his command things have gone sour. In fact, I resigned from the Grays. I'm fixin to join Lige White's boys."

Amanda was certain that Boyd was not telling the whole story. But it would not do to explore that subject just now. Instead, she meekly observed, "They're a good group of boys. You'll know many of them, of course, boys from both sides of the river. And it will mean you are closer to home."

"That's right. I signed on to defend our homes, and the Thirty-fifth Battalion usually operates in Loudoun, so I reckon I can do exactly that."

Boyd reached back to his saddlebags and pulled out his flask. Amanda gently placed her hand on his arm.

"Boyd, I'm a little worried. You know how papa is losing his battle against drink. It seems to run in our family. Grandpa Holland drank an awful lot, and Grandma used to say that his father did the same. I worry about you."

Boyd jerked his arm free. He fixed her with a hard stare. Amanda saw that his eyes were bloodshot and that his hand uncorking the flask trembled. "You women don't know nothing about what this war does to a man. I've seen things too awful to tell. If this," he nodded toward his flask, "helps me get through it, so be it." He took a long swig and said, "Why I recall you were proud as the day was long to give us the flag that said 'Go and Fight'. Well God damn it Amanda, that's what I'm trying to do!"

Amanda reached out to hold her brother's arm again. She tried to will her strength and love through her fingers and into Boyd. "I know, honey, I know."

Amanda planned to conclude the scout with a visit to her Aunt Tilly. As was the case with Aunt Althea, Amanda had not been particularly close to this relative. She was stubborn, and not particularly clever, and these traits made her suspicious that the world was trying to pull something over on her. She had instilled a prideful belligerence in her two sons, and to Amanda's despair, the three of them dominated her uncle. At age fifty-four, Uncle Edward was a kind, generous man who somehow managed to maintain his sense of humor in spite of his wife's hectoring.

They found Aunt Tilly sitting in a rocker on her porch. She was alone. After they exchanged greetings Amanda asked where Uncle Edward was.

"Round about Richmond I suspect, least that's the last I heard about the Fifty-Sixth Virginia."

"He's in the army?" Boyd burst out.

Aunt Tilly gave Boyd a withering look.

Amanda spoke: "Your two sons are already in the army. Won't you be uneasy without any men about?"

"Yes indeed, but you know he ought to go. Them wretches must be drove away!"

There was little to say after that. They sat on the porch and rocked slowly in silence. Aunt Tilly did not seem inclined to offer refreshments and so, after an excruciating five minutes, and then five minutes more, they made their farewells and departed.

"That's terrible news about Uncle Edward," Amanda said.

"He won't last long," Boyd sourly replied. He took a pull on his flask and then visibly brightened. "Tell you what, Mandy, let's stop at the Beckers. It's directly on the way."

Amanda was tired and ready to go home. Becker made her uncomfortable, she plain disliked his daughter. But Boyd had gone wherever she had wanted and more important, she believed that if they had rebuilt a bridge, it was still fragile. She did not want to overload it before the bonds had set. So, reluctantly she let her brother lead her to the Becker farm.

Boyd seemed to have discovered some inner spring of vitality. It communicated to his horse who picked up the pace. At the long curve leading to the Becker place, Boyd turned off into the woods. Puzzled, Amanda followed and discovered a narrow track that followed a straight course to the barn and orchard behind the Becker house. From a distance they saw Rachel Becker feeding the chickens in the side yard and the shape of Sigmund Becker disappearing around the corner into the front yard.

"You'd best tell the old fart we're here, Sis," Boyd said. "He don't take kindly to surprises."

Amanda caught up with Becker just as he was climbing the porch steps. After an exchange of civilities: "My brother and I were just out exercising the horses," she explained — it would hardly do explain Boyd's interest in his daughter — and then Amanda felt an awkward silence descend. She cast about for something to say: "What do you make of the war now, Mister Becker?"

"I only know what I read." He paused. "And you?" he inquired.

She mimicked the slow drawl of the local planters and said, "Well, I reckon that Manassas and Ball's Bluff set the proper tone."

Becker's nod showed that he understood her mocking jest; their parochial neighbors seldom looked beyond events along the Potomac to form their views. He said, "I'll concede that in Virginia our government has yet to find the proper combination, and with one exception, progress we have not yet made."

198

Amanda was astonished to see a hint of amusement in Becker's eyes. Did this dour man possess a sense of humor?

Becker continued, "However, consider recent events in the west: Grant's capture of forts Henry and Donelson, Buell's capture of Nashville."

"Albert Sidney Johnston will straighten things out in the west. But what is the exception you allude to; what significant Union success has there been in Virginia?" she asked.

"The inauguration of Jefferson Davis," Becker replied.

In spite of herself she grinned.

Boyd and Rachel appeared from around the corner. Amanda saw Becker look at her brother with intense loathing. Boyd did not notice. For the first time in the two days they had spent together he seemed relaxed, even pleased. Amanda switched her gaze to Becker's daughter and saw in her eyes a mirror image of what she had seen in Becker; amusement, satisfaction. Only Rachel was staring straight at her alone. Their eyes locked and neither wavered. Oblivious, Boyd walked between them toward his horse. "Come on sis, we'd better hurry along."

Amanda considered: He was tense and eager to visit. Now he's relaxed and eager to leave.

"What do you think about the news, Miz Holland?" Rachel asked.

The game had shifted onto some new ground, Amanda realized. "The news, Miz Becker?"

"They say that the Loudoun Rangers guided the men who conducted the recent raids."

"I don't know anything about it," Amanda coolly answered. She saw a glint of triumph in Rachel's eyes.

"I thought you knew who commanded one of the groups?"

Sigmund Becker called out sharply, "Rachel!"

"Oh," she covered her mouth in an unconvincing display of contrition.

"You might as well let her tell me, Mister Becker. I am sure to find out eventually," Amanda said.

Rachel continued: "I heard that the officer planning the raids was a Captain Carter. I wondered if that might be your cousin Armistead."

Mustering every ounce of her willpower, Amanda replied in a flat, neutral tone, "I am sure I do not know. Good day, ma'am, sir."

She mounted her horse and saw the hand holding her reins was trembling.

Chapter 18. Valley Pike to Rude's Hill, April 1862

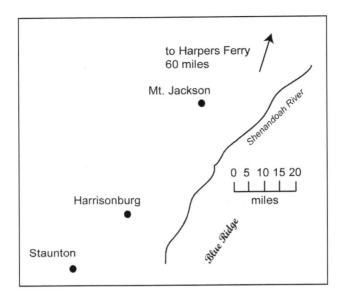

The locomotive appeared like the chrysalis of a giant, ungainly insect. Machinists had stripped it of everything they could; piston rods, pumps, sand box, even the bell, in an effort to lighten the load. Still, the iron skeleton of the Ross Winans camel-back locomotive weighed close to fifty tons. One hundred feet in front of the locomotive stood ten, four-horse teams, selected from the strongest draft stock in the Valley. Teamsters aligned the horses in ranks, four abreast, with an ingenious rig of chain and harness linking the teams to the locomotive. Chief Engineer Hugh Longust nodded and the teamsters mounted. At the signal, the mighty horses pulled.

They had pulled the plow through the heavy, rain-sodden clay of early spring; competed at county fairs in late summer to haul loaded sledges just a little farther than their rivals, skidded mighty chestnuts off mountain slopes in the last days of autumn. Never had they pulled against a weight like this. The chain straightened until it was arrow straight. The strain was enormous. Some teamsters cracked whips, others cursed. The teamster riding in the third rank from the front knew that his horses were strong and willing. Calmly, with little inflexion, Armistead called out: "Ho there Bob, Ho Sam." And to the horse next to him, who cleverly gave every evidence of pulling without actually doing so, "Come on there Lady, you lazy hussy."

Just when it seemed that they could do no more, the huge rear driving wheels began to turn. "She moves!" someone shouted. Accompanied by the screech of metal on macadam, the procession began its slow progress up the Valley Pike.

Just south of Mount Jackson came the first serious obstacle, a hill with a short but steep descent. The horses laboriously hauled Locomotive 199 to the crest. Armistead and the other teamsters unhitched their lathered animals and paused to watch. No one knew what would happen when the giant machine began its downhill run. It started to move, slowly for a brief moment, but only for a moment. The wheels turned faster, and faster still. Locomotive 199 plunged down the slope. An engineer applied the brakes. A piercing squeal came from the wheels. A thickening plume of gray-white smoke appeared and still the locomotive gathered speed. It was as if a great, iron beast had slipped its shackles.

"She's busted free," a teamster said to Armistead.

Armistead rolled the tobacco plug into his cheek. He spat in the red clay dirt and said: "Looks like a runaway team."

To his disappointment, Locomotive 199 came to rest upright. An overseer barked a command and slaves ran to the nearby river to fetch water. By the time Armistead had led his team past the locomotive, the slaves were tossing buckets of water against the white hot brakes. A bare chested slave, his back showing ugly welts from a recent flogging, emptied his bucket, and paused to let Armistead proceed.

Armistead hitched his team and waited. Of the three places he thought might defeat them, the Mount Jackson pitch was the easiest to overcome. He had higher hopes for the tall bridge a quarter mile ahead. It spanned the Shenandoah's North Fork, and although it was solidly built it had never been intended to support such a weight. They pulled the locomotive onto the bridge until Longust shouted, "Stop!" The weight threatened to collapse the bridge. Its timbers groaned and sagged but the indefatigable engineers were equal to the task. They rigged a complicated maze of chains and pulleys to ease the strain. Then, slowly and carefully, the slaves heaved in tandem with the horses to pull Locomotive 199 onto the south bank.

The spring flood had apparently undermined the bank because here the locomotive broke through the macadam surface and listed heavily to one side. Armistead's hopes briefly soared until again the engineers intervened. They directed the slaves to use jacks and timbers to right the monster. Armistead could not help but admire their skills, while also feeling a spurt of pride.

Back in Harpers Ferry, Means had introduced northern railroad men who had openly mocked southern enterprise. The notion that the South was reduced to using horse teams and laborers to try to haul Baltimore and Ohio rolling stock overland along the Valley Pike made them laugh.

"They'll never figure out how to unbolt the extra weight."

"Unless a skilled nigger shows them."

After a volley of great, gasping guffaws, a fleshy railroad executive commented, "Wish I could be there to see it."

"Oh, but you can," Armistead said.

The man had flushed with surprise, indignation, fear. He sucked noisily on his cigar, composed himself, and replied, "Oh, I think we are agreed to leave these little feats of derring-do to you soldier types."

During this time, Means had been silent. He had seen Armistead steadily stiffen as the soldiers and civilians became lubricated with whisky, brandy, wine, and competed to heap scorn upon the South. He recognized the dangerous look in Armistead's eyes and spoke. He addressed his question to a stocky, dark bearded figure who had heretofore been silent, except for the nervous drumming of his fingers: "Colonel, would you please tell Captain Carter what is at stake?"

Without false modesty, but also without braggadocio, the intense Colonel Herman Haupt explained that he was both a West Point graduate and formerly chief of transportation and chief engineer for the Pennsylvania Railroad. "As we learned at cost at Bull Run, this war runs on the railroads," Haupt said. "The South is short of rolling stock, but it particularly lacks motive power. They will find it difficult to keep locomotives running because spare parts are manufactured in the North. They will find it harder to build many, or large locomotives, and impossible to build one like Locomotive 199."

Armistead had quickly grasped that he was in the presence of a man who understood his business. He listened carefully while Haupt explained that Locomotive 199 had been the pride of the Baltimore and Ohio. Stonewall Jackson's men had captured it in nearby Martinsburg. Since Union forces controlled the adjacent rail lines, it looked like the Confederates would be unable to make use of their prize. "Until," Haupt said, "we learned," he made a slight nod toward Means, "that the rebels were trying to move the locomotive directly along the Valley Pike all the way to Staunton. Staunton, as you know, is on the Virginia Central. If it gets there, it can go anywhere in the South."

Haupt paused and looked Armistead squarely in the eye, "That locomotive is worth a division to Jeff Davis. We're hoping you can stop it."

Although he had anticipated that this was coming, Armistead's stomach still knotted painfully. He supposed it could be done. He knew the Valley people and their ways. He could probably intercept the locomotive somewhere along its route. Beyond that, it was impossible to predict. The risk was crazy, but he found that he really didn't care. Besides, he knew that stubborn pride made it difficult to back down before these people. He sighed inwardly, I imagine Means counted on this as well.

The casual way these yankees had dismissed this undertaking as a "little feat of derring-do" irked. He spoke to the group as a whole but looked directly at the little railroad executive: "You know they will hang me if they catch me. So what happens if I don't feel like taking the risk? Will one of you go?"

The railroad executive looked away while fidgeting nervously with his papers. Armistead glanced around the table and one by one they avoided his eyes. His challenge hung on the air unanswered until Means spoke again: "Liverne Taylor will go. If not with you, then he said he's willing to try it alone."

To reach the rendezvous, Armistead passed the turnoff to Fountain Rock. The sight released a flood of memories of the ring tournament and all that had followed. With some effort, he firmly swept them back behind the dam and rode on to find Liverne in an abandoned spring house, cooking a meal over a small fire. After they ate, they settled around the coals, passing a flask of applejack back and forth.

Armistead stared into the fire's remnants. The applejack seemed to release the unbidden memories; the joust against Turner Ashby, Amanda, the Queen of Love and Beauty, Amanda again. "What could I have been thinking? What did it matter now?" An impossible divide separated them. He had tried to bridge the void by forthrightly expressing his longings and his regrets, and had met scornful silence.

"It seems like the blue dogs have bit you," Liverne said.

Armistead gave a thin sigh.

"A woman, I reckon," Liverne said.

"It's that obvious?" Armistead asked.

"You want some advice?"

"Sure."

"Get over it," Liverne said with a laugh. "If a man is going to let himself get down every time a woman disappoints him then he might as well just call it quits."

The next morning they moved on to a Quaker home near Mount Jackson where they collected the draft horse team and prepared their disguises. It was easy enough for Armistead to pass as a patriotic farmer come to help in the grand effort to move the locomotive. He already had calloused hands, bronzed skin, and stained work clothes. A battered slouch hat and a plug of tobacco completed the picture. It had been Liverne's idea that Armistead offer him to the work gang as his "uppity manservant" who had forgotten his place. "A little hard work would serve well to remind him," Armistead would tell the overseer.

The stripes on Liverne's back had been another of Liverne's ideas and it caused their first serious disagreement. In the end Liverne prevailed: "I'm not suggesting I look forward to this, but you know what they'll do to me if they catch me. If I look like a fresh beat slave who needs more of the same, they will see me that way. After that, they will never give me another thought. Then I'll have a chance to recruit some help among the slaves."

Chapter 19. Rude's Hill to Staunton, April 1862

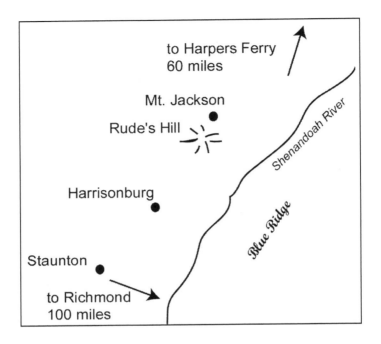

to Harpers Ferry
60 miles

Mt. Jackson

Rude's Hill

Shenandoah River

Harrisonburg

Blue Ridge

Staunton

to Richmond
100 miles

The Valley Pike ascended a thirty-degree incline at Rude's Hill and here Armistead invested his best hope. His hope plunged when he saw the enormous throng standing at the base of the hill. It appeared that every able-bodied civilian in the area, along with hundreds of soldiers, had assembled for the struggle to haul Locomotive 199 up Rude's Hill. The men took hold of the dragropes, the draft horses leaned into their harnesses, and the fight began. They measured progress in small gains; sweat-soaked men and beasts plodding one step at a time; a collective, gasping effort that finally gained the summit of Rude's Hill. It had taken all day to move the locomotive two miles. Ahead lay forty more miles of toil across an increasingly rolling landscape.

All along the route, day after day, curious children, frantic dogs, and old men who said it was madness to drag a locomotive across country, lined the Valley Pike to watch Locomotive 199 slowly advance toward Staunton. During the day, to avoid any chance of being recognized, Armistead stayed way from the crowds. He even avoided the tables laden with refreshments that patriotic ladies served to the hard working crews. "Bad for my stomach," he told the boss man as he sat with his team munching on hardtack, the slouch hat pulled low onto his head. Likewise, at night around the campfire he stayed away from the card games, the drinking, and the cock-fights. "Got to keep up with my sleep," he said.

Three times he managed to talk with Liverne. The first time Armistead asked him whether he could bring anything for his sore back.

"Oh, that wasn't no kind of whuppin. I've felt much worse. The work don't bother me. It's the attitude of these dumb niggers. Most of 'em reckon that they're helping 'massa' win the war, and it makes them happy."

The second time came after days of labor that had brought Locomotive 199 half way to Staunton. "I didn't think they'd make it this far," Liverne said.

"Neither did I," Armistead replied.

Liverne confirmed that they could expect no help from the slaves. With some embarrassment Liverne added, "I ought to tell you that it was because of me that Means got you into this. Back during Christmas I saw what you could do with pulleys and levers and what not, so I figured that this whole deal would be easy."

Armistead gave Liverne a wry look. "When I saw what you could do with pulleys and levers and what not, I knew I couldn't leave you here on your own."

The third conversation came on the expedition's last evening. "So it looks like we get to Staunton tomorrow," Liverne casually stated.

"I know. I've thought about this from every angle. I can't be sure that fraying the harnesses will cause them to break at the right time. Stampeding the horses might work, but I can't figure how to do that without calling a whole lot of attention to us." He nodded toward the picket line where the draft beasts stood eating their evening ration. "Besides, I would hate to see them hurt.

"No, ever since that hill outside Mount Jackson, the same idea keeps coming back to me."

The brakes?" Liverne asked.

Armistead nodded. "The brakes."

Armistead approached the boundary where the fire light met the evening dark. The scrape of the fiddle and the banjo's sweet burble provided a cheerful undertone to the gathering around the campfires. If the gambling was more subdued — the unlucky and unwise no longer had money to wager, the sharps were satisfied to keep their profits close in their pockets — the drinking was more boisterous. Everyone knew that they had over-come daunting obstacles to bring Locomotive 199 to the edge of Staunton, and they were pleased with themselves. They showed their pleasure by sharing canteens, flasks, and bottles. Soon the fighting would begin.

It was time, yet Armistead found himself unwilling to leave the anony-mous safety of the shadows at camp's edge. He fingered the wrench in his pocket and considered. Later, when the alcohol took its toll and the camp fell silent, there would be fewer people moving about, perhaps no one at all. But if he encountered anyone, it would be harder to explain why he was still awake. Worse, during tomorrow's inevitable investigation someone might recall seeing him prowling around the locomotive. The fiddler launched into a reel. His bowing was unpolished, but the banjo's percussive notes smoothed the music's rough edges to create a soaring, spirited sound that compelled a response. As the men around the fires began to dance, Armistead headed toward the Valley Pike where Locomotive 199 rested.

Even stripped of all extraneous weight, the locomotive still looked like a mighty slumbering beast. He approached the side and slipped between the massive wheels at the rear of the machine. Kneeling beneath the engineer's compartment, he reached up until his questing hand found the brake linkage. He ran his fingers along the linkage until he felt the twin hexagonal nuts and lock washers used to adjust the tension. Eight and one-quarter turns caused the linkage to sag to the point where any pressure on the brake handle would cause it to disconnect.

A pair of voices grew louder, and louder still. Armistead waited motionless. The men stopped just on the other side of the rear driving wheel. Armistead saw their legs silhouetted against a gray-black background.

"I reckon I'd better oil her one last time," someone said.

Armistead's stomach clenched, the fear bile rising to attack, burn, and unman. He slid the wrench into his pocket and reached for his knife.

"I'll help you out," spoke a badly slurred voice.

I'll take the sober one first, Armistead thought. The splash of liquid spray on steel caused him to relax his grip. He waited until the men departed, counted to one hundred, and crawled out from beneath Locomotive 199.

The dawn bugle woke the teamster camp. Around the fire rings, shattered, crapulous figures struggled to their feet. Since they were volunteers and therefore outside the bonds of military discipline, they might have ignored the bugle's summons. But this was the last day on their contract, the payday, and therefore worth rising.

The servants rekindled the camp fires to boil coffee. Awake, if not restored, the teamsters formed a ragged circle and discussed future prospects. Most had volunteered their time and their teams out of a sense of patriotism. The generous pay, an even ten dollars — nearly a month's wages for a soldier in service — had tipped the scales for the indecisive.

"It won't be coin, of course," a grey-haired driver said.

"So what?" a young farmer replied. "Money is money, and me and the missus will be needing all we can get to buy seed. We figure on planting fence row to fence row and selling to the army contractors."

The grey-haired man looked at him with a mix of contempt and pity. "My great granddaddy hauled grain for Washington. The army men paid with paper. We still got a bunch chinking the logs in the smokehouse if you be needing some." The grey-haired man gave a thin screech of laughter that dissolved into a dry, hacking cough.

A Mennonite farmer spoke: "What worries me are the prices. Around Staunton and Lexington, what cost a dollar last year costs two dollars now."

"Well I don't give a damn. I got plenty."

Armistead turned to glance at the speaker, a weedy, unshaven figure with darting, red-rimmed eyes.

Another teamster, a heavily bearded, burly man with an ugly scar jutting from his bloodshot left eye to his jawline, spoke, "I reckon you do Weasel. Least after last night's game you got all of mine."

Several teamsters hooted. Armistead heard someone mutter, "First Archie couldn't hold his liquor, then he couldn't hold his cards. Could see everyone of 'em when it mattered."

"Whole family is like that. His daddy is just a toper. The sons mostly the same. Only thing they're good at is starting a scrap. Don't know about young Travis. He done picked up and left one day after his daddy pulled out the whip one time too many. Travis busted up old Junius's face pretty good before he left."

"Probably improved his looks," someone added. Again there was general laughter.

Archibald Kirwin seemed oblivious to the crowd. He took a long pull from his flask. Some liquid slopped from the flask, spilling onto his beard to mix with the tobacco juice and spittle that already flecked his beard. He ignored the dribble and fixed Weasel with a malevolent look.

Weasel seemed to enjoy the attention. He stepped into the center of the circle and pulled a fist full of notes from his pocket. He turned to face Armistead: "Say mister, you want to sell your nigger?"

"Now that he's learned to work again, I don't reckon I do," Armistead replied.

"Best be careful with a big buck like him. I'd flog him regularly. A good purge is good for 'em my daddy always said."

Before Armistead could respond, Kirwin interjected: "You had a daddy, Weasel? I declare that's news to me. I always figured you sprung full grown from under some rock."

The men standing near to Kirwin backed away uneasily. Weasel's entire demeanor transformed. Armistead saw that his eyes ceased their wild, spasmodic movement. His face relaxed, except for the veins above his temples. They became engorged and an angry red flush spread down across his neck. The hand holding the money barely wavered, but the other hand slid slowly into his trouser pocket.

A hint of a smile creased his face and then he turned with amazing speed. His left hand and arm were almost a blur. Armistead registered something shiny flash from his hand and then heard an agonized shriek. He saw Kirwin stagger, his hands briefly clutch at his throat from where twin jets of blood spurted from either side of the blade, and then collapse.

Weasel turned back to face Armistead. "So, like I was saying, flog him regular and if you should ever change you mind, I might be interested in buying."

Armistead and Liverne watched from a hillside overlooking the Valley Pike. They saw Chief Engineer Longust supervise the remaining teamsters and the uniformed soldiers as they prepared Locomotive 199 for its descent into Staunton. The Pike ran down a moderate slope before bending around a marshy bottomland and continuing into the city. The locomotive slowly gathered momentum. The wheels rotated faster and faster, like a giant pinwheel. Shouts, increasingly strident, then a drum, a bugle, two bugles; the noise merged with the shriek of metal on macadam to create panic-tinged cacophony. Locomotive 199 was now clearly out of control. It reached the bottomland, failed to negotiate the curve, and plunged over the verge. It came to rest on its side and slowly settled into the marsh.

Armistead exhaled slowly. He had not realized that he had been holding his breath. "I reckon we best avoid the Valley Pike until we pass beyond the picket posts," he said.

"I agree, but I'll be turning off here," Liverne replied.

"You're not coming with me?" Armistead asked in surprise.

"No, I have in mind to visit a special lady," Liverne casually said.

Images of the Taylor family, Liverne playing with his children, Jolina, passed through Armistead's mind. He coldly replied, "I trust you don't have to go far."

"It would help if I could take the cars, but that don't seem in the cards."

"Stop teasing me, Liverne. Either you are going to tell me where you're heading or you're not."

"Richmond."

"Richmond!" Armistead exploded. "Good God, man. You do like courting danger."

"I'm not going to Richmond to court," Liverne answered.

"But you said it was to see a special lady?"

"Yes," Liverne said. "I won't tell you her name, but she used to operate a station. Sometimes she supplies us with very detailed information about rebel movements. Too detailed, some say. But Means insists that she is reliable. I have to go find out."

Armistead reached out to shake hands. "Be careful, Liverne."

"I always am," he replied.

Chapter 20. Loudoun County and the Shenandoah Valley, April 1862

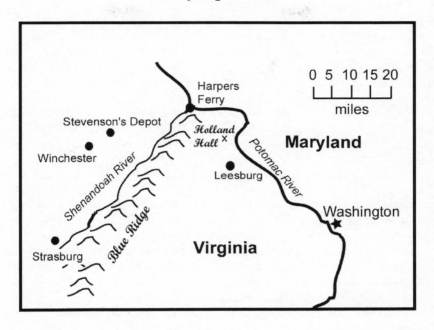

General Pierre Gustave Toutant Beauregard's appeal for plantation bells and metal to be cast into cannon and munitions came to Loudoun County in late April. The local congregations donated their church bells. Tenant farmers sacrificed preserving kettles for manufacture into percussion caps. When the collection wagon came to Holland Hall, Amanda insisted that they give both. A little negro child saw the servants load the preserving kettle onto a wagon and asked, "But what shall we do for preserves?"

"My child," answered Squire Holland, "we think now only of preserving our country."

That evening, Amanda sat at her desk to sort again through the plantation's accounts. Rich in land, rich in slaves, cash poor; it had been that way for as long as she could recall. She knew that next week the note covering her father's unwise investment in more slaves came due. He had never told her the amount, but it hardly mattered because there was no money with which to pay. We will have to give the bank some more land, I suppose, Amanda bleakly reflected. Hopefully Rixey will be content with that scrub land on the ridge. Since we logged it, it's not been much good for anything but it's adjacent to the parcel he bought last spring so I imagine he will be glad enough to nibble another bite from us. I wonder why Rixey has been sniffing hard around our borders this past year. That odious, grasping, she paused, not proud of the word half-formed in her mind. Then she resumed her angry flow: that toad seems always to know just when we are desperate.

Footsteps interrupted her train of thought. She saw her father weave his way into the library. Usually by this time he was asleep in bed. She saw he had a paper in one hand and an empty glass in the other. He walked with sagging shoulders, taking short, halting steps, looking haggard and old beyond his years. He pulled himself erect when he saw Amanda and visibly brightened. Still, he spoke with something of a slur, "That was a noble thing you did today, my daughter. I am proud of you."

He leaned to kiss her on her cheek, his breath reeking of brandy. "That poor child," Amanda said, "when she saw the preserving kettle disappear she looked crushed. I don't think she understood your explanation. She probably thinks the country is some kind of giant, preserved peach."

The Squire retreated to the sideboard to refresh his glass. Amanda saw that the nearly empty bottle came from a select stock reserved for special occasions. She started to ask her father why, but he interrupted, "I know you will preserve Holland Hall, Amanda. Whether it is for Boyd or your own children, I know you will do what must be done."

She gazed at him quizzically, but she had learned that there was no point in serious conversation when he was disguised with drink. She was still working at her desk an hour later when a muffled explosion brought the household running to her father's bedroom.

He sat in his favorite rocker, the article of furniture he valued above all others because it had once belonged to his wife's family and dated back to 1649. He had sat in it while paying court to his future bride, rocking on her porch during languid summer evenings, hovering close to the fire when winter cold drove all indoors. The chair had been beneath the mistletoe when he had first kissed her, and it had been in the shadows at crowd's edge during a July barn dance and here she had first kissed him back. It had come as part of her dowry because he insisted. He said that he had spent so much time in it pursuing his wife that they had established a special bond. It would be disloyal to abandon it now that he had won his prize. He had joked that he would probably die in this chair, and he had.

The next morning she returned to his room. He had apparently tried to ignite a fire in the hearth. Several documents had been completely consumed but two had merely burned at the edges and remained legible. Amanda read them and it was as if she had struck by a blow. She staggered backwards and collapsed heavily onto his bed.

Time passed. James came and was told to leave, then Nell, then, much later James again. He found her sitting in the rocker gazing out the window at the mountains to the west. "I am alright, James. I am sorry to have been rude, but I am fine now."

They buried him on the hillside plot where his wife had been waiting these past three years and more. A surprising number of people found their way to the service, for he had been well liked. Many remarked upon Amanda's resilient composure, a few detected chilly politeness when they pressed close to express their sorrow.

The next week Amanda returned to her diary. "May has arrived late but now it is here," she wrote. "The terrible fall of New Orleans comes so unexpectedly. What a blow! Sugar gone, Texas beef gone, leather, horses, all lost to us. Now begins the War of Endurance. Let me write the names of my commanders. Endurance — Patience — Faith — these be the captains under whose banner I enlist."

On the northern outskirts of Winchester, Min waited while the farrier fitted a new shoe for his horse. He leaned against a post to watch the Valley Army march by. They bore scant resemblance to the regiments that had passed through Winchester almost one year ago. Their patched and stained uniforms looked like beggars' clothes. They were lean, weathered, hairy; many were barefoot. Yet they marched with the swagger of the victor, men who had recently defeated the enemy and were certain that they would do it again. Indeed, they had almost trapped Union General Nathaniel Banks' army at Strasburg and recently ejected him from Winchester. They were supremely confident in their own General Jackson while Banks was the object of their derision. They called the yankee general 'Commissary Banks' because captures from his army — food, ammunition, wagons — provided for most of their needs. However, Old Jack wanted more, which was why he was driving them hard toward Harpers Ferry.

Min observed that the pace was taking a toll. A handful of men collapsed by the road while many footsore soldiers simply sat down to rest. A faint, distant yell came from back along the Valley Pike. The infantry on either side of the road stirred as the shouts grew louder. The tired men stood as word spread along the column: "It's Jackson! It's Jackson." A lone rider galloped into view. Soldiers lined the pike to wave their hats and cheer. Looking neither left nor right, Jackson passed at a furious pace. The cheering subsided and then he was gone.

His passage energized the column. The soldiers resumed the march with spring in their step. Most of the stragglers hurried to join them. They passed a knot of women and children standing outside a brick house. The civilians waved tiny Confederate flags. The seated figure of a young man could be seen behind an upstairs window. The soldiers began to jeer:

"Does your mother know you're up there?"

"It's safe. You can come on down. These children will protect you."

"Come join the cavalry, we always have a heap of fun."

Some began hooting like an owl. With heavy stress on the first word, they chorused, "Who-are-you?"

The figure stirred from the upper window. Laboring awkwardly, he propped himself upright on a crutch. He was missing a leg. Deeply shamed, the owl calls turned to cheers. The nearest unit paused to present arms and salute. Then the march north resumed.

Unnoticed amidst the commotion was the figure of Jason Taylor. The black youth recorded the numbers of men and cannon in the way that he had been taught, until the last rank of soldiers passed. He slipped through a back alley, mounted a horse, and rode hard toward Harpers Ferry.

Min rejoined the Loudoun Grays on a hilltop near Stevenson's Depot. In the bottomland below, some Federal cavalry had deployed on either side of the Valley Pike. They stood about three hundred yards in front of a bridge spanning a small creek. On the bridge's far side was another unit in column, apparently stationed as supports.

"It looks like they mean business," Min said to Travis. Travis grinned and spat. The deep voice of Colonel Dulany spoke: "Attention Seventh Cavalry. Draw sabers. Charge!" The bugle sounded and the line surged forward.

For Min, the next two minutes passed as if he had entered nightmarish world where sense of time and space yielded to a demonic passion to kill and chase and kill again. At first it looked like the opposing horsemen would advance to meet the Seventh Virginia. As Min urged his horse from a trot to canter he saw the yankees begin a slow forward movement. Colonel Dulany, leading from the front as always, struck his horse, Black Hawk, with the flat of his saber and the horse accelerated into a gallop. The Virginia troopers cheered and the noise appeared to unnerve their enemies. What had been a neat line of opposing horsemen suddenly dissolved into a disorganized mass as individual troopers wheeled about and rode hard for the bridge. Then the Confederates were on them.

Min saw a blue coated trooper just ahead. The man was obviously a poor rider. He was clinging with both hands to his horse's mane, his saber, attached by a cord to his wrist, banged against his mount's neck, causing the animal to jig sideways. As he had learned in his fencing lessons, Min delivered a stiff-wristed strike against the man's exposed side and felt his blade glance off of a rib and plunge deep into the torso. His horse's speed carried him past and allowed him to pull his saber free. Min briefly registered the fact that a bright red color stained his saber's point and then he found himself abreast another foe.

This man was armed, but like the first opponent was no rider at all. He had lost the rhythm of his horse so that his bottom slapped hard against his saddle with every stride. As Min presented his saber he saw a wild-eyed look of terror, framed by long black hair and thick beard. The man tried to parry Min's stroke, but Min easily slipped his guard and plunged his point into his breast.

212

Min heard the bugle sound and saw Dulany motioning for the regiment to wheel to the right. The yankees were jammed up against the bridge. Min understood Dulany's intent. He screamed his order, "Follow me Loudoun Grays, we're going to outflank them."

A two-hundred-yard gallop brought them to a ford. They splashed across the creek and climbed a ridge parallel to the Valley Pike. Min saw that the yankees had entirely lost their order. They looked like a mob of leaderless men, riding fast toward Harpers Ferry. A bugler sounded the charge. Again Min found himself riding in the midst of the Union cavalry. Most of them had discarded their weapons and seemed intent upon escape. Min saw Lieutenant Granville Smith slash with his saber repeatedly. Smith's strikes left bloody welts on back and shoulder but otherwise had little effect. Min heard someone, he thought it was Dulany, shout, "Use your pistols boys, kill them all!" In response, the Confederate troopers took up the cry "Kill! Kill! Kill!" Later, Min recalled that he too was shrieking the same.

Min passed a Union trooper, lowered his revolver, and shot him in the hip. "Surrender you yankee son of a bitch!" Min saw the man merely spur his horse harder and so fired a second time. He hit him in the neck, causing him topple from the saddle. On and on Min galloped, shooting one man in the back, missing another but hitting his horse; unholstering his second revolver to shoot until there were no more to kill.

The Loudoun Grays reformed near the bridge. The exhilaration of victory was on them. They laughed and swapped stories. Typically, Bush Underwood had a small crowd gathered around him as he described his exploits. Underwood explained how he had just come even with a yankee and was in the process of finding out how hard a blow to the head a yankee could take without falling, when the bugle sounded the recall. Some troopers laughed. Others looked down at their feet or turned away. Min realized that he had not seen Underwood at any time after the initial charge.

"Where's Travis?" he asked Kinlock.

"I thought he was with you," Kinlock replied.

They found him face down on the earth. Min knelt and gently turned him over. His head lolled unnaturally, an unfocused, already lifeless look in his eyes. Min stood up unsteadily and startled to feel pressure against his shoulder. It was the boy's horse. The roan nickered gently and then pawed the ground near his rider. Leaving the horse to stand guard over the fallen figure, Min staggered a few steps away and wept.

Chapter 21. Shenandoah Valley, May 1862

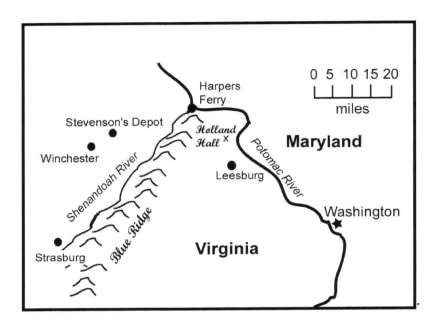

They buried Travis where he fell. That night it was Kinlock who figured it out. While sifting though Travis's meager possessions he came across a neatly folded piece of paper. The paper had been torn from what was apparently a family bible. Someone literate, probably a reverend or preacher, had recorded the family tree. His name was Travis Kirwin, the fourth of five sons born to Junius and Josie. Opposite the family tree was a crude sketch of two men standing beneath the banner of the Winchester Rifles.

Later, Fatty Dudley provided the rest. A return for Company F, the Winchester Rifles, Second Virginia Infantry, Stonewall Brigade listed two Kirwin brothers. A clerk had recorded their occupations: farmer; laborer. One had died at First Manassas; a second had lost a leg and an arm at the Battle of Kernstown in March 1862 and died in late April.

The next day the chase continued. Shedding men and equipment, 'Commissary' Banks fled north to safety over the Potomac. Since it seemed unlikely that Dulany's cavalry would have any duty for the next few days, except to gorge on oysters, tinned meat, and exotic delicacies 'liberated' from a sutler wagon, Min received permission from Turner Ashby to do what had to be done. He wrapped Travis's possessions in a blanket roll, placed a lock of his hair in a watch fob he purchased in Winchester, and rode toward the western mountains to notify the Kirwin's of their most recent loss.

On the second day of the ride the forest track narrowed and began to climb more steeply. God damn pig path, reflected Min sourly. Beneath the dripping canopy of trees, the shadows merged to form a gray-black, all enveloping shroud. Somewhere in the distance the seven-note query of a great horned owl probed once, and then once again. "Damnation!" Min muttered wearily, "it's growing late." His empty belly rumbled. It had been a taxing ride, made easier only by the occasional pull on the flask of newly distilled corn mash that Kinlock had pressed upon him.

Finally the deeply rutted track entered a clearing. Draining the flask, Min studied the terrain. From somewhere ahead a smoke plume rose listlessly above the trees. As he emerged from the forest gloom into the twilight, Min's spirits lifted. Straightening himself in the saddle he wondered if the family might feed him.

"Mama, Mama! There's soldiers again. I believe they're us uns."

Min saw a slender, gangly youth running toward a log cabin at the far end of the clearing. His shouts brought the figure of a woman to the cabin's door. Riding toward the cabin, Min passed between a sparse field of stunted wheat and a torn pea patch whose few thin vines were almost engulfed by a robust crop of weeds. A short section of locust rail fence remained intact. It paralleled the track, running from the cabin toward the clearing where it stopped abruptly. From that point on were charred rail ends, ashes, and piles of fresh animal bones. Min passed a hog pen. It was empty. Farther along he saw a chicken coop, its door hanging from one broken hinge, two scrawny birds pecking forlornly at the ground. Min dismounted in front of the cabin, drew himself erect and saluted. "Ma'am, I'm looking for a Mister and Miz Kirwin."

She was a small woman. Perhaps once she had been pretty. Now she merely looked old, her face lined and worn, a bonnet pulled tight against her skull beneath which fell a few tendrils of dirty grey-brown hair. Her thin arm draped around the youth who now stood by her side. She mumbled, "Yes sir, I be her."

Min caught himself staring at the woman. When her mouth opened to speak it showed a gaping dark hole, its outline relieved only by the presence of one stained front tooth. A flea crawled along the furrows of her forehead.

Min spoke again. "Seems like you've had visitors."

She opened her mouth to reply. A rancid odor struck Min's nostrils. "Yup. Yankee cavalry. Three nights ago they come. They done ate my pigs and chickens, trampled my peas, and used my fence rails for campfires. The mister, he bin gone for nigh on five months now. Wasn't no count no how. Three my five boys went off with the army. Archie is driving horses for Genril Jackson. Harry here couldn't do nuthing to stop 'em."

"I see." Min paused and tried to collect himself. "Uh, I'm sorry to have, er, to have to report, ma'am." Min's voice trailed off.

"It's about Travis, ain't it?"

She gave Min a hard look and then flatly declared, "He's dead."

"Uh, yes mam." Pulling out a sheet containing the standard phrases, Min read the brief message. As the last words, "your gallant son thus fell while helping earn a most important victory," Min's eyes lifted to look at this Confederate mother.

She blinked once, and then again. "I figgered that's why you cum." There was a long silence.

Awkwardly Min said, "I'm so sorry missus. Travis had become a friend to me." He looked away.

The owl cried again. On the wing now, its call came more clearly. From the nearby farm pond the broken banjo string sound of the green frogs provided harsh counterpoint.

Finally the woman spoke: "Travis, he be the third son I've lost." Her voice faded, another pause, and then: "You tell Genril Jackson that as soon as I can get a few things together, he shall have Harry too."

Chapter 22. Loudoun County, May 1862

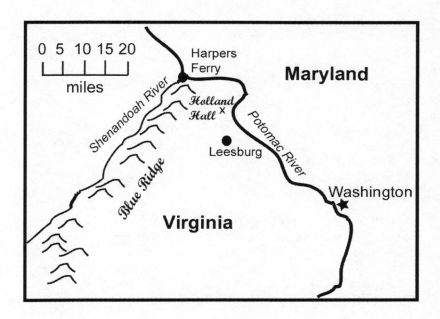

The death of her father removed a major source of companionship. Old family friends came when they could, and them she welcomed. But their visits were infrequent, in part, because they too had recent sorrows to cope with. Also, the war had interrupted the flow of commerce upon which isolated farms depended for both their livelihoods and for news of the outside world. Consequently, visits from men of business, however sporadic, were usually welcome. But not today. Clarence Rixey had come to discuss the future of Holland Hall. He insisted that Gordon be present, and made his demand with an affected warmth that Amanda found chilling.

His appearance surprised her because she had supposed that Rixey would wait a decent interval following the death of the Squire. But she knew that he would come sooner or later and understood that her private chess match was entering the end game. She composed herself, rang for a servant, and told her to bring some cheese and nuts. Then, Amanda herself went to the cabinet, selected an indifferent bottle of brandy, and poured two brimming glasses. She excused herself — "you had a daughter, Mister Rixey, I am sure you understand" — and departed. She left them puzzled, but she also left them with an open decanter.

When she returned, the decanter stood empty. No food had arrived. "Where is that serving girl?" she angrily asked. "I'll have the hide off her."

In fact, she had ordered the kitchen to bring neither food nor water. She sat down and studied her opponents. An alcohol flush showed on both men. Perspiration beaded on Rixey's forehead. He was plainly nervous.

She looked at him expectantly.

"Amanda...I may call you that may I not?"

She sat impassively.

"Your father and I were very close. And I know that he wanted me to look after you. So, I am here today to make an offer to purchase Holland Hall."

"All of it?" Amanda asked.

Her question seemed to startle him. "Why, er, well yes," he stammered.

"And where would I live, Mister Rixey? Not to mention Boyd."

He reached for his glass, saw that it was empty, and reluctantly replaced it. "Er, well, I should think that a, uh..."

"Spinster, Mister Rixey?" As she intended, her hectoring knocked him off his stride. He was flustered and then angry, although he tried to conceal it.

"Now Amanda," his friendly tone had returned, "I have known you and your family root and branch. I have nothing but your best interests at heart in making what I must say is a magnanimous offer."

"You needn't proceed, Mister Rixey, we are not interested."

He sighed dramatically in an unsuccessful effort to convey sorrow and reached into his valise. Amanda saw Gordon's habitually indolent posture become alert. My, said Amanda inwardly, his eyes positively gleam with greed.

Rixey proceeded: "I am sorry to have to bring this note to your attention, but I have a duty to my bank and its investors." He handed Amanda a legal document.

Had she not already known the sum required, her nerves might have balked at the staggering figure. Instead, she cast her eyes quickly over the document and laughed.

"Really, Mister Rixey, you needn't have gone to all the trouble of delivering this yourself. Howsoever, since you are here, I believe we can meet this obligation straight away." She went to her desk and unlocked a drawer. She knew that she had their complete attention but carefully positioned herself to obstruct partially their view. "Oh, silly me, I am distracted today. Is that note for fifteen hundred or fifteen thousand, Mister Rixey?"

The alcohol had nearly reached full flood. Rixey looked bemused, his pendulous lips and mottled face reminded Amanda of one of the small-mouthed bass that she and Boyd used to catch in the Potomac.

"It is for fifteen hundred, Miz Holland," Gordon flatly declared. The gleam was gone, replaced by a quizzical look.

"Oh, indeed." She ostentatiously replaced several stacks of bills into the drawer and returned with an envelope which she handed to the banker.

Although she pretended to watch Rixey as he opened the envelope, her sidelong gaze focused on Gordon. She had the satisfaction of seeing a look of pure surprise cross the Englishman's face as Rixey's thick fingers extracted a pile of United States greenbacks.

"If I am not being indiscreet, Miz Amanda, may I ask where this came from?" Rixey inquired.

"Oh, but you are, Mister Rixey."

There was a long silence. Then Rixey spoke again and this time all warmth was gone from his voice: "This is most excellent, of course. What you may not know is that I, or rather my bank, holds several more large notes and that another comes due..."

"On September fifteenth," Amanda interjected. "Fortunately, business has improved and my South Carolina kin have kindly repaid a few of their own notes that my father, in Boyd and my names, underwrote sometime ago. Now gentlemen, if that is all?"

Their departure left her drained. For a moment she considered pouring a glass for herself but managed to check the impulse. She returned to the drawer and removed the money. A single greenback wrapped around a stack of depreciated Confederate currency composed each bundle. Likewise, her story about her South Carolina relatives was hollow. They lived near the coast and Aunt Tilly's letters informed her that because of frequent raids from the Union navy, their situation was, if anything, worse than her own. Instead, the money she had given Rixey came from Baltimore.

Brook Morgan had eventually recovered from his wound and departed for his Maryland home. They had managed to stay in touch and he had been eager to repay his obligation for the care he had received. A courier had taken a parcel with her mother's jewels to him during a trip north. Three weeks later he returned with a letter from Brook of surprising tenderness as well as the precious money.

She reconsidered and poured herself a small glass of Madeira. She took it upstairs to her father's room and sat in the rocker. Her defense hinged on a gambit of extraordinary risk: the strategy that her opponents would concede or accept a stalemate if they believed that she possessed bountiful reserves. The sacrifice of one of her capital pieces had surprised them and given them something to consider. It had certainly bought time, but she well knew that she had little more to sacrifice and that her king now stood exposed. She despondently acknowledged to herself that her gambit was more akin to a card game of bluff than to scientific chess.

Outside the red-brick building that served as Gordon's office, the Englishman looked at his ally with contempt. Rixey was sprawled in his carriage, fast asleep and snoring loudly. Gordon instructed the driver to take him back to Leesburg. He did not provide an escort. The driver raised an eyebrow in surprise and opened his mouth to speak. Gordon snapped, "You heard me. Get on with it," and gave the team a stinging slap. He didn't particularly care if Rixey safely reached his destination because the man had outlived his usefulness.

Gordon lit a thin cheroot and considered: "A good tumble with one of the girls at Meme Richard's would set me up just fine," he thought. "Business first though." He sat down to think. He well knew all the details of the Squire's outstanding notes, or so he had thought. Once Rixey gained control, Gordon possessed knowledge that Rixey could never afford to have revealed. Instead, the banker would have conceded control of Holland Hall to him alone. Somehow, the bitch had thwarted him.

To date he had refrained from directing Overmeyer's raiders against Holland Hall. It was tempting now to settle scores. Patience, my lad, patience, he said to himself. Won't do to depreciate a valuable asset. He puffed contemplatively, idly blowing smoke rings that drifted toward the open window. He glanced outside to see Gwen walk past, carrying a bucket of slops for the hogs.

Gwen stepped lightly over the stile leading to the hog pen. She moved with unconscious grace and although her figure had not completely filled, Gordon observed a pleasing curve to her chest and hips. Her long legs emphasized her firm, high bottom. I wonder if she is still fresh, he thought. Gordon involuntarily rose to summon her. Her image, firmly bound and gagged — don't want her screams to interrupt me — almost drove all else from his mind. She disappeared around the corner and he paused.

Ever since his proclivities became known, his contract specified that he refrain from using the slave girls. Thereafter, the knowledge that they, and all other property would be his alone, had compelled adherence to the rules. "Meddling bitch!" He angrily tossed away his cheroot and composed himself. So those Carolina relatives had repaid some note to Amanda and her brother. Her brother; heretofore he had given little thought to Boyd. Why not invite the boy to come along to Meme Richard's? The outline of a new plan took shape. Gordon smiled and lit another cheroot.

Chapter 23. Shenandoah Valley, June 1862

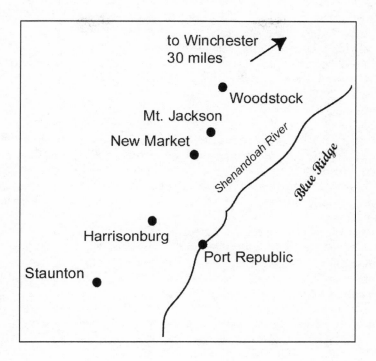

The Confederate cavalry deployed astride the Valley Pike. They were the rear guard, the soldiers entrusted with preventing the pursuing Union army from destroying Jackson's retreating army. The retreat had begun on May 30 when the Union forces reversed their exodus from the Valley and instead prepared a trap. The hunter became the hunted. Although he recognized that the strategic calculus had shifted, Stonewall Jackson was loath to discard his campaign's booty. Consequently, an immense jumble of captured U.S. Army wagons, civilian buckboards, surreys, coaches, and carts accompanied the Valley Army. The army marched south from Winchester through Strasburg, Woodstock, and New Market; and always Ashby's vigilant rear guard stood between its slow moving mass and the enemy.

Wherever the terrain favored the defense — along streams, atop ridges, in woodlots bordering the Pike — the Confederate cavalry stood as if to fight. This forced the pursuers to move off the Pike and deploy into long battle lines in preparation for attack. But just before the overwhelming blow fell, the cavalry nimbly retired, only to do the same thing again a few miles farther south. It took skill to select the right positions and a great sense of timing to know when to retreat. Because he possessed these talents, Turner Ashby was in his element.

He was recently promoted. Just two weeks ago orders had come from Richmond that assigned Ashby to command all Jackson's cavalry. He responded with renewed zeal. He was the first to arrive on the battlefield to scout the enemy and the last to depart after he ordered a withdrawal. He rode a magnificent black stallion and wore a beautiful plumed hat, an unmistakable presence to friend and foe alike. And that was what Andrew Bennington was counting on when he left his plantation to ride to Winchester, dressed in a Union cavalry uniform.

Armistead leaned forward to stroke Blue's neck. His stiff, new uniform restricted his reach. He recalled the pride he had felt when the tailor had sewn on the shoulder straps with their two, gold-embroidered leafs indicating his promotion to major. He wondered if he stood out among the officers who accompanied General George Bayard's cavalry brigade as they marched along Winchester's Main Street, and hoped that the answer was no.

The crossroads town of Winchester sat at the bottom of the Shenandoah Valley, its location like a cork in a bottle. To exit the Valley and go north or enter the Valley and head south, one had to move through Winchester. Since the war began, the town had changed hands repeatedly. It must be a trial, Armistead reflected, to go to sleep safely in the possession of a friendly army and to awake to find the enemy at the door.

The column was just passing the Taylor Hotel. Nearby stood a small group of anxious looking women and children. Armistead heard a woman ask, "What regiment is that?"

One of Bayard's officers replied: "First Pennsylvania."

"Hurrah for Pennsylvania! Hurrah for Pennsylvania!" the women chorused. The children's high voices joined in. The timing of one little boy's cheer was slightly off. As the cheer faded, his thin voice piped, "Hurrah for Pennsylnanee Sout Caliny!"

"Hush, hush, hush!" his mother scolded, but it was too late.

One of Bayard's aides commented, "Well, the cat is out of the bag now."

Armistead saw the Union troopers accept it with good humor. As each company filed past the red-faced woman, the soldiers cheered, "Hurrah for Pennsylnanee Sout Caliny" and presented arms in salute.

The cavalry departed Winchester to continue south on the Valley Pike. The detachment from the Loudoun Rangers remained with Bayard's headquarters group because the general wanted men who possessed local knowledge to guide him as he chased down Jackson's army. It began to rain. But the sight of abandoned baggage, broken down horses, and ever more frequent Confederate stragglers informed them that Jackson's army was not far off, so Bayard's men pressed ahead with vigor. To their frustration, although they came close several times, they seemed unable to force the foe to fight. Instead, they followed in Jackson's wake, like a tireless, questing pack determined to run the fox to ground.

Across the mountains to the east, Amanda sat alone in the rocker listening to the noise of the rain-lashed roof. She reminded herself that the sound of wind-driven droplets on the roof always made the storm seem worse then it was. Still, the unrelenting drumbeat of rain made it hard to look at the future with confidence.

She had lost her brother and doubted her ability to recall him. A short time ago it had appeared easy. When she explained their position, Boyd had loudly proclaimed that he would step into the role of Squire of Holland Hall. Thereafter, Amanda tried to involve him in the plantation's business, but he showed neither interest nor aptitude. Instead, she observed that he began spending increasing amounts of time with Gordon. Indeed, he responded to her challenge to help save their home place by asking, "Why study sums and papers when we have paid Gordon to perform this work?" Boyd also claimed that his military duty required much of his time, but Amanda heard that he passed most evenings in the local taverns.

Her journal sat in her lap. Unlike the gift Armistead had given her a lifetime ago, this journal contained no fine paper with beautiful scroll work etched along the borders. Nonetheless, the ordinary, ruled pages, the printed month and year in the upper right corner, gave order in a world set on end. By the light of a single candle she entered the date: June 1, 1862. The entry brought a pang of hurt. Nearly a year ago — the lifetime ago she now wished to forget — she had journeyed to Turner Ashby's celebration of midsummer's night eve, and there had failed to find what she had sought. Regardless, she understood that her worries then and now were small compared to the events taking place all around her.

She began to write: "In these war times, when we have no visitors to receive and no visits to pay, when books seem impossibly foreign, and only the newspapers hold my interest as I try to follow the path of our armies and the fate of our neighbors and friends, I believe I shall keep a journal. I shall confide in my journal as I would a friend. The question presents itself: what sort of friend will I choose? A respectable maiden aunt? Aunty Hag would be perplexed by the anxieties I feel. A discreet female? I know none. An intimate school mate? He has gone to war. An older and attached governess or teacher? I am now the same age as my childhood tutor, Miss Letitia. Why do I not have her wisdom? Still, upon reflection, I think my confidante shall be a female, older than myself and far wiser. She has the sweet nature that I wish were my own, and a loving interest in my family that induces me to share my thoughts. I have never had such a friend and I shall love her so much."

Amanda set down her quill and read what she had written. She felt shame for her weakness. She reached to tear out the page but checked herself by an act of will. Surely, she thought, to be intimate with her imaginary friend was harmless. She resolved to continue her journal, if only from time to time, because she realized that without such a friend she could not endure.

For the officers serving under Turner Ashby, the previous days had been an exhilarating mix of sudden, rapid movement and occasional brief, fierce fighting. Not even the incessant rains had dampened their spirits. On the morning of June 6, between Harrisonburg and Port Republic, the retreat ground to a halt when Jackson's eight-mile-long wagon train became stuck in the mud. Upon hearing this news, Ashby summoned his officers to conference.

Recently there had been little time for rest and less for meals, so the smell of fresh biscuit, ham, and coffee caused Min to salivate greedily even before he dismounted. A broad smile opened in the middle of Ashby's thick beard. He gestured to a camp table: "Come, my friend, share breakfast with us while I explain what we are about."

Min eagerly joined the other officers at the table.

"Gentlemen, our army is bogged down and in peril," Ashby said. "It's up to us to hold here until it can move to safety."

Ashby pointed across a valley to a wood line where a Union force had begun to deploy. "And, as you see, the yankees are up to something."

The boom of artillery fire resounded from the trees. A shell exploded nearby and then, in quick succession two more.

An anxious staff officer spoke, "Sir, I believe they are sighting in on our headquarters."

"Never mind that. I am very hungry," Ashby replied. He sat down and began to eat, utterly indifferent to the rain of shells. In between bites he told Min, "I never worry about the bullets that are aimed at me. It's those random shots I fear, they always seem to hit someone for whom they were not intended."

Shortly thereafter, the Union fire trailed off and the rest of the morning was quiet.

Armistead had learned that Bayard's officers neither liked nor trusted the Loudoun Rangers. Whenever something unpleasant had to be done, they selected a ranger to do it. An aide instructed Armistead to guide several companies of Union infantry on a scout of a nearby woods. Armistead mildly observed, "I've never been here before."

With obvious distaste, the aide replied, "So?"

As they worked their way deeper into the trees, Armistead admired how the infantry moved with the practiced ease of stalking hunters. Then he noticed that each soldier wore a deer tail attached to his kepi. He learned that they belonged to Colonel Thomas Kane's Pennsylvania Bucktails, select soldiers recruited from experienced outdoorsmen, the deer tail a badge symbolizing their status as crack marksmen. The Bucktails silently passed into the shadows, their white buck tails rising above the underbrush like vigilant deer with tails raised in alarm. Absorbed by their presence, Armistead did not notice a squat, red-faced Union cavalry trooper who flitted nearby as he carefully moved to a position behind a split rail fence. Andrew Bennington steadied his Sharps rifle on a locust rail and waited.

Some seventy yards away, Armistead reached the woods edge. Nearby, skirmish pairs belonging to the Bucktails knelt behind a fence. From this position they overlooked a field about three- hundred yards wide. The entire Union line comprised only one hundred men. They waited patiently, motionless, nearly undetectable in the dappled sunlight that filtered through the branches overhead. The woods adapted to their presence and the birds began to sing again.

After twenty minutes a solitary rider emerged from the far tree line. He rode a black stallion. He paused to study the woods where waited the Buck-tails and apparently failed to detect them. Closer and closer he came until he was within forty yards of the Union line. Armistead's heart sank. He saw the nearest pair of Bucktails level their rifles at the unsuspecting rider. Suddenly a Union officer appeared just behind them. He hissed an order which Armistead could not hear and the sharpshooters reluctantly lowered their weapons. Another long minute passed before the rider departed. Armistead breathed a sigh of relief.

Bennington had also seen the rider conduct his personal reconnaissance. He tracked him with his rifle but a slight inequality of the ground prevented a clear shot. When the rider retired, he cursed and reached for his hip flask. Then he remembered and checked himself irritably before resuming his vigil.

Eight hundred yards to the north, Armistead waited at Bayard's headquarters to report. The officer who had prevented the Bucktail sharpshooters from firing stood nearby. Armistead spoke: "Colonel, the name's Carter. I was just at the front where I saw you stop some men from shooting. May I ask why?"

"My name is Kane, major, and my regiment has been chasing Turner Ashby for what seems like an eternity now. He is too brave to die in that way."

Chapter 24. Shenandoah Valley, June 1862

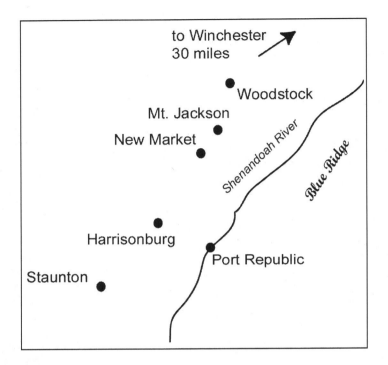

The afternoon wore on uneventfully. Min and his fellow officers loafed around headquarters while their horses grazed nearby. A courier appeared, dismounted, and handed Ashby a note. Flashing his characteristic smile, Ashby spoke: "Gentlemen, Major Harmon reports that the blessed sun has dried the roads sufficiently and the trains are moving clear. I think it's time to stir up the yankees and see what they are about. Here's my plan."

In broad outline it was the same plan they had executed successfully in the past, only this time Ashby had borrowed some Virginia and Maryland infantry to assist. The Loudoun Grays along with the rest of the cavalry would lure the yankees along the Harrisonburg Road. "Let's see if the creatures have learned anything," Ashby said with a mischievous gleam in his eyes. The infantry would occupy the woods adjacent to the road — "I was there recently and did not see a soul," Ashby added — and take the enemy in the flank when they chased the Confederate cavalry.

A Maryland colonel hesitantly inquired, "Turner, shouldn't we scout the woods again, we've seen the yankees massing along the road and maybe they have moved into the woods as well?"

Ashby looked slightly irritated. "If they are in the woods all the better. It saves us the trouble of having to look for them. I'll tell you what Bradley, you take your Maryland boys around the side of the woods to flank 'em out if they'll there. Y'all be safe enough then."

Min winced at Ashby's sarcasm. Bradley Johnson flushed angrily and with visible effort composed himself to ask, "And you, sir?"

Ashby breezily replied, "Oh, I reckon I'll lead the Virginia infantry straight at them."

Bayard's aide ordered Armistead to return to the woods to watch for a Confederate attack. Arriving in position, Armistead gazed across the empty field. A flock of crows rose suddenly from across the field. Their raucous alarm calls announced the presence of intruders. Armistead saw an uneven line of sparkling light moving through the trees as the sun reflected from scores of rifle barrels. Then the men themselves appeared. They wore torn, dirty uniforms colored in every shade and hue of grey and brown. At this distance Armistead could see few details except that the slouch hats they pulled low onto their foreheads barely contained their unruly masses of hair and beard. The Confederates formed an irregular line. A standard bearer uncased his flag. It unfurled in the gentle mountain breeze and Armistead recognized the flag of Virginia. The breeze also brought the deep voiced order repeated all along the line, 'Fix Bayonets!' The soldiers reached into their scabbards to take eighteen-inch steel knives and attach them to the tips of their rifles.

A black horse carrying a compact, dark-bearded rider emerged from the trees to take position in front of the standard bearer. Armistead heard Ashby cry out, "Follow me!" The Virginia infantry raised their rifles to present a gleaming hedge of polished steel. A demonic howl issued from their throats and the soldiers began walking straight toward him.

Armistead had neither seen nor heard anything like it and the effect was terrifying. He felt frozen to the ground as certain doom approached with implacable stride. When they came closer, details emerged: the tall sergeant next to the flag bearer walked with a limp; the blanket roll draped from one man's shoulder to his waist had once been elegant floor rug; the smallish soldier was a beardless youth. And, ahead of them all rode Turner Ashby.

Colonel Kane's voice jerked Armistead out of his trance. "Boys, pick your man like a squirrel in a tree. Fire!"

The Bucktail's volley exploded around him. Armistead saw numerous Confederates collapse and the entire line stagger. Above the din, Armistead heard Confederate officers rallying their men. He thought he heard a well-remembered voice shout, "Forward, my brave men!" Then the Virginians fired and Armistead's perceptions became confined by noise, smoke, and pain.

Bennington had seen Ashby emerge to lead the charge. He sidled along the fence line looking for an unobstructed shot. The Confederate battle line approached with alarming speed. Their yells were unnerving and the sight of their bayonets reminded Bennington that he wore a blue uniform. He felt an uncomfortable churn in his stomach and halted. This will do, he said to himself. He knelt and steadied his Sharps rifle on a fence rail. The Confederates were about sixty yards away. Bennington sighted his rifle on the rider atop the black stallion.

The first volley from the Bucktails almost caused him reflexively to squeeze the trigger. The smoke cleared. Bennington saw that Ashby remained unscathed. God those men were coming close! Bennington breathed deeply and partially exhaled. The familiar hunter's ritual failed to calm him. He registered the fact that the Confederate line had raised their weapons to the firing position, and pulled down on his trigger. Elated, he saw Ashby tumble from his horse. Then the smoke from the Virginians' first volley obscured his view.

Bennington half-stood to see above the smoke, took a quick step toward the rear to begin his escape, and stopped. Ashby's great stallion lay writhing on the ground. Ashby himself struggled to extricate himself from his stirrups, stood, drew his sword, and began running forward. Bennington cursed aloud and quickly reloaded.

Nearby, Armistead fell heavily when the minie ball grazed his temple. He lay momentarily stunned. He pressed his hand against his wound and felt fresh blood warmth. He put his hand in front of his eyes. The image slowly came into hazy focus; blood, but not a great deal. Armistead rose unsteadily to see the outnumbered Bucktails running to the rear. A wave of nausea overcame him and he knelt to vomit. He rose and began stumbling after the Bucktails.

He saw Colonel Kane leaning against a tree, looking toward his left where a line of Confederate infantry was coming hard. As Armistead staggered past, he heard Kane call out, "Give them hell boys!" and then the firing resumed.

Bennington saw Ashby running toward him. He carefully sighted and again pulled down on the trigger. This time he was sure. He nodded with satisfaction, and headed rearward. The noise of battle receded. Panting hard, Bennington reached a clearing where he paused to regain breath. He was reaching for his flask when a nearby voice called for help. It came from a wounded man who was struggling to rise to his feet. Bennington looked toward him and their eyes met. For a brief moment a flicker of recognition, surprise, seemed to register on the wounded man's face. Then he fell again, leaving his back facing Bennington.

Bennington took a long pull from his flask and considered. He realized that he too knew this man and that he would have to hurry because the Bucktails were falling back yet again. He ran over, knelt, and drew his hunting knife. A small knot of blue coated soldiers burst into the clearing.

Several glanced his way and Bennington resheathed his knife. Using his best northern accent, he shouted out, "This one is beyond hope." He rose and resumed running. He disliked leaving unfinished business but consoled himself with the thought that Armistead Carter was unlikely to live.

A quartet of Bucktails, who saw a wounded officer as a passport to safety, carried Armistead to the field station where he passed into and out of consciousness. Oddly, some part of his mind reverted back to the day of Turner Ashby's Ring Tournament. Confused fragments; Ashby dressed as a knight; Ashby on a black horse leading a line of infantry, drinking mead while competing to capture the rings, a blue uniformed cavalry trooper in a clearing drinking from a flask.

A pair of hospital orderlies roughly set him atop a plank table. Another orderly, a black man, brought a bucket of water and a rag. He swabbed the side of Armistead's face. "It ain't nothing much, sir. Looks like you just bin pinked."

He held a glass so that Armistead could see. The bullet had plowed a shallow furrow over his temple and pierced his ear. The furrow was bruised and swollen, the ear dripped blood. The screams of the wounded going under the knife interrupted his examination. How long was I staring at myself? Armistead asked inwardly. To the black orderly he said: "Don't reckon I need a surgeon for a scratch like this."

He plunged his head into the bucket and shook it vigorously. It still felt like he was someone else, someone watching this scene at one or two removes, but he rose from the table and stood. The orderly said, "Wait a minute, sir."

He took a crude bandage from his pocket and wrapped it tightly around Armistead's wound. "You'll be just fine, but keep this tight and soak it in cold water as often as you can."

"Thank you, sir," Armistead replied.

Although he felt light-headed and sleepy, Armistead managed to find Blue. He rode back along the Turnpike to search for Bayard's headquarters. In the gathering dusk, he encountered a hard-marching infantry column. Dust coated the soldiers' sweat-soaked faces, giving them a ghostly appearance. A chill passed over him. That's silly, he said to himself. They are men of course, nothing more.

Confederate soldiers wrapped Ashby's body in a flag and carried him back to Port Republic. Min was among those who came to view the body and to mourn. Many sobbed openly. Others vowed revenge.

When the army commander heard the news he observed to an aide, "I regarded his promotion to general as a calamity. He attached so little importance to drill and discipline that I could not trust him. But his men loved him. I must think." Jackson retired to his room and locked the door. His staff heard him pacing for a long, long time.

Across the Blue Ridge Mountains, the sun had just set. Amanda and two friends sat on the balcony. A bright light in the sky caught their eyes. "Look, it is Venus, the evening star, flying," said Lucy.

The object grew brighter, bigger, moving in a gentle arc along the horizon. "Surely it is not Venus," replied Amanda. They watched awestruck as the comet grew larger, soared past and disappeared.

"Perhaps it is a ball of fire, sent by the Lord to destroy Washington," said Elizabeth.

"More likely," observed Amanda, "some infernal yankee machine."

"No," said Lucy decisively, "It is the spirit of one of our heroes, ascending to heaven on a car of flame."

Chapter 25. Loudoun County and the Shenandoah Valley, August 1862

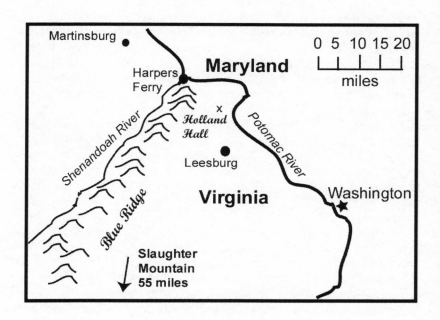

"Parcel of lies," Boyd snorted.

Amanda smiled and continued to read from the Washington Chronicle. Lately, the people of Loudoun County relied on northern papers for war news. Those papers reported a parade of Federal successes.

"It appears, brother mine,"Amanda said, "that McClellan's host is snug up against the Richmond suburbs and another Union army is somewhere south of Loudoun County marching to join him."

"What does one of ours say?" Boyd asked.

With normal communication disrupted by the movement of the armies, it was difficult to obtain southern newspapers. When one arrived, it passed from neighbor to neighbor until the paper itself disintegrated. Anxious family now turned to the casualty lists before reading anything else. Amanda read aloud from the Richmond Enquirer. Boyd listened morosely while slouching in his chair. "Here is General Jackson's epitaph for General Ashby," Amanda said. She read: "As a partisan officer...what is a partisan, Boyd?"

"A ranger or a guerrilla," he replied. "Go on," he ordered with an irritable edge.

"As a partisan officer I never knew his superior; his daring was pro-verbial; his powers of endurance almost incredible, his tone of character heroic."

Boyd nodded with approval. "Handsomely put," he murmured.

"How can we replace him?" Amanda asked.

"I told you before, he was nothing special. Others will rise Amanda. You can depend on it."

Boyd appeared anxious and distracted. It was not the right time to discuss some of the things that needed discussing, so Amanda postponed the disagreeable encounter and retired to her office. She watched the sun dip below the mountains. Storm clouds were building in the west. As the sky darkened she saw jagged streaks of lightning. The animals sensed the storm's presence. The nanny goat butted her reluctant kids into the barn; the jenny escorted her foal into the cedars; Rex, the watchdog, who feared neither man nor beast but who shivered uncontrollably in thunder and storm, slunk into his hidey hole. In the gardens the birds found their evening perches and a heavy stillness set in. Already the ground mist was rising from the hollows even as the clouds raced east to contribute a dense, enveloping murk.

I hope the storm holds off until the girls arrive, she thought. She opened her journal and perused the recent entries. July 21, 1862, the anniversary of the Battle of Manassas. "No one would have thought one year ago that this war would still be raging and the blockade still unraised." She began a new entry: "August 12, 1862. Rumors of another battle south of Culpeper. The name itself, Slaughter Mountain, promises more sorrow."

She paused. Had she heard the hoof beats of a fast-moving horse receding in the distance? Why would anyone be about on a night like this? Rex did not bark. Perhaps it was thunder, she decided, and returned to her journal.

In the woods on either side of the Martinsburg Road, light from camp-fires spread as the Grays established their bivouac. The sight often made Min pensive. Here were the campfires of soldiers, real living soldiers, and he was one of them. A year ago he had imagined how it would be. Now he was veteran enough to know. Perhaps some time in the future he would remember this scene, the tramp of soldiers marching, the gleam of the fires, the voices of comrades in arms. Yet, for the present he could not shake a perception that it was all somehow unreal.

A murky gloom gathered in the low spots. Clouds obscured the night sky. Bush whined to no one in particular that he smelled rain coming. Min silently agreed. It was unfair. The Grays had been on duty all day and would now have to suffer for it because by now the infantry would have begged or purchased all available cooked provisions from the local inhabitants. Facing another hungry night, Min summoned Olin Luckett. At age fourteen, he was the youngest trooper in the company. Min peered at him. Except for a hideous bloom of pimples, he seemed the least likely to appear threatening. Min carefully rehearsed the boy how to act and what to say. He was to take off his hat, and respectfully ask for water. If successful, he was then to ask for food. Finally, if the farm woman seemed obliging, he was to ask if the men could camp in one of the barns. They combed his hair as best they could, brushed the mud off his pants, and sent Kinlock with him to visit the nearby farms.

By the time Min returned from delivering his report to headquarters, the rain had begun. The Grays were where he had left them; gathered around their sputtering fires to complain about their plight.

"All right, Kinlock, what happened?"

"There weren't much to git, Min. We got a bit of flour from the first place, the next two was deserted and there was nothing to find. Jackson's boys had already been there. At the last place a sour-faced woman met us at the door holding a big metal fry pan. Behind her stood a young boy with a shotgun. I pushed Olin forward to say his piece and the idiot blurted it out all at once: "Please, ma'am, give me a drink of water I'm so hungry I ain't got no place to sleep." Kinlock laughed a bit, and then his laugh turned into a wracking cough. When he had regained breath, he concluded, "Then she slammed the door in our faces."

"What are we going to do, Lieutenant?" asked a trooper.

Bush interrupted. "Olin says they heard some chickens clucking at that first place. I say we go back and git 'em."

Min felt the rising tension. I can lose them here, he reflected. He slowly filled his pipe to give himself a chance to think. Unlike the areas where they had served in the past, the people living in mountains west of Harper's Ferry did not welcome their presence. Few inhabitants owned slaves. Consequently, although some had volunteered for the Confederacy, most remained Union loyal. The locals attributed their plight to the wealthy Tidewater elite who had led Virginia out of the Union; a distress made worse by too frequent visits from soldiers on both sides — foragers, requisition teams, and worst of all lawless deserters operating between the shifting boundaries of blue and gray control. Min considered, did the disloyalty of the locals perhaps justify foraging? The word itself stuck in Min's mind: hogs turned out for the winter foraged; for soldiers it was just a fancy word for theft.

He removed the pipe from his mouth and gathered breath.

Kinlock had been watching him closely and spoke first: "Boys, it hurts me to have to admit it, but my folks sent me a package and told me to share it out. Now, I was mightily tempted to keep it for myself, but my high breeding interfered." Kinlock started to laugh but instead was overtaken by a coughing spasm. Although unable to speak, Kinlock theatrically presented a set of tinned delicacies.

Min spoke: "Now Bush, you git busy with that flour and make us some of your special johnny cakes and we all can have ourselves a feast."

Bush looked surprised. Slowly his habitual glower receded. He began snapping out directions. Min exhaled. Speaking to Bush had been a gamble. Underwood had his supporters within the unit. If he had objected again, the Grays might have splintered. Instead, Bush was now invested in making the supper a success.

Min ducked into the tent he shared with Kinlock. The tent, made from captured yankee half-shelters, was already leaking. Min rummaged through his blanket roll and extracted two bottles of peach brandy. "Here's a little bit of cheer, boys, to help spice the feast," he announced.

Everyone, except Bush himself, knew that he was the poorest cook in the company. Oblivious, Bush took a long pull and set to work. His cousin had provided two turtle shells that Bush used as bowls to knead the dough. He wrapped the dough around the carbines' ramrods and supervised while his followers turned the dough over the fire until Bush proclaimed it done. The thin spread of Kinlock's jams failed to disguise the singed flavor of the dough balls. Min's gut-wrenching brandy partially overcame the fact that the cakes were raw on the inside.

Because the rain intensified throughout the meal, the men retired to their shelters as soon as they had eaten. Min wrapped himself in his blanket and snuggled against Kinlock for warmth. Kinlock's wracking cough, the steady dripping from the leaky tent, and an uncomfortable sense that Bush's cakes were somehow expanding in his stomach prevented sleep. It was close tonight, too close, he mused. What about tomorrow? He rolled onto his stomach to try to relieve the strain and found himself sinking into the sodden soil.

Chapter 26. Loudoun County, August 1862

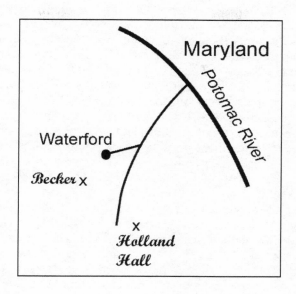

Captain Robert Duchesne waited at the intersection of the Ferry Road and the path leading to the Becker barn. No sound. No pursuit. He doubted that anyone had seen him, but the regular couriers had warned that Lige White's men were increasingly active in Loudoun, so it made sense to be careful. Normally Duchesne managed his business from a safe remove; sorting, evaluating, and passing his findings on to Pinkerton's people. The perils of field service were for the expendable but there were exceptions, and the courier's description of Becker's daughter had fired his imagination.

The fog thickened during the five minutes that Duchesne waited. The path itself became indistinct. Duchesne rode along the gently descending path until he came to a slight curve. He dismounted and reached into his saddlebags. He had learned about this trick from a New Jersey officer. That officer reported that it put an end to the annoyance of rebel cavalry creeping up on his pickets and ambushing them at night. Duchesne looped and knotted the telegraph wire around a sturdy sapling. He carried it across the path, pulled it taut around another tree, and knotted the wire. He repeated the process in reverse. One for the horse, one for the rider, he chuckled to himself. If anyone is tracking me, they are in for a surprise.

Duchesne mounted and rode on. Ahead, he saw a dim light glowing from an upper-story window.

The warm night air brought the scent of trumpet vine and moonflower wafting into Rachel's room. The moon passed behind some clouds and the whip-poor-wills resumed their courtship calls. A stack of envelopes sat before her; many torn and soiled, a handful, the ones she reserved for last, showing stains of blood. The envelopes came from the most recent haul of intercepted documents: some from Confederate mail carriers ambushed along a county lane; most taken from captured Confederate soldiers; and a few, the ones she prized the most, from the wounded and the slain. Abner Means had organized a network devoted to obtaining and examining these documents. Because they possessed local knowledge, Rachel and her father were supposed to peruse those pertaining to northern Virginia and to record all military references. Apparently people up north compiled this information into something they called orders of battle. Rachel dutifully obliged, but only because it gave her access to things she found more interesting; gossip, indiscretions, windows into the secret lives of her neighbors.

She opened the first envelope. It was from Mariah White to her husband Souther. The name was familiar. She recalled him as a gangly, ill-looking boy with ravaged skin. Once, out of boredom, she had given him slight encouragement and then relished his whipped-puppy look when she suddenly lashed into him with mocking, and very public, venom. Mariah was a newly married eighteen-year old bride; plain, pimply like her husband, and obviously lonely. She read: "You know well, my dear Souther, how I feel. At times I can scarce sustain the frame which bears such an aching, sorrowful heart." The words sounded well, Rachel reflected.

Rachel read through the entire bundle and found little of interest. Frustrated, she returned to Mariah's letter. Whereas Rachel loathed letter writing, this doting bride possessed a way with words. She knew that the courier would come tomorrow or the next day and it reminded her of unfinished business. She carefully copied Mariah's letter, substituting Armistead for Souther, put a hint of perfume on the paper and sealed it.

She looked outside and saw that clouds now completely obscured the moon. Like groping fingers, tendrils of fog reached out from the low spots and entered the barnyard. All the better, she thought. She placed the lantern in the back window. He might not be able to see the signal, but she was certain he would come regardless.

The humid air sat heavy and still on the surrounding countryside. Perhaps the storm had passed elsewhere, Amanda thought. Inside the great room at Holland Hall, her friends sat sipping sherry and eating cake. Their unfinished knitting festooned their chairs. Amanda spoke: "Lizzie, thinking about your Captain Houston. It seems to me that no one really knows the person they marry until it is too late. Gentlemen are actors who hide their real feelings and characters. If you marry for love you are sure to be disappointed. After marriage, the gentleman you thought you knew is not at all what you expected. If you loved him, you cannot help but feel very bitterly. However, if you merely liked him and were disappointed, it does not touch your heart."

"Oh Mandy, such stuff," Elizabeth Milton protested with a frown. "Don't you believe in romance, in love itself?"

"I am speaking about marriage," Amanda primly replied. As she expected, her remark elicited giggles. She continued: "Sure, I am not a romantic creature but I think that very few people can expect happiness after they marry. Whereas a wife's love becomes deeper, the husband's love invariably cools. At best what is left is a patronizing friendship. If the husband cares for his wife at all, it is only as a sort of servant, a being made to attend to his comforts, beget children, and then keep the children out of the way. After a year or so, a wife becomes little better than a slave."

"Perhaps you are right," Lucy sighed.

"I know that I wish I were a man!" Letty Smallwood interjected. "I would make my wife so happy. She should never regret having married me."

"I don't know about that," Kate Luckett snapped.

"Sometimes I think we are like a flock of clucking hens, pecking at the barren dirt trying to imagine what men want," Lucy commented.

"I know what my man wants," Letty began.

Amanda interrupted by ringing the small, silver servant's bell. James appeared carrying a fresh tray. "James," Amanda said, "Would you please see if my brother is at leisure. Tell him that confusion has overtaken a coven of women, and the head crone hopes that he, a man, with impeccable logic, can set us straight."

"Boyd, logic. My, my." Lucy laughed heartily. She wiped her eyes with her handkerchief, tried to speak, and resumed laughing.

Amanda looked at James expectantly. "Missy, he left some time ago. He said he was going visiting."

A sudden gust caused a loose shutter to bang against the house; thunder, followed by the sounds of rain lashing the roof.

It was going well, Duchesne thought. His appearance at the Becker home had initially frightened the old man. But Duchesne had quickly provided the current sign and countersign. Thereafter his obvious knowledge about the details of the Union espionage network in northern Virginia had reassured Becker.

The old man was hungry for current war news from north of the Potomac. The girl obviously found the topic boring. More puzzling, when

Duchesne tried to engage her with talk she should find interesting, what the ladies were wearing in Washington and Baltimore, gossip about the affairs of well known actresses, she did not attend. Instead, she fidgeted and often she rose from her chair to peer out the window. Her behavior annoyed Duchesne until he decided that she was probably flighty by nature.

During the tedious hour of small talk, Becker ordered her to fetch a decanter of applejack. Duchesne briefly considered compelling him to match glass for glass so as to be rid of him but decided that such a trial might interfere with his subsequent plans. At one point Becker asked if the Potomac fords had been heavily guarded.

"Exceedingly. I had to use all my skills to outflank them. I counted ten pickets at one post. Since the odds were in my favor I would have attacked had not my duty called me here."

Becker's eyebrows shot up in a gesture Duchesne interpreted as admiration. Rachel asked, "Did you not know fear?"

"Fear? No. I have never met fear. Who is he?" Duchesne was ready to grin and wink depending upon Rachel's reaction. He gauged her look and again saw admiration. So, the gallant cavalier, he concluded inwardly.

Soon thereafter, he rose to make his farewell. "I must depart early, before the patrols become too thick. I shall sleep in the barn."

To his surprise, Rachel objected strenuously. A fierce argument between father and daughter ensued. "Oh, worry not on my behalf, I have made do with far worse," Duchesne interjected. He shook Becker's hand. He clasped Rachel's hand. He noted that her concern for his well-being and anger at her father had imparted a most pleasing blush. Taming this creature will be amusing. I wonder how experienced she is. He spoke with his best continental accent: "I look forward to meeting you again soon, mademoiselle, in what are certain to be much happier circumstances." He brushed his lips across the back of her hand and departed to make his preparations.

After clearing the dishes Rachel walked to the back room. What a foolish little man, she reflected. Moist palms. Bah. She extinguished the lantern and went to bed.

The flow of rough corn mash trickled to a stop. Boyd flung the jug into the bushes. He searched for the break in the trees. All he saw was an indistinct pattern. The anger came as it always had. Childhood memories of Amanda and her friends calling out while he blundered around in futile search. When he finally tore off the blind they would be standing in a circle around him laughing, unless they had already abandoned him in the dark glade.

The fog presented an opaque shroud. "God damn it!" he muttered. He kicked his horse into motion. The animal knew the way and suddenly turned off the road to enter a gray portal leading to the Becker place.

The last time he had visited she had allowed him to go farther than ever before. Then, abruptly, she slapped him. He had made a fist and hesitated. "Go on," she taunted. Her mocking laughter echoed from the rafters as she skipped out of the barn.

He had never struck a woman, at least not until recently when Gordon invited him into a private room at Meme Richard's. The naked woman was bound to a column of the four-poster bed. When Boyd entered her eyes widened; excitement? fear? He was uncertain. A gag prevented her from speaking. "She likes it rough," Gordon said, "so she will need a little stirring up. Like this." He hit her hard, gave Boyd a leering wink, and left them alone.

Boyd could not recall exactly what took place thereafter because he and Gordon had drunk a tremendous amount. He did remember that although confined in her movements, she had tried to turn away from his mouth. After a few blows she had yielded. Later, he recollected a loud scene downstairs with Meme Richard. Somehow Clarence Rixey had been present. But in between had been his first time.

Rachel will find me a different man, Boyd enthused. She won't be able to say I'm inexperienced. Boyd raked his spurs along his horse's flanks. The animal was unused to such treatment. Startled by the unexpected pain, it began running down the gentle slope toward the place where the path curved.

Mounting his horse, Duchesne forlornly looked back a last time: no sounds, no movement. He retraced his route until groans caused him to check his horse, draw his revolver, and dismount. The crippled body lay by the side of the path. Duchesne examined the wires. In the early morning light he saw that he had improperly positioned them. Although the lower wire contained blood and hair, the horse had struck it after the rider had already contacted the upper wire. Apparently, the horse was gone. He coiled the wires and hung them on his saddle.

The temptation to leave was strong. It would compromise the old man and his bitch daughter. He looked more closely. The man's face was swollen and blood-encrusted. One eye protruded from its socket and hung by a thread of muscle. Still, the face was somehow familiar. Duchesne tore a strip of cloth from the man's shirt, poured some water from his canteen onto the face, and began wiping away the blood. The eye detached and he flicked it to one side. He sensed in the man's remaining eye recognition. The man began to mew loudly. Duchesne stuck the cloth into his open mouth to dampen the noise.

He recognized the face that emerged from beneath the blood sheen. He drew his knife. He put his foot on the man's chest. The eye tracked his movements and registered terror. With his left hand Duchesne seized his hair and tugged the head backward. With his right hand he severed the jugular with the same motion he had once used to slaughter hogs at his home place in Maine. He hefted the body onto his horse and secured it.

He was in a better mood now. As he rode, his thoughts returned to Rachel. Next time will be different, he resolved. She will not refuse such an invitation again.

He came to the river where he untied the body and shoved it gently into the current.

The rules established by the War Department were quite clear: each cavalry trooper had to provide his own horse. If he could not, then he was eligible to be drafted into the infantry. The horse owned by Corporal Isaiah Clemmer of the Second Virginia Cavalry had broken down. He knew that the chances of securing a remount were poor in this ravaged county. He had heard that although Loudoun's Quaker community had often been the target of Confederate confiscation teams, some crafty farmers still managed to retain their animals. It was just light enough to see so he began walking. He did not fancy himself a thief, but resolved to take his chances at the first likely looking farm.

The animal's whicker came as such a surprise that Clemmer stared in disbelief. Ten paces away stood a horse. Clemmer approached cautiously. The horse carried a saddle. I reckon the rider is in the bushes with a running gut, he said to himself. He quietly offered the horse a handful of oats. As the animal lowered its head he grabbed the reins and prepared to spring into the saddle as soon as the rider reappeared. The horse methodically chewed the oats and lifted its head to ask for more. It had a kind eye and except for a gash across its chest appeared sound.

Clemmer stroked the horse's neck while listening intently. "Maybe you broke free and run here," he said. "Ain't a war horse though, you're in much too good condition. Well, you're mine now."

Clemmer mounted, applied gentle pressure, and rode toward the river to rejoin his regiment.

240

Chapter 27. Richmond, August 1862

The three-story brick warehouse squatted beside the canal at Twentieth Street. The early morning breeze was long gone, apparently stunned by the broiling sun, yet still the prisoners pressed against the windows in hopes of finding relief. At the entrance, a pair of women carried bundles of books and flowers past the bored soldiers who stood guard. They paused to chat and the older woman handed each guard a slice of cake. The women proceeded through a brick archway beneath a faded inscription of an anchor denoting that the building had once served as a ship chandler's loft.

A careful observer might have seen that the lettering above the anchor read Libby's Warehouse, and in fact, someone had already noted this detail along with much else. Liverne stood across the street watching intently until the women disappeared inside. He scanned the area for any other watchers and then settled into a corner to wait.

Inside, another set of guards ushered Elizabeth Van Lew and her mother into the office of Brigadier-General John Winder. Winder was a bulky, imposing, silver-haired figure who had served in the U.S. Army for more than forty years. Although the experience had coarsened him, he retained a sense of proper manners. Winder courteously motioned for the women to sit. After a few minutes of inconsequential chat, Elizabeth Van Lew fixed him with an adoring gaze and spoke, "General, your hair would adorn the temple of Janus, it looks out of place here."

Winder swelled with pleasure and allowed as how no doubt President Davis would soon give him an even more important duty. "But for the moment", the general continued, "with the vandal horde pressing near our gates, this city must be ruled with an iron hand, idlers put to work preparing our defenses, spies detected and shot, prisoners guarded closely. For these reasons and more the President has chosen me provost marshal."

Amazement over the extent of his burden, awe for his talents, and then Van Lew asked if she and her mother could deliver a few comforts to the yankee prisoners.

"I am sure that can be arranged," Winder replied.

"Ah, but army paperwork must take time," Van Lew said, "And I know an order in your hand, the hand that commands Richmond's fate, would be absolutely persuasive."

Winder sat up even more erect, brushed some imaginary dust from his lapel, and called for his aide: "A blank pass, Captain Archer." Winder wrote a couple of lines and pushed the form across his desk. "Will that do?"

The younger woman read, "The bearer, Elizabeth Van Lew, may visit the prisoners and send them books, luxuries, delicacies and what she may please."

She again looked adoringly at Winder, "General, that is most generous. We thank you and if there is some small service either my mother or myself can render, please do not hesitate."

Outside the prison, Liverne realized that he was hungry again. He had finished the last of his travel rations two days ago. He believed that by passing himself as an idle laborer, one of many among Richmond's numerous free blacks, he could circulate freely throughout the city. However, Means had told him that food prices in Richmond were high and climbing fast. Lacking specific knowledge about what goods cost, he had resolved to refrain from commercial transactions in order to avoid a simple blunder that might attract attention. Moreover, he had also decided to carry little money so, in the event of arrest, he could more plausibly maintain his cover as an itinerant day laborer. But hunger had upset his planning. Since the women were unlikely to reappear anytime soon, he followed the now familiar steps to Auntie's Kitchen. As he turned the corner he was rewarded with the appetizing aroma of fried sweet potatoes. His mouth watered and he slowed his pace.

Something was amiss. The usual crowd was not present. He saw one of the serving girls glance out the window in his direction. He gestured and saw her eyes widen with surprise before she discreetly touched her neck and then the back of her left ear. In times past, whites occasionally ate at Auntie's Kitchen, in which case the entire front room was off limits. But blacks could still eat in the kitchen yard. But not today. For some reason today he would be at risk. He silently thanked the girl for signaling the old warning and headed toward Church Hill.

From the cemetery of St. John's Church, Liverne studied Elizabeth Van Lew's Church Hill mansion. The property covered an entire city block. It was one of the finest homes in a proud city's most exclusive neighborhood. A cobbled driveway led to a Greek temple-like entrance. Twin curved stairs climbed the front porch where three pairs of tall white columns supported a massive portico. The main structure was likewise built on a grand scale that only the wealthy could afford. It had an open balustrade stretching above the eaves of the roof and ending at an enormous stepped gable. An ornate wooden fence bordered the impeccably landscaped front lawn which featured pruned hedges, rose of sharon, and oleander. It was too exposed for Liverne's liking so he waited until full darkness before walking down a side street in order to enter through the terraced back gardens overlooking the James River.

The gardens were in deep shadow, all light blocked by the broad magnolia canopies. The highest terrace nearest the house encompassed a boxwood garden. Here Liverne paused to listen and heard nothing exceptional. If the house was being watched, he concluded, then the watchers possessed tireless patience. He shrugged and walked up the back steps to knock on the door.

A black maid answered. She assessed him warily and seemed oblivious to the sequence of coded words embedded in his salutation. An unseen female voice said, "Let him in. We haven't heard those words since well before the war but you are welcome nonetheless."

Up close, Elizabeth Van Lew was a small woman, almost birdlike in appearance, her pale blond hair done up in ringlets, yet judging from her unadorned fingers, apparently a spinster. Her maid brewed tea and served Liverne ham biscuits. However, after he had established his credentials, he found that he was barely able to eat because there were few gaps between her rapid-fire volley of questions. Finally, blessedly, she realized his distress.

"You must excuse me, Mister Taylor, I am as starved for news as a traveler is for food. Please eat."

Once sated, Liverne managed to turn the conversation to local events. Her blue eyes blazed with indignation as she related how Confederate press gangs had swept the streets of all negroes, whether free or slave, and marched them to work on the fortifications guarding the city.

Liverne felt a cold chill descend his spine. He had noticed the scarcity of black men but had not altered his plan. He had been more lucky than he had realized and repeated his thanks to the girl at Auntie's Kitchen. He resolved to be more disciplined because survival should not be a matter of luck.

Although she was obviously a shrewd woman, his passing emotion seemed to go undetected. Instead, Van Lew was musing with real anguish, "Why oh why did McClellan not attack? The city was his for the taking. We told the authorities in Washington how few rebels were here and later I learned from the officers held in Libby Prison that McClellan outnumbered them vastly."

"I cannot answer, Miss," Liverne responded with a rueful smile, "President Lincoln does not choose to confide in me."

"We must all be careful now," she replied. "You are right to be fearful. What was called loyalty is called treason. They suspect where my sympathies lie. I have had gentlemen who I have known since childhood shake their fingers in my face and say terrible things. We have had threats of eviction, threats of fire, and threats of death. We look under our beds for spies and informants."

So she had noticed, Liverne concluded inwardly. "How have you managed to avoid arrest?"

"Ah, is that what they sent you here to find out?"

Liverne realized that this woman could see through his every deception and replied, "Yes."

"Before the war my family and I enjoyed a certain status in this city. This enabled me to approach directly the appropriate officials and ask to serve as a nurse to the Union prisoners. I also provide comfort for our poor boys, but mostly I played the coquette; flattering them all shamelessly, whether General Winder or that odious Lieutenant Todd who commanded the prison guards. By the way did you know he is our president's brother-in-law? And, I must add, my mother is a superb baker. Still, they do not let me do much, but I can take the prisoners a few comforts such as food and books. It is a start."

From the street outside came the clatter of hoof beats. Liverne saw the maid startle. Van Lew spoke calmly, "Sally, go take a look through the peephole."

Van Lew quickly collected the dishes while continuing to speak: "In the past week they have been here twice: once to take my man servants, although they seized no others on Church Hill, and a second time to search for deserters. There was nothing here that could compromise me."

"But there is now," Liverne softly said.

She seemed not to hear but instead said to the returning maid, "Another patrol?"

Sally nodded.

"Which is why we must hide you," Van Lew said. "Come."

She led him upstairs even as Sally began slowly unbolting the front door. Liverne heard voices, sharp questions, but Van Lew appeared untroubled. She led him toward the front portico.

Van Lew deftly pushed aside a chest of drawers and opened a thirty-inch, spring hatchway, its mechanism concealed by the intricate, carved wainscoting. She motioned toward the darkness within.

For a very long time Liverne had confronted danger. He would never have described himself as a fearless man, but in most things he had learned how to manage his emotions so as to be able to do what needed doing. Since childhood, for a reason he only dimly remembered, one fear remained above all others. Liverne stood as if paralyzed.

She spoke in a near whisper: "They have been here before and they have not found it. They will not find it this time." She motioned again.

Perhaps because it was her first display of anything like anxiety, Liverne responded. With great reluctance he crawled into the three foot high chamber. She sealed off the entrance and he heard her depart. As the walls themselves seemed to close inward, Liverne shut his eyes and tried to remember to breathe.

Chapter 28. Loudoun County, September 1862

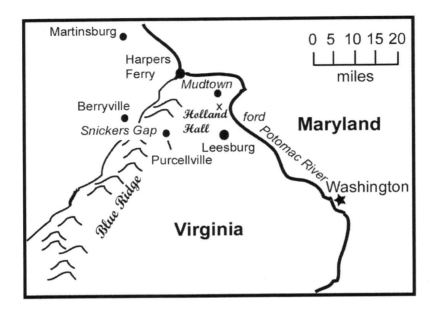

Again armies were on the march. After a terrible drubbing at Second Manassas and a confused battle at Chantilly, fought in darkness during a thunderstorm, John Pope, the general who boasted that he came "to you from the West, where we have always seen the backs of our enemies" and had pledged to do the same against Lee's veterans, ordered his demoralized army to scuttle back to the safety of the Washington defenses. Everyone expected a pause now, a time for both sides to reorganize and refit from the exertions of incessant march and battle; everyone except the one man who mattered. And that man, Robert E. Lee, having triumphantly "suppressed" the detested Pope, ordered the Army of Northern Virginia to take the war onto enemy soil.

During the first days of September, Confederate soldiers splashed across the Potomac fords and marched north. They were in high spirits; laughing, shouting, singing, supremely confident in themselves and in their leader. Only an observant few noted how thin were their ranks. Among them was Major Moxley Sorrel of General Longstreet's staff. Sorrel stared pensively at the returns listing the numbers present for duty and frowned. Battle casualties, straggling, desertion: never before had there been so many men separated from their colors. A band struck up "Maryland, my Maryland" and Sorrel turned his horse into the waters of the Potomac ford and headed for the far shore.

Upstream, a footsore Louisiana private sat soaking his feet. In the backwater above an eddy, a tangled mass of flood debris had created a snag. Sycamore limbs dipped low over the water, their branches festooned with green thorn and ivy. They reminded the private of his native bayous. He was an experienced hunter, attuned to nature's signals. He watched the turkey vultures wheel and soar in effortless flight without beat of a wing. Probably feeding on a dead animal, he reckoned. But this war had shown him that often the dead animal was human and the discovery sometimes proved profitable.

He waded through the shallows and as he approached, the vultures fixed him with malevolent glares before reluctantly taking to the air. The body bobbed gently among the debris. Advancing, the private disturbed the feeding turtles who slid off and disappeared into the depths. He hauled the body onto the mud shore. It hadn't been in the water too long, he judged, probably ten days or so. It wore civilian clothes, which briefly gave the private hope of finding something uncommonly valuable. He turned the body onto its back. The black slash across the throat was not pretty, but the battlefield always presented sights far worse. Without great hope, he sifted through the pockets. To his delight, the inside vest pocket yielded a few coins. Better still, he found a silver timepiece. It no longer worked, of course, but it alone would provide a sufficient stake to enter tonight's game. Deeply satisfied, he stood up and looked at the vultures perched on the nearby limbs. "I reckon he's yours again," he said, and headed back to the ford.

Gordon sipped the French brandy. It came from the last of the Squire's bottles. He had intended to drink it in celebration. Instead, he had cracked the bottle last night because he needed to think. At least the brandy had helped him sleep. Last night he dreamt again that he was Squire of Gordon Hall. The wealthiest neighbors came to him for advice, to propose business deals, to parade their young daughters in hopes of forging a business dynasty based on blood. But when he woke, another day had come and his rightful place receded toward some unknown future while he remained plain Mister Gordon, hired man to that Holland bitch.

He needed the brandy now because he had to plan clearly and the god-awful throbbing in his head made reason impossible. Gordon drained his glass, stared sourly at the empty bottle, and hurled the glass into the brick hearth. He had been close, oh so close. He had patiently secured a great deal from the Squire, but not quite enough. Then, he had arranged Boyd's encounter perfectly, complete with ironclad witnesses. The boy was certain to give him the balance to avoid scandal. And then the young idiot had disappeared.

He could no longer afford patience. When the war began he had speculated aggressively. At first he realized easy profit. But he had failed to anticipate the ruinous inflation, and heavy obligations came due at this year's end. He needed a clear deed to the land to stave off creditors, the deed that had been so nearly his. The injustice of his situation boiled up anew. Gordon swept the dishes onto the floor.

The crash brought an anxious black face to the doorway. "Is anything the matter, master?" the boy asked. Gordon fixed him with a bloodshot glare and hissed, "Get out, get out now or I'll have the hide off you!"

He lit a cheroot. The soothing smoke caressed his mouth and nostrils. Composed, he sat down to write the coded message. It had always been one of his choices, albeit the last, least-favored. But he consoled himself with the thought that once he assumed title he could rebuild what they destroyed.

The sun set behind the Blue Ridge and the air fell silent. The days are already getting shorter, Amanda reflected. Soon it will be time to harvest. Her inner voice asked, how will we possibly manage that?

In the past this had been Amanda's favorite time of day, a period of calm and reflection. Too often now she found it a time of brooding anxiety. As the days passed without any word from Boyd, she grew increasingly apprehensive. None of the neighbors had seen him recently. She visited the Beckers: the old man sharply answered that Boyd was not welcome on his property and that he had not seen him since the time of his visit with Amanda. Then, realizing that he had given offense, he remarked that long intervals often passed without hearing from his son Charles, so she should not worry.

Rachel too had denied having seen Boyd recently, but Amanda did not believe her. Unfortunately, Amanda had failed to hide her skepticism, and then Rachel had grown close-mouthed.

Amanda next sent James to make inquiries around Mudtown. A message from the proprietor of Meme Richard's told her that if she wanted to hear about Boyd, she should visit in person. With great reluctance, Amanda went. She learned, in far more detail than she would have chosen, about Boyd and Gordon and her father as well. Amanda considered if and how to reply. Although she chose her words carefully she also chose candor. "I have no money to pay damages," she said, "but Gordon will be dismissed at year's end." Before Amanda departed, the woman had surprised her by saying that if she loved her brother she should keep him away from Gordon.

Amanda looked outside again. It had grown dark. Soon it would be safe enough to finish her chores.

The Loudoun Grays passed through Berryville on their way east to Loudoun. The townspeople turned out to cheer, and better yet, to press food, sweets, and surreptitious jugs into the hands of friends and relatives. Among the crowd was Souther White. Kinlock leaned from his saddle to shake hands. "What you about, boy? Haven't seen you in a coon's age."

Souther waited until Kinlock stopped coughing before replying, "I'm with Jackson's foot cavalry. We'uns do some real fighting while y'all go gallivanting around the countryside chasing after the ladies."

Kinlock tried to respond, but speech seemed to make him cough more readily so he merely grinned.

"Here's one lady you won't catch. This here's my wife." Souther draped an arm around a young girl and proudly announced, "Mariah just told me that God willing, in five months or so she's going to give me a son."

Kinlock managed to congratulate the couple. The young lady appeared terribly shy. Kinlock was struck by the way she clung hard to Souther's hand, as if attached to a lifeline.

The bugle sounded. "I've got to go," Kinlock said.

"I'm just here for a visit," Souther replied. "Pa will loan me his horse so I can catch up with my regiment this evening. Kinlock, we're going to win the war on the other side of the big river and then we can all come home."

The Grays' march resumed, up the mountain through Snicker's Gap, east toward Leesburg. Progress was slow. Not only were the roads clogged with regiments, batteries, and wagons heading north toward the river, but the paths and byways were crowded as well. Here were hundreds of gaunt, barefoot soldiers wearing ragged trousers, stained, dirty jackets, the brims of their old slouch hats pinned up with a thorn, a begrimed blanket folded into a roll over the shoulder, a grease-smeared cotton haversack contain-ing, if they were in luck, a few green apples or ears of unripe corn. They belonged to no formed units. Instead, they moved like shorebirds following the tide line, shifting first one way and then the other, buffeted by the force of the latest rumor about where a farm might provide food.

They were men who had fought to save Richmond and then followed Jackson and Longstreet on the hard march north. They had fought again at Slaughter Mountain, Second Manassas, and Chantilly, and by so-doing had sent Pope's hated minions back across the Potomac. They had come to Virginia to defend their homes from the invader, and with duty done many now balked at crossing the river to invade Maryland.

Progress was so slow that the Grays made it no farther than Purcell-ville, where they camped for the night. After supper, Kinlock asked Min to accompany him on a walk outside of camp.

Kinlock began coughing violently. Min supported him with both arms. When the seizure ended, Min asked, "What's on your mind?"

"The boys have been listening too much, Min. All these stragglers have given them ideas and they've begun talking among themselves." Kinlock stumbled to a pause and resumed coughing.

"So they've been talking," Min prompted.

Kinlock looked miserable. He stared at the ground and spoke: "They say that now that Virginia is free they've done what they set out to do. If they march north they'd be no better than the yankees."

"And what do you say?"

Kinlock painfully gasped for breath. He slowly raised his head to look at Min squarely. "I reckon I agree."

"My friend, I might agree also, but my opinion don't signify. Why don't you go back and tell the boys that they might want to reflect on something. Neither Bush Underwood, Kinlock Barton, nor Arminius Carter commands this army."

Kinlock straightened up and snapped a salute, "Yes sir!"

"Tell me Kinlock, if we are ordered north, will you come?"

Kinlock uncomfortably shifted from one foot to the other. "I'm hoping you'll not ask."

Min lay awake worrying deep into the night. Except for Turner Ashby, he had never met any of the army's famous leaders. But if Stuart, Jackson, and most importantly General Lee, deemed a march north wise, how could he, a mere lieutenant, gainsay them? Yet it still did not seem right. Would not the northerners fight to defend their homes with the same savage ferocity displayed by Lee's proud army? And wouldn't they be in the right? He looked at the problem from all perspectives and found his thoughts looping in a circle, beginning and ending at the same place, constant movement that never approached an endpoint, turmoil that produced nothing except sleeplessness.

A bugle sounded boots and saddles. He crawled out of his tent. It was still dark, without hint of a new dawn. Instead of brewing coffee and cooking breakfast, camp servants were busy packing the pots and kettles. Min recognized a staff officer hurrying by. "What's this all about, Drew?"

"We're going back to Martinsburg. It must be important, because we're supposed to get there in a big hurry."

The Grays stood next to their horses while Min briefly inspected them. Kinlock's wracking cough had settled deep in his lungs and seemingly grown worse. "Sergeant, I want you to report sick."

"No sir. I'm feeling better," Kinlock wheezed.

Min reluctantly passed along the line before addressing the Grays. He saw the tension in their faces. "Boys, the fair maidens of Martinsburg can't make do without us so we've been recalled. Bugler, to horse!"

He felt the tension release. They were with him again, but he knew that the bond was frayed thin.

Chapter 29. Harpers Ferry, September 14, 1862

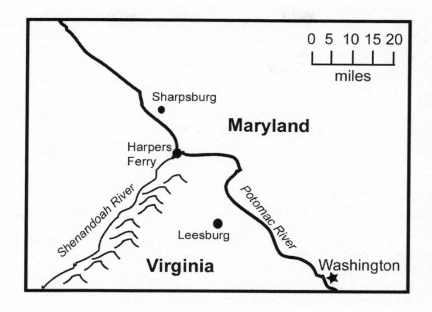

The Union soldiers manning the lines on Bolivar Heights were uneasy. The news that Stonewall Jackson was marching hard toward Harpers Ferry had spread like wildfire, and, like all camp gossip, grown with each retelling: "He's coming with twenty thousand, I heard it from Colonel Miles' orderly."

"I heard at least thirty thousand rebs for sure including Hill, Ewell, McLaws and Hood."

"My cousin at the telegraph office said forty-five thousand certain."

From what Armistead had learned, regardless of the number of rebels, the position of the ten thousand-man garrison was not good. High ground surrounded Harpers Ferry on three sides. Yet, instead of defending the commanding heights, the garrison commander, Colonel Dixon Miles, insisted on keeping most of the men close to the town. Armistead saw for himself that the fortifications at Camp Hill, which were supposed to defend against an attack from the west, were poorly laid out. A belt of woods that could conceal a large hostile force lay a half-mile in front of the works. Armistead had asked an infantry major why no one ordered the trees cut down. The major had rolled his eyes and replied that Miles did not think the effort worthwhile. Armistead reckoned that the garrison was half beat already.

It certainly seemed to be the opinion of the black teamsters who were cracking their whips to urge their teams to move faster as they recklessly drove down Washington Street toward the depot at the old United States Musket factory. Armistead jerked his horse off the street to avoid a careening wagon. He was about to curse the driver when he heard a familiar voice.

"Mister Armistead, Mister Armistead!"

The voice came from a group of Sibley tents alongside the street. A small black figure wearing blue uniform trousers with red piping stood waving, an uncertain smile on his face.

"Wellington, what in the blazes are you doing here?"

"I'm with the army now. I'm practically a soldier," Wellington proudly replied.

Armistead shook his hand. Wellington explained that he had been in Harpers Ferry for about a month and that he helped cook for an artillery battery. "When did you learn to cook?" Armistead asked. "Oh, never mind, you always were a scamp. I have to report to headquarters for some damn fool reason. Probably forgot to sign the ration slips in triplicate or something. I'll come back this evening and catch up on news." Armistead paused for a moment and pressed hands firmly with the boy. "Wellington, I truly am happy to see you safe."

Pleasure showing on his face, Wellington replied, "And I'm happy to see someone from home."

A cavalry orderly ushered Armistead into Colonel Miles' headquarters. Armistead saluted, but Miles took no notice. Armistead realized that he had interrupted a conference that was growing more heated by the minute. Apparently several cavalry officers wanted to try to escape from Harpers Ferry and Miles was unsure if the undertaking was wise.

Armistead recognized Colonel Benjamin Franklin Davis of the Eighth New York Cavalry. He had heard only favorable reports about the thirty-year-old, 'Grimes' Davis. Davis was said to be a strict disciplinarian, yet men and officers alike trusted him. The scars from an Apache arrow marked his service in the Indian Wars and testified to his courage. A New York volunteer officer had assured Armistead that in spite of Davis's West Point education, he possessed common sense.

When Davis spoke, Armistead was surprised to hear a deep-south drawl. Davis argued that mounted men could be of little use sitting behind fortifications. Miles could hardly disagree, but the idea of losing any of his forces on the eve of fighting against the mighty Stonewall Jackson clearly worried him. Miles spoke, "Colonel Davis, it would discourage the men left behind to see your troopers cut and run."

"Perhaps sir, we could lead the way for the entire garrison to escape."

"Stuff sir, simply stuff," Miles responded archly. "Infantry and artillery could not keep up with the mounted forces. Besides, my orders are clear."

252

Miles reached for a paper on his desk. "This was my last dispatch from Washington before the rebs cut the telegraph line. It's from General Halleck himself: "it is important that Harpers Ferry be held to the latest moment.""

Davis interrupted Miles, "Sir, the latest moment has come and passed."

"Don't tell me my job sir! I believe that forty years in the regular army of the United States has taught me how to evaluate the strength of a fortified post. We will hold here until McClellan relieves us."

"If you are to endure a siege, my troopers and their horses will only be more mouths to feed. If, in spite of all your best professional efforts, the rebs capture this place, the horses and equipment would make some very valuable prizes."

Armistead looked intently at Miles. If the man could tolerate interruption and sarcasm from a junior officer, he was unlikely to prove much of a match for Stonewall Jackson's soldiers. He should place Davis under arrest now, Armistead thought. That would help stiffen the garrison's resolve.

Instead Miles appeared to be considering seriously Davis's plan. "How do you propose to escape if, as you say, the rebs already have us surrounded?"

Davis answered confidently: "I have located two guides, both local men."

This time Miles interrupted. With a scornful snort he said, "Splendid, you are going to rely upon a pair of rebels to lead you to safety."

"Actually sir, only one of the guides is a southerner and he, like you, proudly wears the national uniform. May I present Major Armistead Carter."

Armistead stepped forward and again delivered an impeccable salute. He had the satisfaction of seeing an embarrassed look cross Miles' face.

Amidst further rankling among the senior officers, a plan emerged. Moving as silently as possible, some fifteen hundred cavalrymen would cross the pontoon bridge to Maryland. Armistead recommended that the column turn left, move between the canal and the bluff, and then follow a seldom used farm path until it intersected the Sharpsburg Road.

Miles inquired sharply, "You are confident you can find this route in the dark, are you sir?"

Armistead firmly answered, "Yes sir I am."

During the ensuing long pause, Armistead saw the frown on Miles' face transform into something else. The haggard visage of a confused, anxious, old man emerged. With a notable effort Miles shook himself into the present, "Very well, Colonel Voss is the senior colonel and will command the breakout. Voss, I authorize you to take only your own Illinois regiment, Davis' New Yorkers, and that Virginia and Maryland rabble." Miles looked pointedly at Armistead. Failing to elicit a response he continued, "I need everyone else to defend this post. Move quickly and silently. No bugle calls. If my garrison learns that you are abandoning them they might stampede to join you. Dismissed."

As soon as they had left Mile's headquarters, Davis seized Armistead's hand. Pumping it firmly he said, "Well done, major. You stood up to that old fool. He tried to bait you there at the end. It's a shabby business when a superior officer tosses off insults, knowing full well the target cannot defend himself. We're well done of him. Now, because of this night a pair of southern boys can give back to Old Abe the services of two fine cavalry regiments."

In spite of himself Armistead found that he was grinning back at the gregarious Davis. The man was a born leader. "Sir, I have one concern. I can find the Sharpsburg Road. But after that I do not know the land so well."

"Don't worry about that. My other guide knows Maryland like the back of his hand. You might even know him since he claims that he hails from hereabouts. A little, sly looking, dark fellow named Means, Abner Means."

The September sun disappeared behind the mountains leaving the town of Harpers Ferry in shadow. The growing darkness perfectly matched the mood of the defenders. Many had traveled long distances to arrive at this place; easterners from New York, western boys from Ohio and Illinois. There were also hundreds of Maryland soldiers and they perhaps were the most anxious of all. They knew that somewhere just across the river the rebel army was even now occupying their home places and the knowledge ate at them.

As the shadows deepened, a line of rebel campfires began to glow on the surrounding heights. They appeared like giant fireflies dancing above the river mist as they spread along Maryland Heights to the east, Loudoun Heights to the south, and Bolivar Heights to the west and north. The flames clearly signaled that the great grey machine was closing the vise on Harpers Ferry with appalling precision.

An enormous list of tasks left Armistead with no time to appreciate the grandeur of the scene. Tonight he would delegate responsibility for his company to his second in command because he would ride in the van with Davis, and, he supposed, with Means as well. It would be the first time he had encountered Means since he and Liverne had sabotaged Locomotive 199. Dear God! that seemed like a different age, Armistead reflected. He briefly wondered how Means would react and then realized that he hardly cared. Means had repeatedly and expertly manipulated him. He considered Means a dishonorable scoundrel, but he himself had been a fool.

Before preparing his unit for a difficult night march, he resolved that one thing he could do was bring Wellington along with him to escape from the trap at Harpers Ferry. If anyone asked why, he would say that he needed Wellington to help recognize the route north. Miles had strictly enjoined everyone to keep the attempt a secret. It was one of his few statements with which Armistead agreed.

Chapter 30. Maryland, September 14-15, 1862

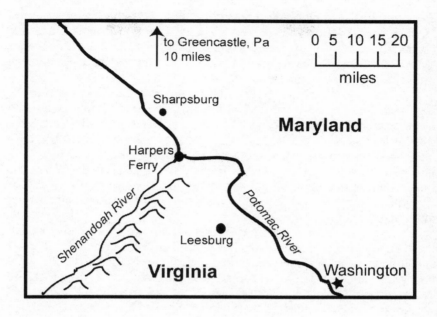

Colonel Arno Voss waited until full dark before assembling the regiments on the Ferry Lot across from the Wager House. The troopers mounted, formed a column two riders wide, and rode toward the pontoon bridge spanning the Potomac River. The Loudoun Rangers were part of the rear guard. As the first Ranger pair approached the bridge an army sutler stepped off his wagon and offered his hand.

"It's my finest tobacco. Better you have it then the damned rebels."

The troopers eagerly grasped the little tin foil wrappers. Henk remarked, "It's an omen boys. When tight-fisted, egg sucking, pond scum become generous, you know our luck has changed." Henk accepted the offering. He resolved to keep this small treasure: It will be my good luck charm, he thought. He carefully placed the wrapper inside his vest pocket.

Upon reaching the Maryland shore, the column turned north and followed the towpath alongside the Chesapeake and Ohio Canal. Skirting the canal locks, the column moved slowly until it reached the perimeter of the Union line. Here a pair of infantry pickets stood aside to allow the cavalry to pass. Voss nodded and Davis moved near to Armistead and whispered, "We're in your hands now."

It was a moonless night, difficult to see far because of the shadow cast by Maryland Heights. If trouble came it would begin somewhere along here, at the forward edge of the Confederate picket line; a ringing challenge or perhaps just the flash of powder followed by the detonations. Instead, there was only the sounds of hooves on hardback and the rushing of water over rock.

Scanning the cliff Armistead saw a dark patch of ground that stood out because it was a denser black than the adjacent terrain. It wound up slope like a black serpent climbing the heights. With the lightest pressure from his knee Armistead moved Blue onto a rugged farm path and up a ravine toward the summit of Maryland Heights. It is like entering the door to a crypt, Armistead thought. He found himself bracing for the expected blast of musketry and forced himself to relax.

Midway up Maryland Heights the path turned north to parallel the ridge line. From here Armistead could see Confederate campfires grouped in irregular clusters along the crest. Occasionally the sounds of voices came to Armistead's ears, once the rhythmic burble of a banjo. Either they don't know about this road, they're too tired to guard, or they're waiting to bag the whole lot, Armistead concluded. They passed four sets of campfires, the fourth so close that the fire light reflected in the treetops above the riders. Then, there were no more, no light, no sounds, just the occasional noise of hoof striking rock.

The head of the column reached the Sharpsburg Road without challenge. Davis reached over and touched Armistead. He whispered, "Now we should hurry when we can. Remember, the column is stretched out mighty thin all the way back across the bridge. We don't want the rebels waking up and trapping the poor fellas at the rear."

Armistead knew that neither regular army officers nor their men thought highly of the Loudoun Rangers. They would be stationed at the rear of the column; most likely to be captured, least likely to be missed. Armistead wondered, was Grimes Davis reminding me that my own men are still in grave danger?

Davis set a killing pace; long stretches at a fast gallop interspersed with short periods at the trot. Inevitably, the riders began to separate when the less fit horses faltered. Scared troopers drove their mounts furiously to close the gaps, sometimes colliding with their file leaders. Oaths, the sounds of men and horses falling, sharp orders: "Close up! Come on!" Armistead remembered that until recently Davis's New Yorkers had been serving as infantry. Clearly, some could barely ride.

The first contact occurred when they approached Antietam Creek. Blue's head came up and his ear's pricked. His high-arched neck twisted slightly from side to side. There was a momentary break in the rhythm of his legs. Armistead felt a change in the tension of the reins. He checked and looked intently: blackness, shadow, a sudden burst of flame followed by detonations. A kneeling rifleman was briefly lit by his own musket. Several more figures came running.

Davis appeared next to Armistead. "Is there another way?"

"Not that I know of," Armistead replied.

"Then we will cut our way clear. They will not stand." He seemed utterly confident and from his tone Armistead sensed that Davis was pleased.

Drawing his saber, Davis shouted, "Eighth New York! Column of fours. Follow me. Charge!"

Side by side, Armistead and Davis galloped toward the Confederate pickets. Behind them came a solid column of cheering troopers. Within seconds they were close enough to see that a group of men stood as a barrier blocking the road. Several were rapidly reloading their muskets, their arms pumping like pistons as they plunged their rammers down the barrels. A soldier in the front rank dropped his weapon and tried to stand. An unseen force from behind pushed him back into place. Most of the rebels were sighting down their weapons, preparing to fire. Forty yards separated the riders and their foes, thirty, twenty, closer still.

Pale faces emerged from the shadow of slouch hats, ghost-like figures to kill or be killed. The gap rapidly closed, yet for Armistead it seemed like motion slowed to a span contained by a single heartbeat, a universe compressed to an immediate, terrifying present. Armistead's whole being focused on a pair of kneeling figures directly in front of him. Both held weapons and both were aiming straight at him. He had time to register that one soldier wore a slouch hat and had a blanket roll slung across his chest while the other had a full beard and was hatless. Then came twin jets of flame and the sounds of exploding powder.

Armistead heard something pass close to his left ear. He felt something else pluck at his right sleeve. Then he was upon them. His cavalry instructors back at Carlisle taught that a saber's edge could cut, but it was the tip that killed. In his excitement, Armistead forgot nearly everything. He slashed down viciously into the full-bearded face of the bareheaded man. He felt his blade cut through something soft and then strike bone. He did remember to turn his wrist slightly to disengage his blade. He lifted his saber to strike again and sensed a warm drip against the back of his hand. He was through. No pale figures pointing death in his direction. He felt a cramping in his gut and tasted bile.

"Look, they're running. I wish we had time to chase. Are you all right?" Grimes Davis's reassuring voice helped Armistead compose himself.

Armistead swallowed painfully and gasped. "Yes thank you, I guess I am."

"Don't worry," Davis replied. "You get used to it, far more quickly than you can imagine." And then mercifully Davis rode off to rally his men, leaving Armistead alone to be sick.

The column continued at a rapid pace until reaching the outskirts of Sharpsburg. A sharp-eyed Illinois trooper detected a picket line on the edge of town. Davis gathered the troopers at the front of the column. He warned that they were near McClellan's army now, so they should respond to any challenges in order to avoid being shot by friends. Davis jocularly inquired, "Any volunteers?"

Armistead answered quietly, "I'll go, sir."

Davis shook his hand and Armistead set off. Again his horse saw them first; shadowy figures deployed across the road. One of them called out something indistinct. Armistead replied, "Friends of the Union."

A dancing orange flame split the darkness as the Confederate pickets opened fire. Armistead ducked low and waited for the inevitable impact. He heard the balls pass overhead and noted with surprise that they did not particularly frighten him. Then he heard Davis's voice roar the order to charge.

The Confederates were cavalry videttes, their job to detect an enemy's presence and then withdraw. They retreated rapidly toward Sharpsburg. Occasionally one or two riders turned to fire at their pursuers. Their delivered their Parthian shots in haste, their intent to induce caution and thereby slow the pursuit. The killing would come at some indefinite future.

The rebels failed because the thrill of the chase was upon the Union cavalry. The inept and inexperienced had long ago fallen behind. Those who remained were cavalry troopers. Among them, riders and horses were as one: hunting teams in perfect coordination, troopers half-standing in their stirrups, balanced, poised, keen; horses stretched out, ears erect, muscles taut, tails streaming. Furlong after furlong they pursued the fleeing rebels with their colonels, standard bearers, and buglers vying to take the lead.

Suddenly, a single rider emerged from the shadows to block the road. And then Confederate artillery erupted. The sputtering shells arced across the sky. One exploded in the air some twenty yards behind the rider. Its detonation backlit him, revealing a small, hooded figure in dark, civilian clothes. He spoke in German and Colonel Voss answered in the same language. Voss, Davis, and the unknown rider held a hurried consultation. Then Davis stood high in his stirrups and shouted, "We're heading right into Lee's army. About face!"

The hooded figure led the column off the road, across fields, and along woodland paths. From time to time the blue coated riders passed so near to Confederate bivouacs that they could plainly see the lounging rebel soldiers gathered around campfires. But they passed like bloodless wraiths, neither seen nor heard until finally they picked up a hard surface road. Only then did their guide slow the pace, turn in his saddle, and again speak: "It's the Hagerstown Turnpike, Carter. If anything happens to me, continue north across the Boonsboro Road to Greencastle. We separate now so we don't both get hit at the same time."

Armistead nodded and reined to a halt to allow the leading squadrons to pass. Even before Means had called out in German, Armistead had recognized him. He wasn't sure how he had known although, of course, he had been expecting him. Somehow, it was as if he could sense his presence, even in the dark. The arrival of the Loudoun Rangers interrupted Armistead's musings. To his surprise he found Hathaway leading the unit.

"Where's the lieutenant-colonel?"

"He's sick, or at least he reported sick. I reckon you're in command now."

"You have the boy?"

"No sir, he would not come. He said he was with the artillery now and it wouldn't be right to run just before a battle. He said they was "fixin to whup rebels" come morning. He said he's a freeman now and a soldier as well, and won't take no orders from any white man except his officers or President Lincoln. He asked me to thank you and said that you'd understand."

Chapter 31. Maryland, September 15, 1862

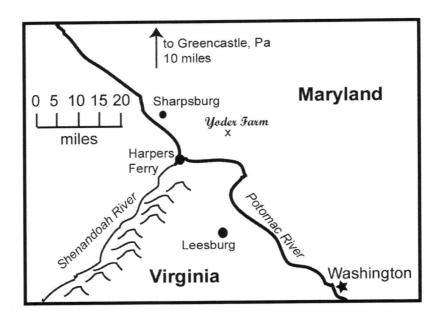

to Greencastle, Pa
10 miles

0 5 10 15 20
miles

Sharpsburg

Yoder Farm
X

Maryland

Harpers
Ferry

Shenandoah River

Potomac River

Leesburg

Virginia

Washington

On through the darkness rode the blue column. The Rangers passed beleaguered troopers standing by their broken down horses. Some begged for rides, others seemed too exhausted to even speak. A stout handful walked along the road, incredibly one or two carried their bridle, reins, and saddle. Probably old regular army cavalry, Armistead reflected. Troopers trained in the hard western school of Indian fighting, soldiers who accepted discipline and knew that the cost of lost equipment would be deducted from their pay.

Dawn's half-light found them passing smoldering fires from another large Confederate camp. The familiar military route march, with its start-stop-start rhythm, had almost lulled Armistead to sleep when the column halted. Officers trotted briskly from the van to the rear; hoarse whispers, electrifying intelligence: contact with the rebels just ahead.

Armistead strained to listen. He could hear the low rumbling of wheels on pavement; artillery or wagons? The Union cavalry deployed: the Eighth New York on the north side of the road; the Twelfth Illinois on the south, the remainder including the Rangers in reserve behind the New Yorkers. An officer rode just behind the two-deep line, pausing to give instructions and words of encouragement. He inquired softly, "Major Carter?"

Davis explained the situation. Scouts had detected a Confederate wagon train trundling slowly along the Sharpsburg Road. There was no easy way to avoid contact, so they were going to rely upon surprise and charge. "It will be like Hannibal at Lake Trasimene," Davis enthused. "You smoke the reference, Carter?"

"Yes sir. We wait until the whole column is parallel our position, charge out of the mist to cut the van and rear, and bag the whole lot."

Somewhat abashed, Davis replied, "Just so. Surprise is everything. No bugles, no cheering, sabers not pistols. Your men do have sabers do they not Carter?"

"The 1840 Dragoon Saber, sir."

"Then remember Carter, this time points not edges."

Now it was Armistead's turn to feel chagrin until Davis softened his words an infectious grin. Before disappearing into the half light he added that he was first going to try a scheme to capture the rebel train without a battle.

The creaking of iron-shod wooden wheels rolling up the slope announced the arrival of the wagon train. Teamster curses, the crack of whips, the lowing of a herd of cattle; obviously the rebels believed themselves safely within their own lines.

To Armistead's amazement, Davis appeared out of the murk and stood in the middle of the road. He saw Davis speak to the lead teamster and point to a fork in the road leading into a small woodlot. Armistead was too far away to hear the Alabamian's deep South drawl, but he saw the wagon dutifully turn as directed. He then saw Union troopers quietly take control of the wagon.

Without firing a shot, the Union cavalry captured Longstreet's entire ordnance train. A delighted New York officer whooped, "Boys, a change of governments was probably never more quietly or speedily effected." Armistead understood when he saw the wagons up close. Most had the white letters "U.S." painted on their sides indicating that they had been recently captured at the Battle of Second Manassas. Now they again resided with their original owners.

The bright morning sun found the Union cavalry escorting the wagons across the Pennsylvania border. Ahead lay the town of Greencastle. Panicked civilians thronged the streets. They carried trunks, boxes, bundles, packages tied up in blankets and quilts. Shop owners in shirt sleeves feverishly loaded carts, housewives buried the family silver in back yards, boys herded horses and cattle to safety. Men drove over-loaded wagons full of household furniture, their wives and children perched on the top, kettles and pails dangling beneath their feet. Some headed for the rail station, others went along the roads leading north or west. Once they realized that the column was not Confederate raiders, everything changed. They lined the road to give the weary troopers pails of water or buttermilk, fruit, cakes, and pie, and to praise them as heroes.

Whereas before they had been slumping in their saddles with fatigue, now Armistead saw his men straighten in their saddles and puff out their chests; fourteen hours of exertion, fear, and silence now finished. They talked, joked, and bragged about their exploits. Even more remarkable was their response to Grimes Davis when they paraded in Greencastle's main square.

Davis told them that they had captured Longstreet's ordnance train with nearly one hundred heavily loaded wagons, each drawn by a six-mule team, along with the escort of some two hundred and fifty infantry, and a herd of beef cattle for good measure. "We can proudly call ourselves the Harpers Ferry Skedaddlers," he told them, "because we fought our way clear from the rebel trap and we didn't lose a man doing it. You did well and are becoming soldiers. But boys, wars ain't won by retreats. Next time we meet the rebels we are going to lick 'em in a standup fight!"

The jubilant cheers of fifteen hundred troops filled the square. The voice of a newly confident cavalry major joined without hesitation.

Liverne was more tired than he could ever recall. His journey from Richmond had been long, but now, as he traversed the familiar lane leading to the Yoder Farm, he was almost home.

He recalled the seemingly endless time spent confined in Elizabeth Van Lew's hidden room, and his strained laughter upon being told that the patrol had departed after a perfunctorily search lasting only ten minutes.

"I recommend that you stay here until I can arrange things with my friends," she had said. "We can make it quite comfortable. It can hold over twenty men."

"Thank you, but no," he had answered.

He agreed to wait until the next evening before departing but steadfastly refused to return to the hidden room. Like the good agents they both were, neither one had divulged much about their activities. Nonetheless, he had learned that Van Lew and a network of Union sympathizers were in regular contact with Union prisoners and that they had hopes of helping them escape. More than this, she would not say.

He had slipped out through the back gardens and followed the James River to the landing at Rocketts. In times past, friendly captains had carried fugitive slaves down the river to safety. No longer. Confederate engineers had obstructed the river to block the ascent of the Federal fleet. He considered trying to skirt the flank of the Confederate army defending the capital in order to reach Union lines. He learned that the region was infested with wary, hair-trigger patrols and so dismissed this route as well.

Van Lew had recommended traveling west where eventually he would find people sympathetic to the Union. But a black man moving through country where very few blacks traveled was sure to attract attention. Moreover, Liverne had long ago learned about the gulf separating people professing good intentions and people willing to take personal risk to assist a black man on the run. So, he resolved to return more or less the way he had come.

His departure from Richmond previewed how difficult the journey would be. Evidently something big was being organized because the army had clamped down hard on all intercourse between city and country. There were many more checkpoints, far more patrols, and all displayed a vigilance unlike any he had seen before. He eventually found a way out but not until he had consumed all the provisions Van Lew had provided.

And then his real troubles began. He almost made it to the Valley before he fell ill. He had hoped the sickness would prove mild, but something sunk its claws so deep that he had to seek refuge in a shallow cave overlooking Rockfish Gap. He remained there for a very long time, subsisting on moisture from a seep dripping from the rocks and the pale, boney fish that lived in the pool below. Sometimes, when the fever receded, he dragged himself outside to gaze forlornly at an isolated farm in a nearby hollow. He saw that a woman and two small children lived alone there and that it was the children's duty to gather eggs from the hen house hidden in a grove of chestnuts out past the field of sparse corn.

When the fever broke he went there and greedily ate one egg after another. He wrung the neck of a chicken, and carried it no great distance away, plucked the feathers, and ate it raw.

Diversions and delays followed him north until he neared Harpers Ferry. Here Confederate cavalry compelled him to swing west into the mountains. Eventually, during the second week of September, he crossed the Potomac well upstream at Hancock. He discovered that the intelligence bureau remained at the same address. His passwords were long out of date but fortunately an old operator recognized him. He bathed in comfort for the first time and thereafter slept from one morning to the next.

A final, unexpected hurdle came when he found the Confederate army occupying the area around the Yoder Farm. But here he was on totally familiar territory, having guided fugitives from the slave catchers and their bloodhounds across this very ground. Throughout the ordeal, the image of family and home had served as his lodestar and now he had arrived. The rapturous greeting fulfilled his every hope. Frederick, his youngest son, initially responded with measured dignity, acting as if he had grown to become the man of the house in the space of one short summer: "I trust I find you well, sir?"

"Come son. Let me have the feel of you." Frederick hugged him tightly, his muffled sobs the sounds of a man-child become a boy again. Next appeared the twin girls who launched themselves into his arms with abandon, trying to describe all the amazing things they had done and seen, in one, long tumbling breath before the other interrupted. Then came his wife; serious, as always, with relief and love showing in her eyes, and something else as well that he could not decipher. He kissed her fully on the mouth. When they unclenched, he asked, "Where's Jason?"

She stood holding both his hands and replied, "I found him listening to the meeting of the Committee. Mister Means was telling the others how a few of the young blacks were proving exceptionally useful. They could sometimes move more freely than the soldiers. Jason burst into the room and volunteered immediately. You should have seen him, Liverne. You would have been so proud."

The knot of fear, his utterly reliable tell-tale, came. "And," he softly prompted.

"He went with my blessing. He's at Harpers Ferry working with Mister Means."

Liverne disengaged from her grasp. "Good God, woman! Do you know what they do when they catch someone spying? If it's a nigger they don't even wait for a soldier's trial, they just string him up to the nearest tree."

"Do you think I made this decision lightly?" she snapped. "Of course I know the risks. He went with my blessing."

"Have we, you and I, not done enough? Have we not lost enough comrades? Have I not taken enough risks to satisfy you?"

"Stop Liverne. Stop. Our son is almost a man and in these times when freedom lies in the balance, the god of war cannot pause to count the ages of those who enlist. The cost of freedom is high, my husband. We all must pay what we can."

She reached out to him and he pushed her hands away.

For the children's sake he strove hard to restore normalcy to the remainder of the day. Now that he understood his son Frederick's new role, he set to work distilling the obligations of manhood, knowing that time was short and that the vessel's capacity uncertain. Too soon it was time to put the children to bed. They said the familiar prayers and closed the door to the children's room. Jolina looked at him expectantly.

"I'm going to fetch Jason. I'll be leaving before dawn. You needn't see me off." He walked past the door to their room and continued down the hall.

He long lay awake until he heard her footsteps. "May I come to your bed?" she whispered. He knew how difficult such a request was for her. Later, as they lay still entwined, she said, "Had I not bid him permission he would have gone anyway."

"I know my love. Hush. Here is the sun. Let us salute the dawn."

Chapter 32. Harpers Ferry and Loudoun County, mid-September 1862

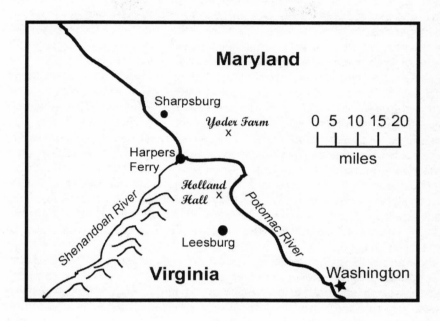

The Loudoun Grays entered Harpers Ferry during the late afternoon of September 15. According to Jackson's men, they had not missed much of a fight. Sly Old Jack had set up his artillery on the commanding heights overlooking the town. A brief bombardment, a push from the woods against Bolivar Heights, and the yankees had shown the white flag. Apparently their commander, some officer named Miles, had been mortally wounded by one of the first shells.

What had taken place after the surrender proved more interesting. When Jackson rode into the town he passed hundreds of blue coated prisoners. The Union men noted the contrast between Jackson and their own leaders. Jackson was shabbily dressed. A battered, weather-stained kepi worn low on his forehead exhibited his seeming indifference to martial display. His craggy features, full beard, and the burning intensity of his eyes made Jackson appear like a warrior from the Old Testament. Scores of yankees showed their respect for the Confederate leader by saluting. Jackson, in turn, invariably returned the salutes. A Union soldier remarked to his comrades, "Boys, he's not much for looks, but if we'd had him we wouldn't have been caught in this trap."

After Jackson passed, the rebels exchanged their threadbare, patched jackets and trousers for new and better-made yankee uniforms. The Grays passed camps littered with cast-off clothes. Here the stripped prisoners milled about shamefaced and anxious. Farther along were the stores of a magnificently equipped army: laden wagons groaning under the weight of their cargoes; sleek mule teams fitted with shiny new harnesses placidly grazing along the sides of Washington Street; deserted tent cities with countless stands of stacked muskets standing as mute guards; complete batteries of rifled artillery arrayed rank after rank. Min marveled at the contrast with the barren campsites of the lean rebel soldiers.

The Confederate infantry in town belonged to A. P. Hill's division. They were the lucky ones who could devote the remainder of the day to enjoying the fruits of victory. They filled their canteens with molasses because Jackson had ordered the whiskey collected and preserved for the medical department. They loaded haversacks with cigars, coffee, French mustard, writing paper, silk handkerchiefs. Most of all they filled empty bellies with unfamiliar foods; pickled oysters, canned lobster, game birds preserved in aspic, and better still, light breads so different from the coarse, dark loaves served by the army's bakers, so different and enjoyable that they ate them like cake. Best of all, a fortunate few beat the provost guards to the officers' quarters where they washed down their feast with Rhenish wine and champagne.

However, most of the victors had little chance to partake. It seemed like Old Jack was not content with what had been done. Already long columns of sweat-stained infantry were departing to rejoin General Lee who was said to be offering battle along the banks of Antietam Creek near the little market town of Sharpsburg.

Around Harpers Ferry, Min saw provost guards roughly herding blacks off the street corners. "What's this about sergeant?"

"Runaways, sir. Major Harmon wants them gathered up quick."

Min knew that Harmon was Jackson's highly respected, hard-bitten chief Quartermaster. "Treat 'em easy, sergeant. They are people, frightened people. Treat 'em easy."

The Grays settled into the cavalry stables. Min made sure that the men were grooming and feeding their horses before he set out to search for rations. Groups of soldiers marched purposefully through the streets. Officers carrying reports and orders hurried into and out of headquarters buildings. Dust-covered couriers galloped by. Evidently everyone had a mission yet no one had made any arrangements for the Loudoun Grays. Min reflected angrily that here in the midst of plenty, no one gave a damn whether his hungry men ate. He finally managed to secure a box of hardtack and a side of raw bacon from the hands of a grasping, skeptical commissary sergeant. After depositing them with his men, Min and Kinlock went looking for orders. His queries led him to the Gault Hotel.

Inside, a splendidly uniformed staff captain sat alone at a linen covered table. On the table were two place settings, baskets with bread and rolls, numerous covered dishes, and a decanter of wine. The officer daintily lifted a silver lid and inspected the dish. The smell of glazed ham wafted into the dining room. Min heard the captain remark with disdain, "Pork again. I think not." He then looked up and Min recognized the face.

Captain Otis Polk's eyes ran from Min's battered slouch hat down to his patched and faded trousers. He did not seem to remember their previous encounter at Piedmont Station on the day when the battle at Manassas Junction occurred. With evident distaste Polk said, "Well?"

Min stiffly provided a formal report. The captain impatiently interrupted. "Loudoun Grays you say?" He sighed loudly and opened a leather valise. He found a set of orders and briskly explained that the Grays were not selected to join the march north. Instead, they were to work with Jackson's quartermasters. Polk explained that selected officers were to write the paroles issued to some eleven thousand Union prisoners, count the thousands of captured muskets, and assign guards to protect the newly acquired supplies. Min complained irritably, "Good God! First we ride all over tarnation looking for yankees when everyone knows that all of them are right here in Harpers Ferry, then we are put to work as clerks."

The captain primly replied, "Actually lieutenant, you and your company have a different assignment. Seems like we captured between five hundred and a thousand niggers, likely all runaways." The captain took a delicate pinch of snuff, sneezed, and then looked at his sheaves of paper. "Since you come from around here, Major Harmon figured that you would be most suited to sort out the claims. "

"Claims, sir?"

"Yes. Owners are already showing up in town looking for their property. Major Harmon wants the runaways given back to their legitimate masters but he also wants to impress as many as possible to serve as teamsters. We're called the foot cavalry, you know lieutenant, and we rely upon the wagons keeping pace. It's a very important job."

"Yes sir, I understand. We are not to serve as clerks like you, another very important duty I am sure, but rather as slave catchers."

Min delivered his best salute, half turned, and felt Kinlock's nudge. "What about rations sir?"

Min faced Polk again and spoke, "Sir, can you tell me where I can find rations for my men?"

The captain looked up with open contempt. "Surely you know that rations are the domain of the commissary officers and I, you see, am in charge of the quartermaster department."

"Yes, I see," Min answered.

"I see too," Kinlock said. He paused to cough and then pulled back the chair opposite the captain. He sat down and eyed the dishes hungrily.

The captain icily inquired, "Sergeant, are you aware of whom you are dining with?"

"Well," Kinlock replied, "before I came soldiering I used to be particular who I ate with, but now I don't care a damn, so long as the victuals are clean."

Without bothering to conceal his amused grin, Min left the dining room and walked back to the stables. He saw from a distance the rear of a shuffling column of black men trudging up Shenandoah Street. He did not notice that among them was the forlorn figure of Wellington Holland. Nor did he observe that roped together with the other blacks was a tall youth who held his head high in an act of defiance that he hoped hid his fear.

September had begun with high promise. The Richmond papers became available again and Amanda read that Confederate arms everywhere were ascendant. The Southern Illustrated News reported that out West, General Bragg had liberated Kentucky and captured Cincinnati, while in Virginia, General Lee had driven the yankees across the Potomac and stood poised to liberate Maryland and perhaps invade the North.

While neighbors told of columns of lean, barefoot rebels marching north across the Potomac fords, at Holland Hall Amanda saw a different side of war. Every day numerous stragglers appeared at the door and always their tale of woe was the same: "We're powerfully hungry, ma'am, can't you give us something to eat?" At first, Amanda ordered the servants to feed all who came. But as the days passed, and Lee's army moved farther north into Maryland, the requests only increased. More worrisome, Amanda saw that the soldiers were without supervision. They formed bands who drifted from farm to farm, descending like voracious locusts to consume everything and then demand more.

Already James and two of the field hands had had to brandish her father's old hunting rifles to see them off. So far there had been no violence, but she wondered how long it could last.

Gordon had surprised her by offering his assistance and she had surprised herself by being tempted to accept. Surely he could be trusted with routine farm management and it would relieve her of an enormous burden. But when James represented to her that the darkies would only obey Gordon with extreme reluctance, she knew that it was work she had to perform herself. Accordingly, she directed the necessary precautions; ordering seed stock, smoked hams, preserved fruit, apples and the like hidden in places no forager was likely to find. There were countless tasks that did nothing to increase production at Holland Hall but at least protected what remained.

After Amanda explained to Gordon that acting as overseer was far beneath his station, he continued to handle the accounts. Nightly, she continued to double check his work. She also hinted that there were some other tasks he could perform if he were willing. He told her he would think about it. Thereafter, it annoyed her greatly that while everyone worked long hours, Gordon did not participate. He typically emerged from his cabin late in the morning and spent the day resting in the shade of the huge chestnut that stood sentinel over the smoke house. Occasionally he rose to stroll about and observe the work and sometimes, the servants told her, he set off on nocturnal visits to places unknown. During it all he seldom appeared sober. Amanda again considered turning him out, but the terms of his contract clearly stated that he had the right to room and board until year's end. Holland Hall could not afford the cost of breaking his contract and she knew that Gordon knew this as well. In the absence of reliable men, she desperately longed for Boyd's return. In the absence of any information, she had concluded that he must have accompanied Lige White's cavalry on the march north. No one had any idea when they might return.

Chapter 33. Shepherdstown and Loudoun County, September 18-19, 1862

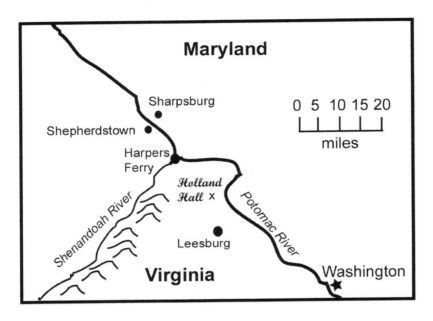

On Thursday, September 18, Min received orders to march the Loudoun Grays to Shepherdstown on the southern bank of the Potomac. The Grays entered the town with difficulty. Ambulances and farm wagons carrying wounded soldiers jammed the streets. There was a continual din as teamsters wrangled and cursed, officers galloped about trying to restore order, and women moved from building to building carrying bandages, medicines, water, and food. Confederate wounded filled every structure: the town's six churches, the Odd Fellows' Hall, the Freemasons' Lodge, the unfinished Town Hall. They overflowed into the surrounding countryside to occupy farm houses, barns, corn cribs, and pigsties. Min saw that every structure no matter how dilapidated was filled past capacity. Yet, it made no difference because fresh wounded kept arriving.

For the remainder of the day the Grays occupied positions guarding Shepherdstown. During the night, the Army of Northern Virginia crossed the river. By Friday's first light, General Lee and those parts of the army that remained under control had marched south. Hundreds of hungry stragglers remained behind; gaunt, hollow-eyed, nervous, their presence a burden to a town already strained far beyond its capacities. Soon thereafter, McClellan's army appeared on the Maryland side of the river.

Min watched a Union battery unlimber on Douglas's Hill and begin shelling the town. Confusion gave way to terror. Panicked solders and some civilians fled. Min saw that the artillery fire was not indiscriminate, the yankee gunners were aiming at the army's rear guard. "They don't realize the whole town is a hospital. Spread the word to raise yellow flags over every building. When the yankees see them they'll know. Kinlock, you get down to those old warehouses in the ravine. I'll take Main Street. We meet at Town Hall. Go!"

In less than fifteen minutes, strips of yellow rags flew from rooftop and chimney. Yet still the shells whistled and shrieked and the town descended into chaos. The hospitals emptied as anyone who could walk began hobbling away. Those who remained begged for someone to carry them to safety. Terrified civilians poured from their homes. Min shouted to them to stay, telling them that they were safer in their homes than in the open on the roads. He argued, threatened, ridiculed, and it was in vain.

Shouting men, crying women, screaming children, white and black alike, became wedged among the wagons and ambulances in a giant, struggling mass that was beyond all control. Most of the shrieking shells flew well overhead. Clearly they were aimed at the disciplined soldiers who provided the rear guard. But some fell short to explode in adjacent fields, in front lawns, and sometimes in the streets themselves. It was one of them that sent a flying piece of metal into Min's thigh.

It knocked him backward into his saddle and his horse jigged wildly. He quickly regained control and looked down at his wound. Blood spurted from the jagged tear above his knee where the fragment had gouged out flesh and muscle. He reached for the bandages that Amanda had made him promise he would always carry. He pressed the rough linen against the wound and rode back toward the Town Hall to search for a surgeon. At first he felt light-headed, and soon thereafter very, very thirsty.

The Shepherdstown Town Hall had stood half-built for a long while, as townspeople argued about how to pay to complete it and who should do the work. Hospital orderlies had thrown rough fence boards over its beams to provide a crude roof and filled it with straw. Scores of wounded lay within and here the surgeons worked. A line of wounded men waited their attention. As he stood in line, a freshly bandaged infantryman limped by. Catching sight of Min he exclaimed, "Say mister, I'll give you fifty dollars if you'll go back to camp with me!"

"And why is that?" Min responded.

"Oh, it's simply a business proposition. I know I can easily get one hundred dollars to show the boys a wounded cavalryman." Chuckling with delight, the soldier moved on.

Min shuffled his way up the line. From beneath the planks he heard the call, "Next!" with monotonous regularity as the surgeon completed operation after operation. From time to time a negro emerged, balancing a pair of large buckets filled with amputated limbs. Two soldiers carried a man out on a crude stretcher. Min saw that he was missing a leg. He was young, barely more than a boy. He looked exceedingly pale. As the stretcher passed, Min overheard him mumble, "I'll just lay down to bleed awhile, and then get up and fight again."

Another stretcher, another missing leg, but apparently something else was missing as well. Between clenched teeth the wounded man hissed, "It's over for me, boys. Now I'll never marry."

One of the stretcher bearers replied, "Come on, Briscoe. It ain't nuthing more than a proud cut. You'll get along fine."

Min winced. Back at home when they gelded horses they performed a proud cut, thereby rendering the animal no longer potent but still in possession of its male energy.

He finally reached the front of the line and descended beneath the planks into the Town Hall. Inside was heavily shadowed. Light from a flickering lantern caused him to blink. He stepped on something and a soldier groaned. Min saw that the floor was alive with the writhing shapes of the tightly packed wounded. The motion and the odor reminded him of the worm-infested bowels of a freshly killed deer. He realized that he had joined another line and sat down to rest.

He woke when someone trod heavily on his hand. An orderly motioned for him to come and sit on a crude table formed by a door laid across some empty hardtack boxes. Min saw the surgeon approach. His blood-splattered apron and the clots of congealed blood on his hairy forearms made him look like a slaughter house laborer. "What have we here?" the surgeon inquired. Min smelled a strong aroma of liquor.

"I don't know that it's much, but I can't seem to make it stop bleeding."

The surgeon refreshed himself from a hip flask, probed Min's wound, and said with a slur, "I take it off and it stops bleeding."

Someone nearby screamed. An anxious hospital attendant appeared to summon the surgeon. Min saw the surgeon weave as he made his way among the injured. Min stood. Again he felt light-headed. He leaned against the table. His mind began to float. The surgeon's voice drew near. Min staggered back outside.

Evening had come. Some negro servants had ignited fires around which lay the wounded. Min heard a voice, "Mister Carter? Mister Carter?"

With great effort he knelt by the figure, but did not recognize him. "Who are you?"

"Why, I'm Souther White from Berryville. "I'm' kin to the Whites who live at the Ferry. I seen you there. You was racing on a beautiful dapple gray. As fine a horse as I've ever seen. I seen Miss Amanda there too. How are they?"

The boy spoke in a restless, disjointed manner, the air catching in his throat and causing him to gasp and cough. Min could see that he had been shot through the shoulder and lungs. Min did not recall having ever met him. "Of course, I remember you. They are fine, just fine. Is there anything you need?"

"I'm real thirsty, and powerful cold."

Min shared his canteen but the boy had great trouble swallowing. Most of the water leaked down his cheek. Min saw that the person lying next to Souther was dead. He removed the blanket from the body and covered the boy with it. Souther grabbed his arm. His touch was icy cold. "Don't go, Mister Carter."

Min rose unsteadily and motioned toward a nurse. "It won't be long now," the nurse said.

Min knelt again and held Souther's hand. Souther was trying to tell him something. Min recognized Kinlock's name, and something about a son, a woman's name, Mary perhaps, but most of the words no longer made sense. "Remind me to Miss Amanda, oh what a fine horse, oh Ma! Ma!" A liquid gurgle in the boy's throat interrupted his chant-like repetition. Souther's hand jerked once, twice, and fell still.

Min shook his head, trying to clear it. Amanda's name seemed to hang in the air and Min made his decision. He asked one of the negroes to bind his wound hard. It slowed the bleeding. Using the last coins in his pocket he found a literate corporal to write and deliver a brief message to Kinlock.

The moon appeared above the horizon. It was a color that he had once called blood red. Now he knew otherwise. He mounted his horse and rode east toward the rising moon, east toward Leesburg, east toward home.

Anne Rix had held little hope that her birth record might still exist. In exchange for the usual favors she had once sent a respectable client to search the records at the Leesburg Courthouse. As she expected, he found nothing. But she paid her barkeep well because he was in a unique position to acquire surprising information that often proved profitable. She never imagined that his diligence would assist her own particular quest. When Billy told her of an unguarded conversation in which Gordon boasted about his prior employment as clerk of registers, she resolved to meet with him.

Gordon's visits were less predictable than they had once been. But she was a patient woman, when patience furthered her aims, so she bided her time until he reappeared. He was intoxicated, but still able to talk. "I have a business proposition to discuss," she told him.

He was taken aback. "Now Meme Richard, Gordon's been a good boy," he whined.

"That's why we let you in. Billy, pour Mister Gordon a brandy. It's on the house."

"I've had a spot of trouble with Mister Clarence Rixey. I've heard that he was a bit wild in his youth and spread his charm with less care than he might wish to be known. There should be some records, but there are none. I imagine he paid you to burn them."

"Oh, I never destroyed documents," Gordon replied, "Why it would be quite against the law."

With considerable effort she controlled her breathing. "Then perhaps we can make a deal."

He too knew how to bargain and his price was high. After he had his way with the girl she would be of little use for several weeks, but she had been planning to dismiss Luinda anyway. The gold she was more loath to concede.

"Only if it is a fully certified original, Mister Gordon."

The next day Gordon returned. The document was authentic. As he left he commented with a smirk, "They still won't believe you, you know."

I'll settle accounts with you later, my friend, she thought, but she said nothing. What Gordon did not realize was that she needed the proof to convince herself.

Her childhood memories were indistinct, made unclear both by the acts themselves — which at the time she had not thought unusual — and by the threats made later. The visits stopped around the time she was eleven, she supposed. He always gave her special presents before he departed, and she recalled missing them, especially the Dutch chocolate. When she asked her mother why he no longer came, she had grown angry and beat her. Later, she told her that it was because of her that they had to move to Wheeling and that she must forget all about him.

Now her father was a regular client. He consistently preferred the company of the younger girls and more than once hinted about the availability of Anne's nine-year-old daughter. Her breath caught and she considered. She told herself that her dislike for her daughter had nothing to do with her decision. If revenge required such a price, it was worth it. Besides, Clarence Rixey undoubtedly possessed a great deal of money. How much will he give to prevent exposure? A wave of pleasurable anticipation swept over her. She poured herself a drink and began writing sums on a discarded piece of paper.

Chapter 34. Boteler's Ford, September 20, 1862

Armistead guided the One Hundred and Eighteenth Pennsylvania Regiment toward the Potomac ford downstream from Shepherdstown. It was a lovely morning, the quiet broken by the one-sided conversation conducted by Lieutenant Colonel James Gwyn, the regiment's second in command. Armistead had learned that different men steadied their nerves before battle in different ways. Gwyn did so by talking, his Irish accent growing more pronounced as his irritation increased. He told Armistead that the regiment comprised mostly new recruits. Their first taste of war had come three days earlier at Antietam. But they had been in reserve the entire time and had not even fired their weapons.

"You would think," Gwyn said, "that a unit named the 'Corn Exchange Regiment', would receive sufficient financial backing from its sponsor. But no, we have these miserable Enfield rifles that have been condemned, condemned sir, by the inspector-general!"

Armistead heard the words, but barely attended. He was over tired, and what energy he possessed he directed toward the far shore. Virginia again, he reflected.

The ford was deep. The soldiers held their Enfields high over their heads and carefully filed through the water. Armistead led them up a ravine and toward the right. Upon reaching the bluff, he glanced toward the regiment's commander, Colonel Charles Prevost, and said, "I believe this is your station sir."

The escort company of Maine cavalry led the civilian to General George Sykes' headquarters. The general was busy speaking with his aides while consulting a map. The civilian impetuously moved toward him until a pair of troopers pinned his arms, bringing him to an abrupt halt. "Civilians don't interrupt generals, mister," a trooper hissed in his ear.

The commotion attracted Sykes' gaze. "What is this about sergeant?" he asked.

The civilian seized his chance. "General, your men are walking into a trap. Not a mile from your picket line is the whole rebel army. A.P. Hill is already advancing to attack your right flank."

"Good God!" Sykes exclaimed. "Who do we have there?"

"The Corn Exchange Regiment, general."

Sykes groaned. "My poor regulars. I knew it was a mistake. The Virginia side of the river is no place for troops until a proper reconnaissance is made." Sykes lowered his head and pressed his hands against his temples. After a long pause he looked up and spoke: "I can't withdraw the troops until I consult General Porter."

"It's too late for that," the civilian said. Sykes ignored him. The general summoned an orderly to bring his horse. "It's too late, you fool," Abner Means muttered, but in the flurry of activity around the headquarters no one attended.

"I wonder if we should not advance to that belt of trees." Colonel Prevost commented.

A crackle of musketry interrupted Armistead's reply. Emerging from the tree line came a heavy battle line of rebel infantry. They obviously outnumbered Prevost's men. "Deploy!" Prevost screamed.

Armistead was unsure where his duty lay. It seemed cowardly to abandon the regiment at the moment of crisis, but his orders merely required him to lead the Corn Exchange Regiment to its designated position. He remained on his horse just behind the center of the regiment.

The sounds of battle intensified. Far to the left a federal unit appeared atop a knoll. It was a regiment of United States Regulars, professional soldiers renowned for their discipline. They marched toward the river and away from the rebels. Then, like a finely tuned machine, they halted as one and faced about to confront the Confederates. Their front rank knelt, the second rank raised their muskets to the shoulder. An officer chopped downward with his sword and the entire line disappeared in a thick cloak of smoke. Before the smoke dispersed, the regiment was moving backward again; marching with firm, even steps, toward the safety of the far shore.

The regulars' withdrawal exposed the flank of the Corn Exchange Regiment. A rebel battle line, banners waving, crested the knoll that had been abandoned by the regulars. Armistead saw Prevost gallop off to position personally his three left-most companies. In Prevost's absence, Lieutenant-Colonel Gwyn ordered the center companies to open fire. A feeble popping ensued. Armistead guessed that not more than one in two of the defective Enfields actually discharged.

The volley had little effect. The howling rebels pressed hard against the regiment's center and left and the raw Pennsylvania soldiers wavered. Prevost returned. To rally the regiment he ordered the colors to advance. The colonel rode forward with the color guard only to topple from his saddle. He rose, badly wounded, and began limping to the rear.

Gwyn immediately replaced him and shouted, "Forward boys! Follow me!" Inspired by Gwyn's example, perhaps two hundred stalwart soldiers advanced over the crest toward the Confederates. The balance hung back; uncertain, fearful, trusting neither their weapons nor their leaders.

The charge of the Corn Exchange Regiment momentarily checked the Confederate advance. But the rebels who overlapped the regiment's left flank made an oblique turn to face the Pennsylvanians and opened fire. Gwyn's men began to fall and he ordered them back under the brow of the hill. The reverse slope of the bluff provided a sheltered place for the regiment to reform. Above the din, Armistead heard Gwyn telling the remaining officers to prepare to charge again.

"You sir," he shouted to Armistead. "Ride back and bring up some supports."

Before Armistead could comply, a blast of musketry came from the knoll on the left. Armistead saw the knoll crowded with Confederate soldiers as successive waves of troops appeared. He counted three, four, six battle flags. The noise doubled, and then doubled again.

He rode Blue down the bluff toward the river. It was a relief to escape from the terrifying din. He saw the last of the regulars tramping across the ford to safety. From the heights on the Maryland side, federal batteries fired furiously against targets he could not see. A rider splashed across the ford. "Orders for the One Hundred Eighteenth. Can you tell me where they are?"

"Follow me," Armistead replied.

At the top of the bluff, the Corn Exchange Regiment was grimly holding its position against worsening odds. Armistead saw the three companies on the regiment's left flank bent back like a hinge but fighting tenaciously still. The noise was so loud that the messenger had to lean sideways in his saddle to shout in Colonel Gwyn's ear. He apparently told him to withdraw because officers began moving along the line, tapping men on the shoulder and gesturing to the rear.

Until this point, the regiment had performed admirably. But an orderly withdrawal in the face of an enemy who had closed to point-blank range was beyond its powers. The Pennsylvanians scrambled wildly down the precipitous slope while Confederate marksmen, like hunters killing the game they had flushed, methodically started picking them off.

Once before Armistead had seen how quickly a disciplined group could dissolve into selfish mob. Accordingly, as soon as he saw the regiment start to withdraw, he turned around and began his descent. Blue was a sure-footed animal, so Armistead let him find his own way across rock ledges and through bush and briar until he reached the road to the ford.

Above him, panic-stricken soldiers heedlessly plunged down the slope; tripping, falling, discarding muskets and canteens to make flight faster. On the Maryland side of the river, the Union artillery intensified its cannonade in an effort to check the Confederates. Whether it did any good, Armistead could not tell, but when he heard the tempo of nearby bullets increase, he put Blue into a fast canter for the ford.

The passage to the ford, he later decided, was akin to running a hellish, dreamlike gauntlet in which his momentum slowed in spite of his efforts to accelerate. Scores of soldiers converged on the ford to form a jostling, cursing mob intent only on crossing the water. And all the while the Confederate marksmen, aiming with deliberation from the bluff, decimated the mob. Because he was mounted, Armistead was able to stay ahead of the flying soldiers. He reached the shallows on the far shore and looked back.

The infantry struggled through the ford, their legs pumping furiously in the knee-deep water. Each step saw a reduction in their numbers as men fell, their wounded bodies sometimes floating on the surface, sometimes disappearing beneath the water. He saw a wounded man struggle in the water. He desperately clutched at the greatcoat of a comrade. Rather than help, the man shed his coat and kept going. Armistead saw a young soldier, more a boy than a man, pitch forward into the water and then rise. One hand reached out to beg assistance, the other pressed against a dark and spreading stain on his chest.

Armistead dismounted. He slapped Blue vigorously on the rump and shouted, "Go!" The frightened animal looked at him with extreme reluctance, but years of training told and Blue trotted north through the mud shallows and onto dry land.

Armistead saw the wounded boy being driven under by the human tide. He forced a passage toward the stricken soldier. Running soldiers impeded his progress and blocked his view. Something, a bullet, grazed his cheek. He collided with a fear-crazed soldier and nearly fell. He recovered, and with elbow, shoulder, and fist, bulled his way ahead. A gap emerged. He was only ten feet from the boy. The gap filled. The man in front of him screamed an oath and fell heavily. Armistead shouldered his way past and then he was there. Their eyes locked.

The boy's hazel eyes opened wide. In them, Armistead saw fear, shock, despair. Armistead reached to clasp his hand when the minie balls struck. One grazed his face, the second tore into his left shoulder. The blows drove him into the water. He rose unsteadily to find himself surrounded by a horde of fleeing men. He tore off his neck cloth and stuffed it into the gaping wound. The bright red blood quickly soaked through the cloth. A near blinding pain stabbed at him. He tried to find the boy but could make out nothing except the movement of the trampling mob. Finally, amidst a knot of pumping legs, Armistead saw the boy's face, his hazel eyes plaintively looking straight at him. Then he was gone as the blue tide again enveloped him. It surged against Armistead and he was too weak to resist the pressure.

He reached the shallows, collapsed, and, prepared to die. A familiar whicker brought him to fuller consciousness. He saw Blue standing like a breakwater as fleeing soldiers dodged around him. A stirrup dangled close to his face. He reached for it, pulled himself upright, and staggered another few steps onto the shore. Here he fell again and this time he did not move.

He remained unconscious until the rough jostling of the hospital orderlies woke him to a howling universe of pain. They set him on a plank table and tied his arms and legs securely. The last thing he heard before he smelled an unusual, strong odor and fell into blessed sleep was a voice saying, "It will have to come off."

Chapter 35. Maryland, October 1862

He rose toward the surface, toward the light that he sensed but could not see. He struggled but came no closer and so he gave up. The now familiar, fearsome images returned. They grew, changed, became more terrible still, and took over all except a corner of his mind. In the distance, he heard screams.

Sometime later he sensed the light again, only this time it was no longer a white horizon but rather a mere pinpoint centered at the end of a long tunnel. The tunnel was warm, far more inviting than the chill that enveloped him. Images appeared in the tunnel, indistinct at first but then filling into horror shapes. They advanced toward him. He was too weak to challenge them, so they came closer. He fought against the urge to cry out until the horror reached out to take him. He heard screams and realized they were his own. A voice, indistinct as though at some far remove, but insistent and somehow soothing, then coolness, then sleep.

When he awoke again his temples throbbed with an ache unlike any he had experienced. He sensed that it was dark but that somewhere nearby was a feeble, flickering light. He considered it for awhile but was unable to bring it into focus. I'll just rest awhile and wait for my head to clear, he said to himself. He felt a chill emanating from his left shoulder. It spread and intensified. The light faded; faint, grey, almost gone.

He heard his name being called, gently at first then with increasing urgency. He made out a voice. It called, "Armistead, come back!" With that part of his mind still capable of thought, he considered: Perhaps later, and started to drift. He felt a stinging pain. What now? Leave me be. But the pain continued so he opened his eyes to seek its source.

Darkness filled the space around him but there was a lantern nearby. He shifted slightly to examine it. Between him and the light stood a figure, a woman, her hand open, her arm descending rapidly toward his cheek. His eyes opened wider and the hand slowed. "Thank God!" the voice said. "I thought we had lost you for good."

During the night the fever abated and he awoke lucid. Someone was sitting next to him. Judging from his dress, he was a Quaker. Armistead started to ask him a question, but the figure rose and hurried way.

He looked around and saw that he lay in a row of beds. Surrounding him lay others, some jerking convulsively while mewing with pain, others motionless and silent. A hospital, I suppose, Armistead thought. He began to reconstruct events when he heard someone approaching rapidly.

It was Jolina. She carried a metal pan in one hand and a bucket in the other. Her hair was tucked into some kind of white bonnet. She wore a splattered, apron-like garment that reminded him of a butcher's garb. She had apparently lost weight, but most of all she looked exceedingly tired. She put down her burdens and reached to embrace him gently. "Our prayers are answered," Armistead heard her murmur.

He waited until she had finished her short prayer and had stood up again. "So, you finished your studies and you are a nurse I find."

"They don't trust me to do much. So I bring food and take away." She paused. The odor coming from the pan next to his bed completed her sentence.

"I sat with you whenever I could. I am so glad to see you on the mend at last."

"Where are we?"

"Near Sharpsburg."

"What day is it?"

"The second of October."

"How long have I been here?"

"Twelve days."

He tried to work it out, but his mind still seemed dumb and slow. I'm like a little child, I shall have to count on my fingers, he said inwardly. He counted to five on his right hand and shifted to his left. And then he understood.

The touch of a water-soaked, cooling cloth woke him. He waited, his eyes still closed, for the pain to attack. It came in waves, but the first blow was less than what it had been, and the subsequent ones less still. They subsided into a pulsing throb that no longer required all of his energy to endure. I can manage, he thought and opened his eyes.

Jolina stood near his bed, her hand poised to swab his brow again. "Hello, Jolina," he said. He saw that she look startled. Her arm dropped to her side. "You recognize me?" He considered a joking response but found the effort somehow beyond him. Besides, something in her tone told him that she needed reassurance so he simply answered, "Of course." Her face relaxed.

"How long have I been here?"

"Twenty days and today is the first time in eight you have talked sense. I will go tell Hannah."

"Wait. Would you please bring me a mirror?"

The reflection he saw did not appear to be his own. A scar extended across his face where the bullet had gouged a runnel from above his ear to his chin. It left an angry red welt that contrasted with his pale skin. It had also left his face half-frozen in an ugly leer. He tried to smile but the muscle did not answer. "Rather horrid, isn't it? Perhaps I shall grow a beard."

"It's not and yes, you would look most dashing with a beard." The voice that answered was not Jolina. He turned to see Hannah standing alongside Jolina. Her face carried a welcoming smile but Armistead saw that her eyes were blinking hard; blinking in an unsuccessful effort to conceal tears.

He stirred again to Jolina's voice. "Armistead, wake up, you have a visitor."

He opened his eyes to see a tall, gaunt, careworn man. His dress was somber; a black suit topped by a tall, black, silk hat. A full beard and thick, bushy eyebrows completed the picture of a troubled, disturbed figure, yet he smiled when he saw Armistead focus upon him and Armistead liked the look in his eyes.

"I understand, colonel, that you are one of the loyal patriots from Virginia. On behalf of the nation, I want to thank you for the sacrifice you have made."

"I reckon the folks back home only regret that I did not make the supreme sacrifice," Armistead replied softly.

The tall man gave a high pitched laugh. "Yes, it's strange times indeed. My wife's family wishes the same for me. They say that my own brother-in-law is a jail keep at a Richmond prison."

Armistead felt a sense of kinship, but failed to find the words to express himself. He seized upon the familiar: "I believe you have it wrong, sir, I am a major."

"Ah, you are like all the other military men, I see," the tall man said with a chuckle. "They are always telling me that I have it wrong. However, in this case I must insist that I am in the right. You see, I promoted you myself."

The tall man leaned down to place a colonel's shoulder strap on the sheet covering Armistead's body. Armistead struggled to extend his hand toward the man only to be betrayed by weakened muscle.

The man moved closer and bent down to clasp his hand. A serious expression crossed his face. "Let us have faith that right makes might, and in that faith allows us to dare to do our duty as we understand it."

He passed on and Armistead fell back asleep. The man left the hospital looking pensive and sad. Waiting outside was a small entourage, among whom was an old friend from Illinois. He summoned his friend and together they walked to a commanding rise. They stood as if on an island surrounded by a sea of army tents. And moving through this sea was the might of a nation: thousands and thousands of blueclad soldiers performing the impeccable drill maneuvers which so pleased their general; enormous herds of horses, mules, oxen hauling laden wagons filled with foodstuffs and munitions to feed this host and to allow them to continue the killing; the black and bronze muzzles of hundreds of cannons, silent now after their recent death feast but unsated.

Gesturing to the sea around them, the tall man asked his friend, "Do you know what this is?"

"Why it is the Army of the Potomac," the friend answered in surprise.

"So it is called, but that is a mistake," the tall man replied bitterly. "It is only McClellan's bodyguard."

Corporal James Gooch slowly tapped the butt of his revolver against his canteen according to the familiar pattern. He had come here often enough that it all seemed unnecessary, but the British fellow insisted.

The unseen voice spoke: "The guide has the directions."

Gooch replied: "The provider has the gold." He rode forward to the base of the stone chimney and waited until the figure emerged from beneath the nearby trees.

"Colonel Overmeyer ain't too happy. Last few places we visited, weren't much of nothing left at all to pluck."

"Tell your colonel that he should be more thorough. Here's a new list. Tell him to make a better job it. Tell him it's a test. He has one week. He passes, and next time I bring you something much, much better. Tell him if he wants it, he will have to come himself. At the new moon."

Gooch chuckled, "The colonel ain't much for taking risks."

"There's no risk if he does what I say."

Kinlock's rasping voice woke Min from a wonderful, deep sleep. He lay between linen sheets on a feather bed and at first did not know where he was. "Go away, Kinlock. I'm in heaven and don't want to leave."

Kinlock uttered a strangled laugh. A second voice added a richer, throaty chuckle. Min opened his eyes and saw Moxley Sorrel.

At first, Min felt constraint. His part in the campaign had been small and not particularly glorious whereas he knew that the men who fought in Maryland had paid a terrible price. Yet Sorrel had the gift of putting him at ease, so slowly Min told his story: the drunk surgeon; Souther's death; Kinlock finding him collapsed by the roadside, his horse stolen, stripped of his possessions including his boots; convalescence at the home of an attentive farm family near Martinsburg; travel, by easy stages to here in Berryville.

"And you Moxley, you were at Sharpsburg, I collect."

"It was pounding, Min, terribly hard pounding. They came at dawn in waves; first to assault our left, then our center, and finally our right. Desperate fighting and all the while their artillery thundered from across the stream to dominate the field."

"In Shepherdstown I saw more injured men than I ever could have imagined," Min observed.

"Maybe three thousand killed, nine thousand wounded. We were blooded at First Manassas. At Sharpsburg we were bled white," Sorrel said.

"Did we win?"

"We did not lose. At the end of the day we occupied the same ground that we held in the morning. General Lee must be the most audacious officer on the continent because the next day he offered battle again even though our ranks were depleted while McClellan had reserves in hand. The yankees declined."

"But here is some good news demonstrating our undiminished spirit. General A.P. Hill repulsed a yankee probe at Boteler's Ford. Let me read you his report: "Then commenced the most terrible slaughter that this war has yet witnessed. The broad surface of the Potomac was blue with the floating bodies of our foe. But few escaped to tell the tale. By their own account they lost 3,000 men, killed and drowned from one brigade alone. This was a wholesome lesson to the enemy."

"Wholesome indeed!" Kinlock chuckled.

"Surely the armies will now go into winter quarters?" Min asked.

"General Lee does not consult me about every decision," Sorrel's smile belied his pompous words, "but with both armies so fearfully hurt, I think there must be a lull."

"Where is our army?"

"Wherever there's food," Sorrel replied. "And now I must be off. What's next for you?"

"The sergeant here needs to recover his health. Our company is below half-strength. I intend to ask to go home on recruiting duty for a spell."

"I have some influence, I'll see what I can do." Sorrel said. "Meanwhile, see if this doesn't help y' all along." Sorrel placed a small brandy bottle on the bedside table. "Take care of yourself, lieutenant."

"And you general."

Sorrel gave Min a quizzical look.

"Not yet, perhaps, but soon," Min explained.

"I'm not sure if this army is ready for a smart-ass Jew to be made general." Sorrel grinned, winked, and departed.

Kinlock looked astonished. "That was a Jew?"

"They say that Major Sorrel is the brains in Longstreet's headquarters."

"I don't believe I've ever met a Jew," Kinlock continued.

"And?" Min inquired.

Kinlock considered. He reached for the bottle, uncorked it and sniffed. "This here's the real stuff Min. I reckon I like Jews."

Jolina visited whenever her duties permitted. They enjoyed an unusual relationship, Armistead reflected. They shared long intervals of companionable silence, a silence many would have found uncomfortable. When they conversed, Armistead discovered that he often learned more about Jolina from the things she left unsaid.

Today she looked troubled. She had been in contact with Liverne, how she did not say. Liverne wished him a quick recovery, of course, and wanted to remind him that it took only one hand to raise a glass. Jolina relayed this last bit of his message with distinct disapproval. She added that Liverne would visit as soon as he could. Armistead surmised that he was across the river again trying to learn what had happened to their son Jason. It was apparent from Jolina's expression that the news so far was not good.

He detected something else, something unfamiliar, and concluded that her visit today was a burden. So, he invented the excuse that he needed to visit an old comrade who was about to depart to rejoin his regiment. The play of emotion across her face remained unfathomable until he saw her reach an inner decision and visibly relax. She rose from her chair and said in a false voice, "Oh, I almost forgot. This is for you."

Jolina handed Armistead a letter and, with a knowing smile, departed. A distinctive scent rose from the envelope, a scent he had last inhaled long ago in a different world. His response surprised him. I am still a man, I find, he remarked inwardly.

Rachel's words presented a second surprise: "You must know, my dear Armistead, how I feel. At times I can scarce sustain the frame which bears such an aching sorrowful heart because you are not nearby."

Armistead gazed at the ceiling for a long time. Perhaps he dozed, but some part of him remained conscious, because when he heard the sound he had been listening for he called out to the orderly. "I find I need to have my beard and hair trimmed. Is there a qualified barber hereabouts?"

His strength returned more rapidly than he had dared hope. Still, many common tasks were awkward, some remained outside his ability. At those times he showed an impatient anger. "This is not a healthy change," Hannah gently chided during one of her visits. He acknowledged that she had the right of it, but found, in spite of his repeated resolutions, that he could do little to control his temper.

The next time she visited she brought him a gift: "When you find yourself becoming angry, touch this."

She handed him a small, ornate wooden box. Armistead held it to the
light and admired the craftsmanship. "It is old," he commented.

"Yes," she replied with a smile.

He opened the box to find a gilt disk. In the center of the disk was some
sort of coat of arms with a crown atop a shield. Inscribed around the outer
perimeter of the disk were the words FUR GOTT UND VATERLAND. A
gilt clasp connected the disk to a faded red ribbon with green stripes.

Armistead gently lifted the medal from the box. He looked at Hannah
with a quizzical expression.

"It belonged to my great-grandfather. Like you, he fought against
oppression. In 1814 he was part of the army that liberated Paris from the
tyrant Napoleon. Duke Ernest of Saxe-Gotha ordered that this medal of
military merit be given to his soldiers."

She leaned forward to fold neatly the left sleeve of his tunic. She
opened the clasp on the medal and used it to secure his sleeve to his breast.
She kissed him gently on the forehead.

Armistead's breath caught. "I am honored," he said.

Although the army's movement north had brought a host of unantici-
pated troubles, it also permitted the return of mail service. Earlier in the
day a Confederate mail carrier had visited Holland Hall. Amanda saved one
letter as a reward to be enjoyed after completing the day's chores. She had
not quite kept her pledge: the animals still had to be hidden. But dusk was
an hour away and trouble typically only came at night.

She smiled as she recalled the dour aunt who had sent this letter. From
her South Carolina coastal plantation, Aunt Tilly invariably reported that
everything was always awful and getting worse fast. Long ago she had
decided that Amanda was a bright child with a mind that merely required
learning in order to counter her brother, the Squire's, sanguine outlook. To
impart fully life's despair, Aunt Tilly chose frequent letters as her means of
instruction, letters of wit and insight written with acid pen. This letter was
different; devoid of hyperbolic complaint, it instead provided a straightforward recitation: "The Yankees swooped down on us and we had to flee
inland. They sacked houses, breaking everything they could. They built
fires out of doors and furniture, cut up and trampled the corn crop. Killed all
of the fattening hogs, sheep, and cattle. They took all the horses and mules,
even the carriage, and of course took off the darkies. How we will endure
I do not know. Salt is our greatest want, aside from the suffering caused by
loss of friends. There is not a white soul within five miles of me."

Troubled by her aunt's uncharacteristic words, Amanda picked up her
knitting and promptly stabbed herself. With difficulty, she checked the
curse forming on her lips. But she had seen so many poorly clad soldiers

that she was determined to complete a self-imposed quota of socks each day. Sometimes, when I am knitting alone, she morosely thought, I feel so old and grave. I see myself like Grandma Holland. All I lack is her spectacles and a cap.

To rally herself she began to sing a new song that Aunt Tilly had provided in a previous letter. Her aunt recommended it on the grounds that it appeared to comfort the young, empty-headed, soon-to-be widows she had recently met.

> "My homespun dress is plain, I know,
> My hat's palmetto, too;
> But then it shows what Southern girls
> For Southern rights will do."

She paused for a moment. Had she heard Rex barking? She listened. Nothing. She continued.

> "We have sent the bravest of our land
> To battle with the foe
> And we will lend a helping hand —
> We love the South you know."

Her voice trailed off. Rex bayed a warning. The guinea fowl emitted their alarm calls. Amanda set down her sewing and looked out to see a group of blue-clad riders entering the lane. Their leader signaled and four troopers dismounted while the others held their carbines at the ready. The dismounted men split into pairs, each pair cautiously exploring the nearby barn and stable. When they reappeared and shook their heads, the mounted men lowered their weapons and relaxed. The leader signaled again and the rest of the troopers dismounted and began to spread around the outbuildings. The leader himself headed toward Gordon's cabin.

Amanda composed herself and walked onto the veranda. She stood there until the yankee officer saw her and spurred his horse into motion. As he approached, she saw two men emerge from the hen house, one carrying a handful of eggs and the other swinging the squawking hen until her neck broke.

"Good evening, ma'am," the rider leered. Amanda saw he wore a faded shell jacket, with three yellow bars embroidered on the sleeves. So, she thought, a sergeant, not an officer. A cold chill passed through her.

She curtsied and primly replied, "Good evening sir."

The guinea's distress calls came loudly. Amanda and the rider looked toward the barnyard to see a group of soldiers trying to surround the excited birds. The guineas nimbly evaded while two soldiers dove at them with clutching hands. One soldier stood, cursed loudly, and pulled out his revolver. The rider spoke sharply, "Ralston, put that god damn gun down.

You fire a shot and we'll have every rebel within earshot down on us in a heartbeat."

He turned to face her. "Pardon the language, but they're hungry you see. Thomas Parks, Loudoun Rangers, at your service."

"Oh my yes," Amanda responded. "Some of the local boys serve with you. I dare say you are familiar with a Captain Carter?"

"Yes, of course."

A soldier approached him. "Tom, we've bin lied too. There ain't much here. This place must have been plucked before."

Parks asked Amanda, "You had visitors lately?"

Amanda looked past him to see several troopers heading toward the smokehouse. In a simpering voice she replied, "It's been right lively here. Yesterday Lige White's boys came and I had to feed a parcel of men. They liked my cooking just fine and said they would be back this evening. But there's not a lot left. However, the hogs recently died of cholera so we started to make up some lard. I could bake us up some fine biscuits. They taste real good browned in lard."

The rider snapped out a command: "Cholera! Ralston, Jenkins, hold hard!" Amanda saw a pair of troopers pause outside the smokehouse.

"How many was they?" Parks demanded.

"Oh, only the two old sows for sure. But I fear the young uns catched it too."

"No, damn it. How many of your cavalry was here yesterday?"

Amanda had counted all of the visible riders and observed nine men. She began to recite slowly the names of the boys and men who lived on neighboring farms. Parks stared at her impatiently: "So with the Beattie twins, oh, and Min, there weren't many, maybe twenty or twenty-two."

A whoop of pleasure came from the barnyard. A soldier emerged from the dairy barn pulling the milk cow by a lead rope. The balance of the troopers had returned to their horses, some empty-handed and some carrying chickens, hay, or grain.

"Sir, old Bossy there, she's about all we have left. But I can milk her and bake you up something fine right quick." She saw one of the troopers walking toward the cow holding a long knife.

"It's a terrible pity, but we got orders to seize all the livestock hereabouts. Can't have it be feeding the rebels. And while we are at it, we had best take a look inside." Parks motioned toward the manor house.

Suddenly Rex bayed again. Amanda knew it was his welcoming bark. She thought she heard the faint sounds of galloping horses. A trooper kicked at the dog, but the hound only redoubled his barking. Parks looked at Amanda and then back toward the road. A cloud of dust was rising above the west woods. "Riders!" Parks exclaimed. "Let's get out of here fast."

The yankees ran toward their horses. The man with the knife paused for a moment, slashed with his blade across the cow's throat and laughed. As he ran towards his horse he called out, "We'll be back!"

The troopers galloped down the lane and turned east, away from the approaching dust cloud. After a brief gurgling bellow, the cow collapsed in the dirt. "Yankee Bastards!" she shouted and ran to cradle the animal's head during its death throes. The animal struggled briefly and then was still "Bastards!" she hissed again.

Min had visited three times since the evening when he and his men had appeared unexpectedly. At that time he had found her standing in the barnyard wearing a calico dress splashed with the blood of her slaughtered milk cow. She had snapped out orders like a drill sergeant, telling him that yankee raiders had taken off toward the poplar springs, telling him to pursue them immediately, telling him to kill them all.

They had chased hard but failed to catch the raiders. The next morning he glumly reported that they seemed to know the local terrain as well as he himself knew it.

"That's because they are local men, or at least their leaders are," she replied.

"Are you sure?"

"You remember my Aunt Althea?"

Min winced and gave a wane smile. "As a child I remember her firm right hand when she used to thrash me and Armistead."

"It may not show, but she is a shrewd woman. I asked her how the raiders were able to hit us where we were weakest and escape with ease. At that time we suspected someone was betraying us. She said I should figure out who made money from these operations. For a very long time I worked on this without success. Last night convinced me that for once Aunt Althea was wrong."

She handed Min a letter. "Read this."

Min's face paled as he read Armistead's letter promising to bring "ruin and death" to the rebels who opposed the Union. Amanda saw the muscles around his jaw tighten when he came to the concluding boast: "Defend yourself if you can, we are coming, carrying the sword and buckler of the lord."

"We've always known it had to be someone local. Armistead obviously both knows the terrain, how to enlist local help, who is weak, and how to exploit it."

Min shook his head sadly. "I reckon he's a changed man, Mandy."

"I need to take safeguards against when he sends them here again."

"What can I do to help?" Min asked.

Along with his growing physical strength, Armistead's interest in the outside world also returned. He avidly read the papers and learned that since Antietam, the Army of the Potomac had remained inert around Harpers Ferry. Meanwhile, Jeb Stuart had embarrassed the northern cavalrymen again by raiding north into Pennsylvania and making a complete circuit around McClellan's army. It surprised Armistead how easy it was to follow McClellan's movements by reading the papers. The war correspondents speculated about pending maneuvers and backed their speculations with comments from senior officers and congressmen in Washington.

So, Armistead learned that as soon as the October rains relented, the Union army intended to march south. In the meantime, there would be a series of small scale forays across the Potomac to keep the rebels off balance. "We might as well tell Bobby Lee exactly when and where, so he can be good and ready this time," Armistead muttered disgustedly.

He began to take short rides, trying each day to stretch his limits. He even attempted a few jumps. Blue's quizzical turn of his head, his obvious contempt for such insignificant heights, made him laugh aloud. He later reflected that it was the first time he had laughed since his wound. Riding sometimes made his wound seep, but he successfully hid this from Jolina and the other hospital attendants.

Later, he recalled these days as a recovery period when time was suspended. Yet the visible signs of the passage of the season were all about him; the green leaves retreating before the onslaught of yellow, brown, and red; the afternoon heat rising to summer-like heights, but holding there only briefly before retreating; the wind from the north hinting of the winter to come.

On the third Wednesday in October, he returned from an invigorating canter over freshly fallen leaves to find a note from Henk. Overmeyer was leading increasingly destructive raids into Loudoun and he generally used Loudoun Rangers for scouts. He was sorry to say that Jimmy Gooch had boasted that he reckoned that Overmeyer was soon going for Holland Hall. "I promise I'll do what I can," Henk concluded.

Armistead wrote a short reply, crafting it in guarded language that only Henk would completely understand. He paid a sutler's boy to deliver it to the Ranger's camp, changed into a clean uniform, gathered his possessions, and walked toward the stables.

Chapter 36. Loudoun County, October 1862

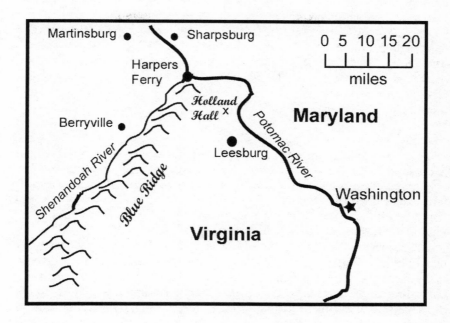

From the moment he crossed the Potomac, Armistead felt as though he was entering a dream world; a completely recognizable place at first inspection, a place of hidden menace when viewed more closely. Cavalry patrols, whether Confederate or Union he knew not, forced him off the main roads. Near a farm where he remembered drinking juleps after a long June day spent haying a bottomland pasture, a shotgun blast, delivered from an unseen shooter sent him cantering to safety. At a crossroads where once had stood a bustling inn, a blackened chimney loomed above the encampment of an ugly looking band of deserters.

Evening came. The fatigue; unwelcome, even unacceptable, but real in spite of his resistance, played a part in his decision. How much her letter influenced him he did not know. Armistead smiled as Blue recognized the turning place and strained against the bit. He at least, seemed certain of his welcome.

The farm appeared unchanged. Smoke rose from the kitchen chimney. Most likely a baking fire, he decided, and realized that he had not eaten all day. The orderly ranks of late season crops; squash, pumpkins, onions, potatoes, marched in carefully tended rows. As he came closer he saw the small changes: newly hewn locust rails patching gaps, created, undoubtedly, by visiting soldiers who saw no need to search for firewood; the absence of animals in the paddock; and the bent figure of a woman, methodically working her hoe around an earthen hill. She chopped angrily at the weeds in the unskilled way that removed the tops but left the roots, the technique employed by someone whose goal was to appear finished even though the task remained undone.

Perhaps she sensed his gaze or maybe she simply paused to rest and happened to look up. Her eyes met his and he saw that her face had matured. The bloom of youth remained, but it had become something different, pretty adolescent shaping into mature beauty, a girl becoming a woman. His presence surprised her. He saw recognition, calculation, welcome, and then, as he came closer, horror.

Min divided his money between two pockets. His right pocket held his ready money, the sum he was willing to risk at tonight's game. His left pocket held his reserve, an inviolable sum, he told himself, not to be used unless he saw a sure thing. Card playing was a weakness, he knew, probably a sin like the preachers said, and he loved it dearly. Furthermore, he reminded himself, he was never going to grow rich on a lieutenant's pay.

The notion of being rich was appealing. Had he been born to money he would have already proposed. But the absence of wealth made him both embarrassed and shy. He wondered if she even knew his feelings. Her family had money. The possibility that they, or the community at large, might think he was marrying to become rich, horrified him. He supposed that if he was clever he could speculate profitably, like Amanda's apparent beau, Brook Morgan. But he wasn't clever, at least not in that way. I may not be clever, Min mused, but when it comes to cards I'm lucky, and that beats clever every time.

He'd heard that they played for high stakes at Meme Richard's. He handed his horse off to one of stable boys and noted that there were a surprising number of horses tethered to the rail. "More sheep to fleece, Min told himself.

He entered the saloon and fought his way to the bar through a crowd of boisterous soldiers. After fending off the girls, he ordered a cherry flip and asked about the game. The barkeep gave an assessing look, "House rules. Ready money only. Greenbacks or coin."

The man's demeanor slightly dampened Min's soaring spirits. He considered a comment about the house's lack of patriotism for refusing Confederate script, but the barkeep's gimlet-eyed stare changed his mind. Instead, he simply nodded.

With a jerk of his thumb the barkeep motioned to a door.

A carpet-lined, narrow passageway led to the gaming room. A collection of knives and handguns sat on a side table. "Y'all mustering in a new regiment?" Min asked the large black man who had opened the door.

The man grinned, "Can't have no fighting. Meme Richard gets right cross when blood spoils the carpet."

A woman sat behind a desk at the end of the passageway. Her raven colored hair contrasted dramatically with her pale, white skin. She wore a low cut, tight fitting, white dress that revealed more than it hid. He handed her the money from his right pocket. She leaned forward to count, her scent rising to him, a slightly musty mix of perspiration and expensive French perfume. He stared down the rouged curves of exposed breast and swallowed hard. She handed him a stack of chips, gave him a long-lashed look, and said in a thick accent, "My name's Meaghan. I'm just spotting old Laudable for a spell and then maybe you might like to buy an Irish lass a drink."

Min smiled in a way that he hoped looked merely friendly. "Meaghan, I'm afraid I am a married man."

She gazed at him appraisingly. "That don't bother me none."

"Yes, but it might annoy Missus Carter."

"She's fortunate to have such a handsome husband. If you should change your mind..."

Impulsively Min shoved a chip back toward her. "Wish me luck, Meaghan."

Her face hardened for a moment. "You won't be needing luck, Mister Carter. You'll be wanting the cards."

In some ways it was as before; hearty German cooking, Sigmund Becker keen to discuss national affairs, the wine steadily drunk, the air oppressive with the promise of storm. Yet there was an underlying tension that was entirely different, as different as the mellow Rheingau they had shared back before it all began and the slightly astringent Chambourcin from Becker's own vines they now drank. Rachel did not appear to attend to the conversation and said little. She responded tersely to her father and spent long intervals away from the table. She displayed no interest in Armistead at all.

Still, it was as close to home as Armistead had been for a very long time. He felt a comfortable glow spread from his belly. His muscles slowly unknotted and he relaxed into the conversation as Sigmund related his views on the war. Finally the German turned to local affairs, the telling of which Armistead had been patiently waiting for all evening. The words tumbled from Sigmund's mouth, and it was all news to Armistead: his own farm, stripped, first by Confederate confiscation teams then by foragers and bandits; Becker building the concealed storage room in the disused spring-house where he now kept provisions; the Loudoun Grays fighting staunchly but suffering steady attrition; local boys come home, much like Armistead, injured and sometimes maimed; some killed including boys Armistead had grown up with and one or two he considered friends.

Perhaps hardest of all, Becker related, was the absence of news. Becker expressed genuine sympathy for Armistead's cousin Amanda, who had yet to hear from her brother. "Why just last week we finally received a letter from Charles. The young fool joined a Virginia battery that transferred out west to someplace called Vicksburg." Sigmund sighed heavily. He took a sip of wine and brightened, "At least he is out of the infantry and well away from the carnage here."

Boyd missing. Poor Mandy, Armistead reflected. He realized that he had not been attending. "You were saying..."

Suddenly Rachel burst in from the kitchen: "Riders!"

"Again, Mein Gott!" Becker exclaimed.

"Father, go conceal his horse." She quickly began removing the dishes, cutlery, and glasses. "I'll show," she paused in an apparent effort to find the right word, and then spoke with special emphasis, "him, the hiding place."

Anne Rix drained her glass. Must be something I ate, she said inwardly. Stomach aches, head's pounding. She seldom drank during business hours, but already she had swallowed a third of the decanter.

She reviewed her plans. It's still going well enough, she told herself. He had come in response to her invitation, only to be diverted by the game taking place in the back room. She knew from experience that some men were more attracted to gambling than to her girls. She had learned to take advantage by increasing the house's percentage. But tonight, of all nights, she thought. I'll tell Billy to keep the drinks flowing back there. Someone will lose big quick, and the game will bust up.

Time mattered because everything upstairs was ready. It had not been hard to introduce Elsie to the dress up games. Little bitch probably dressed up behind my back anyways, Anne thought as she took another sip. Elsie enjoyed dressing to look like the older, working girls. She's middling attractive, Anne acknowledged. Wait till her curves come in. She'll have the boys lined up with their peckers hanging to the floor.

But Elsie would not stay in the room forever. Right now Rita Mae was doing her hair up French style. And then?

Anne fingered the little vial. She had secured it from a Union army doctor, one of her customers who came when Overmeyer's men raided. When the time came, she'd dose Elsie. It would be easier that way and Rixey wouldn't care. How much had the doctor said he used?

She couldn't quite remember. She finished the contents of her glass, put the vial in her pocket, and ascended the back stairway to check that the witnesses remained sober.

Chapter 37. Loudoun County, October 1862

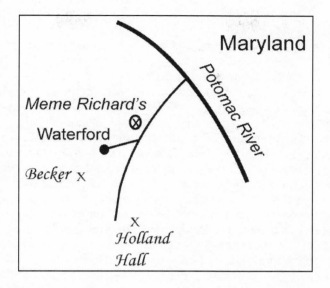

Three Confederate cavalrymen rode up the lane toward the Becker farm. Two held carbines at the ready. Their heads swiveled alertly as they searched for hidden danger. The third rider, an officer, nonchalantly brandished a revolver. He almost looked bored. Rachel appeared on the porch and his demeanor changed.

In the fading light Rachel saw that he wore a black plumed hat, oversized buff gauntlets, a gray shell jacket embroidered with a great deal of gold trim, and calfskin breeches stuffed into gleaming, knee high riding boots. A yellow cravat matched the sash he wore around his waist. With great self-assurance he introduced himself as Captain Otis Polk.

He told her that after a day spent hunting yankees, he was desperately hungry. Rachel simpered and allowed as how it would be an honor to help feed her gallant protectors. His manner around the supper table was much like his outward appearance. He dominated the conversation with stories about his exploits, eagerly displaying a canteen and saber that had belonged to a federal officer he had shot earlier in the day. Scratched into the canteen's metal surface was the name "J Gooch."

I wonder if that is the same Gooch who lived over near Purcellville, Becker mused inwardly. He found Polk tiresome. He silently willed the man to leave. Rachel, he noticed, seemed to find his talk absorbing. She followed Polk's stories as if spellbound, and even asked questions that demonstrated a surprising knowledge of military nuance. For this Becker was thankful. Rachel's behavior permitted him to sink deeper into his own thoughts. He had not realized how far his attention lapsed until he felt his daughter's none too gentle prod.

"Father, bid this brave man goodnight. No doubt he and his men are on their way to slay countless more of those vile Yankees. I'm stepping out to show Captain Polk where we store the corn we managed to hide from the Yankees. He must feed his horse so that it will be as strong as he is."

Rachel's remark brought Becker to full awareness. What is that girl doing giving the enemy sustenance from the carefully hoarded grain? he asked himself. With grain prices climbing fast around the Confederate camps in Warrenton and very attractive rates across the river in Maryland, he had meant to sell soon. Damn it, he depended on her. She was one of the strong knots that held his plans secure. He would, he would...

Exactly what he would do he did not decide because there was Polk's outstretched hand bidding farewell. Collecting himself, he clasped his limp hand and wished his men good hunting. He saw Rachel lightly skip outside, only to pause on the veranda to offer her arm to Polk. He saw them walk, arm in arm, down the steps toward the abandoned spring house.

As they proceeded, Rachel remarked that tonight there was a new moon and how such complete darkness always made her feel weak. As she expected, Polk slipped his hand around her waist and pulled her closer.

"I'll protect you my dear."

"How much grain will you require, Captain? As you know it has become terribly scarce, but if you have a long way to travel."

There remained enough light for Rachel to see Polk wrestle with a response. He started to open his mouth and then tightened his lips with a small shake of his head.

Rachel spoke again: "We figure the Yankees will look here," She pointed to the entrance of the partially collapsed spring house. "So, we store it back here." She led Polk behind the building.

"If you pull away this brush, you'll see father dug out a whole new cellar. It looks like a solid stone wall, but if you take out the fourth stone from top left, the others fall away easily to reveal a door. But you might have to guess where the key is."

She slipped around Polk and stared up at him invitingly. The upper half of a leather thong that looped around her neck was visible. With a slight gasp, Polk placed his hand on her neck and followed the throng downward. When his fingers came to the top of her breast, Rachel placed her hand atop his. She could feel the man actually trembling. She held his hand in place for a moment and then slid out from his reach.

"I should relish the chance to get to know you much, much better Captain. In the meantime, let me help you." She pulled the key free from her bodice.

"Take what you need," she said as she twirled the thong around her forefinger, "but I have something to ask in return. We can afford the loss of most of what the yankees took, but one officer, oh I will never forget his terrible face, took a family heirloom, my grandma's brooch, that I value above all else. I would give anything, Captain, anything to have it back. I am such a weak female. I cannot quite remember the unit's name. But I know I'll recognize it if I hear it again."

"The Loudoun Rangers?"

"Yes, yes that's it!"

"We're going against them tonight. Their officer's name is Carter, Armistead Carter."

"That's him," Rachel squealed. "I heard one of the men call him Colonel Carter."

After that, Polk's words poured out fast and full. By the time Polk and his men had taken down the false back of the spring house and filled their saddle bags with grain, Rachel possessed the complete plan for the ambush and destruction of the Loudoun Rangers.

He kissed her lightly on her hand and then mounted. Returning his plumed hat to his head, he jested about his banditti appearance.

"It doesn't do, you know, to dress well to fight yankees," he laughed. Polk wheeled his horse and led his escort down the lane. He turned back to call, "We will meet again soon," and was gone.

"I rather think not," Rachel softly said. She hurried back to the house where she interrupted her father before he could begin venting his anger. "Be quiet, father," she said firmly, "There's work to be done."

There were five players already at the table. Among them Min recognized the corpulent features of Clarence Rixey. The banker's presence surprised him for he had not expected to compete against anyone he knew. Min took his place at the table and the play resumed. The game was seven card stud.

The drinks and fast pace of play eliminated three players within thirty minutes. Min had been lucky. He was enjoying what the card sharks around camp called the rush, and he had parlayed his good fortune into a considerable stack of chips. As a rule he never counted his chips until the game ended. Still, he knew that he must be up several hundred dollars. Federal money, he reminded himself. He took a small sip of whiskey.

They were now playing a game in which each player received two cards that remained concealed and then shared four common cards that the girl revealed one by one. After some uneventful hands, the pot started to build. The first common card, a seven of diamonds, appeared to help no one. The boy bet on the second common card, a jack of clubs. Min's two cards were weak so he folded to what he supposed was the boy's pair. Rixey called. The girl revealed the third common card, a three of clubs, and Rixey made a large bet. He's trying to scare off the boy,' Min judged. Throughout the evening the boy had played cautiously. Now his hand reached quickly for his chips and with great confidence he raised Rixey. Clearly he now held two pairs, jacks over threes.

Min was pleased. He did not much care for the fat banker. Before the war, Rixey had relentlessly squeezed many small businessmen and farmers, including some of his friends. His poker style was much the same. He used his deep pockets to drive opponents from the pot. But Rixey had obviously made a mistake and would now fold. Instead the banker called.

The girl exposed the last common card, a five of hearts. The boy made a robust bet. Without hesitation Rixey made a huge raise and spoke, "Son, I'll tell you what. You give me five of those red chips of yours and you can see either one of my cards, whichever you choose."

After a long interval, the boy tossed over five chips and pointed at one of Rixey's cards. Rixey turned it over, a five of spades.

Min involuntarily sucked in his breath. The only possible explanation for Rixey's offer was that his two hole cards were the same. Since the boy presumably held two pairs he would lose to Rixey's three of a kind. A long minute passed. At last the boy spoke, "Don't reckon I'll play." He took his small pile of remaining chips and stalked angrily away.

With a laugh, Rixey revealed his remaining hidden card and raked in the stack of chips. Min startled. The card was a seven. Rixey had been running a colossal bluff.

"Now Mister Carter," the banker said, "I feel pressed for time. I suggest we conclude with a faster game, five card stud. Table stakes, no refreshing."

Since the age of seven Min had been playing stud poker. He was confident in his ability. Table stakes was something else altogether: bets limited only by the money each now possessed, winner take all. It was madness. If he walked away now he took away a handsome profit, far more than a year's army salary. Even as these thoughts flashed through his mind, he felt his hand reach into his left pocket and heard his voice saying, "Very good."

Six hands later came the decision. Min's concealed card was an eight of spades, his exposed card a six of diamonds. Rixey showed a five of diamonds. Rixey was low man. By house rule he had at least to match the ante. Instead he doubled it. Min matched him.

The girl dealt a three of diamonds to Rixey and an eight of hearts for Min. With a pair in hand Min considered. I'll set the trap, he decided. He pretended to hesitate and then nervously drummed two fingers on the table indicating no additional bet. Rixey aggressively pushed forward chips. Min matched him again.

Rixey received a seven of clubs, Min a two of spades. Rixey's chance for a flush was gone, the odds of a straight, remote. Nothing he could have beat Min's pair of eights. Again Min did not bet and again Rixey made a heavy bet. Elated that his trap had worked, Min emptied his left pocket to make an enormous raise. He tried to ignore the value that the chips represented and instead focused solely on Rixey's expression. Rixey gave nothing away. He sat erect and stared with unblinking eyes. He accepted Min's bet.

The girl's eyes grew wide. Her hand slightly trembled as she dealt the last cards. Rixey received a jack of clubs, Min a useless three of hearts.

"Mister Carter," the banker softly said, "I believe I have a jack in the hole." He pushed forward all his remaining stack of chips.

Min's gut clenched. Has Rixey played with nothing except a concealed jack, paid this huge sum simply in hopes of outdrawing me, and made his pair? Min wondered.

He knew that if he folded now he still preserved a reasonable profit. But he had not come to Meme Richard's to make a reasonable profit.

"Mister Rixey, if you got a jack down there, you're liable to win yourself one hell of a pot."

Rixey gave a faint smile. Min called the banker's bet and turned over his hole card to reveal his pair of eights.

For an achingly long moment Rixey did not react. Finally, he pushed back from the table. "I reckon the pot is yours. I welcome the opportunity to meet with you again."

Chapter 38. Loudoun County, October 1862

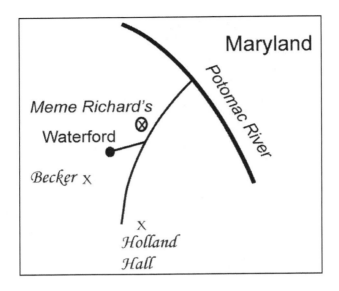

The autumn sun set behind the Blue Ridge and the air fell silent. Amanda paused and listened intently. Nothing. She cautiously worked downslope toward the horse enclosure. The raid against Holland Hall had exposed vulnerability. Whether it was lawless bands of deserters, grasping Confederate requisition agents, or yankee raiders mattered little. They all wanted, and prime horseflesh topped their lists.

With the help of Min and the remaining field hands, she had built a crude corral in a creek side ravine. Here they hid the most valuable animals. Her horse heard her coming and whickered a greeting. She reached out to stroke the mare's neck. Buttercup's questing lips searched her hand and then her pocket. "No sugar, pet. But I brought you this, you greedy hussy." Buttercup gently lifted the apple from her hand.

Amanda absently stroked the horse's neck while the mare rested her head on Amanda's shoulder. From far away came the sound of thunder. Amanda sighed and took a backward step. Buttercup gazed at her skeptically. "I know pet, you want to go back to the paddock. But it's not safe right now." Amanda cast an assessing eye at the other animals; the carriage horses and draft mules had all put on weight. Their glossy coats indicated inner vitality. Already their long, winter coats were growing in. They were entering the cold season in superb condition, but the enclosure would not sustain them. They would need much more space to forage.

She carefully backtracked, making sure to sweep away her foot treads with a cedar bough. She heard Buttercup's reproachful whinny as she ascended the ravine. She paused again, to listen and to gather breath. The evening shadows thickened. The days are getting shorter, she thought. Soon it will be time to prepare the fields for next year's crop. Her inner voice asked the question she had so often asked, How will we possibly manage that?

"Scarecrow," the voice said. Only one person had ever called him by that name, long ago in childhood.

"Advance and be recognized, Slow Belly."

"God Damn, Armistead! It's good to see you," Henk said. "I wasn't sure you would make it. It seems like every swinging dick in Loudoun is out on patrol tonight." There was a distant mutter of thunder. "God damn storm coming too," Henk added.

"Dulany's Confederates are setting a trap," Armistead said. He told him what Polk had divulged. "Here's what we'll do, Henk. You ride like hell and intercept the Rangers. Tell Hathaway to retreat immediately. Get back over the river, back to camp. I'll go warn the guide."

Henk looked unhappy. "You go back with the boys. I can get to the guide and be well clear before Polk's men show up." Henk paused, and then awkwardly added, "My horse is fitter than yours."

Armistead looked fondly at Henk. Bluff, honest, direct; Henk had never been able to lie plausibly. "Old friend, my arm, or what's left of it, is fine. Besides, well, it's just something I need to do myself."

Henk silently reached out to clasp his hand. They grasped palms for a beat longer than usual and Armistead spoke again: "Henk, I'm not foolish enough to linger. But promise me, if I don't show up in camp, neither you nor anyone else is to come looking for me."

Henk shifted uncomfortably.

Armistead continued: "Look, nothing is going to go wrong, but I need your promise. It's one less worry and I don't have a lot of room to take on more worries just now."

Henk squeezed his hand harder. His voice caught, but he collected himself and answered, "I promise."

Meaghan was gone, her place taken by a dissipated man who sat hunched over the desk. He looked up, a flicker of recognition crossed his face, and then he resumed counting the money. Min paid him no heed. But, as he returned to the saloon, he thought that probably Meaghan's absence was for the best.

The crowd at the bar was mostly composed of cavalry troopers belonging to Dulany's regiment. They proudly related their successes against the Yankee raiders who crossed the river to plunder Loudoun County farms.

However, beneath their boasts was a sober tale of fruitless patrols against an enemy who always seemed to be one step ahead.

"We set ambushes and they avoid them. Worse, while we're covering Point of Rocks they come over Noland's Ferry, we picket the Old Carolina Road and they cross at Point of Rocks. It makes you wonder," a sergeant complained to Min.

The sergeant spat disgustedly into the fire. "But I reckon we'll catch 'em tonight."

Min gestured to the barkeep and ordered two more drinks. The sergeant nodded his thanks and continued. "We strung up Jimmy Gooch. Before he swung, it 'pears like we got some special information. Maybe this time it's accurate. Them filthy Loudoun Ranger bastards are coming tonight to meet up with their guide. If our fearless captain can pull his pants on in time, we should be in position to intercept them before moon rise."

The sergeant's tone surprised Min. He had heard that the unit's captain was well respected. "So you don't think much of Captain Blackwell?"

"Old Blacky? He's fine, or at least he was till them Rangers bush-whacked him one night. Gut shot. He lived eight days, each one of them a living hell. It was a blessing when he passed."

The sergeant stared sadly into the fire and drained off his glass.

"Richmond sent us a new man. Before now he was a staff officer but we hear that he got in trouble over some missing money so they sent him into the line. He looks pretty and is real popular with the ladies. But Captain Polk don't suspect nuthin about nuthin. We'll see if he knows how to fight."

Min stepped outside. The air was hot, oppressive. Overhead, a few open patches of starlit sky remained. Even as he watched, he saw a fast moving bank of clouds engulf them. He walked along the picket line. The horses were unexceptional, a few blooded animals for the officers, some reliable quarter horses, a hock-kneed piebald that looked like it was fixing to go hooves up. He stopped abruptly. A trooper was curry combing a gleaming animal. It was the boy from the poker table. The boy asked conversation-ally, "What do you think?"

"That's a mighty fine horse. Where did you get him?"

"Won him off a Virginia fella named Clemmer. We was across the river near Frederick. I joined a game of bluff. Clemmer had been drinking and I fleeced him good." The boy sighed and gestured toward Meme Richard's. "They play a different game in there."

"You ever hear the name Boyd Holland?"

"No, don't reckon I have."

"I might like to buy that horse."

The boy's expression changed. "Mister, until tonight he weren't for sale." He resumed his combing. After a long silence he asked, "They got another game worked up inside?"

"They're just getting started."

"I reckon I'll take your money, mister."

Armistead dismounted at the clearing's edge. He was early so he would have to wait. Clouds covered the sky. In the distance he saw lightning strokes. "Let the storm rage," he muttered. It was too easy to feel sorry for himself: the perfumed letter; her contemptuous dismissal, "I don't expect a cripple can do much to stop Polk's gang, but maybe you can at least warn the Rangers."

He was unsure how much her taunt had influenced him. Maybe he would have come here anyway to warn the guide that Gooch had betrayed him. Her words, with the precise emphasis on the word cripple, returned, again and again.

He heard the sound of hooves on gravel, drew his revolver, and listened hard: one rider only. Armistead tapped the butt of his revolver against his canteen as he had been instructed.

The unseen voice spoke: "The guide has the directions."

Armistead startled. "Where have I heard that voice?" He composed himself and replied: "The provider has the gold."

Armistead advanced toward the stone chimney.

The voice called out sharply: "Stop right there! You're not Corporal Gooch."

Disguising his voice and taking care to remain in the shadows, Armistead laughed and said, "Gooch's bowels are leaking like shit through a goose. So the colonel sent me."

"Overmeyer was supposed to come himself." Gordon emerged from beneath the trees. He leveled a small hand gun at Armistead's breast: "Show me the gold."

Becker had reluctantly given Armistead all of his ready money. It totaled barely half of what the guide expected. Armistead had put the gold coins in one leather pouch. A second pouch contained metal shards from Becker's forge.

Armistead awkwardly shook both pouches. He placed one pouch in his left armpit and tossed the second to Gordon. "Count it, it's half. They told me to get your directions before giving you the rest."

Gordon unshuttered a dark lantern. While he carefully counted Armistead studied his face. The Englishman had always been somewhat of a dandy. The lantern cast enough light to show an unkempt beard, hollow cheek bones, a stained cravat. Broken capillaries around a swollen nose completed the picture of dissipation; a toper falling fast. Armistead saw that the hand holding the pistol was shaking.

Gordon pocketed the pouch and produced a piece of paper. "So, you want to play a game with me. Very well. You have two targets. My map here shows where they've hidden some very valuable horses. It's a fine hiding place; water, concealment, a nice mossy rock to sit on and soak your feet. But you will never find it without my map. Your other target is Holland Hall. Burn the outbuildings but look under the floor boards in the smoke house. You'll have to move the old hay piles first, but it will be worth your trouble. Leave the manor house alone. They've hidden valuables somewhere inside and we'll never get them if we have to shift through the ashes."

Gordon continued, "So, give me the rest of my money and you get the map. Oh, there is something, or perhaps I should say someone, else. I know that Gooch would have found her quite the prize." A knowing leer crossed Gordon's ravaged face. Armistead felt the blood rush through his temples, anger mounting toward barely controllable passion. He forced himself to say, "Go on."

"So you might be interested? I thought so. Oh she's quite the piece, is Amanda Holland. Willing, they say, even more than willing. But she likes it rough."

Armistead ducked low into his saddle while simultaneously reaching for his revolver.

He saw Gordon's eyes widen and then his arm give a convulsive jerk as his finger pulled down on the trigger. Gordon's gun discharged and Armistead felt a burning pain as a ball grazed his right rib. He raised his revolver and aimed carefully. "You miserable bastard," he said, and then a bugle sounded.

Gordon saw Armistead hesitate, and seized his chance. He hurled his lantern even as a cacophony of sound descended: riders charged into the clearing, their voices baying the fox hunter's cry; Otis Polk shouting, "give them cold steel, men!"; the snap of Armistead's trigger; the explosion when hammer struck the percussion cap. Shouts, movement, confusion, and Armistead was off, riding fast for the shadows.

The whole affair has been bungled, Min lamented. Because of Polk's dalliance they had arrived late at the rendezvous. Then the fool had ordered his bugler to sound the charge before his troopers had time to surround the clearing. Consequently, at least one yankee had escaped the trap. Regardless, Polk's troopers gathered triumphantly around the wounded man. He lay face down, bellowing with pain. Blood flowed profusely from the exit wound in his upper torso. A trooper lit a torch while someone examined the injured man. Given that the bullet had struck below his right shoulder, it appeared to Min that the wound was not fatal.

"Secure him to a horse and we'll take the traitor back to Meme Richard's. If he don't die on us we'll make him talk," Polk ordered.

They roughly lifted the man upright. Min stared. It was Gordon. "You son of a bitch," Min hissed.

"You recognize him, Carter?" Polk inquired.

"Yes. He's the manager at Holland Hall."

"That's most convenient," Polk said. "She, I mean Holland Hall was on my list of appointments."

As he spoke, a jagged streak of lightning crossed the sky. Thunder followed.

"But it won't do to get wet. So Meme Richard's first and we'll get this yankee dog to tell us what he knows."

"Sir," Min said. "I'd like to proceed to Holland Hall. My cousin lives there without the protection of white men."

Polk considered. Another peal of thunder, this time closer. "Certainly lieutenant."

With a sketchy salute Min departed. Polk turned to his escort. "Follow him wherever he goes."

Chapter 39. Loudoun County, October 1862

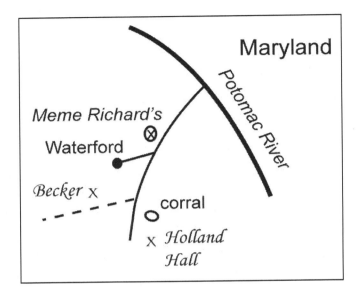

Min slowed his horse to a walk when he neared the crossroads. His left hand held the rope attached to Boyd's horse. Although they had not come far, the led horse was already panting hard. Like so many of the cavalry horses who had returned from Maryland, Boyd's animal had lost condition. Min reconsidered his plan. He had intended to go to Holland Hall. Perhaps it's best to take him to Mandy's corral, he decided. Strokes of lightning cut across the sullen sky. Unusual for this time of year, Min said to himself. He turned away from Holland Hall and approached the turnoff leading to the corral. His horse's ears pricked. Min stopped to listen.

He heard the sounds of riders moving along the woodland path. He eased to the side of the road, drew his revolver, and waited.

The mossy rock Polk had divulged could only mean one place; a secluded ravine with a spring fed pool, a secret childhood place known only to the cousins. Blue's whicker of greeting, answered by unseen animals lower in the ravine, confirmed Armistead's deduction. He knew that he had to hurry, because whomever had interrupted his meeting with Gordon would find the manager's map and come here next. Armistead opened the corral gate and clucked to the horses. Buttercup came immediately and buried her head against his chest. The other animals seemed wary. There was no time to tie them together. "Come on y'all, you know Blue."

He felt certain that they would follow, particularly when they realized that he was leading them home. And indeed, they climbed up the ravine in his wake. He turned Blue onto the road and glanced back to make sure they were still coming.

The metallic sound of a revolver being pulled to full cock came just before the voice: "Good evening cousin. Out doing a little horse rustling on the side?"

Somehow, she thought, he must have sensed her impatience, or perhaps he was just drowning his anger after losing a sum that meant something even to a Leesburg banker. Regardless, Rixey ignored Anne's invitation and instead sat at the bar drinking. Finally he slid unsteadily off his stool and nodded. She led him toward the stairway. Shouts from the tavern yard caused Rixey to stop. She tugged on his arm. He grabbed her wrist with surprising strength and said, "Quiet."

A group of Dulany's cavalry entered the great room. The saloon fell silent. Otis Polk sauntered in, fully conscious that all eyes were upon him. "We got the filthy traitor," he said with a satisfied smirk. A pair of troopers carried a bloodied civilian through the door and dropped him heavily. A crowd gathered around the prostrate body. "It's that Englishman who works at Holland Hall," someone said. The volume of noise rose.

The heavy retort of a Colt naval revolver silenced the crowd. Polk stood over Gordon's body, the barrel of his Colt leaking smoke from the shot he had fired through an exterior wall. He looked at Meme Richard: "Find someone to patch this bastard up. Just good enough so my sergeant can get him to talk. Now, won't someone buy me a drink? Hanging traitors is thirsty work."

Even before Polk had completed his speech, Rixey released his grip. She looked at her father and was surprised to see him turn visibly pale. Beads of perspiration formed along his brow and jowls. Rixey pushed his way clear and walked quickly into the tavern yard. Anne followed and saw him mount and depart at a furious gallop.

Old Doctor Ferguson had been one of three witnesses waiting upstairs. The gunshot brought them all to the common room where Ferguson took charge. He ordered the soldiers to carry Gordon into a side room. While one of Polk's men stood guard outside, he examined the injury. It did not appear life threatening. A series of orders brought the barkeep with a surprisingly complete medical kit, including a small, stoppered beaker with laudanum. Ferguson methodically cleaned and bandaged the wound. He opened the beaker and sniffed. His eyebrows shot up in surprise. He hadn't encountered undiluted laudanum since the beginning of the war. He poured a small dose into Gordon's mouth. "I'll come back and give him another if this don't take."

He rose stiffly and walked to the door. "You find me someone to sit watch" he told Billy.

A feminine voice replied, "Me sir, I know a little about nursing."

Ferguson glanced at the girl. She seemed to be in a high state of nervous excitement. Her flushed cheeks contrasted with the pale skin of someone who seldom ventured into the sun. At one time she had undoubtedly been pretty. She was probably still quite young. However, the hard set to her mouth and expressionless eyes properly belonged to a much older person. They age fast here, he observed inwardly. "What's your name dear?"

"Luinda"

"I'm sure you'll do, honey," he said kindly. "All I want is for you to watch for a bit. If he starts dancing around, sing out and the guard will fetch me."

Luinda found Gordon motionless, snoring lightly. Using the silk veil and leather thongs that were sometimes part of her trade, she gagged and tied him tight to the bed. She slapped his cheeks hard. "Don't be dead yet. I want you to see me first," she hissed. He groaned and opened his eyes. They appeared slightly unfocused so she leaned closer. She saw his eye's widen in recognition. "That's right, it's me, your little slut." She ripped open her dress to expose her breasts and dangled them before his face.

Initially he appeared confused, and then stimulated. She drew the butcher knife from her waistband, reached between his legs, and began to saw.

Min slid his revolver back into its holster, reached for his saber and said, "Draw and be damned!"

Overhead, the new moon danced in a gap in the clouds. It provided enough light for Min to see that Armistead remained stock still, as if stricken. Min lowered his point and closed the distance between them. "Draw you yellow-bellied traitor or I will cut you down."

Clouds obscured the moon. The wind intensified. Lightning, quickly followed by thunder; it began to rain. Min ignored it all and instead listened intently for the metallic scrape as Armistead's blade cleared its scabbard. He drove his horse closer until he could see Armistead's pale blade and initiated a series of feints and blows that both men knew preceded a killing stroke.

Armistead replied skillfully. They were evenly matched. Min quickly perceived that his cousin was content merely to parry his thrusts. During a brief instant when their blades locked hilt to hilt, Min hissed, "Fight you bastard!"

The rain increased. Now, the horses occasionally slipped as their riders maneuvered for advantage. Feint, parry, thrust: both men were breathing hard. Min felt the muscles in his arm burn. But when the locked blades again, he measured Armistead's strength and knew that his cousin was defeated.

308

A spectacular burst of lightning revealed Armistead's open mouth gasping for air, his officer's insignia glittering on his right shoulder. But what caught Min's eye was a heretofore unseen gilt object; a medal disk attached beneath Armistead's left shoulder that secured an empty sleeve against his cousin's tunic.

Armistead had employed all the skills learned on the Carlisle parade ground. He searched for an opportunity to disarm his cousin, but no such chance came. Then, as he felt his strength flagging, he fought to survive. The thought came that he knew of no trick that could save him. Then, a lightning flash so intense that it apparently interrupted the rhythm of his opponent's swordplay. He lunged inside of Min's guard, rotated his wrist, and send his foe's saber flying.

The sudden turn of fortune appeared to astonish Min, because he failed to move. Instead, he opened his mouth, and later Armistead decided that he had heard the question, "what?"

Armistead spoke rapidly: "Gordon has betrayed Amanda. I came across Buttercup and the others. They recognized Blue's scent and came running. I was taking them back to Amanda. Surprised?"

"So you say Gordon is betraying Holland Hall?"

"Yes."

"Convenient," Min replied. "I catch you stealing Mandy's horses and you blame someone who is in no position to gainsay you."

"Another thieving yankee brigand?"

"Yes."

"Believe me or not," Armistead said. "I have traveled a long way and I intend to complete the journey. Come along if you like."

He lowered his saber and turned Blue in the direction of Holland Hall. A pair of riders came from the shadows. The sound of the storm had muffled their approach. They passed on either side of Min. He saw that they held revolvers.

Min shouted a warning but his words were lost in the noise of thunder and the twin explosions from the revolvers.

At least one of the shots grazed Blue and startled him into a gallop. There was no time to react. All Armistead could do was settle into Blue's stride as the frightened animal stretched out.

They were moving fast, following the dark, rain-soaked road as it wound through the trees. Armistead's cape streamed behind him. In the intervals between the sounds of thunder he heard his pursuers fire their weapons. He recalled Sergeant Hathaway's admonishment: "a foolish waste of ammunition, no one can deliver an aimed shot while galloping."

They're playing for the lucky, random shot, Armistead concluded. Then he sensed Blue falter.

The hitch in his gait was on Blue's left rear. Armistead placed his reins in his teeth and reached across his saddle with his right arm. He turned to extend his reach until he felt the warm, sticky blood spurting from Blue's wound. He felt Blue react to his probe by jigging awkwardly away from the pressure. Blue turned his head to ask why. Armistead saw his wide, frightened eyes. He looked back to see that his foes were coming hard.

Armistead turned Blue off the road and reached for his revolver. His weakened horse slipped on the slick embankment. The riders came near. Armistead turned to face them.

They fired at the almost stationary target.

Armistead felt his horse stagger beneath him as he pitched awkwardly from the saddle.

Amanda looked at the date in her diary. October 15, 1862. Yet summer seemed unwilling to release its grip. The day had been unusually warm; bruising heat, oppressive, sultry air that promised a storm. Her quill scratched across the page:

"The army's retreat from Maryland comes so unexpectedly. Another blow! I look back at these pages and find that last spring I enlisted under Captains Endurance, Patience, Faith. I will honor my contract, though sometimes I cannot see how."

She closed her journal. Tomorrow promised to be a trying day and she had resolved to retire early. She reached for the decanter of port and poured. She had found that it helped her sleep, helped her prepare for another day. Tonight the port failed her. She tossed fitfully in her bed, her over busy mind making lists, arranging chores. She was considering going back to the port when the banshee-like cry came: an unearthly scream, a pause, and then the reassuringly familiar 'who...who... who-who.' The servants claimed that the owl only appeared to signal a change, a curse, a death. Amanda sat up and shook her head. "Omens," she thought, "Bah!"

Even here at Holland Hall the negroes had never completely shed their primitive superstitions, she reflected. Maybe those who said that the South was performing a Christian duty, a charitable act, by both providing for them and keeping them from returning to their heathen ways had the right of it. If so, then it was one more reason to fight to preserve Virginia's way of life, another reason to fight for freedom, one more reason to accept the cost.

But the price had already been high and the final reckoning was as yet unknown. The owl called again. Many whites she knew also believed in signs and prophecies, and the thought unsettled her.

The banging shutter woke her from an uneasy sleep. "Damn that lazy girl. I shall have such words with her," she said out loud. Then she remembered that Lilain was gone, having run off with the yankees. She rose to secure the shutter and looked outside. A line of clouds came scudding across the sky. The Tennessee coffee tree trembled as the wind strengthened and shifted into the north. Probably bring a storm, she thought as she returned to her bed. She fell into a deeper sleep.

The muscular rider galloped along a narrow, winding road. His cloak flowed in the wind, his dark horse stretching out with great, ground-eating strides. Bright flashes lit the sky behind him. He wore a kepi pushed down over his eyes to cover part of his face. A thick, full beard obscured the rest. He held his reins in his teeth because he had only one arm, and that arm reached across for a revolver. He turned to point the gun and by so doing clearly revealed his face. Scarred, drawn, but his face for sure. A terrible crash and Amanda awoke with a start.

Wind-driven rain lashed at the windows. A peal of thunder, and then another: the storm had come.

Chapter 40. Loudoun County, October 1862

By the time Min arrived, Armistead's assailants were hovering over his prone body. One of Polk's troopers was obviously searching Armistead for valuables. Nearby, Blue lay on the ground, his flanks shivering, an unearthly sound issuing from his mouth. Min brandished his revolver and shouted, "Back away! This one's mine."

The trooper looked up but did not move. Min fired. His shot kicked up ground near where the trooper knelt. The soldier reluctantly stood and moved away.

Min dismounted. He kept his revolver pointed at the troopers and moved to Armistead. All the while Blue's anguished screams continued. He knelt and gently probed. Armistead groaned.

Min looked at the troopers. "He's my cousin, leave us alone or I'll kill any son of a bitch who interferes!"

"Steady, mister. Steady. This ain't our fight"

Min s asked Armistead: "Are you all right?"

"I think so. Is that Blue?"

"Yes, and I think he's badly injured."

"See to him, Min, and if you have to..." Armistead's voice trailed off.

Min hurried to Blue's side. He was writhing convulsively and his front shoulder was sticky with blood. He seemed to be choking as well. Min reached a hand into Blue's mouth. It came away covered in blood-flecked foam.

Min leaned forward, whispered in the great horse's ear, pointed his revolver, and killed him.

Before Min could stand they were on him. A pair of troopers quickly disarmed him. Additional riders appeared. Someone raised a torch to illuminate the still prone figure of Armistead.

"And what have we here?" Polk demanded.

Min pushed aside the men restraining him and replied, "It's a Union officer whose been injured. We're taking him to get care."

"It's the lieutenant's cousin, sir," a trooper interjected.

"And what do you propose to do with him, lieutenant?" Polk asked.

"We're near Holland Hall. Another of our cousins lives there. She'll provide whatever is needed."

"Are there any large trees around Holland Hall?" Polk inquired.

"Excuse me, sir?" Min asked in disbelief.

"Trees, lieutenant, like those." Polk gestured toward the maples flanking the road.

"Well, yes," Min slowly responded.

"Very good," Polk said. "You see lieutenant, after your cousin fixes him up enough so we can, ah, interview him, we'll need a large tree to hang him from."

The cavalry marched steadily toward Holland Hall beneath an intermittent rain. Min wasn't sure that his luck was still in, but he could see no other way. He waited until another shower began pouring a drenching deluge and pulled his horse to the road side. "What's wrong?" his escort shouted.

Min dismounted and quickly bent over to pick up a fist-sized rock. "She's pulled up lame. I think it's a damn loose shoe. I'll just pull it off. You got a tool?"

"Yup." The trooper pawed into his saddle back and reached down to hand it to Min. "Hurry, mister. I'm fixin' to drown."

He wasn't a bad sort so Min felt a tinge of reluctance as he grabbed the extended arm and pulled the trooper from the saddle. He struck him hard enough to stun him, took his revolver, and dropped him onto the ground. "Sorry brother. It ain't personal."

No one appeared to notice. Min waited until the column passed around a bend and then set off in a fast canter toward Meme Richard's. He had covered about two-thirds of the distance when they sprang the ambush.

It came at a stream ford and was so professionally performed that Min had no chance to resist, even though he confronted only three riders. Their leader, a large, burly man, unshuttered a dark lantern and waved it in Min's face.

"God Damn! It's Min Carter!" Henk roared.

"Hendrick Kupper!" Min exclaimed. "Good Christ!"

Min's words poured out fast. "Polk and his men are taking Armistead to Holland Hall. I sent them the long way but when they get there they plan on hanging him."

"How many?" Henk asked.

"Too many," Min replied. "I was heading to Meme Richard's to round up enough to stop them."

Henk looked at his men. Min saw them nod. "We're with you, Min."

"But, but," Min stammered.

"Tonight we're all on the same side."

"Your uniforms?"

Henk looked slightly abashed. "As for that, we can, ah, pass for rebs."

"Alright then," Min concluded. "An armistice for tonight. Let's get moving Sergeant!"

Amanda sat in the Squire's rocker, a shawl pulled over her shoulders. She had awakened with a start, the image so vividly present that she did not even attempt further sleep. She sipped from a wine glass and saw that her hand trembled. This won't do, she said inwardly and prepared to drag herself to her work desk. A single candle cast bizarre silhouettes on wall and ceiling as wind blown drafts leaked through the windows to twist the flame. Outside the lightning and rain returned. A powerful gust doused the flickering candle. She sat in the darkness, her every sense alert.

She heard Rex bay and forced herself to stand and look outside. Riders, whose and how many she could not tell. She took a last, long sip and slowly walked to the head of the stairs.

From below came muffled banging of fist on door. A light appeared. She exhaled. It was James. She called down the stairs: "You may as well open the door, James, I imagine that they are coming inside one way or another."

A pair of soldiers pushed into the hall, rain dripping from their capes. "Is Miss Holland here?" The accent was southern, but Amanda had learned that this meant little.

"Who wants to know?" she answered.

The soldiers startled. They stood in a pool of light cast by James's lantern. Hesitant, uncertain.

An imposing figure shoved his way inside. He wore a black plumed hat and a bulky, black cape trimmed in scarlet that concealed the rest of his uniform. One of his men gestured up the stairs. He swaggered into the brightest pool of light, looked at Amanda, and removed his hat and bowed. "Captain Otis Polk at your service, ma'am. Although after tonight's exploits I am certain it will be Major Polk."

He stared at her appraisingly. "And you no doubt are Miss Amanda Holland. I have been looking forward to this meeting."

Amanda stood transfixed. The posture, the jowly face and thin lips, the close set eyes sunk too far into the skull; it was the man from the slave auction in Alexandria. She heard him bark out a command.

"We have a surprise," Polk smirked.

Two pairs of soldiers entered the hall hefting a blanket bundle. They released their hold and a bound figure rolled heavily onto the pine floor.

"You recognize this traitor?"

He lay face down, his torn riding cloak covering his body. She knew without looking who it was.

Polk waited expectantly. When she failed to answer he snapped, "Sergeant, turn him over."

The sergeant kicked Armistead heavily in the ribs. He groaned but did not move. He kicked again but before he could kick a third time Amanda said, "Do that again and you die."

"I admire a woman of spirit," Polk drawled. "Ralston, listen to the lady and turn him over gentle like."

The sergeant's name, the memory of the raiders arriving in late afternoon, a man, this man, wantonly killing her livestock and promising worse. She turned to fetch her father's LeMat revolver

314

"I think not, Madam," Polk said. He had drawn his revolver and stood poised over Armistead with the gun pointed at his head.

The sound of the trigger pulled to full cock arrested her steps. She stood motionless, her every sense quivering.

"That's better," Polk said. "I'm sure we can sort out this little confusion before we hang the traitor. After all, we're all on the same side, aren't we?

"I'm sure we are," Min said as he entered the hall from the kitchen passage.

There was a stirring along the many passages that led to the main hall. Men emerged from the west veranda, the library, and the front door. Polk's troopers were the first to appear. Some looked sheepish, others relieved. A few were obviously angry, but none carried weapons. Amanda saw that behind them came the brothers and sons of families she had known a lifetime: neighbor boys home on leave; convalescents like the limping Archibald Luckett, home recovering from yet another wound; a schoolmate from Upperville, his once handsome face horribly scarred; two Berryville relatives, almost crippled from their service in the Thirty-third Virginia; Marylanders from across the river and many, many more; and they all had weapons drawn.

"Now Captain, this is hardly the place to question the ah," Min searched for the right word, "ah prisoner. So, I suggest we gather in the library in say five minutes, and James no doubt will bring us coffee and perhaps something to eat. The servants can clean up the prisoner, assisted by one of your men and one of mine. In the meantime, Sergeant Barton here will show you the way while I see to Miss Holland."

He climbed the stairs and found that she had retreated out of public view. He opened his arms and she staggered against him. She sobbed convulsively before gradually collecting herself. "I'm sorry for being such a weak creature."

Min held her until she had stopped shaking and then gently disengaged. He escorted her to the rocker.

"Cousin," Min said, "There's one more thing. It's about Boyd."

"He's dead isn't he?" she asked.

"I don't know." He described his encounter at Meme Richard's and how he had found Boyd's horse. "We know he made it to Maryland. He might have been taken prisoner there."

"We don't even know that, Min," Amanda replied. "His horse was in Maryland and that's all we know."

He started to object, but reconsidered and instead looked at her closely. He had failed to notice the changes. She was thin, almost frail, yet still sat erect with a straight back. He saw dark pouches below her eyes, which rest, no doubt would remove, and he saw newly formed lines and creases that were now a permanent part of her. He saw a younger image of Auntie Hag and wished he could hug her until her old self returned. "I'd have given a lot to be able to come tonight with better news, Mandy," he softly said.

"You and the boys have already given much and we are thankful. If we; you, the Loudoun Grays, the people of Loudoun County, have to give more, I trust we will not be found wanting."

He walked to the window and stared outside. "Let me see if the storm has passed."

It gave her time to gather herself in private and she was grateful. She returned from an inner room and spoke without emotion, "I am ready. I have no more tears to shed."

Chapter 41. Loudoun County, October 1862

Armistead sat in a straight backed cane chair with a soldier on either side. Polk occupied the settee opposite him. He had helped himself to the decanter.

When Amanda entered the library Polk stood, "Please madam, join me and we will conclude this ugly business." He gestured toward the settee.

"I will sit here," Amanda replied and lowered herself onto the front edge of a straight-backed rocking chair.

"Very well," Polk snapped. "The situation is simple. My men intercept a yankee agent. He divulges the plans of this man's unit, the Loudoun Rangers, the spearhead of the enemy raids into Loudoun County. We catch him meeting with a yankee spy. He flees. We catch him again, this time he has descended to horse thief. We will hang him as a warning to the others. At least in his death he will provide some service to the people he has betrayed."

"Is it true, Armistead?" Amanda softly asked.

"Am I a Union officer? Yes. Have the Loudoun Rangers been in Loudoun County? Yes."

Polk began to speak but Amanda interrupted.

"Have you been directing these raids?" she asked.

"Would you believe me if I answered?" he challenged.

"I would believe the truth," she replied.

"A Union officer named Overmeyer directs operations against Loudoun County. His objective is personal gain."

"But what about the letter?" Min asked.

Armistead looked surprised. "What letter?"

"The one you wrote Mandy. She showed it to me."

"I've written several letters."

"I've only received one, Armistead," Amanda replied. "In it you boasted, 'we are coming, carrying the sword and buckler of the lord.'"

"I did not write such a letter."

There was a lengthy silence, punctuated by the sound of Polk slapping his gloves against his thigh and the scrape of wood on wood while Amanda rocked back and forth.

At last she spoke: "I am sorry that I burned it."

She looked at Armistead and shrugged. "You see, I was so angry. But even at the time there was something odd about it."

Min saw that for the first time a hint of a smile, or was it relief, play across her face.

"I did not remark upon it to you Min, but it was the spelling."

"The spelling?" Min asked.

"Unjustifiable was misspelt, an error Armistead would never make. I now wonder, who wrote it?"

Polk started to stand. "Enough of this..." he began to say before Kinlock's and Henk's firm hands pressed him back down.

"Do you know how Overmeyer knew where to strike?" Amanda asked.

"Gordon was betraying you, although why I don't know. Why don't you bring him here and ask?"

"He's dead, Armistead," Min related.

Polk exploded. "So this traitor's defense relies upon a letter that has been burnt and a witness who is dead."

The circle of soldiers pressed inward and a discontented murmuring began. Armistead realized that he possessed the courage of the condemned who no longer valued life. Yet her opinion still mattered and he felt suspended in time as he waited for her judgment, her answer that would determine all that lay ahead.

Amanda looked straight at him. He returned her gaze and their eyes locked. He searched for her answer. The cold chill of premonition rose from his spine and he fought to avoid displaying any emotion.

"Armistead, I believe you."

"Well I don't!" Polk snapped. "And as senior officer what I think matters most. Out of deference to the lady, we won't hang him here."

"We hang spies. This officer is not a spy. He is a prisoner of war under my charge," Min said. "He will be handled like all such prisoners."

Polk looked around the circle and saw that Amanda's statement had carried the group. "I find that I am outgunned, so for the moment I yield." Polk stood face to face with Min and stared hard, his eyes almost reptilian with cold menace: "I will remember you, lieutenant," he hissed.

After Polk departed, Amanda looked toward Min. "I am so proud of you."

"And I am sincerely grateful for you saving my neck," Armistead added. "That man means you trouble."

"No doubt," Min replied, "but I reckon he'll have to get in line first."

Armistead gave a wan smile. "Well, let's not make things worse and keep him waiting."

Amanda interrupted, "Min? May Armistead and I have a word before he," she hesitated, seeking the right word, "has to go?"

Min looked at her and then quickly broke contact. It had always been there, he later decided, only he had been too foolish to recognize it. "Of course. I'll be outside," he said.

Min gestured to Henk. They walked to the side yard.

"God damn close back there," Henk said.

Min nodded, "God damn right!"

"What happens now?" Henk asked.

"It's prison for Armistead, there's nothing I can do about that Henk. Hopefully he'll soon be exchanged."

"Exchanges ain't so easy anymore," Henk replied. "It helps being an officer, of course, but we hear that it's pretty rough in the places y-uns put us."

Min felt his temper rise, "It's no picnic at Fort Delaware, Henk."

He saw Henk swell up but before he could speak Min interrupted, "I don't reckon we can settle everything here tonight, but you're right about prison. That, at least I can help fix. I won a pretty good stake at Meme Richard's tonight. I thought I would be needing it, but I don't reckon that's the case anymore. I'll pass it on to Armistead. Money talks in Richmond. It will make sure he's heard. Now you'd best skedaddle."

Henk visibly relaxed, "You probably won some of what I left there. Goodbye Min, keep your rebel ass out of harm's way."

"And you keep your fat Dutch ass between you and our bullets, Henk. God speed!"

"Armistead, I am so terribly sorry you've been hurt like this," Amanda said.

He exhaled slowly. "For a time, too long really, I felt sorry for myself." Like a flood wave surging across a shallow-water ford, his words poured out unchecked. "But while I was recovering I saw others who were hurt far worse. I saw only one hospital. After Antietam, Amanda, I'm told that the wounded were beyond number, blue and gray alike, and that all the hospitals could not begin to cope."

"I was at Piedmont Station after Bull Run. Even then we were overwhelmed. I did not think it would come to this."

"No one did."

"Yet I foresaw part of it, Armistead, although I did not know it at first. I saw a soldier in my dreams, riding through a storm. I saw his missing arm. I dreamt it again tonight, and for the first time I saw that it was you."

She had leaned forward in her chair while she described her premonition. Leaned forward close enough to almost touch him.

She saw him wrestle inwardly, the passage of some thought as obvious as speech, and then his expression hardened. The gulf that she prayed had closed, widened once more. And she felt an emptiness so profound that she could not imagine anything more painful.

Armistead stood. "I'm afraid I must go."

"Is there anything I can do that will help?"

"It's kind of you to offer. There is something I am loath to lose. May I write a short note?"

Amanda swallowed her surprise and retrieved a pen and paper.

Armistead leaned over the desk unsteadily and began to write. Amanda politely looked away and she heard him scratch out a few lines.

"Thank you," he said and she turned to see him awkwardly folding the paper. He reached across his chest and tugged at an ornament of some kind that secured his sleeve. She had not previously noticed it.

"Hell and damnation," he muttered as he fumbled at the clasp.

"Let me help you. For God and the Fatherland," she read in a puzzled tone.

"It dates back to Napoleon's time and is a family heirloom. I should not like to, ah, lose it. If something happens and I don't come back, would you send it on to the person whose name and home place I have written on this card?"

"Of course." She studied the medal and ribbon. "It is striking, almost beautiful. Is she?"

She winced inwardly to see her shaft strike home.

He hesitated before answering: "Yes."

She caught his tone but still could not help herself: "Do you have a special understanding?"

He breathed deeply and tried to think.

Someone rapped on the door. A voice spoke. "Missy, the guests are growing anxious."

Hearing James's voice resolved Armistead's uncertainty. "Yes, we understand one another."

He took her hand and lightly kissed it. He saw her eyes tear up. He squeezed her hand, willing what little strength he still possessed to flow to her before releasing her hand and departing the home where they had so often shared so much.

She watched him leave, and even then one part of her tried, in spite of all else, to remain appraising, analytical, detached. She stared at his retreating back, his still muscular legs, the empty sleeve. She wished that she could ask again and hear a different answer.

Min saw him appear with unsteady gait, his shoulders slumped. "I'd better go with you Armistead," Min said.

Armistead gave a slight smile. "Thank you cousin, but Kinlock and the boys can protect me. I'd be happier if you would see to Amanda." He extended his hand toward Min.

He saw Min reach into his pocket, his lips pucker, a finger press against his lips, warning him to be quiet. His palm pressed against Armistead's palm and Armistead felt something being passed.

Very quietly, Min spoke, "I'm told it can be rough where you are going. This can make all the difference."

Min closed Armistead's fingers around the purse and withdrew. His voice caught, "Take care cousin."

He turned quickly away before Armistead could reply and climbed the steps into Holland Hall.

Epilogue: Washington, December 1862

Abner Means entered the chamber where the intelligence committee held its periodic meetings. The two senators were typically late so Means sidled into his chair and listened to the gossip about the recent conscription act passed by the rebel congress. A Massachusetts congressman described the exemption law that kept the overseers on the big plantations from being drafted. "They're still worried about a slave revolt," he said.

"Worried that some big buck nigger will visit the missus while they're off in the army," an Illinois congressman sniggered.

"Those idiots," the government man interjected with a hearty laugh. "If we can just keep from losing this war, the southern people may do our job for us and hang Davis and his crew."

"You people in Washington still don't understand, do you?" Means interjected. "One of my patrols intercepted a rebel scout. Among his belongings was this." Means removed a torn, blood-stained letter from his valise. "I've found example after example of this sentiment. Why don't you read it aloud?"

The government man handled the letter with extreme distaste. He held it carefully at a distance and read: "Dear Henry, I feel more lonely and sad than I have been in some time. Oh! that I knew what the termination of this awful conflict would be. Henry I want to see you but dont you come. Join for the War if tis forty years if you get killed tis the most honorable death. If you escape I will rejoice. I love thee still."

"There may be complaints throughout the South about a 'rich man's war, poor man's fight,' gentlemen, but the vast majority of the common people, the families who provide the soldiers, see this as a life and death struggle to defend their homes. When there is any wavering, the women provide the rallying voice and these women have spines of steel. They will not quit until we burn their factories and farms, destroy their armies, and capture their cities. And before that happens, our own people might give up," Means said.

"Come now, Means," a general said irritably. "Surely we have as much backbone as they do."

"If they were invading our country, general, I am sure the answer would be yes. But we are fighting for something less tangible, to preserve the Union, and now our president has changed the terms of the fight by adding emancipation and I am not sure how this is going to go down."

"Not well at all, I fear," a New York colonel observed. "While you, Mister Means, have been collecting our enemy's letters I have been," he paused and coughed as if to clear his throat, "ah reading some of what our own men write. The volunteers of sixty-one joined to save the Union. It appears that they don't want to die to free the slaves. Neither do the men who signed for two years. They are not re-enlisting. What will happen when the three-year men, the soldiers who now compose the balance of our armies, come to the end of their terms, I shudder to think."

"What we need is an inspired stroke to show the world that black men are willing and able to fight for their own freedom," Means said.

"The darkies won't fight," the general muttered.

Secretary of War Stanton ignored him. "You have something in mind, Means?"

"If the blow were struck in the enemy's capital, might not the world take note?"

"Well?" Stanton asked, looking directly at Means.

"Sir, the rebels are short of iron manufactures. Their main factory, the Tredegar Works, is in Richmond."

"Get to the point, man," the general interjected. "We know all of this."

Means ignored the interruption. "A well-planned mission might destroy Tredegar. My agents inform me that it is not well guarded. An intrepid handful, perhaps even a mere pair, like those who destroyed Locomotive 199, could burn Tredegar to the ground. If one of the agents was a negro, think how that would play in the press!"

"It would play even better if the rebels hung them afterwards," the Illinois congressman proclaimed.

"Remember John Brown!" the Massachusetts senator added. "He did more for us by the way he died than by anything he accomplished while living."

"A nigger and one of ours, side by side at the gallows after a feat of surpassing heroism," the government man enthused.

"It could be arranged," Means said.

"Hold hard, Means. Didn't you tell me that this officer, let's see, what's his name?" The secretary's voice trailed off as he shuffled through his files.

"Carter," Means said. "Colonel Armistead Carter."

"Yes! That's the man." the general said. "Wasn't proper at all, promoting a southerner in that way. Why the man never even attended West Point! A colonel! Forsooth." The general took a large pinch of snuff and sneezed.

"Just so," Stanton said. "But you told me he was taken prisoner recently?"

"Yes," Means replied, "taken prisoner and conveniently shipped to Richmond, from where, when I give the word, he can be sprung."

"Gentlemen," Stanton intoned, "I believe we have a consensus. Carry on, Mister Means, carry on."

FINIS

Historical Note

In a work of historical fiction some readers may care to know how closely the story line mirrors real events.

The historical events, large and small, are derived from period sources. For example, VMI cadets from my home town were present at John Brown's execution and left vivid, although unpublished, descriptions that provide the basis for my depiction. Inspiration for Rattler's ride at Bull Run came after reading Captain John F. Lay's Report in the *Official Records of the War of the Rebellion*, Series I, vol. 2; August 15, 1861, p. 572: "Dispatching three couriers under a forced and rapid ride to Piedmont at night to communicate with General Johnston's command. In this ride a very valuable horse was seriously injured." Turner Ashby died under circumstances as described. Then and thereafter participants were uncertain who shot him. The events at Shepherds Ford are based upon the various reports in the *Official Records*, Series I, vol. 19, part 1. General Sykes wrote, "Knowing that the Virginia side of the river was no place for troops until a proper reconnaissance had been made, and several reports from citizens inducing the belief that a large force of the enemy was moving upon us." One might surmise that Abner Means, whose name does not appear in recorded history, was one of those citizens.

In addition, I have borrowed fragments from diaries and letters in order to reveal better the characters of the men and women who lived during this time. At the Battle of McDowell, a soldier of the 12th Georgia explained why his regiment disregarded orders to retire: "We did not come all this way to Virginia to run before Yankees." I have a Georgia officer belonging to a regiment that was present on Henry Hill speak these words. Min's letter to Amanda describing his feelings during battle utilizes a Texas cavalry officer's letter relating his experience at the Battle of Corinth.

In a few instances I have strayed outside the strict bounds of historical place and chronology. Thus, the incident where the rebel zouave murders a wounded Union soldier at Bull Run actually took place later on the Peninsula. The episodes regarding the murder and flogging of blacks at my Camp of Instruction actually took place at Camp Stone near Edwards Ferry in the autumn of 1861. The words I have Frederick Douglass speak in Carlisle in 1861 were delivered as a eulogistic address to John Brown on May 30, 1881. Jackson's raid on Martinsburg and the subsequent movement of Locomotive 199 down the Valley actually took place in the summer of 1861. Birders will recognize that the plagiarism committed by my Robert Duchesne was committed by Audubon himself who lifted the illustration of the Mississippi kite from Alexander Wilson.

Although I anticipate my story somewhat, I want to note that Elizabeth Van Lew was surely one of the most remarkable women of the war. While

U.S. Grant may have exaggerated by calling her the war's most important yankee spy, her northern admirers had it right when they contributed a plaque for her Richmond gravesite that reads, "She risked everything that's dear to man: friends, fortune, comfort, health, life itself, for the one absorbing desire of her heart: that slavery might be abolished and the Union preserved."

Lastly, I want to acknowledge my debt to *The Journals of Amanda Virginia Edmonds: Lass of the Mosby Confederacy*, the inspiration for Amanda Holland. Meeting Amanda's granddaughter in 1984 began a journey that is a privilege to share with my readers.

About the Author

James R. Arnold is the author of more than twenty-five books devoted to military history and leadership. His published works include *Presidents Under Fire*, a study of how American presidents perform as war leaders, *Grant Wins the War*, a campaign study of Vicksburg, and *Jeff Davis's Own*, the story of the future Civil War generals who served on the Texas frontier during the Indian Wars. Arnold is the founder of Napoleon Books, a niche publishing venture originally devoted to Napoleonic studies. His most recent book, *The Moro War* (Bloomsbury Press, 2011) examines the first U.S. war against an Islamic insurgency. He has also written forty-two library reference books for young adults that address the social and historical events associated with colonial America, the American and French Revolutions, the Industrial Revolution, and the American Civil War. Arnold and his wife live on a farm in Virginia's Shenandoah Valley.

53069917R00202

Made in the USA
Lexington, KY
21 June 2016